"MY GOD, THIS IS GOOD. YOU COOK LIKE AN ANGEL."

Samantha sighed as she savored each bite. "Do you always feed your business partners this well?"

Gabriel lifted his eyes from his plate. "I haven't agreed to any business arrangement yet, Samantha. But I did want tonight to be a little special."

"You're trying to impress me?" she dared lightly.

"I'm trying to seduce you," he replied, his eyes never leaving her face.

Samantha dropped her fork halfway to her mouth. It clattered rudely on the white plate, and she mumbled a hasty apology.

"Why the panic? S-surely I'm not the first to pose the question."

She took a grip on her resolve. "Of course not. I just wasn't expecting it from you."

He smiled bleakly. "Still trying to dress me in a halo and wings?"

DOUBLE DEALING

Jayne Castle

A DELL BOOK

Published by
Dell Publishing Co., Inc.
1 Dag Hammarskjold Plaza
New York, New York 10017

Dell ® TM 681510, Dell Publishing Co., Inc.

ISBN: 0-440-12121-3

Printed in the United States of America
First printing—August 1984

For my editor, Anne Gisonny,
who gave me my first chance and who,
still undaunted, is giving me another

CHAPTER ONE

"My God! You're killing me!" The therapist ignored the protest, continuing to sweep the length of her client's bare back with a heavy hand, her palms sheathed in textured mitts. Chin resting on her hands, eyes squeezed shut against the breathtaking discomfort of the vigorous rubdown, Samantha gritted her teeth and willed herself to endure. The pain was not lessened a bit by the knowledge that she was paying a small fortune for such refined torture treatments.

"It is absolutely imperative to exfoliate the skin completely, madam," the therapist proclaimed, making a serious effort to remove an entire layer of flesh with a single sweep of the mitts. "The skin must be thoroughly cleansed of dead cells before it can be properly cleaned and oiled!"

Samantha bit back another moan, having learned during the past twenty-four hours that it was useless to argue. The fiercely strong and fanatically dedicated middle-aged woman working over her body was not about to cease and desist because of the protests of a weakling. The client had paid good money for the spa treatments, and Miss Carson saw to it that weaklings like Samantha got their money's worth. Miss Carson was a professional.

"I'll kill that travel agent when I get back to Seattle," Samantha muttered darkly. But she knew in her heart that it wasn't the agent's fault. It was Samantha who had come across the article on elegant spas in a fashion magazine, and it was she who had convinced her travel agent to move heaven and earth to get her reservations. Who would have guessed it was the most exclusive, incredibly overpriced torture chamber on the California coast? It had all looked so marvelously relaxing and serene on the pages of the magazine. Perhaps she could sue the publisher for misrepresentation.

All around the large, white-tiled room other women, all paying the same exorbitant rates, submissively complied with the demands of the attendants. Several were stretched out on massage tables, draped as Samantha was in only a fluffy white towel across their buttocks. Others alternately froze or steamed in the hot and cold plunges or subjected their muscles to the throb of a whirlpool bath.

At the far end of the room, glass-walled booths provided a choice of sauna or steam heat. Down a corridor to her right, Samantha had learned to her cost, was another room full of exercise machines which appeared to have been bought at a dungeon yard sale. Elsewhere on the grounds of the extravagant facility was a restaurant which served from a menu featuring largely sprouts and yogurt. Samantha had been so disgusted at not finding even the most modest of wine lists at dinner the previous evening that she had seriously considered sneaking out at midnight to find a fast-food restaurant.

If her plans for Gabriel Sinclair had not jelled by this afternoon, she promised herself silently, she would follow through on the scheme to slip away for a decent meal this evening. It would be tricky. A large, hulking type was always on duty at the front desk in the lobby, and getting past him would be a feat. Furthermore the southern California coast was rather wild and desolate in this area. No telling how far she'd have to drive in order to find something to eat besides roughage du jour.

"Now, madam, back into the hot plunge. We must open the pores one more time!" Miss Carson administered one last punishing slap to Samantha's thigh and stepped back.

"Anything to get off this table," Samantha muttered, trying to sit up and finding her muscles strangely rubberized. "I can't move!" she squeaked in horror as the fluffy towel across her derriere fell away.

"Of course you can! Soon you will move better than you ever have in your entire life!" The stocky woman took hold of one of Samantha's arms and pulled her ruthlessly away from the support of the table. The towel, which had been the only sop to modesty, fell aside completely as Samantha stumbled in the wake of her martinet of a therapist. She was beyond caring about modesty, however, other than sending up a silent prayer of thanks for the fact that the spa catered only to women.

The incredible weakness which assailed her limbs was claiming her full attention.

"I'm not kidding," she breathed in her soft, slightly husky voice. "I think you've ruined me. Every muscle feels crushed."

"In you get," the older woman ordered, ignoring the protest and the fact that she literally had to support her client with both hands under Samantha's armpits. "You will feel much better after the hot and cold plunges. Everyone does!"

"This bath is steaming more than the last one," Samantha observed dubiously as she carefully stuck a toe into the pool. "I think it's a little too hot." And then, as her toe jerked back out of its own accord: "It *is* too hot! Listen Miss Carson, I'm really much more of a shower person. Couldn't we try that instead?" She turned pleading eyes on her attendant and saw no pity in the firm, determined features. Samantha was learning that the staff was obsessed with a mission, and nothing could alter the course of a true believer.

"The Swiss showers come later. Now you plunge!" Quite forcefully Miss Carson propelled Samantha into the hot water, an action which drew a gasp of startled dismay from her victim.

"I'm going to be boiled alive! Really, Miss Carson, I just read somewhere that hot baths can be dangerous. Bad for the blood pressure. Oh, Lord!" Her protest trailed off into a squeak of pain, her body now fully immersed. Up to her chin in the steaming pool, Samantha glared helplessly at her tormentor who, in turn, studied her victim's form with professional detachment.

10

The shoulder length, seal-brown hair was drawn into a severe knot and secured with a wide terry band. The strict line revealed the gentle planes and angles of a face which, had it not been animated by intelligence and a subtle hint of passion, might have been deemed ordinary. But the lack of perfection in the features was just as well. It allowed full scope to the flare of intellect and lively awareness in the gold and brown eyes. A firm nose and chin gave evidence of the willpower which guided the basic intelligence, but there was a nuance of recklessness in the faint tilt of the tortoiseshell eyes.

At twenty-nine years of age it was a face which reflected character and a sense of self-identity, qualities which had been developed early in Samantha's life under the auspices of a mother who had distinct, if unconventional, ideas on how to raise a daughter. Yet underneath the strong elements lay a betraying softness, a strange vulnerability that contributed an emotional element to her nature which Samantha knew she could not blame on either of her parents. It was, unfortunately, a unique and dangerous quality with which she had been cursed.

But it was the body beneath the face which was Miss Carson's responsibility. Her assignment was to strengthen the slender form which was a bit too rounded at hip and thigh, according to the spa analysis. With an experienced eye Miss Carson identified and cataloged the small, high breasts, the full hips, and the slight curve of her client's stomach. Too much softness, the therapist decided.

By the time Samantha left the spa, Miss Carson

11

decided, the curve of the stomach would be quite flat, and inroads would have been made into the creeping cellulite at the thighs. But nothing, the therapist knew, would permanently slow or alter the quick impatient way her client moved. There was a sense of reckless energy about Samantha Maitland, a dynamic, almost rash force which, Miss Carson realized, was an intrinsic part of the woman's nature. It was temporarily muted now by the extreme effects of the massage and thermal plunges, but it would return in force once Samantha had recovered. Miss Carson idly wondered just how much energy her client burned away in simply controlling her natural impulsiveness. Inefficient.

"Come," Miss Carson ordered briskly, stepping forward to assist, "time for the cold plunge."

"Hell! It's like ice water!" What had Miss Carson done before she got this cushy spa job? Interrogation for the CIA perhaps? "I'll talk!" Samantha had the urge to blurt out as her body received the full impact of the cold water.

"Enough of the cold." Miss Carson held out the white towel. "The pores have now been tightened again. The cleansing gel is next and then a mist of water-holding oil will be sprayed on the skin. You will feel like a new woman!"

"Good. Right now I feel like a nearly dead woman," Samantha muttered as she struggled shakily from the tub. She was appalled at the unsteadiness of her muscles. It was a little frightening to find oneself so weak. "I also feel like I need a drink. If I slipped you ten bucks, could you find me a margarita or a cold beer?"

"The alcohol promotes cellulite!"

"You know, Miss Carson, before I came here I didn't even believe in cellulite. I hadn't realized that there were people like you around who have dedicated your whole lives to fighting it," Samantha grumbled dryly.

Miss Carson permitted herself an indulgent chuckle as she settled Samantha back on the table. "Just wait until this is finished, madam. You will thank me before you leave the spa. All my clients thank me!"

Samantha withheld her private opinion on the matter, too weak to argue. What had she done to herself? But it had all seemed so convenient. So well suited to her scheme. The consummate businesswoman conducting her affairs in the plush setting of a luxurious spa was just the image she wished to project. Besides, it would be fun to treat herself while she waited for the reaction to the bait she had dangled in front of Gabriel Sinclair, Samantha had decided, and the spa was conveniently close to Sinclair's home on the California coast near Santa Barbara.

It had been unbelievably complicated pulling even such minor details as an address for Sinclair out of the computer, Samantha reflected as she gritted her teeth against Miss Carson's pounding. While building his financial empire, the man clearly had spent a lot of time and energy staying out of the media spotlight. The very opposite of Drew Buchanan, who gloried in having his carefully orchestrated deals reported on in *Forbes* or *The Wall Street Journal*. That thought made her frown even more than Miss Carson's less than gentle ministrations did.

13

No, there had been very little on Gabriel Sinclair in the various computerized data bases she had searched. And the very paucity of information on him had intrigued her. His name had been one of only a handful of possible people.

For hours her fingers had moved across the keys, drawing forth information from the computer terminal with the practiced ease of a musician coaxing a melody from an instrument. Behind the lenses of the pair of chic designer frames she normally wore, Samantha had eyed the green words which formed on the screen in front of her. The search had been exhausting, but at long last she had managed to narrow the list of names down to five.

The winnowing process had been painstaking, the search requiring all her ingenuity and the full resources of the data bases to which she had access. But four days ago it had finally come to an end.

On that last afternoon in Seattle a gentle northwest rain had pattered on the roof of the wraparound porch which cozily encircled the old Victorian house. The roof of the porch formed a balcony for the bedrooms on the second level. The rain was a comfortable and familiar sound now to Samantha, as comfortable and familiar as the computer terminal at which she worked.

During the past three years Samantha Maitland had become accustomed to both the rain and the technology. Around her that afternoon the Puget Sound island home creaked as if it needed to yawn and stretch occasionally while waiting for the summer warmth. The house was in no rush. It had sat through a good many Seattle

14

winters, doing its job of protecting the various inhabitants with the gracious if slightly supercilious manner of an old family retainer who knows he'll be around to serve the next generation.

It was true the house had never been called upon before to shelter anything like the consoles and computer terminals which now occupied the back parlor, but the current human resident was quite acceptable. A bit eccentric, highly independent, and capable of the Grand Gesture on occasion and once, three years ago, a Grand Passion, Samantha Maitland felt right at home amid the quaint gingerbread trim and the underlying solidity of the old house. She knew the house liked her and was privately convinced that was the only reason it tolerated the electronic hardware she'd moved into the parlor.

But Samantha had been totally unaware of her surroundings that afternoon four days ago. Instead, with a mounting rush of barely suppressed excitement she had entered one command after another into the terminal. Finally, after taking a few nanoseconds to consider the matter, the machine had responded by reducing the names on the screen until there remained only two.

Absently she had chewed her lower lip as she viewed the final results of her search. The computer had helped her narrow the choice, sorting through the information at its disposal in response to her orders until the list had been cut down to two names. But it didn't contain sufficient data to select between the final choices. Some human decision-making was going to be called for in the last analysis.

William Oakes or Gabriel Sinclair. The computer knew very little about either man. But as she sat staring at the names, Samantha's frown of concentration had abruptly cleared, and her mouth had moved upward in a wry smile. A little divine intervention might be useful for what she had planned. And if ever a woman needed an avenging angel, she did. Samantha had pressed the enter key one more time and was left with only one name on the screen. It seemed entirely appropriate that her financial angel should be named Gabriel.

It was not untypical of Samantha, having relied on technology to get that far, to rely on pure intuition to make the last decision.

With a feeling of cool anticipation she had stretched out a hand to the telephone beside her. It was only as her travel agent came on the line that Samantha had remembered reading that article on spas.

Now she could only regret the spur of the moment decision which had put her into the clutches of the zealously devoted staff of health enthusiasts. And there was no immediate relief in sight. One could hardly look forward to dinner around here, and Samantha could not check out until Sinclair got in touch. This was the address she had given him in the short, hopefully intriguing note she had sent to him.

"Ouch! I thought all that was left was some kind of cleansing gel," Samantha protested as the attack on her body intensified.

"But it must be properly applied," Miss Carson admonished, pummeling the muscles in Samantha's legs.

"It does no good to pour it lightly over the skin. It must be worked into each and every pore."

Gasping for breath, Samantha shut her eyes and then automatically opened them again as a collective murmur of surprise went through the room full of near-naked women and their attendants. Even Miss Carson paused in her assault, joining to look toward the door.

A man stood there, gazing around the room with an expression of surprised interest. Several women adjusted their towels, a few nonchalantly slipping them aside.

"The owner of this place?" Samantha inquired, reaching down to her hips to make certain her towel was securely covering the rounded curve of her bottom.

"No, it's certainly not Miss Fortune," Miss Carson huffed. "I'm not sure who it is. Probably some lost husband come to collect his wife and wandered into the wrong room!"

Samantha was about to reply to the comment when quite suddenly the intruder glanced in her direction. Something about the intensity of the gaze made itself felt, and she instinctively reached for her glasses which were lying on a small shelf attached to the table. She prodded the frames onto her nose with an automatic gesture and discovered that the man was watching her even though he was now being approached by two determined attendants.

Samantha smiled in spite of herself as the image of the stranger jumped into focus. In the white-tiled room full of white towels, white uniforms, clear crystal pools and nude female bodies, he managed to convey the impression of a satyr who has just succeeded in crashing a party of sea nymphs.

There was something very solid and substantial about him, Samantha decided as he looked away to speak quietly to one of the attendants. He wasn't fat or soft or particularly tall, just very much *there*. An uncompromising, rather unyielding male presence. Then Samantha blinked in sudden intuition as the intruder followed the nod of one of the attendants and glanced again in her direction.

"Oh, no! It couldn't be! Surely he wouldn't just walk in here unannounced." The words were spoken on a weak hiss of dismay as the man started toward her with a resolute stride. Just from watching him walk Samantha got the distinct impression he did everything resolutely. "Oh, hell," she murmured in frustration.

"You know him?" Miss Carson demanded as she returned to work with a vengeance.

"I'm not sure, I . . . Please, Miss Carson, could you stop that for a moment? I can't think when you're pounding on me!"

"You are here to exercise the body, not the brain!"

Skirting the hot plunge, the stranger was rapidly nearing Samantha's massage table. She found herself desperately wishing for more covering than the towel provided and grimly reminded herself not to raise her bare upper torso far from the surface of the table.

This wasn't going at all as she had planned! If this was Gabriel Sinclair, things were already veering disastrously from the course she had charted. Samantha groaned to herself, and this time the exclamation was not caused by Miss Carson's tender touch. How could everything have gone so wrong? How had Sinclair gotten past that hulking desk clerk in the lobby? Why hadn't she been paged?

Of all the stupid, ridiculous situations! It looked very much as if she was about to be forced to begin negotiations on the deal of a lifetime while her body was being pummeled. Talk about not being firmly in control of a situation!

Frantically, recognizing that she simply could not get up and flee into the woods like any other respectable nymph would under such circumstances, Samantha tried to concentrate on what she knew of Gabriel Sinclair. If she was going to survive the encounter without a total loss of dignity, she had better get a firm grip on her flustered thoughts.

The problem was that there wasn't a great deal of information to marshal and collect in her head. From the beginning Samantha had realized she was going to have to play the opening scene by ear. The computer had contained so few personal facts on this man that she hadn't even been able to guess his age.

Now Samantha eyed the firmly etched brackets around the hard line of his mouth, absorbed the impact of the quiet, controlled solidity of him, and pegged the years at thirty-seven or thirty-eight. There was a restrained, shuttered look about the stranger, as if he did not allow himself to become too involved with anything or anyone around him. It would take that kind of aloof arrogance to stride through a spa room full of naked women, Samantha decided grimly. The impression was reinforced by the knife blade of a nose and the cool, watchful expression which schooled the bluntly unhandsome features.

"What do you think, Miss Carson?" she heard herself demand with false flippancy as the intruder neared.

"He looks in fairly good shape to me," the therapist allowed judiciously as she concentrated on kneading her client's right thigh.

"Yeah, I had the same impression," Samantha drawled wryly. Trust Miss Carson to view everyone from her own peculiarly limited viewpoint. In that moment Samantha could have used a little insightful input from the other woman, and all she got was an analysis of whether or not Gabriel Sinclair was a candidate for treatments!

Damn it to hell! Hadn't she seen movies in which powerful corporate heads or prominent underworld figures conducted business in the surroundings of a health club?

Yes, she had, Samantha thought nervously. And in those films there had usually been a dead body or two lying around after the mist from the steam bath had cleared! She didn't even have the advantage of a cover of hot steam. Instead she was going to confront Gabriel Sinclair while wearing only a towel and a massage table. Well, she would just have to strive to be as brisk and calm and as coolly professional as possible under the circumstances. So much depended on subtly gaining and keeping the upper hand with Sinclair.

Samantha managed to summon a graciously aloof smile, hoping her inner agitation did not show in her eyes. It was tricky maintaining the serene, faintly inquiring expression while keeping her chin planted firmly on her stacked hands. Miss Carson industriously ignored the potential interruption as the man came to a halt beside the table. Her continued assault was going to make conversation as well as the gracious smile rather difficult to maintain, Samantha acknowledged ruefully.

"From that rather cryptic little message you sent, I somehow pictured you in a gray pinstripe business suit and a pair of low-heeled pumps, Miss Maitland." The man's voice suited him, a low, soft drawl that held the essence of stones on a riverbed in its depths. "The towel adds a whole new twist to the picture."

Good God! He was so *substantial*-looking. The impression of solid, granite-hard immobility was unnerving. How did one get the upper hand with this type? It took a fierce effort of will for Samantha to maintain the smile. "I was led to believe that Californians appreciate a touch of novelty, Mr. Sinclair. You are Gabriel Sinclair, aren't you?" She tried to inject a hint of admonishment into her voice. After all, he hadn't had the good manners to properly introduce himself. But, then, someone with good manners would have backed out of this room full of naked women as soon as he'd blundered through the door!

He inclined his head in acknowledgment. Before Samantha could continue, Miss Carson chose to take temporary charge of the situation.

"My client is occupied at the moment, Mr. Sinclair," she announced, turning violent on a particularly stubborn bit of cellulite. "And gentlemen are not allowed in the treatment rooms."

"I am a friend of Miss Fortune, the owner," Gabriel murmured absently. His gaze was focused on the portion of Samantha's anatomy presently under attack.

"And that gives you the right to just march in here?" Samantha demanded coolly, annoyed as she sensed a flush rising into her face. Heaven only knew what other parts of her were also turning pink under the interested perusal she was undergoing.

"Frankly, I didn't ask." Gabriel smiled down at her, a small, faintly amused smile that increased Samantha's feeling of unease. "I just came looking and here you were."

"I see," she retorted repressively. "Do you make a habit of staging such grand entrances for every business appointment?"

"As you said, Californians are fond of novelty."

Samantha eyed him warily. She mustn't let him think he had intimidated her with his unexpected appearance. She had enough instinctive business sense to know the value of holding her own, especially when dealing with a successful businessman. Such males were natural competitors, natural hunters. They survived precisely because they knew how to zero in on weaknesses in their opponents. The one thing she must not do was appear weak. On the other hand, she didn't want to alienate him, either. His cooperation was all that stood between success and failure for her. A delicate situation.

The worst part of the whole thing, Samantha thought irritably, was that he had succeeded in his obvious attempt to catch her off-balance. "A robe," she muttered, "my kingdom for a bathrobe. Miss Carson, would you kindly fetch that robe you took from me earlier?"

"We are far from finished for the day, madam!" Miss Carson protested, redoubling her efforts.

"I think I'm finished for the rest of my life! Miss Carson, please do as I ask. I have a business appointment with this gentleman." Samantha tried to infuse her voice with authority. Damn hard to do from her position on the massage table, she discovered. She was vividly conscious of Gabriel Sinclair's silent amusement.

"Tell him to come back later. You are here at the spa for physical reconstruction, not business!"

"My God, I don't believe this," Samantha gritted. "I feel as though I've been trapped in Dr. Frankenstein's spare parts room."

"Would you like me to draw up a chair so that we can talk here while you are being, er, reconstructed?" Gabriel asked very politely.

His smooth taunt was too much. Damned if he was going to stand there and silently laugh at her predicament. Forcing a cool, challenging smile, Samantha lifted her head just far enough to meet his assessing eyes. "I really don't think I can concentrate on business while this person is intent on working me over as if I were a particularly tough cut of meat. Why don't you be an angel, Gabriel, and make Miss Carson go away? Show me you wield a little clout here in California!"

Samantha felt the sudden hesitation in him and felt a rush of satisfaction. Excellent. She had succeeded in taking him back a bit with her taunting request. It was time she regained the initiative Sinclair had stolen by approaching her in the manner he had chosen.

But Sinclair, to give him credit, recovered immediately. With a polished gesture he peeled off the expensive, lightweight jacket he was wearing and held it out with a flourish. "I s-s-shall be happy to do my best, Miss Maitland."

Samantha's tortoiseshell eyes widened at the solution he was offering even as her attention was momentarily caught by the unexpected stutter in Gabriel's voice as he hit the "sh" sound. Sidetracked by it she had to refocus on the offer of the jacket.

"That's the best you can do?"

"I'm afraid so. It's either this or walk out of here wearing that little towel. Your Miss Carson doesn't look as if she's going to back down."

Indeed, Miss Carson was viewing the entire proceedings with a baleful eye. "Miss Maitland can't leave yet! We have only begun to properly cleanse the pores and rejuvenate the muscle tone."

Gabriel cocked a dark brow inquiringly at Samantha. "Take your pick. Miss Carson or me."

"The devil or the deep blue sea," Samantha complained. Miss Carson unloosed a decidedly savage attack on the left hip, and Samantha made her decision. Extending a hand, she snatched at the proffered jacket.

Only to have it held just out of reach. "Allow me to assist you, Miss Maitland," Gabriel insisted far too gently. His eyes gleamed, and Samantha noticed for the first time that they were a deeply gold shade of hazel. The kind of eyes that could reflect any emotion or an absolute

24

lack of same. She couldn't begin to read anything beyond flickering male amusement in them now.

But she knew when she had been backed into a corner. Thoroughly annoyed and not a little embarrassed, Samantha recognized that the only way out of the untenable situation in which she found herself was bold action. She would not let him win this ridiculous confrontation.

She could only hope that his business acumen far exceeded his limited ability at gallantry. Grabbing for the towel across her buttocks, Samantha sat up quickly, holding it in front of her, and then came lightly down off the table in a hasty rush. The least he could have done, she thought seethingly, was look away as she slipped into the jacket. But of course, being a man intent on establishing dominance in the small power struggle being waged, Sinclair didn't bother to glance away.

"I wouldn't look so pleased with myself," she advised sweetly as she wrapped the too-large jacket around her body. "The inside of this coat is never going to be the same."

"I doubt that I s-s-shall mind having the essence of your perfume clinging to the inside of my jacket," he mocked, studying the way the garment fell to her thighs.

"It isn't the essence of my perfume you're going to be stuck with," she assured him with grim cheer. "It's the sticky remains of Miss Carson's cleansing gel!"

Satisfied at having had the last word, Samantha spun around on her bare heel and strode regally out of the steamy, tiled room. The dark satyr followed silently in her wake. Miss Carson watched them both depart with a distinctly dissatisfied expression. Since when was business more important than fitness?

Disdaining to acknowledge the curious glances of several people who were checking into the spa, Samantha sailed through the serene Japanese garden atmosphere of the lobby. She was all too conscious of the man pacing behind her and of what he must be thinking as he trailed her bare-legged figure down the tiled hallway.

Gabriel must have had a fairly good notion of what she was thinking also because as she came to a halt in front of her room he murmured gently. "Perhaps you s-should have thought twice about requesting my assistance back there in the spa, Miss Maitland. Summoning angels can be as uncertain a business as summoning demons. Didn't you know that?"

"I shall try to remember that in the future," she retorted briskly, taking the key which had been attached to her wrist with a band and inserting it forcefully into her lock. "Do you behave like this regularly, Mr. Sinclair?" She pushed open the door and stalked into the room.

"No."

The brusqueness of the admission surprised her. Turning to glance at him, Samantha suddenly realized that he was telling the truth. Gabriel Sinclair was not at all accustomed to impulsive action on his own part.

The realization helped restore her own sense of humor as well as giving her a feeling of being back in control. She was extremely grateful for both.

"The problem in this instance," he went on thoughtfully as he stepped into the room, "is that I find myself responding to a deliberately baited hook. I don't care for such devices, Miss Maitland."

Samantha's eyes narrowed fractionally. "My note?"

"Your *cryptic* note," he clarified coolly.

"You don't appreciate a hint of a puzzle?" she dared, stifling a tiny smile. After all, whatever he thought of her provocative note, it had the merit of having been effective. He had sought her out at the spa as she had hoped he would.

"Let's get something clear between us," Gabriel drawled, taking a chair beside the window which overlooked a small patio garden. "I don't like puzzles. I don't like unknown quantities. I don't like deliberately dangled lures."

"How very unadventurous of you." But her tone was light, not mocking. If he thought she was genuinely laughing at him, he might simply turn around and leave and then she would be in one heck of a mess. "I shall try to remember that in the future. Now if you'll excuse me, I'll put on something a little more, uh, businesslike." She glanced down in disgust at his jacket wrapped around her body and started for the dressing room.

"What's the matter, Miss Maitland?" he asked quietly behind her. "Afraid I might mistake *you* for an interesting little puzzle in that outfit?"

Samantha paused momentarily in the doorway of the dressing room before shutting the door behind her. "Not at all, Mr. Sinclair. The very opposite, in fact! Thanks to the way you introduced yourself there isn't anything left of me which might still be an unknown

27

quantity. You got an eyeful, didn't you?" The door closed with a bit more force than she had planned.

At once she went limp with reaction, sagging momentarily back against the closed door and shutting her eyes while drawing a long, steadying breath. It was difficult to tell if her weakened condition was due to Miss Carson or from the shock of having Gabriel Sinclair materialize in that spa room. A little of both, probably. Good lord. What had she gotten herself into?

Well, there was no time to stand around worrying about the unorthodox way her business with Sinclair had begun. He was here in response to her note, and that could only be a hopeful sign.

Staggering a little, Samantha straightened away from the door and reached for the first thing that looked easy to slip into. She really was feeling quite limp, and the thought of struggling with tight jeans or a lot of buttons was simply too much. Miss Carson had a lot to answer for with her clients!

Dropping the jacket, Samantha pulled the cotton knit crew-neck dress over her head. It was a bright summer white, California white, she had decided when she'd purchased it in Seattle, and it was banded at hem and sleeve with bright stripes of turquoise. Bracing herself with one palm against the marble counter framing the sink, Samantha lifted her other hand to slip off the headband and the pins that held the tight bun.

The curve of shining brown hair swung down around her shoulders, and Samantha couldn't restrain another groan, this time one of relief. The severity of the required hairstyle had been slowly contributing to a headache. The new result wasn't as businesslike as she might have wished, but after all, this was California.

"And after what that man has seen of the rest of you," she lectured herself in the mirror, "he's not likely to be too impressed by a somewhat belated attempt to make yourself look as though you just walked in off Wall Street." The thought made her grimace, and she wrinkled her nose and narrowed her eyes behind the lenses of her glasses. The whole matter had gotten off to a horribly ridiculous start. It was going to take all of her energy and skill to get things back on course.

And Gabriel Sinclair did not appear to be a man who was easily pushed onto a desired course.

Squelching a small sigh of regret over the way she had loused up the deal thus far, Samantha opened the dressing room door and walked barefoot into the sitting area of her small suite. Sinclair was seated at the round table in front of the window, just as she had left him. But now he was sipping tea from a delicate china cup as he gazed out into the private little garden. Samantha's eyes widened in astonishment.

"Where did you get the tea?" she demanded, coming forward to take the opposite seat.

"I ordered it sent to the room while you were getting dressed. You looked as if you might need something reviving, and I think tea is about all that's allowed in the way of stimulants around here." To Samantha's surprise he set down his own cup and poured her one, handing it to her with grave politeness.

"Thank you," she murmured, unaccustomed to men

who knew how to pour tea. "My mother would love you," she added unthinkingly.

Gabriel's hazel eyes lifted quickly, something close to humor moving in their depths. "Your mother?"

"Umm." Samantha took a long, satisfying sip from her cup and settled deeply into the chair, bare legs stretched out in front of her. "My mother is a woman who appreciates men who don't have role problems. She's one of those who read Simone de Beauvoir's *The Second Sex* in the original French."

"An early feminist?" Gabriel seemed mildly curious.

"An early everything." Samantha smiled reminiscently. "An early beatnik, an early environmentalist, an early antinuclear power type, an early women's rights person. You name it."

"A natural revolutionary?" Gabriel asked dryly.

"A natural independent," Samantha corrected him. "She could never become a true revolutionary because, although she loves causes, she also likes people. Real revolutionaries have to be willing to sacrifice people to a cause."

"I see. A humanist, not an urban guerrilla." Gabriel nodded, as if finally satisfied at having pegged the unknown woman.

Samantha shrugged. "You may be right." Humanist would be a good term to describe Vera Maitland, Samantha thought. "She'd probably like that." Did Sinclair have to label everything and everyone? He'd said himself he disliked unknown quantities. Perhaps it was his instinctive way of maintaining control over situations. But he must be something of a fanatic about

30

summing up people and stuffing them into their proper niches if he went so far as to categorize a woman he was never likely to meet! What a neat, analytical, methodical sort of mind he must have, Samantha thought in silent amusement.

She sincerely hoped she could resist the temptation to occasionally provoke him. People with neat, methodical, pedantic sorts of minds did not appreciate being baited, she knew from experience. It was a pity that they made such irresistible targets to people like herself who preferred to move through life at a much more hectic pace, relying on intuition as much, if not more, than analysis.

"What does your mother do when s-she's not out demonstrating?" Gabriel asked calmly, blithely unaware, apparently, of her thoughts.

"Teaches socioeconomic theory at a small college back east."

"And are you truly your mother's daughter?" he startled her by asking.

Samantha slitted her eyes briefly, caught off guard. "If you mean am I cause-oriented, I'm afraid not," she finally said remotely. "I seem to have inherited a fair share of my father's interest in the more self-serving world of business." But I *am* Vera Maitland's daughter, she told herself silently, fiercely. And you, Gabriel Sinclair, are going to help me prove it!

"Perhaps it's just as well you don't s-s-share your mother's devotion to causes. I get a bit nervous at the thought of doing business with radicals. So unstable. So

31

unpredictable," he added, frowning. It was obvious he didn't approve of unpredictability in any form.

Samantha's mouth curved faintly at the corners as she realized that she was finding his slight stutter almost endearing. A stupid reaction under the circumstances, actually. The man was anything but endearing! His financial success alone was proof of that. Men as quietly successful as Gabriel Sinclair couldn't afford genuinely endearing weaknesses. She mustn't let her imagination paint him other than what he obviously was.

But it was odd to find herself discussing such a personal subject as her mother's unusual career with a man she intended to know only on a business basis. How had they gotten started on such a personal topic?

Gabriel's strong, square hand reached for the teapot, clasping the delicate curve of the handle and pouring tea with a precision and innate grace which made her think of a Japanese tea ceremony. Every movement had meaning and no motion was superfluous. He was that kind of man, she realized. Every action would be planned and executed with an absolute efficiency. The knowledge sent a small chill down her spine. It was going to be difficult curbing her own far more dynamic, often impulsive methods. She couldn't afford to scare him off with such hints of "unpredictability."

"How are you feeling? Recovered from your therapist's S and M techniques?" Gabriel broke into her musings to inquire politely.

Samantha winced, remembering. "My first experience with a spa, I'm afraid. I simply wasn't prepared for what I got. I had read this wonderful article about these places in a fashion magazine a couple of weeks ago. 'A time of cleansing for the body and the mind' or some such garbage, I believe was the exact quote." Samantha shook her head in baffled wonder. "Maybe you Californians need Miss Carson and her friends to cleanse the body and mind, but personally, I don't have the stamina for it. I've been here twenty-four hours, and already I'm exhausted. Also starving to death," she tacked on with feeling. "I must thank you for rescuing me, even if you didn't choose the most gallant method!" She fixed him with a deliberately charming smile.

Gabriel stared at the smile for a moment, as if that, too, had to be assessed and pigeonholed. Then he nodded once. "If it's any consolation, I surprised myself as much as you. I'm not normally the impulsive type."

"No, I don't imagine you are," she managed lightly. "What type are you, Mr. Sinclair?"

"Merely a businessman. Like your father, I imagine. How does he tolerate your mother's passion for causes, by the way?"

Samantha went still, the charming smile tightening into a cool, too-civil line as she began to realize how very many questions Gabriel Sinclair was inclined to ask. She had already revealed more about herself than she had ever intended. It wasn't that she particularly cared if he knew about her background, she told herself, it was simply that the matter was largely irrelevant to the issue at hand. "My father's tolerance for Vera's passions was not a problem. My parents were never married, Mr. Sinclair," she stated very neutrally. "He had no say in what she chose to do."

There was a pause, and then Gabriel probed carefully. "You speak of him in the past tense. Your father is dead?"

"My father was several years older than my mother. He died two years ago in his late seventies."

Sinclair must have finally sensed her desire to close the discussion about her parents because he acceded politely to the firm tone of her words. For a long moment they continued to sip their tea in silence, each waiting for the other to establish the new direction of the conversation. There was really only one other topic that was appropriate, of course, and Samantha realized that Sinclair was going to let her be the one to bring up the business between them. It was a subtle but effective method of telling her silently that he wasn't dying of eagerness to hear the details, she decided wryly. Had Gabriel Sinclair ever been overly eager or enthused about anything in his entire life, she wondered.

In the small, quiet space of time it took her to marshal her thoughts, Samantha took a moment to analyze the man opposite her. The impression of solid, even stolid presence which she'd had from first sight of him was stronger than ever. But now she had time to note other details. The conservatively cut hair was a deep, dark shade of mahogany, a shade repeated in the heavy eyebrows. The hazel eyes were as politely unreadable now as they had been earlier in the spa room, but there was no doubting the intelligence behind them. She had the feeling that his smiles would be infrequent and would rarely reach those assessing eyes. The clothes were casual, but they, too, were conservative, considering the fact that he was a Californian. A button-down oxford cloth shirt worn open at the throat and subdued slacks clasped with an unadorned leather belt went with the quietly styled jacket she'd "borrowed" earlier.

A conservative, cautious man in all things, she thought in fleeting frustration. Why couldn't he have been more like herself? Matters would have been so much easier.

"About that note I sent you," Samantha finally said, taking the plunge. "I assume from your presence here at the spa that you're interested in what I have to say?"

Gabriel shifted his glance briefly from her face to the small garden and back again. "I wouldn't say that I'm particularly interested in doing business with you, Miss Maitland, but I will admit to a certain curiosity."

Samantha resisted the impulse to clench her teeth. Getting a commitment out of this man was going to be difficult. And she had so little time.

But what had she expected? Men like this did not automatically grab at every deal that was offered. She had been hoping, though, that the bait she had used in this particular instance would give her an edge on gaining his agreement. It struck Samantha as she watched his profile that Gabriel Sinclair's physical solidity had an intellectual counterpart. He would not jump into anything, nor would he be pushed. But he had an ego, she reminded herself. Every man had an ego, and it was invariably his weakness. Which did not mean that he would understand or sympathize with her own weaknesses, so she must maintain the strictly business facade. He must never suspect for a moment that her motivation stemmed from an emotion as dangerously unpredictable as revenge. Nothing would have been more likely to make such a man shy away from this deal.

"As I explained to you in my note," she began industriously.

"Your *cryptic* note." Why did he have to harp on that?

"If it was a bit, er, cryptic-sounding, I expect it was because I was in something of a hurry," she apologized airily.

"It was cryptic because you were trying to interest me in the deal without giving too much information away at the beginning," he corrected softly, hazel eyes gleaming.

"Perhaps," she conceded with a shrug and then smiled engagingly. "Whatever my motives, you're here."

"Don't congratulate yourself yet," he advised blandly. "I have a great many questions which I would like answered."

I'll just bet you do, Samantha thought grimly. Outwardly she maintained the smile. "Of course you have questions. And I shall be more than happy to answer them." Damn it, he *was* interested. He had to be interested or he would never have bothered to turn up at the spa, seeking her, Samantha assured herself, trying at the same time to stifle the rush of excitement which was bubbling up inside. She must not get in a rush and ruin everything through her own eagerness. But it was so difficult to be calm and businesslike when she was so close to the end. So many months of careful planning and investigation were nearing the finish line, and she could destroy all her own efforts by letting the hopeful exhilaration show. She just *knew* that kind of enthusiasm would make this plodding financial angel take wing. Samantha's fingers clenched around the handle of the teacup in her hand as she forced herself to remain cool and restrained in front of Sinclair. Everything depended on handling this man properly.

"First, I would like to know a little more about your business, Samantha. I may call you Samantha?"

"By all means," she hastened to assure him, smiling brilliantly.

He blinked with decided wariness under the flash of the smile, and she instantly modified it into a polite, tempered expression. Gabriel poured himself another cup of tea and met her eyes deliberately. "What does Business Intelligence, Incorporated actually do?"

"Oh, I'm a sort of information broker," she explained, resigning herself to the fact that this man would do everything in a prudent, step-by-step fashion, attending to each detail in turn. There would be no hurrying him. Would he make love to a woman in the same deliberate fashion? she found herself wondering with a flash of inner humor. She could just picture him in bed, going step-by-step through the procedures outlined in a sex instruction manual. "While kissing left breast, locate sensitive area of partner's inner thigh and massage slowly. After three minutes repeat, alternating to right breast and left thigh."

Brushing aside the image, Samantha hurried into a further description of her work. "I supply my subscribers with news and information which might affect their businesses. Sort of a glorified librarian. Through a computer I can collect a huge amount of information and process it down to a manageable level. It's like being paid to sift through *Forbes, The Wall Street Journal,* and *Business Week* with a yellow highlighter and a pair of scissors," she summarized.

"Your system is computerized?" he demanded, frowning slightly.

She nodded quickly, wanting to get off the subject and on to more important things. "There are literally hundreds of computerized information retrieval services that anyone with a good home computer can subscribe to. Indexes to all the major newspapers, for instance, lists of research being done in almost any field you can imagine. Analyses of stock market activity that go back to the beginnings of the exchange. . . . And a lot of other miscellaneous information," she added with deliberate vagueness as she realized the direction of his questioning.

"The sort of miscellaneous information that helped you track me down?" Gabriel drawled with far too much perception.

There was no point denying it. "Yes, as a matter of fact," she admitted with a cool smile. "That sort of miscellaneous information. But if it's any consolation to you, there was very little to be had on you, Gabriel."

"Just enough to make you guess I might be interested in a deal involving the Buchanan Group?"

"Just enough." Samantha felt as if she were walking on eggs. "Was I right?" she finally dared to breathe after a moment.

"I will have to know a great deal more before I can give you that answer. Tell me about this real estate venture you're trying to involve me in," he instructed calmly.

Samantha took a deep breath and crushed down her disappointment. "It has to do with a site assembly project which is currently underway in Phoenix for the Buchanan Group's latest development."

"Buchanan is picking up properties in Phoenix? How did you find out about that?" They both knew that Buchanan and others like him usually stayed well hidden while their people quietly acquired the individual parcels needed for a development. Once the individual owners who occupied the properties realized just how important their particular hunks of land might be they were more than likely to ask an astronomical price.

"Of course he tries to keep his company's name out of sight," Samantha replied with a small grin. "Even one holdout owner can ruin a multimillion-dollar deal if the land he's sitting on is needed for the development."

"I think I'm beginning to get the drift," Gabriel murmured. "You haven't answered my question, though. How did you find out Buchanan was involved in an assembly project?"

Questions, questions, questions! Didn't the man ever just jump ahead to the important things without climbing each individual step along the way? Samantha closed her eyes briefly, taking a tight rein on her own restless anticipation.

"Buchanan is well hidden on this project, as usual," she said in what she hoped was a sedate tone. "I would never have found out about his plans if a few odds and ends of minor information hadn't cropped up in a couple of the data bases I routinely monitor." She saw no point in telling Gabriel that she automatically devoted a portion of her time each week to searching for any and all information on the Buchanan Group. It would be difficult to explain, in light of the fact that the company was not among her subscribing clients. Fed even a small tidbit like that, a man like Sinclair would immediately start sniffing around for further information, and Samantha had no intention of explaining her personal interest in Drew Buchanan.

"So"—Gabriel sat back and gazed at her interestedly— "You managed to discover that a secret assembly project was underway. And then?"

"I'm sure you've already guessed the rest," Samantha said demurely, sipping tea. "I quietly went in and picked up an option on a little restaurant situated right in the middle of the area Buchanan needs. That was several months ago, after I'd determined the general area of Phoenix that Buchanan's people were working in."

"I see."

She could read nothing in his stolid words. Resolutely Samantha continued. "Buchanan's real estate people have begun to move. Quietly, of course. They're using a variety of dummy corporations and a lot of different attorneys and real estate brokers to cover up who is doing the buying, but the buying has started."

"But as far as the general populace of Phoenix is concerned, what's taking place are simply a bunch of small, individual real estate deals. No one knows one developer is behind all of them."

"Nope. Except you and me," she said cheerfully. "Only we know how absolutely crucial that little restaurant is going to be. Without that piece of property a major development project which has been on the drawing boards for at least two years will have to be canceled. I can't see Buchanan letting his plans for downtown Phoenix be frustrated by one tiny Mexican restaurant."

"You're going to wait until he's bought up almost everything and then confront him with a ridiculously high price tag?"

"Ridiculously high," she agreed happily.

"But you need me," Gabriel pointed out softly.

"I'm afraid so." She sighed.

"Because your time is running out on the option for the restaurant, right? You need cash and a lot of it to close the deal with the present owner?"

Samantha raised one eyebrow above the frames of her glasses. "I need a financial angel to help me close the deal. I simply don't have access to the kind of cash or credit it will take to buy a restaurant. As a professional venture capitalist, you do. You make your living by financing ventures like this one."

"You think Buchanan's people will pay your asking price rather than wreck the whole project?"

"Of course. They're committed financially to the development project. They can't back out now, not without losing a tremendous amount of money, far more than I'll be charging for that damn restaurant!"

She could see him taking it all in, grinding it up,

41

rearranging the facts into little patterns in his head. Samantha would have given a great deal to be able to read his mind. As it was, it was like watching a blank brick wall. Was he even interested? She decided to press a bit further.

"I will make a tidy fortune out of this, and you will receive a healthy percentage of return on your invested money. As my silent partner I promise you will be amply rewarded, Gabriel," she told him earnestly. "It should be a quick, clean kill. When the big developers run into a snag just as they're nearing the end of a site assembly like this, they'll pay unbelievable amounts to buy up a crucial chunk of land. You know that as well as I do. I'll do all the work. All you have to do is put up the money and forget about it until the payoff."

Finally an emotion flared briefly in the hazel eyes, and Samantha cringed inwardly. He was laughing at her. God, she mustn't come across as naïve; that would be the kiss of death as far as he was concerned. He wouldn't risk his money in the hands of a naïve businesswoman. "Just how long will I have to forget about my money?" he inquired gently. Too gently.

"Buchanan is starting to move. I'd say someone will make an offer on the restaurant in the next few weeks."

"Tell me something, Samantha. You knew when you picked up the option to buy that restaurant that you were going to need a source of cash to close the deal with the owner when the time came. What was it you found in your computer data banks which led you to choose me as a potential business partner?" Gabriel's bluntly carved features were utterly devoid of expression.

More questions? Didn't the man ever stop asking questions and get to the important stuff? Samantha could have screamed with frustration, but instead she rallied herself to respond calmly. There was something about the solid rocklike deliberation of this man which was beginning to irritate her, though. She found herself wondering what it would take to ruffle or disturb him. The temptation to experiment in that dangerous direction was a strong one and one she repeatedly reminded herself she must resist. She was here to entice the man into her web of business intrigue, not send him plodding off in the opposite direction.

"I discovered your name linked to a Buchanan Group deal that took place four years ago. It wasn't very clear, and the report was only a scrap of news in *The Wall Street Journal*, but I got the feeling from reading between the lines that you and Buchanan had both attempted a buy-out of a small electronics firm in San Jose. Buchanan got it." She waited expectantly. Would he deny the report?

He didn't. He nodded once, complacently, as if satisfied to have one more piece of the puzzle fall into place. One more tiny item cataloged and shelved. "So that's why you dropped his name into your note. Buchanan got caught up in the merger mania which was so rampant then. Started acquiring all sorts of unrelated businesses which, I understand, he's since dumped. I was backing a group of private entrepreneurs who wanted that little San Jose firm. But all the moves were made officially by the people I was backing. I was a very silent partner. I'm surprised you found my name associated with the deal. I congratulate you on your detective work."

"Thank you." She accepted the accolade with a polite inclination of her head, trying not to appear too satisfied. Actually she was delighted he recognized the difficulty it had taken to worm out the details of his involvement in that particular deal. Perhaps it would help elevate his opinion of her business sophistication.

"So now you think I might be interested in a way of evening the score with Buchanan, is that it?"

"It occurred to me that you might find the prospect intriguing," she murmured very casually. "But even if it doesn't appeal from that standpoint, it's still a way for you to make some very easy, uncomplicated money."

"Money in large quantities, I have discovered, is seldom easy or uncomplicated."

Samantha said nothing, nibbling on the soft inner portion of her lip and mentally kicking herself for adding that last comment. Lord, he could be pedantic!

"If something goes wrong with your plan and Buchanan's people never get around to making an offer to you, I would be left holding half interest in a restaurant in Phoenix," he mused. And then, quite unexpectedly, he grinned, a totally astonishing slash of white teeth which made Samantha think of sharks and pirates. "Can you cook, Samantha? I mean, just in case we were to find ourselves running the place together?"

She eyed him owlishly, taken off guard by the humor in him. "I, uh, wasn't thinking of a half interest for you," she finally retorted smoothly, ignoring his question about her cooking ability. "Unless, of course, we *do* wind up owning a restaurant."

"You'll give me a small cut of the profits if you make your fortune and a large s-s-share of washing dishes if you fail, is that it?"

"Would you be willing to agree to a deal like that?" she asked innocently.

"What do you think?"

"I think you're probably not going to be quite that generous," she grumbled dryly.

"You think right." Gabriel sat quietly, clearly going over the possibilities inherent in the offer. The momentary humor had faded completely from his face now, and Samantha knew he was back to being all business. Slow, deliberate, careful business. She wasn't offering him the best deal in his career, and she knew it.

True, they stood to make a great deal of money, but he had undoubtedly made more backing other ventures. Still, he must be somewhat intrigued by the idea of evening the score between himself and Drew Buchanan. He had enough of an ego to want to accomplish that much, surely? It was only a business feud for him, of course, and an old one, at that. As such it couldn't contain the element of calculated revenge it contained for her, but it should be enough to keep Sinclair interested.

Besides, how could she hope for genuine, passionate revenge from a man who poured tea the way Gabriel did? She watched him lift the teapot one last time, a little fascinated in spite of herself with the studied restraint of every move. Did this man even know the

45

meaning of the word passion in business or even in bed? She sincerely doubted it. On the heels of that thought came another: Perhaps he was lucky.

"Well?" she finally couldn't resist prompting after a few more minutes of sustained thought on Gabriel's part.

He blinked and looked across the table at her as if she had interrupted a complex chain of logic he'd been building in his mind. "Well, what?"

She could have slugged him. Instead she sat very still in her chair and forced a tentative smile. "Are you interested?" Why was he dragging everything out like this? Wasn't the beautiful simplicity of the whole thing obvious to him?

"You're expecting an answer right now?" he asked in open astonishment.

Samantha's mouth firmed as she realized he wasn't anywhere near to giving her an answer. "I don't have a lot of time at my disposal." She tried pushing carefully.

"Nor do I," he retorted, rising slowly to his feet with a decisive air. "Which is why I try not to waste time on business propositions which lack important support data."

Oh, Lord, she was losing him! Samantha leaped up, frantically searching for a way to keep him from simply walking out of the room and leaving her high and dry. "This deal has been quite carefully researched," she asserted. "And I have the information with me. Perhaps we can review it over dinner? The facts are impressive and speak for themselves." Was she looking too hopeful? Too anxious? Keep it cool, Samantha. Calm and cool. You're the one in command.

Gabriel arched one heavy mahogany brow. "Dinner. That sounds like an excellent idea."

"Good," she said quickly. "Then I'll make reservations at the restaurant here and we can . . . Oh, no!"

"What's wrong?"

"I've just remembered what a totally horrid restaurant the spa has. You can't even get a glass of wine to go with the sprouts! Do you know of any other place close by?"

"Certainly. My home," he suggested immediately, startling her yet again. The hazel eyes gleamed with remote curiosity as he waited to see if she would accept.

But Samantha wasn't about to hesitate. She literally jumped at the opportunity. "Fine." She beamed engagingly. "If you'll let me have your address, I'll be over at seven."

"I was going to offer to come pick you up," he began cautiously, regarding her eager expression as if she were an overexcited puppy which might leap up on him at any moment.

Seeing the wariness in him, Samantha desperately reined in her enthusiasm. "That's quite all right," she returned sedately. "I'll be happy to drive myself to your home."

Anything to get on with this deal, she added mentally.

"I'll give you directions," Gabriel said politely, drawing a small notepad from his pocket.

Why was he the one suddenly looking rather satisfied with himself? Samantha wondered uneasily.

CHAPTER TWO

An hour after he'd left Samantha, Gabriel Sinclair methodically rolled out piecrust into a near-perfect circle. With each movement, the rolling pin traveled the same distance from the center to the outer rim, and after every three rolls, the piecrust was carefully given a quarter turn on the marble-topped pastry board.

That article in *Bon Apétit* last month had been right. Marble really was superior for working with pastry. The cool surface kept the butter in the dough from melting. Gabriel knew a sense of satisfaction at the perfection of the crust taking shape on the board. It was a familiar feeling, the kind of satisfaction he always took in projects that were under control and turning out as planned.

He hadn't made a lemon meringue pie in ages. But there was something about lemon meringue which made him think Samantha would like it. A bit tart with an underlying sweetness. His mouth crooked slightly at one corner as the image developed in his head. A tart tongue and a sweet ass. Yes, Samantha and lemon meringue went very well together.

God, he was crazy to even be thinking of doing business with someone about whom he knew so little. She was young, and although he didn't for one minute doubt her intelligence, he did wonder at her presumption when she talked of taking on an opponent as formidable as the Buchanan Group. His own memory of attempting to outmaneuver Buchanan four years ago was hardly a pleasant one, and he knew he'd been better equipped, both in terms of experience and financial backing, to enter the fray than Samantha was now.

Without his assistance little Samantha Maitland, regardless of her quick tongue and her daring, would come to the same end. Buchanan would flick her out of the way as easily as if she were a small fly which had had the temerity to land on his custom-made shirt cuff. There would be nothing unduly malicious about the act, simply the inevitable result of a lone player going up against the team effort of a corporation the size of the Buchanan Group.

Clever of her to ferret out his own experience with Buchanan, he acknowledged. And she had been smart enough to get ample play from the information. It had been that oblique reference to Buchanan in her note which had drawn him to the spa that afternoon. He had been curious; curious about the person who had uncovered the facts about the aborted buy-out attempt and even more curious about the approach Samantha Maitland was using to attract his assistance.

Within five minutes of meeting her Gabriel had known

she was not at all the sort of woman with whom he wanted to do business. She was too reckless, too impatient with detail. She wanted to bite off far more than she could chew, and she had every intention of involving him in the potential disaster which might ensue. Correction, *would most certainly* ensue if he were foolish enough to allow her to control the partnership. He liked to cook, Gabriel reminded himself wryly, but he did not particularly want to wind up running a taco stand in Phoenix!

Furthermore, any man dumb enough to get involved in a business arrangement with Samantha Maitland would find himself struggling every minute to stay in charge of the operation. There was no doubt at all in his mind that she assumed she would be giving the orders, even if it was his money being used!

No, as a business partner Miss Maitland definitely did not meet his standards. But he'd stayed long after he'd come to that conclusion. The curiosity which had brought him to see her at the spa had undergone a subtle but definite change as they had sipped their tea.

Samantha Maitland intrigued him.

Hell, he thought roughly as he gave one last turn to the pie dough. She did a damn bit more than intrigue him. He wasn't particularly interested in her as a business partner, but he had sure envisioned her as a bed partner during those moments when he'd encountered her lying bare on that massage table.

When she'd mockingly asked for his assistance, he'd had an idiotic urge to scoop her up off the table and carry her out of the room. He'd never thought of himself as an imaginative man, but in the brief fantasy which had flickered into his head during those moments, he'd almost been able to feel the tantalizing curve of her thighs against his arm. Even now he could sense his body tightening just remembering the images which had flashed through his mind.

She had been annoyed at the way he'd stood there and offered his jacket, not bothering to turn around as she slipped off the table. How furious would she have been if he'd followed through on the fantasy and had carried her off instead?

The jacket. Would she remember to bring it with her tonight? Would it occur to her that he'd deliberately not asked for it before he left? A subtle reminder of his presence while she prepared to visit his home tonight. He liked the way she had looked bundled into the overscaled garment. The conservative cut had surrounded her naked femininity in a very appealing way, making her look a little helpless.

Not that she'd seemed overly aware of her softened status, he thought grimly, sliding piecrust carefully into the pan. She'd remained as regally arrogant throughout. What would it take to break down that feminine arrogance? What would it take to make her go soft and breathless and pliable in his arms?

The mental picture of Samantha Maitland clinging to him and begging him to make love to her was so unexpectedly arousing that his hand shook a little as he set the oven temperature. Good God! What was the matter with him? He hadn't had this kind of reaction to a woman since he was a teenager!

Suddenly Gabriel wondered which of them, Samantha or himself, was left truly vulnerable. No! He could handle his reactions. He was a man, not a boy at the mercy of his hormones.

But he wanted the woman he had met in the spa this afternoon. Wanted her in a way which was new to him. He felt compelled to reach out and take her as if she were somehow his by right.

Hell, he wondered feelingly as he began methodically slicing lemons, had Samantha felt anything at all other than annoyance and startled embarrassment when he'd approached her today? Probably not. He'd read somewhere that it was only men who had such instant, gut-level reactions to the opposite sex. Not that he was any judge of uncontrollable desire, Gabriel thought laconically as he measured sugar with a precise eye. He'd always considered himself very much in command of his own physical needs.

So why was he deliberately setting out to seduce this one particular female who had thus far shown no other interest in him except as a business partner?

Because that's what it amounted to, Gabriel acknowledged as he worked on the lemon filling. He was going to stage a seduction scene over dinner tonight. The realization was enough to make him laugh aloud at himself. Sinclair the grand seducer.

All she really wanted from him was money. A rather large chunk of it. It was hardly fair to lead her on, he told himself as he stirred the bubbling filling with even, controlled strokes. But he had no other hold on her except the promise of financial support. She would never have come to his home for dinner tonight if he hadn't lured her with the business angle.

The least he could do, he promised himself, was look over her information. He nodded once, appeasing his sense of honesty with that thought. He'd look at her facts and figures.

Then he'd try to get her into his bed.

Actually, it had been rather sharp of her to try coaxing him into the deal with her personal angle. Four years ago when he was still smarting from the loss to Buchanan, the revenge approach probably would have held some appeal. But now he felt no overpowering urge to challenge the Buchanan Group. He held no animosity toward the conglomerate. Buchanan's victory had been a thoroughly reasonable one of money, power, and experience over an opponent who'd held much less of all three back then.

It was the way of the business jungle. Hadn't he, himself, used similar advantages over others? And he wouldn't hesitate to use them again.

True, there was money to be made if Samantha's scheme worked. He supposed that to her it seemed a great deal more than it did to him. Money was always a relative thing, naturally.

He had the feeling she wasn't wealthy, by any means. The spa bit didn't come cheap, but she had admitted it was her first visit to one. No, Samantha Maitland wasn't yet wealthy, but she was definitely willing to hustle, he thought with a small smile. If she wasn't doing very well financially ten years from now, it wouldn't be from lack of trying!

What she needed, Gabriel decided judiciously, timing the foaming lemon filling carefully, was someone to take her in hand and guide her naturally aggressive business instincts. She was headed for trouble taking on outfits like the Buchanan Group, regardless of her skill and talent. She needed polish, too. The kind of cool, poker-faced, boardroom sophistication which gave nothing away.

Just remembering how hard she'd had to work trying to hide her hell-bent-for-leather enthusiasm to get on with the Buchanan project made Gabriel's mouth twist in sardonic amusement. Had she really thought she was hiding the reckless daring which seemed to motivate her?

What had he been like at her age? That brash? She was probably twenty-eight or twenty-nine, which meant about nine years difference in their ages. That was a lot of time in terms of business experience. But Gabriel doubted that he had ever been that openly rash in his dealings. Oh, he had been far less street-wise than he was now, but that restless, volatile energy which simmered in Samantha had never characterized him.

Even at twenty-eight he'd been the slow, methodical, plodding type. He'd been born that way!

Gabriel sighed, removing the pan of bubbling lemon filling from the heat. Did the slow, methodical, plodding types ever get women like Samantha into bed? Maybe not, but he'd give it a damn good try, he promised himself a bit savagely as he set the pan down on the counter. The shock of feeling so strongly about the matter caused him to forget his normal caution long enough to singe a finger on the hot metal of the pan.

"Jesus!" He stuck the burned finger under cold water from the tap. What the hell was the woman doing to him? He never had accidents in the kitchen! Wrong question, he decided broodingly. The real question was what the hell did he think he was doing trying to seduce the daughter of some wild-eyed radical even if said daughter did have a delightful backside?

Making a scene in a public place had never been Samantha's style. Oh, the occasional, arrogant Grand Gesture could be quite satisfying, but embarrassing confrontations were quite another matter. If she hadn't had to learn a healthy respect for the value of a dollar during the past three years, she probably wouldn't have fought the battle at the spa's front desk that evening.

But she had learned that respect and learned it the hard way from the time she'd suddenly found herself unemployed after being eased out of Drew Buchanan's life. With characteristic bravado she'd refused financial assistance from either of her parents, flinging herself instead into the task of building her new business from scratch. It had probably been foolish to turn down the offer of help, but Samantha had found it hard enough to accept the fact that both her mother and her father had been right about Buchanan. Pride had made it unthinkable to allow them to assist in her financial recovery. Another of her sometimes costly Grand Gestures.

Two years ago she'd had another opportunity to obtain a solid level of financial security for her struggling young business. Victor Thorndyke had died, and she had been left a sizeable sum in the will. And once again pride had prevented her from taking the money. Pride and, she freely admitted, the sheer unadulterated pleasure of seeing the stunned shock on the faces of the legitimate Thorndykes the day she had regally declined to accept the money in the lawyer's office. The brash, arrogant gesture of refusal had been worth it. She would never forget that scene and neither, she suspected, would the Thorndykes. That Grand Gesture had been worth every cent it had cost.

Samantha had finished with scrimping almost a year later when Business Intelligence, Incorporated, had finally achieved critical mass in terms of having enough clients to begin attracting other subscribers in satisfying numbers. She now had the kind of income which allowed her such interesting indulgences as a week at a spa. But, she told herself as she defiantly faced the desk clerk, she hadn't reached the level of financial casualness where she was willing to kiss a chunk of cash good-bye. Not when said chunk had purchased nothing in return.

"But, Miss Maitland," the muscle-bound desk clerk persisted with hauteur, "surely you understand that the week's package rate was nonrefundable?"

"I certainly did not!" Samantha lied, grimly aware that the travel agent had made some mention of the fact and also aware that she hadn't paid any attention to the agent as visions of conducting business in the manner of the executive elite had danced through her head. She had planned to deal with her financial angel from the depths of a lounge chair beside a crystal swimming pool, a margarita in hand. Samantha now realized that she had confused the realities of spa life with cruise ship living. Next time she would try a luxury liner. In the meantime she had to make some effort to retrieve the money she was about to lose.

"Well, I'm afraid that's the case, Miss Maitland," the overly healthy ex-surfer-turned-weight-lifter announced flatly. The young man was far too large and robust to be a clerk, Samantha decided privately. He would have been better suited to a job as an orderly in a mental institution. "Your travel agent guaranteed a week's stay when she booked the room and I . . ."

"Originally I planned on staying a week, but something's come up. I have business to attend to, and it can't be done here." Samantha tried a reasoning sort of smile.

"You're quite free to leave" was the cold retort, "although I must warn you that once you've gone off the Plan, even if it's only for a meal off the premises, we can no longer promise you the full benefits of the regimen."

"You don't seem to understand! I'm not just sneaking off campus for dinner, I'm checking out permanently! I've had it with all this good, clean living, is that clear?" She knew she was beginning to sound agitated, but she couldn't help it. Already the clock was nearing seven, and the last thing she wanted to be was late to Gabriel Sinclair's. "I want to go back to potato chips and wine and a nice walk now and then for exercise!" If this torture chamber is a sample of what you Californians do for fun, she thought to herself, you're going to count me out of the running in the fast lane.

"No one is stopping you from walking out the front door!" The clerk, too, was clearly losing patience.

"Not without my refund!"

"There are no refunds on the plan you chose. Especially not after we made such an effort to accommodate your agent's request!"

"Don't blame my travel agent for this. It's not her fault!" Samantha gritted furiously. "I want to speak to the manager," she forced herself to add more sedately, chin lifting with as much arrogance as she could command.

"The manager is at dinner with the other guests," the oversized beachboy announced vengefully. He looked very pleased at being able to thwart her.

"Surely he can leave his alfalfa sprouts long enough to attend to this little matter?"

"Perhaps in the morning," the clerk conceded dismissingly.

"Perhaps right now!" Samantha interrupted forcefully, only to find herself interrupted in turn by a low, quiet male voice behind her.

"What seems to be the trouble here, Jon?"

The clerk and Samantha both turned in surprise to see a balding, middle-aged man in a somewhat rumpled dark suit entering the plant-lined foyer. He was not more than a couple inches taller than her own five feet four inches, and what remained of his graying hair had once been midnight black. There was more than a hint of a comfortable paunch beneath the outline of the suit, and the heaviness was repeated in the man's face. Dark eyes studied her from beneath heavy lids, eyes filled with a pleasant, old-world gallantry. He looked, thought Samantha, like someone's grandfather.

"Good evening, Mr. Fortune," the desk clerk said in an astonishingly deferential tone. "Is Miss Fortune expecting you? I'll have her paged immediately."

The newcomer inclined his head, waving off the clerk's offer. "That's quite all right, Jon. I know where to find her." Turning back to Samantha, he repeated his question. "What seems to be the trouble, Miss . . . ?"

"Maitland. Samantha Maitland," Samantha said quickly. "It's kind of you to offer to help, but I'm afraid this is between myself and the spa's management. A slight misunderstanding about billing procedures," she explained dryly.

But the desk clerk was not nearly so inhibited about dragging the innocent bystander into the fray. "Miss Maitland, sir, is one of our guests. She, uh, wishes to check out ahead of schedule, and as I'm sure your sister has probably explained, our policy requires a nonrefundable fee."

"All guests eventually check out, Jon," Fortune pointed out very mildly, smiling gently at Samantha. "Does it really matter whether or not they leave ahead of schedule? Perhaps a slight change in policy could be made in this instance?"

"Thank you very much for seeing my side of this, Mr. Fortune . . ." Samantha began quickly.

"Emil, my dear. Call me Emil."

"Yes, well, Emil, thank you for your interest in the

matter, but you needn't get involved. It's not your problem. I just hope your sister doesn't have the same problem when she checks out!" she added darkly.

"My sister owns this place. She makes the policies," Emil Fortune explained kindly.

"Oh." Nonplussed, Samantha stared at him.

"I gather you have not enjoyed your stay here?" Emil Fortune inquired gravely.

"I am starving to death and sore all over, to be perfectly blunt." Samantha could not resist the opportunity of listing her complaints in front of the desk clerk. "Your sister has built a very impressive business here, Mr. Fortune—but frankly, it's beyond me why anyone would pay good money for this sort of thing!"

"To each his own," Emil Fortune intoned, but his eyes were smiling.

"I suppose," Samantha agreed. "I came to California to attend to some business, and I thought I would be able to do it while staying here, but that's proven to be quite impossible."

"I see," Fortune nodded. "Are you certain you wish to leave tonight, though, Miss Maitland? We're quite a distance from Santa Barbara and the nearest motel."

"I don't mind driving at night," she assured him. "I'm having dinner with my business acquaintance this evening, and I'm sure he'll be able to direct me to a good motel."

"You are doing business with someone nearby?" the middle-aged man inquired.

"Yes, a Mr. Sinclair. He lives a couple of miles up the coast, and I'm sure he's expecting me. I was due at seven." Damn, she hadn't meant to drop Gabriel's name into this mess. Strange how this unassuming little man had her chatting quite freely. But it was getting late. "I really must be on my way. If a refund is impossible this evening," she added with a severe look at the clerk, "then you can count on seeing me again in the morning! Perhaps your manager will see fit to look into the matter."

"I don't see why things can't be settled tonight," Fortune murmured softly. "I'm sure my sister would not want a guest of the spa to be prevented from taking care of their business affairs properly. What do you think, Jon?"

"Uh, no, sir, I'm sure she wouldn't."

"Well, why don't you see if you can't figure out some sort of way around this little glitch?" Fortune suggested calmly.

To Samantha's surprise and relief Jon moved awkwardly behind the desk, no longer the overconfident, supercilious clerk. "Yes, well, if you really think Miss Fortune wouldn't mind. . . ."

"I'm sure my sister will agree with me. In any event, I shall tell her it was all my fault and you'll be off the hook," Fortune said smoothly. He turned to Samantha as Jon began rummaging through the papers on his desk. "And I also don't think we should keep Miss Maitland from her dinner engagement any longer. Gabe will be wondering where you are, Miss Maitland. He's a very precise sort of man, and he doesn't have all that many dinner guests. I wouldn't want to be responsible for ruining the evening for him."

"Why, thank you," Samantha managed, very grateful for the miracle the man had worked on the muscle-bound Jon. "I certainly appreciate your help, Mr. Fortune. I do hope your sister won't be upset. . . ."

"Leave that to me. My sister is a businesswoman. She'll understand." The smile in the dark eyes gleamed more brightly. "I have the feeling Gabe will feed you far better than the chef here. Gabe is a marvelous cook, believe me. I've had the pleasure of dining with him on a couple of occasions."

"You're a friend of his?" Samantha peered at Fortune narrowly through the lenses of her glasses, wondering what sort of friendship her angel had with this pleasantly rumpled little man.

"We've done business together," Emil Fortune explained easily. "And, yes, I probably come as close to being his friend as anyone could be. In turn, he is perhaps the nearest thing to a friend that I have known. Neither of us, I'm afraid, has an abundance of acquaintances with whom we feel, shall we say, comfortable? But, then, how many close friends does anyone ever have?" he continued philosophically.

Samantha smiled. "I'll say hello to him for you," she offered, glancing at Jon, who was still bent over a sheet of paper, scribbling furiously.

"Please do," Fortune returned seriously. "Tell him I'm glad to see he is expanding his circle of associates to include a young woman who has sense enough not to pay good money to have her body abused."

Samantha laughed. "Actually," she confided, "it looked rather appealing in the article I read. But I seem to lack the stamina for it." She broke off as Jon finished his calculations and handed her the voucher marked for a full refund. "Why, thank you very much," she said stiffly, startled at receiving the entire amount back. She snatched the paper from him and stuffed it into her purse before he could change his mind. Then she reached down to lift her suitcase.

"I'll take care of that for you," the man named Fortune said, reaching for the expensive yellow leather case before she could grasp it. Without a word he followed as she smiled and hurried toward the parking lot where her rental car waited.

"I can't thank you enough for your help," Samantha said quickly as she opened the trunk of the sporty little compact and allowed Fortune to put the suitcase inside. Actually she felt a little guilty at having let him carry the case. He wasn't all that much larger than she was! "I'll give your best to Mr. Sinclair."

"He already knows what he can expect from me," Fortune smiled comfortably, "but say hello to him anyway. And be nice to him, will you, Miss Maitland? He needs an interesting woman like you in his life. Perhaps you could jolt him out of his humdrum routine a bit, hmmm?"

Samantha looked up sharply, frowning at the hopeful tone in Fortune's voice. "Mr. Sinclair and I are business associates, nothing more," she told him frostily through the open window.

"And have a little patience with him, too," Fortune advised, just as if she hadn't spoken. "He tends to do things in his own slow but sure way, but they do get done. He is a very thorough man." Fortune nodded complacently. "I think you're going to be very good for him, Miss Maitland. Shake him up a little." Before she had time to clarify the situation once more, he said, "Good-bye and drive carefully. You have the directions?"

"He gave them to me this afternoon," Samantha said vaguely, longing to be on her way. She was late and she had the feeling Gabriel Sinclair wouldn't appreciate tardiness.

"In great detail, no doubt," Fortune chuckled. "A very thorough man, as I said."

Samantha allowed herself a small laugh as she started the engine. "I got a detailed drawing of every bend in the road and every possible landmark between here and his house!"

She just hoped she could remember a few of the details on that elaborate map Gabriel had drawn for her earlier in the afternoon because after taking a quick glance at it, she'd automatically tossed it on the dresser top and forgotten it there. How lost could one get when there was only one road between the spa and his home?

With a last glance in her rearview mirror at the comfortable form of Emil Fortune, she guided the little car out of the parking lot and onto the narrow highway which hugged the coast. Leaving the spa behind her had all the uplifting exhilaration of a prison escape. What a nice little man that Mr. Fortune was. She was really very grateful for his assistance with that bull of a desk clerk.

The decision to check out of the spa had been made almost as soon as Gabriel had left that afternoon. Hiding in her room when she was supposed to join the other inmates in a lengthy jog along the beach, Samantha had come to the conclusion that there was no point torturing herself further. She had achieved contact with Sinclair, which had been her main goal all along.

Taking her time, she had dressed for dinner and packed her suitcase. The outfit she had chosen had been purchased in Seattle. It was a dashing black velvet tuxedo-style jacket and pants complete with a pleated white shirt with tiny, upstanding wing collar and a small black velvet tie. The close-fitting stylish parody of the traditional male evening dress was both tailored and chicly feminine. With her hair coiled neatly into a curving knot at the nape of her neck, Samantha felt suitably attired for an evening of business with her angel.

She grinned to herself as she realized that she was applying the term "angel" more and more to Gabriel Sinclair. Was that because, subconsciously, managing an angel seemed potentially easier than managing a high-powered business barracuda?

The grin faded as she recognized the truth behind that thought. She had certainly not succeeded in managing Drew Buchanan very well! He had sent her life into a tailspin from which it had taken a long time to recover. Revenge was the last link in that recovery. No, managing a cold-blooded bastard like Buchanan was a dangerous business at best. But angels, especially plodding angels, should be a much easier proposition.

Samantha found the nearly hidden drive which led off the main road toward the sea after two or three attempts and a certain amount of backtracking. She really should have brought that damn map, she decided. Half an hour late, she noticed, glancing at her watch as she parked the car in the curving drive of the secluded beachfront home.

Her expression tightened determinedly as she pressed the small bell outside the huge, intricate wrought iron gate which guarded a courtyard paved in pale stone. It wasn't her fault she was late!

The main door to the house opened and her host emerged. Gabriel was wearing a conservatively striped, long-sleeved shirt, open at the throat, and a pair of dark, well-tailored slacks that seemed to emphasize the solid masculinity of his frame. The burnished leather of his shoes and the refined gleam of a gold and stainless steel watch on one strong wrist were quiet evidence of Sinclair's abilities as a venture capitalist. As was the beachfront home, Samantha reminded herself silently. Property along the California coast cost an angel's salary: Gold and stardust.

In addition to the conservative clothing, Gabriel was also wearing a very forbidding expression, she realized, one which brought the excuses immediately to her lips.

"I'm very sorry to be so late," she plunged in chattily, using her most dazzling smile. "There was a little trouble at the front desk of the spa when I told them I was checking out. If it hadn't been for the nicest little man, a friend of yours, I believe, I'd still be arguing with that ridiculous desk clerk. I do hope I didn't spoil your dinner plans? I'm starving!" She tried anxiously to make the smile a very ingratiating one.

Dark lashes lowered to partially conceal the hazel gaze as Gabriel slowly opened the gate. Samantha noted his whitened knuckles against the iron filigree. She studied the rather grim expression on his face and decided that her excuses were being considered very seriously, as if there was some question about whether or not they would be accepted.

"You checked out of the spa?" Gabriel finally asked, apparently zeroing in on the most important piece of information she had given him.

"I had to. Self-preservation," she explained with great feeling as she stepped through the gate. "I've decided I'll find a motel somewhere along the coast highway after dinner," she confided easily. Behind her the heavy gate was swung shut and locked. The solid, rather final sound of the iron setting into place sent a strange shaft of unease through her, and she swung around.

"Something wrong?" Gabriel inquired as he politely took her arm and walked her toward the door.

"No, nothing," she assured him, her mind leaping from the sound of the closing gate to a sudden awareness of the tension in him as he took her arm. Was he really this upset because she was half an hour late? "Believe me, I'm normally a very prompt sort of person," she assured him quickly. "As I said, the scene at the front desk held me up. If it hadn't been for your sweet friend, Mr. Fortune . . ."

"Emil Fortune helped you settle things with the desk clerk?" The surprise in his tone was obvious.

"Yes, he was there to see his sister who owns the

67

place. The desk clerk was very obliging once Mr. Fortune took a hand in the matter."

"I'll bet."

"I beg your pardon?" Samantha wrinkled her nose as she stared up at him.

"I said, I'll bet the desk clerk was very obliging once Emil got involved," Gabriel repeated patiently as he pushed open the door to the house.

"I heard what you said," Samantha retorted in quick irritation. Hastily she stifled the emotion, reminding herself that this man took everything very literally. "I meant, what did you mean by the remark? I'm sure he carries some clout because of his sister, but you make it sound as though the desk clerk might have some reason to be genuinely afraid of Emil."

That brought a tight smile to Gabriel's hard mouth. "Samantha," he said very gently as he carefully closed the door, "a lot of people call Emil Fortune a lot of names, but you're the only one I've ever heard call him 'sweet.'"

"But he was! Very."

"He must have liked you." Gabriel shrugged.

"So?" she challenged. "I liked him, too!"

"That's nice," Gabriel retorted laconically. "So, as a matter of fact, do I. Sit down. I'll get you a glass of wine."

"Gabriel, you're being deliberately cryptic," she accused, glancing around curiously at the cool, uncluttered surroundings. The interior of the house suited the inhabitant, she decided. The ocean side of the modern structure had been opened with decks and balconies and a great deal of glass to take full advantage of the spectacular view of the sea. Natural sisal matting had been used on polished board floors and the walls were sand-colored. The clean lines of the furniture were upholstered in a very restrained palette of earth tones. It rather reminded her of an elegant cruise ship. Expensive and neat with everything in its place. There wasn't so much as the morning paper left lying on a coffee table to mar the tidiness. How depressing it was going to be working with someone who had such a penchant for precision.

"I am never deliberately cryptic," Gabriel informed her as he poured a glass of chilled Cardonnay wine and carried it toward her. "I've told you, I don't like puzzles."

"Then what is it that's so strange about my finding Mr. Fortune a pleasant man?" she taunted lightly, taking the glass and flinging herself lightly down on the nearest chair.

Gabriel watched her sprawl with casual ease, and then he carefully sat down across from her, adjusting his wineglass so that it sat in the exact center of the coaster on the end table. His hazel eyes were hooded as he said slowly, "Emil Fortune's father spent time in a federal prison on income tax fraud charges. The government went to court over the discrepancies in his taxes because the FBI couldn't find enough evidence to pin the more serious charges on him. Emil's brother manages some of the most lucrative casinos in Vegas and Atlantic City. From a discreet distance, of course. Emil's cousin was careless. He's spending ten years in prison on smuggling charges. Emil's lawyer expects to have him out within two years, however. Another of Emil's relatives runs a trucking firm that somehow made a fortune during the recent recession when most trucking firms were losing their collective shirts. Emil's grandfather founded the family empire during prohibition, if that gives you a clue as to the solid financial status of the family."

Samantha stared at him. "And Emil?" she asked very carefully.

"Emil is much more sophisticated than the rest of his family," Gabriel drawled, sipping his wine. "He's into arbitrage. He moves money and securities around on the international market so fast it makes your head spin."

"And makes a nice profit on the price discrepancies between the currencies of different countries," Samantha concluded slowly. "I see." She took a long sip of the wine, trying to square the image of the little rumpled man in the spa lobby with that of an international money broker who had ties to a powerful crime family. "Do you, uh, mind if I ask the obvious question?" she hazarded.

He leaned back in his chair. "You want to know how I got involved with Emil Fortune?"

"Well, it might be reassuring to know you're not in danger of being hauled off to prison in the middle of our deal!" she retorted spiritedly.

That elicited a lazy grin, that rare smile which made her think of sharks. "Emil would never allow that to happen. He likes me."

"Don't be modest," she instructed tightly. "Tell me why he likes you?"

"Nervous?"

"I'm involved in a business deal, not a criminal venture!"

"Sometimes there's a rather fine line between the two," Gabriel noted dryly.

"The line may be fine but I can still see it, and I intend to stay on my side of it."

"Very commendable." He took another sip of wine and eyed her over the rim of the glass. "Okay, I'll set your mind at rest. You're not in any danger of finding my photograph on a Wanted poster at the post office. I met Emil when I got involved with his sister."

"His sister! Oh, I see," Samantha began hastily, aware of a totally unexpected twinge of resentment against the unknown woman. What was the matter with her? Why should she give a damn about Gabriel Sinclair's love life? But in spite of her dismissal of the topic, she once again had a mental image of him making love to a woman in that slow, methodical way of his. What would it be like?

"No, I don't think you do see," Gabriel corrected her mildly. "You asked earlier if it was Emil's money behind the spa. It isn't. It's mine. I loaned the capital to Donna two years ago. It's been a very profitable venture for both of us."

Samantha gave him a sharp look. "You're her financial backer?"

"Ummm." His mouth twisted wryly. "At the time I didn't know who her brother was. By the time I found out, it was too late. I couldn't back out of the deal and leave Donna stranded."

"If Donna's family has so much money, why didn't she borrow from them?"

"Believe me, that's one of the first questions I asked Donna when I found out just what I'd gotten involved with! The simple truth is Donna has spent her whole life trying to break away from the family connections. She wanted her business to be strictly legitimate, funded with strictly legitimate money. When she came to me two years ago, she deliberately neglected to tell me about Emil and the other relatives. The first I knew of it was the night Fortune showed up on my doorstep."

"A shock?"

"To put it mildly. But it turned out he only wanted to make sure I didn't have any designs on his sister."

"Romantic designs or financial designs?" Samantha demanded without stopping to think.

One mahogany brow lifted coolly. "Do you always say the first thing that comes into your head?"

"Not everyone is as deliberate and premeditated as you are, Gabriel," she murmured, ruffled at the implied accusation of flightiness.

"I prefer to do business with people who think and act the same way I do," he warned very gently.

"Then you must find your life a bit dull at times," she snapped.

To her astonishment he considered that. "At times," he finally agreed. "Are you going to liven things up for me a bit?" he asked whimsically.

"Your friend Mr. Fortune thought it might be good

for you," she grinned wickedly. "Don't worry, though. I assured him our association was strictly business."

"That was exactly the type of association I had with Donna Fortune," he said calmly.

Samantha narrowed her eyes briefly.

"Which was why Emil was so concerned. He had visions of some enterprising capitalist getting his financial hooks into Donna and then taking advantage of her. By the time I had assured him everything was straightforward and honest between Donna and myself, Emil and I somehow discovered we had become friends."

"It sounds like a dangerous friendship."

"Friendships, I've discovered, aren't always logical."

"Don't look so chagrined." Samantha laughed. "There are a lot of things in life which aren't logical."

He looked at her. "So I'm learning."

Samantha chewed reflectively on her lower lip and wondered exactly what was going through her angel's very logical, very organized brain.

Gabriel saw the speculation in her gaze and thought he knew precisely what was going on in the lively brain of the sweet witch he had invited to dinner. She found him dull, pedantic, slow, and God knew what else. But she was here, he told himself. She was in his house, drinking his wine, and about to eat the food he had prepared. He was amazed at how territorial and possessive his thoughts were. Even a little predatory.

"It's time to start dinner," he announced, getting to his feet with a decisive movement, feeling a need for some physical release from the tension he'd been under. When seven o'clock had arrived with no sign of Samantha, he'd experienced the most appalling surge of anger. It was an anger which had died quickly after her belated arrival, but some of the tension it had caused persisted. "You can stay here and finish another glass of wine if you like."

"No, I'd much rather watch you at work. Perhaps I'll learn something," Samantha said lightly, rising quickly to follow him into the kitchen.

Indeed, it was fascinating, she decided shortly. Everything went together with a precision and patient skill that Samantha could only admire. She watched as he set a pan of sliced apples in butter to sauté while he put mushrooms into another shallow skillet. When the mushrooms were cooked, he removed them and added more butter to the pan. In this, Gabriel browned several small veal scallops to perfection.

Transferring the scallops to a platter, he added calvados to the skillet, igniting it and shaking the pan until the flames went out. Then he poured in cream and a bit of *glace de viande* and reduced the rich sauce until it was slightly thickened. The result was served over the veal together with the sautéed apples and a salad composed of asparagus, potatoes, and beets.

"My God, this is good." Samantha sighed as she savored each bite. "When I think of all those poor people suffering through lettuce and sprouts tonight back at the spa . . ." She broke off, shaking her head with pity. "Do you always feed your business partners this well?"

Gabriel lifted his eyes from the remainder of the veal on his plate, riveting her attention with the sudden, utter seriousness of his expression. "I haven't agreed to any business arrangements yet, Samantha. But I did want tonight to be a little special."

"You're trying to impress me?" she dared lightly. She refused to be put off by the fact that he wouldn't make a commitment regarding their deal.

"I'm trying to do a little more than impress you. I'm trying to seduce you," he drawled evenly, his eyes never leaving her face.

Samantha dropped her fork halfway to her mouth. It clattered rudely to the white octagonal plate, and she mumbled a hasty apology as she recovered it. *Play this light, Samantha. Give him an out and maybe he'll retreat of his own accord. He's not really the pushy type.*

"I'm sorry, I don't think I heard you correctly. Goodness, I hope I didn't spatter anything on this lovely place mat!" She searched the woven fiber mat anxiously for signs of veal sauce. What was she going to do if he didn't back down? Honesty in a man was far more unnerving and far more difficult to handle than the subtle maneuver!

"You heard me, Samantha," Gabriel said quietly. "Why the panic? S-surely I'm not the first to pose the question."

She took a grip on her resolve. "Of course not. Somehow I just wasn't expecting it from you."

He smiled bleakly. "Still trying to dress me in a halo and wings?"

"Mr. Sinclair, I came here tonight because I hoped we could do business together. I never mix business with my personal life." Not anymore, she silently noted to herself. "And certainly not to the extent you're suggesting. Is that very clear?" No one knew better than she just how disastrous a combination it could be.

"I've been thinking about you ever since I saw you lying on that massage table this afternoon. I would like to take you to bed, Samantha," he said with devastating simplicity.

Samantha swallowed, her fingers drumming on the glass tabletop as she mentally ran through a list of ways to handle this new development. He wasn't going to simply back off. Once started on a course of action, it would probably take a nuclear explosion to deflect Gabriel Sinclair from his chosen path. She had never before experienced such blunt directness and such a deliberate way of doing things in a man, and it temporarily put her off stride. Perhaps the best way to handle it was to be equally blunt.

"Are you saying that our partnership is contingent on my sleeping with you?" Utter disdain permeated her words. "If that's the case, Gabriel, I might as well say good night and be on my way. I don't make deals like that." She wasn't bluffing and it showed. But she couldn't read the thoughts moving behind the guarded hazel gaze as Gabriel continued to search her own fiercely controlled features. Then he lowered his eyes to his wineglass and reached for it.

"Whether or not you'll come to bed with me won't affect my decision on whether or not I'll do business with you, Samantha."

Her eyes widened in sudden perception. "You're not

planning on doing business with me at all, are you?" she whispered tightly.

He hesitated and then shrugged. "I haven't decided yet."

"Terrific!" she muttered scathingly. "Am I wasting an entire evening then? Were you even going to ask to see the information I've collected? Or were you just going to rush me into bed and then send me on my way in the morning without any answer at all?"

Gabriel eyed her thoughtfully for a moment. "Would you like a little career advice, Samantha?"

"Not particularly!"

"Don't worry, it's free. The advice is to watch that temper of yours. Watch all your moods, in fact. You're very volatile, you know. You ought to keep yourself under control when you're trying to conduct business. Don't let your opponent see how anxious or angry or reckless you really are. You s-s-should strive for a little more business poise, Samantha."

She raised beseeching eyes toward the ceiling. "For heaven's sake! I didn't come here for a lecture on professional conduct! I've put a simple, straightforward, potentially lucrative proposition in front of you. Just tell me whether or not you're seriously interested."

"And if I'm not?"

"William Oakes," she said succinctly.

"Oakes?" Gabriel frowned. "From New York?"

"You know him?" she inquired pleasantly enough. "You ought to. He's in your line of work. He was the other man on my list of potential backers."

"Why didn't you select him as your first choice? How did I get so lucky?"

She lifted one shoulder dismissingly. "You were on the West Coast, which made you convenient and less likely to be known to Buchanan's people. You have a low profile in the venture capital world, which means you can make a move without telegraphing it to *The Wall Street Journal* or *Barron's*. You operate alone, which means I didn't have to convince an entire committee of the validity of my plan. And you'd had that previous encounter with the Buchanan Group which I thought might predispose you to want to even the score."

"An excellent line of reasoning. I see you can think logically when you wish." He smiled gently.

"I can work up an equally sound line of reasoning to present to Mr. Oakes, I'm sure," she threatened carefully.

"Stay away from William Oakes, Samantha." Gabriel's voice turned suddenly hard.

"Why?" she challenged.

"Because he'll chew you up into little pieces and spit out what's left. That's why. You'll find yourself coming out of the deal with nothing. He'll take everything."

"Is this professional envy I'm hearing?" she mocked, pleased at having regained some advantage. She couldn't be sure why he didn't like Oakes, but there must be a way of working the information to her advantage.

"It's not professional envy, it's a professional evaluation of a colleague," Gabriel growled. "I mean it, Samantha, stay clear of him."

"I need a backer for my plan. If you're not willing to

78

go into a partnership with me, then I shall have to look elsewhere, won't I?"

"Samantha, Samantha!" He shook his head, smiling faintly. "You're so hopelessly transparent! You're not going to force my hand by threatening to run off to William Oakes, so don't bother trying that tactic. I'm giving you sound advice about the man. Accept it for what it is."

"Just tell me the truth, Gabriel," she demanded. "Are you even considering my proposition? Or was the invitation this evening strictly a play to get me into bed?"

He faced her levelly. "I haven't ruled out the possibility of doing business with you," he said honestly.

"Word of honor?" she pressed.

"Word of an angel," he mocked lightly.

She sat back, somewhat appeased, and picked up her fork. "Then perhaps we could go over the information I've collected after dinner."

"Samantha?"

"Hmmm?" The veal really was quite fabulous.

"If we do wind up in business together," Gabriel began slowly, "there's something we s-s-should have very clear between us."

"Yes?" She waited expectantly.

"You have my word that I will be quite frank with you on all matters. I would want your word in return."

Visions of what this man might do if he knew her true motivation on the Buchanan deal blazed in her mind. It was very clear that Gabriel Sinclair did not approve of emotionalism in business. If he realized just how steep an emotional investment she had in this deal, it would kill any possibility of gaining his cooperation.

"You have my word that I will be quite straightforward with you on all business matters," she stated carefully. And she would, she promised herself. She just wouldn't burden him with a lot of past history about herself and Drew Buchanan.

He nodded once, as if satisfied. "Excellent. Now please relax and enjoy the rest of your dinner. I have a lemon meringue pie for dessert of which I am particularly proud."

Samantha glanced up, smiling again as she sensed that the rough spot in their new association had just been safely traversed. "It's a wonder some woman hasn't chained you to her kitchen sink. A man who can cook like this is prime husband material."

"I was married once," he said quietly, managing to make her feel awkward at having asked the implied question. "The cooking wasn't enough to hold her, however."

"I see. I'm sorry. I didn't mean to pry," she whispered a little stiffly.

"It's quite all right," he assured her. "What about you? I see no ring."

"No. I came close once, but disaster was avoided at the last minute," she told him lightly, having no desire to pursue the topic.

"The marriage would have been a disaster?"

"One of the many things I learned at my mother's knee was that marriage was not one of life's necessities. I think I'm ready for that pie now, Gabriel. And after dinner I would like to borrow your phone, if I may, to make reservations at a motel for this evening. How far is it to Santa Barbara?"

"Several miles, but there's no need to find someplace for the night, and you know it," Gabriel told her bluntly as he carefully sliced the pie. "You can stay here." He set her piece of pie down in front of her with a short decisive gesture as if he were throwing down a gauntlet.

"It's very kind of you to offer me a bed for the night," she began politely, not certain how to take his mood.

"I am not a kind man, Samantha. I am a practical man," he added regretfully. "Quiet, practical, fond of detail, careful, prudent, and a lot of other dull qualities to be's-sure, but kindness isn't among them. I am also not given to assaulting potential business partners. You'll be safe enough here tonight."

Or as safe as I want to be, Samantha found herself thinking. What in hell had put that thought into her head? Too much speculation on what it would be like to have Gabriel Sinclair make love to her. Far too much.

CHAPTER THREE

Stark was the first word that came to mind as Gabriel ushered Samantha into the guest bedroom. It was done in the same subdued tones as the rest of the house, the furnishings comfortable but minimal. No, not exactly stark, she reconsidered as he set her suitcase down beside the bed, but definitely not comfortably cluttered! She had the feeling that her host had never been exposed to the glories of clutter—of cozy chaos. Pity. It might have done him some good. Loosened him up a bit.

"Why the sly smile, Samantha?" Gabriel interrupted her thoughts to ask.

"Does it make you nervous?" she taunted lightly.

"It would probably make any man nervous," he told her seriously.

"Well, don't let it bother you. I was just thinking that you're a very tidy housekeeper. Everything always in its place."

"Feel free to mess up this room if you like," he retorted.

"Thanks, I'll think about it. It has great possibilities, you know. A little sand tracked across the carpet over there, perhaps." She waved toward the door which opened onto a balcony. "Then I could take a few of the books out of the bookcase and fling them around at random. Or I could spill a cup of coffee on the dressing table. . . ."

"Please make yourself right at home," he invited gravely.

She spun around, startled by the hint of humor in his tone. For an instant she stared at him thoughtfully. "Was that a joke, Gabriel? A sarcastic quip about the way you imagine I keep house?"

"Everyone knows witches live amid a certain chaos." He smiled.

"Witch? You think of me as a witch?" She frowned.

"An interesting combination, isn't it? A witch and an angel?"

"Except that it's not a combination. Not yet. You haven't agreed to work with me, remember?"

"I remember." He watched her prowl restlessly around the room. "The bathroom connects through that door."

"Thank you. Actually, it's a lovely room, Gabriel. I'm sure I'll be very comfortable," Samantha said, suddenly aware of being rather tired. It had been a long, frustrating day. She turned away from studying the night-darkened view outside the floor-to-ceiling windows and faced him with a deliberately dismissing air. "Good night, Gabriel. In the morning perhaps we can go over those computer printouts I've got stashed in the car."

"Yes." But he didn't move, and Samantha had the

feeling he was thinking about something other than the printouts. It didn't take any great intuitive powers to read the trace of masculine hunger which came and went very quickly in the depths of those hazel eyes.

Samantha found herself wondering how long it had been since he'd invited another woman to stay the night. Some instinct told her that there probably weren't vast numbers of females coming and going in this man's life. Not because he had an angelic, disinterested view of sex but because of his innate caution.

Gabriel Sinclair would be as careful in his selection of a woman to share his bed as he was in everything else he did. That thought left her intrigued. She had been one of those women he'd selected, and he had made the decision within hours of knowing her. Samantha pondered just what that signified. Rashness of any kind, as he, himself, had pointed out, wasn't one of his normal character traits!

On the other hand, there was no denying the heavy maleness of him. It was a dense, tempered aura that emanated from the man, making itself felt whenever he came too near. But Samantha had the feeling that he wasn't aware of the solid, unyielding power he projected. Or perhaps it only affected her?

Perhaps he wasn't used to the idea of what he could do to a woman's sense of awareness because other women were not affected by the aura of implacable maleness, the waves she felt coming at her across the bedroom.

Were other women immune? Or was she more attuned to this man for some reason?

That last thought was far too disturbing. It was time

to drop the curtain on bedroom drama before it developed into something much more complicated.

"Good night, Gabriel," she said again, this time very firmly.

He nodded once instead of replying, swung around on his heel, and walked out of the room, the sense of him lingering long after he had gone. Slowly Samantha crossed the room and shut the door. After a second's pause she flipped the lock, too. A part of her insisted the man could be trusted not to force himself on her. If she hadn't truly believed that, she wouldn't have accepted his invitation to stay the night.

But a more objective side of her nature reminded her that she knew as much about Gabriel Sinclair as just about anyone else in the world, and that wasn't really much when you thought about it. She might have been a bit hasty in making her decision to stay the night.

Well, as Vera Maitland was fond of saying, to live life to the fullest one must take risks. She could almost hear her mother quoting the words. Samantha went to stand before the window facing the darkened ocean. The problem, of course, was that her mother's notion of a worthwhile risk often differed considerably from that of her daughter.

Vera Maitland was too gloriously self-contained to risk herself emotionally the way Samantha had once done so disastrously with Drew Buchanan. For Vera risk was something undertaken for the sake of a great cause, and when it came to that sort of thing, few people were braver than Samantha's mother.

She remembered the fearless way Vera had joined

ranks of others one dark year to go against the dogs and fire hoses in Alabama. Samantha remembered the incident clearly because Vera had taken her along on the theory that one was never too young to get involved in the things that mattered. It was the dogs Samantha recalled most vividly. She had always loved dogs before that frightening tirp to Alabama; always thought of them as friendly, affectionate creatures, responsive to love and kindness. Since that fateful year Samantha had been wary of dogs and generally gave them all, large or small, a wide berth.

During the march Samantha had been terrified; more than once she had considered letting go of her mother's hand and running. But finally her fear of disappointing Vera by showing herself a cowardly daughter had been far greater than her fear of the snarling dogs. Even at that early age living up to Vera's standards was important.

But nothing frightened Vera except, perhaps, the knowledge that she had raised a daughter who was not cast entirely in her own image. Samantha closed her eyes against the memory of her mother's shocked expression the day she had learned that Samantha was planning to marry Drew Buchanan.

"My God, you can't possibly be serious!"

Samantha met her mother's eyes across Vera's kitchen table and bravely nodded her head. "I'm very serious, Mother. He loves me and I love him."

Vera's finely drawn features were still austerely beautiful even in middle age. Her deep brown hair, which Samantha had inherited, had begun to streak quite dramatically with gray in the past few years in a manner hairdressers envied. That day she had worn it combed straight back, caught with an exotic clip at the nape of her neck.

The clip, Samantha knew, had been given to her mother by one of her economics students. He was the son of an important political figure from an underdeveloped country in Asia. Vera had seen a golden opportunity to inculcate him with her socioeconomic theories for developing nations and had lavished a considerable amount of attention on him. The young man had sent the clip as a token of his appreciation. Samantha knew better than to speculate on whether her mother had had an affair with the young man. Vera was neither promiscuous nor a prude, but she had made it a rule never to become physically involved with her male students. Vera never broke her own rules. Society's on occasion, but never her own.

"Love? Samantha, how many times have I told you that the emotion is a myth—a trap. A dangerous illusion for a woman. A fairy tale that Madison Avenue employs to sell everything from mouthwash to linoleum. It blinds her to reality, puts her in the grip of a man's will, and she is *used*! Enjoy an affair with Buchanan if he attracts you, but don't make the mistake of thinking he seriously returns your affection. He isn't capable of it. Haven't you learned anything at all working with him? He's the original user—using up people and money and anything else he can get his hands on to get what he wants. He's a full-blooded robber baron who would have done very nicely a hundred years ago when there were no legal brakes at all on such men. Even today he's doing very well manipulating everything and every-one around him quite ruthlessly!"

"If you thought so poorly of him, why did you encour-age me to go to work for him when Dad suggested it?" Samantha flung back, already knowing the answer.

"Because I thought, as you've decided to follow a business career instead of an academic one, that you might as well go into a position where you could exer-cise some good influence, however small, over a man like Buchanan. I don't live in an ivory tower, Sam; I'm well aware that sometimes the most important battles are the insidious ones fought from within the enemy walls."

"I'm not working for Drew as some kind of spy!" Samantha protested fiercely.

"But you've already proven you have the power to sway or at least alter the effects of some of Buchanan's decisions. Look at the way you mitigated the effects of his last land grab in Miami! Those people in that apart-ment complex would have been dumped into the street if you hadn't been in a position to assist them. You used Buchanan's resources to find those unfortunate people new housing. That was a brilliant play, Sam!"

Though her mother's praise was rare, Samantha was only temporarily put off her train of thought by the compliment. "Drew *let* me use his company's resources, Mother," she argued back. "If he hadn't cooperated, I wouldn't have been able to alter a thing! He's not what you think he is; he's simply an up-and-coming business-man. We have a tremendous amount in common. . . ."

Vera shook her head sadly. "No, you don't, honey.

You're worlds apart from Drew Buchanan. And I'll bet he knows it, even if you don't. Believe me, if he's actually talked of marriage . . ."

"Talked of it! We're engaged!"

"Then there can be only one reason," Vera shot back coldly. "He believes you can be useful to him as a wife, and we both know there's only one way, don't we, Sam?"

"Mother!"

"He knows you're Victor Thorndyke's daughter. Buchanan is only marrying you for the money he expects you to inherit, Samantha. Use your common sense! If there's one thing I've tried to teach you, it's how to think logically. Kindly do so now!"

"I want to marry him," Samantha repeated doggedly.

"And then what? Quit your job to become the perfect corporate wife? Oh, Sam, you know that would never work. I haven't brought you up to be a good little corporate wife. To dole out your time between luncheons and teas and appointments at the beauty salon. You've been taught to make your own way in the world. To change it for the better if you could. And once outside the corporation arena your influence would be significantly lessened, anyway."

From out of nowhere came the courage to ask her mother the one question Samantha had never dared to say aloud. "Did you ever, even for a little while, imagine yourself in love with Victor Thorndyke?"

Vera sat back abruptly in her chair, staring at her daughter. Then she seemed to gather herself for the answer. She had always prided herself as a mother on the fact that every one of Samantha's childhood questions had always been answered fully and frankly, regardless of the subject matter. Every question was an opportunity to teach and guide. Vera never lost an opportunity.

"Your father and I were physically very attracted to each other, Sam," she began honestly. "But how could it have ever developed into anything more than that? He was diametrically opposite to me in all his political, social, and economic beliefs. For God's sake! The man had even supported McCarthy during those Communist witch-hunts of the fifties, although I'm pleased to say he eventually saw the error of his ways on that issue." Vera hesitated, glancing unseeingly out her window into the kitchen garden. "Frankly, that is Victor's one saving grace. He's a hard man, but he is capable of seeing the error of his ways. His problem was that he had been born into wealth and had always been taught that privileges and power were only his due. Why would he ever entertain the notion of undermining a system that had so lavishly nurtured generations of Thorndykes? By the time I met him, naturally it was too late to expect he would ever change. You have to shock Victor to get him to view his world from the outside if you want him to change his mind about anything."

"And that's why you seduced him? Because it was the one way you thought you might get through to him?" Samantha waited tensely. Her mother had explained years ago that she'd had the affair with Victor Thorndyke while she was trying to convince him not to build the chemical plant he had been planning near a river. She had been successful. Thorndyke had never built the plant. Samantha's conception was the other result of Vera's campaign.

"It's true that none of my logical arguments had worked." Vera half-smiled reminiscently. "And I knew he was attracted to me. But I also knew he was married with two children and under most circumstances I would not have had an affair with another woman's husband. But I was thirty at the time, Sam," she went on gently. "I wanted to sample the uniquely female experience of bearing a child and mothering it. Victor had a great many qualities I admired. He was intelligent, healthy, and physically attractive. It wasn't his fault he had become a product of a system I found morally reprehensible. I decided he would make a good biological father for you, and since I would be making no claim on him later, either financial or emotional, I also decided I would not be a disturbing influence on his family."

"But were you in love with him?" Samantha persisted desperately.

Vera's lashes lowered as she gazed down at her coffee cup. Then she drew a deep breath. "Perhaps, for a while, I made the mistake of thinking that what I felt was . . . love," she finally admitted very slowly.

Samantha stretched out a hand across the table, closing it warmly over her mother's. "Oh, Mom, please don't act as if you've just confessed to some horrendous criminal act. I'm glad you felt that way."

Vera looked up, her expression raw. "Because it gives you an excuse to make the same mistake now?"

"No! Because I like the idea that I was conceived in love and passion, not just cold-blooded mating!"

In spite of herself, Vera's mouth curved faintly. "There was passion, Sam. More than I've ever known with anyone else." Then she shook her head once, very determinedly. "Which is probably what led me into thinking for a while that what I was experiencing was love . . . I don't want you making the same error!"

"If you had it to do over again, would you?" Samantha whispered, searching her mother's features.

"I have never regretted the affair," the older woman said vibrantly. "You are an intelligent, healthy, and independent young woman. I have always been very proud of my daughter."

Just don't screw up now and ruin everything I've tried to do, Samantha finished wryly in her head. "I love him, Mother."

Vera knew her daughter's streak of independence well. Hadn't she deliberately fostered it all during her childhood? It was unfortunate that it was temporarily sending her off in a misguided direction, but there wasn't much point in further argument, and Vera knew it.

Eventually Samantha had departed for Miami never dreaming just how desperate her mother was to prove her point about Drew Buchanan. So desperate, in fact, that for the first and only time in her life Vera had turned to a man for help. And the man she turned to was Victor Thorndyke.

After that, events had moved quickly and catastroph-ically. With a knowledge and complete understanding of Drew Buchanan which stemmed from the fact that Victor, himself, had used many of the younger man's business methods, Samantha's father had moved coldly and calculatingly to bring a swift ending to the engagement. It had taken only one phone call from Vera to send Thorndyke on his way to Florida determined to protect his daughter in the only way he knew.

Samantha did not find out until much later of the way her father had walked into Buchanan's office and bluntly told the younger man that his "bastard daughter would inherit nothing!"

That's all it had taken. Samantha had shortly thereafter found her romantic illusions in ashes as Drew quickly eased her out of his life.

As the truth emerged, the anger set in. At first the heated emotion was directed at her parents, but that hadn't lasted long. She was too logical, too intelligent not to realize that all they had done was show her the truth about Drew Buchanan. If he had loved her, her illegitimate status and the fact that Thorndyke promised to leave her nothing wouldn't have mattered.

The anger became self-directed. It had provided the incredible energy required to start over again in her chosen location in the Northwest three years ago, and eventually the white heat of it had died.

But the need to revenge herself on Drew Buchanan had never burned itself out completely. Samantha's desire to rectify the biggest mistake of her life had remained constant. Even now it made her wince to recall how she had been willing to give up everything for the man she loved. She wanted Buchanan to know that the naïve, emotional woman he had manipulated so easily three years ago had teeth now. She had emerged from the experience older and wiser, and she was going to make Drew pay in the only way he understood. With a huge chunk of money and an even larger slice of masculine ego.

After that, Samantha knew, she would be free. The slate would somehow be wiped clean, and she need no longer see the occasional memory of disappointment in her mother's eyes. She was only sorry Victor Thorndyke had not lived to see his daughter's revenge. He would have appreciated the beauty and simplicity of the plan. He had always appreciated her inborn ability for business. It was the talent she had inherited from him.

Slowly Samantha turned away from the window and got ready for bed.

An hour later she was still awake, staring at the darkness beyond the window and wondering why sleep wasn't descending as abruptly as it should have done, given the extent of her exhaustion earlier in the day. How much longer was she going to lie here going over and over the events of the day?

Groaning in mild self-disgust, she climbed out of bed and went to the window again, her apricot-colored nightgown wafting lightly around her legs as the breeze from the open slider caught at it. She could have done with a bit more of her mother's courage, she decided. Just now she was feeling tense and uncertain about the snag which had developed in her carefully outlined plans.

What was she going to do if she couldn't get Gabriel Sinclair's cooperation? Start over again with William

Oakes? Something in her mind shied away from abandoning the project with Gabriel. It was becoming very important to make it work.

Once again she wondered at how he might react if he were to learn the real reason behind her business proposition. He was already not overly enthused about backing her. Her cause would be hopeless if he discovered the truth.

It wasn't as if the deal she'd put together couldn't stand on its own merits! She was going to use her father's business methods to prove herself her mother's daughter. What fine irony. Why couldn't Gabriel see how much money there was to be made?

And while he was making money, she would be wiping out the recollection of what a fool she had been three years ago. Her mother had raised a daughter capable of total independence, and except for the affair with Drew Buchanan when she had sacrificed her pride for a meaningless passion falsely labeled love, Samantha had tried hard to live by her mother's code. The opportunity to seal the still-open wound in her pride, however, must not be allowed to slip by simply because she couldn't convince one very stubborn venture capitalist to go along with the plan!

Angrily Samantha pushed the sliding glass door open wide and stepped out onto the balcony. Below her the sandy beach met the rhythmically pulsing waves. A yellow glow from the outside lights around the house illuminated the scene faintly, revealing a touch of glittering phosphorescence in the cream-topped breakers. The beach stretched empty for miles. The few other homes secluded along the curving miles of coastline were not even visible from where Samantha stood.

The breeze off the ocean chilled her. She couldn't stand out on this balcony much longer unless she went back inside and found a jacket. Samantha straightened from the railing and stepped back through the sliding glass door.

Her eyes fell on the vague outline of her folded jeans lying in the open suitcase as she walked back toward the bed. On a sudden impulse she reached down and picked them up. Then, without giving herself a chance to think, she whipped the apricot nightdress off over her head. She stepped into the jeans without bothering to search for a pair of panties and felt through her clothes for the cotton shirt she knew was buried somewhere in the case. A few minutes later Samantha let herself out into the beige-carpeted hall.

Shoving her arms into the sleeves of a black leather jacket, she made her way softly through the shadowy living room toward the door which would let her out onto the beach. She needed to walk off her restlessness if she hoped to get any sleep tonight at all.

From his bedroom window Gabriel watched her leave. He had heard her go out onto her own balcony and had known the exact moment she had opened her door and walked down the hall. She had been moving with a purposefulness which had alarmed him.

He had climbed out of bed and had his hand on the doorknob before he realized she wasn't heading for her car. She was going out onto the beach, not running away from him.

96

He had yanked his large, square hand off the door-knob as if it had grown hot beneath his palm, but in truth what had startled him was his rush to the door in the first place. He hadn't stopped to think; he had simply charged out of bed, uncaring of his own naked-ness and prepared to stop his witch if she were indeed intent on taking flight in the middle of the night.

The unexpected rashness of his own actions was unnerving. He crossed the bedroom in three long strides and was mildly disgusted to find his hand was shaking slightly as he braced it against the metal frame of the sliding glass door. Even more unsettling was the surge in his loins as he watched her walk over the sand toward the water's edge. What was he letting the woman do to him, for God's sake?

It was just that he had been too long without a female, Gabriel decided, and knew in the same instant that he was lying to himself. It *had* been a long time, but that was because it hadn't been very good the last time. He had been in no rush recently to satisfy the basic needs of his nature; not when physical satisfaction had to be purchased at the price of feeling empty and emotionally shortchanged afterward.

A man of his quiet, plodding characteristics counted the cost of everything, Gabriel thought grimly. And the cost of taking to bed a woman for whom he felt only superficial desire was painfully steep. It made him feel compromised in a way he couldn't quite explain. He consoled himself with the knowledge that at least the short, fleeting relationships were honest, if unsatisfying and almost boring. But he always felt as though he had paid too much and received too little in exchange.

Watching the woman on the darkened beach, however, Gabriel realized what was so different about the attraction he felt toward Samantha. This time he didn't want to think about the cost. He wanted her. Period. No, not quite period.

He wanted something more. He wanted her to surrender without counting the cost, either.

He had fretted over his uncharacteristic behavior all afternoon, analyzing it, dissecting it, trying to find a rational explanation for it. When seven o'clock had come and gone and Samantha had not yet arrived, a strange kind of panic had invaded his bloodstream only to be followed by an unreasonable anger: anger at himself for having tried to set the trap and at the woman for having evaded it. Then he'd heard the crunch of gravel under her car's wheels and had immediately gotten himself back under control.

Setting snares for women apparently wasn't his forte, however. Look at how he'd nearly ruined everything by trying to put things out in the open over dinner. He'd blurted out the truth about his intentions, and she hadn't hesitated to put him firmly in his place.

Mentally he chastised himself for his own stupidity. How had he expected her to react, for God's sake? He was damn lucky she hadn't walked out then and there. He must have succeeded in allaying her immediate concerns, though, because she had agreed willingly to spend the night in his spare bedroom.

His eyes narrowed as he realized she didn't appear to be particularly wary of him in the physical sense.

That thought brought conflicting emotions. Look at her out there walking along on the beach lost in her thoughts—as if no one of this world had the slightest claim on her. Didn't she sense he was standing here, imagining various ways of pursuing her, dragging her down into the sand and claiming her completely? She ought to be running as fast as she could, not ambling along the waving line of surf.

"Damn!"

What was the matter with him? He didn't want her to run. He wanted to keep her under his roof and within reach as long as possible. "Face it, Sinclair," he growled under his breath. "She's in no danger from you. You've never forced yourself on a woman in your life, and you're hardly likely to start the practice now." But he found himself wanting her to *know* that he hungered for her. He wanted her to be aware of him on the most fundamental level. The strangely possessive, uncomfortably predatory sensations he'd experienced earlier in the evening were growing stronger.

At least she hadn't laughed or teased him earlier this evening when he'd confessed his true intentions. She hadn't played games with him; she'd simply told him to back off in no uncertain terms. Did that mean that she at least took seriously the possibility of his desire?

He watched her adjust the collar of her leather jacket in the pale light of the outside lamp. It was strange how the blatantly masculine lines of her outfit only emphasized her femininity. She wasn't a beautiful woman, but she was a strong, intensely feminine one.

He wanted to curve his hand around the curve of her bottom, find the outline of a nipple under her shirt, and prod it until it was hard with desire. He wanted to jerk her off her feet and stretch her out beneath him, taking her totally.

The palms of his hands were damp. He dried them awkwardly on the billowing curtain. What was she doing out there alone on the beach at night? This was a relatively safe part of the coast, but she was his responsibility. And he always took care of his responsibilities.

Who was he kidding? Gabriel stopped trying to rationalize his own actions as he yanked on a pair of jeans and reached for a dark blue pullover sweater. He wanted to be down there on the beach with her.

Samantha didn't hear him as he came toward her softly through the sand. She could hear nothing above the muted roar of the surf, yet something urged her to glance back toward the house, and when she did she saw Gabriel's dark figure advancing toward her with a purposeful stride that was becoming familiar. Did the man ever do anything without a purpose? she wondered fleetingly. He must have seen her leave the house and been worried about her out here alone. Politely she stopped and waited for him to catch up with her.

"You couldn't sleep?" he asked distantly as he came to a halt in front of her. The wind feathered the dark mahogany of his hair. His face was an unreadable mask to Samantha, who peered up at him questioningly.

"No. I had a lot on my mind, and I thought it might help to walk it off."

His mouth crooked. "Didn't you get enough exercise today at the spa?"

"Oh, my body is worn out. It's my mind that's all tied up in knots."

He fell into step beside her, not touching her as they continued slowly along the beach. He forced himself to think about her real business with him. "If all your facts are correct and you've got the guts to go up against Buchanan when he turns nasty, there's no real reason why your plan s-s-shouldn't work, I suppose," he began hesitantly.

"With your help," she amended pointedly, eyes straight ahead. When he said nothing more, she clenched her teeth and absorbed the sense of him striding along beside her. His close proximity out here on the lonely windswept beach generated conflicting emotions deep within her. In one way he made her feel secure. His solid presence made her feel protected, she realized. But in another way, he ruffled some atavistic, feminine sense of wariness which she didn't understand.

A faint tingling warning came alive in her head.

It was ridiculous, of course. The man was no threat to her. Still, Samantha found herself moving a little way from him as they walked. He was a little too close.

"Samantha?"

"Hmmm?"

"I think we s-s-should start back toward the house." Damn it to hell, Gabriel thought bitterly. Could she hear the extra hard way he was stumbling over the "sh" sound tonight? He never had been able to say it properly, but here on the beach it sounded worse than usual. It was the tension. He would have to select his words carefully. Soon she would be wondering why he was so damn hot and bothered.

"You can go back if you like," she told him in a remote tone, her gaze focusing on the blackness of the endless sea. "I think I'll walk a little longer. It was very kind of you to come out to keep me company."

She had the notion he was gritting his teeth and counting slowly to ten before he said in a very neutral voice, "I've already explained that I am not a kind man."

"Then why are you out here?"

He put out a hand, catching her wrist and pulling her around to face him in a swift, striking movement that caught her unawares. It was rather like hitting the end of a chain which was securely anchored at the other end in rock, Samantha thought in a flash as she was halted immediately in her tracks. He was so incredibly *solid*!

The hazel eyes blazed down at her with an intensity that took away her breath. "You know why I followed you. You're bright enough to figure out something as elementary as that, Samantha Maitland. Please don't play games with me. The one thing I demand from you is honesty!"

"Is that really all you want from me?" What on earth was she doing? Even she could hear the provoking challenge in her words. Stupid fool!

"No," he muttered huskily, dragging her close. "It's not all I want from you, but it's a start."

Samantha knew an instant of sheer panic as she realized he was going to take her mouth. He had been right. On some level at least she had known why he had followed her down onto the beach. She should have run when she'd seen him crossing the sand toward her.

Yes, she should have run. As far and as fast as she was able. Samantha had never been so certain of anything before in her life. But it was too late now. His mouth closed over hers.

It wasn't at all like being pinned against a rock wall, Samantha had time to realize in vague wonder as Gabriel gathered her close. It was more as if she were being absorbed into the dense granite of him.

The unexpectedness of the sensation held her still for the crucial moment it took for him to find her mouth with his own. Gabriel's arms wrapped around her waist and shoulders, and she could feel the hardness of his lower body as he urged her into the heat there.

His need and desire were as blunt and forceful as the other aspects of his character. The solid, uncompromisingly aroused feel of his body sent a tremor through her limbs.

Honest was another word which applied, Samantha acknowledged. This man wasn't playing any tantalizing games. He wanted her and his undisguised, blatant desire was strangely compelling.

Gabriel's mouth moved across hers slowly, determinedly, thoroughly. Refusing him admittance into the dark, warm chamber behind her lips would have been like trying to refuse the sea entrance into a shoreline cave as the tide rose. There was an inexorable quality about the whole procedure, and Samantha again wondered if anything or anyone could stop this man once he had set himself on a course of action. There were tactics which could be used against a devil, but could anyone halt an angel?

The groan came from deep in Gabriel's throat as his tongue probed hungrily into the slowly yielding interior of her mouth. The husky sound had a strange effect on Samantha. Her fingers sank into the material of his sweater, finding the hard planes of his shoulders. Her body seemed to relax of its own accord against him. Once inside the warm dampness behind her lips, Gabriel took his time, exploring and claiming completely.

Half-expecting to find her senses stormed in a rush of masculine aggression, Samantha experienced an enthralling confusion instead as she submitted herself to the slow search-and-seizure operation. Gabriel was as detailed and deliberate as her computer. No point was missed. His tongue swept deeply, seeking out hers for a twisting, writhing little duel which she could not avoid.

When the intimate battle was over and he, clearly the victor, moved on to taste the hollows of the insides of her cheeks, Samantha decided that the computer analogy only went so far. There was nothing mechanical about the way this man was making her feel!

A shock of fierce satisfaction and excitement went through Gabriel as he felt Samantha's response. It fed the new daring, masculine recklessness in him as nothing else could have done. The combined power of the sensations was dazzling. He could feel the softness of her thigh against the hardness of his own and wanted to strip the clothing from her body even as they stood there on the beach. Fantasy and reality merged dangerously. In a few more minutes he would not be able to tell them apart.

Samantha knew she had done far more than allow her body to simply relax against his by the time Gabriel finally lifted his head with slow reluctance and stared down into her face. She was literally leaning into him, using his rocklike strength to support herself. Behind the lenses of her glasses she tried to narrow her eyes with cool, amused detachment as she met his searching glance, but it seemed as if she could only look up at him in dazed uncertainty.

"It's all right, Samantha," he whispered hoarsely. "Forget about the business side of this. Tonight there is only you and me."

"Gabriel," she pleaded, her voice sounding awkward and faintly bruised, "I . . . we can't separate the business from the rest. It's all mixed up together, and I make it a policy to never combine business and . . . and the other."

"So do I," he confessed on a strangely unsettling note of humor. "But it seems as though I don't have much choice in this case. Samantha, I want you. Tell me what I have to do to get you tonight."

Her gaze fell to the level of his shoulder, her senses shaken by the unvarnished demand. "It's not a matter of doing something in order to buy your way into my bed!" she gasped.

He closed his eyes in obvious pain at the mess he had made of the question, opening them again to confront her deliberately. "I didn't mean that the way it sounded," he began thickly, and then shook his head once in exasperation. "Oh, hell, maybe I did. I'm a straightforward sort of man, Samantha."

Her eyes warmed. "Except when it comes to business?" she dared to taunt. "You seem quite willing to keep me dangling on that score!"

"Leave business out of this," he grated, not responding to her poor attempt to lighten the situation. "We'll worry about that part later. Samantha, sweet witch, I'm trying to tell you that I need you tonight. I've been wanting you all afternoon. I'm not used to feeling the way you make me feel. It's not like me to invade spas full of naked women. It's not like me to deliberately set out to seduce someone who doesn't show any signs of wanting to be seduced. And it's not like me to find my hand shaking when I contemplate taking a certain woman to bed! Damn it to hell, woman, I'm half out of my mind with wanting you!"

He had such a way of putting her off guard, Samantha thought desperately, even as she found herself deeply intrigued by his genuine self-confusion. Why did he have to be so blunt about the whole matter? It was much easier and far safer to play small games at a time like this. Games were a way of dancing around the ultimate question if one didn't wish to answer it. And she didn't want to answer it, not tonight, not with Gabriel. Or did she? God, she was beginning to get thoroughly confused herself.

"Are you trying to tell me that I have the power to actually make you behave a little impetuously?" She tried to mock.

He didn't smile. "Yes. Impetuously. Rashly. Impulsively. I'm not normally an impulsive man, Samantha. But around you . . ."

She shook her head, watching him from beneath her lashes. "You'd probably hate me in the morning then. I don't want emotions to cloud our business arrangements."

"I can't seem to think as far ahead as tomorrow morning," he muttered thickly, cradling her head close against his shoulder. He used one square hand to push her head down to the sweater, and although the caress was gentle enough, Samantha realized there was no way on earth she could move from where he held her. "Samantha, I don't want to talk about how or what I'll feel tomorrow. Right now all I can think about is . . ." The sentence was halted abruptly, and Samantha moved uneasily against him.

"All you can think about is getting me into bed?" she finished for him, whispering the words into his sweater.

"That's a relatively polite way of saying it, I suppose," he agreed heavily. Yes, getting you into bed his own thoughts echoed, making you mine, hearing you call my name in passion, making you respond to me, learning what it feels like to have you lying beneath me. "What it comes down to, Samantha," he said finally, "is that I want you, and I don't care how much it's going to cost me."

She froze. "I'm not for sale, Gabriel!"

"I'm not talking about money, damn it," he breathed, catching her chin in the cup of his hand and lifting her face so that she could see the burning intensity in his eyes. "Leave the money out of this!"

107

He bent his head again, and Samantha stumbled slightly as he thrust his foot heavily between hers, forcing her weight against him. He sensed the shiver that went through her and immediately tightened his hold.

"Samantha, Samantha . . ." The masculine groan was half plea, half command.

She felt herself slipping into his sensual trap, her instincts responding to the uncanny pull he was exerting. She had never known a man who made love with this fundamental honesty. With Drew it had been a dance of sophisticated passion, a fantasy of being in tune intellectually and emotionally with the right man. Since the disaster which had ensued in the wake of that affair, Samantha had remained aloof from men. She had not needed one, had not particularly wanted one in any other role than that of casual escort. It had proven easy enough to keep men at a distance, and Samantha thought she at last learned the lesson Vera Maitland had tried to teach. There were far more important matters in life than an ongoing relationship with a man. Someday, she had promised herself, she would take the lesson the rest of the way and allow herself the occasional brief affair. Vera was the last person on earth to suggest that a woman deny herself the physical pleasures of a man-woman association.

But tonight Samantha couldn't seem to think properly. There was something new and different in the charged atmosphere which was enveloping herself and Gabriel. She wanted to fully experience the powerful feelings this man was capable of arousing within her. She wanted to explore the depths of this man's passion. There was nothing wrong with experimentation and discovery, she reminded herself. There was nothing wrong with taking a few risks. So long as one did not surrender completely to the fantasy that was love.

Love. The word flickered in and out of her brain, and instantly she felt more certain of her rationalizing thoughts. There was no love involved here. As long as she acknowledged that, she was safe. Perhaps the time had come to allow herself to venture once more into the waters of sensual fulfillment. As a woman she was entitled to experience the pleasures of a physical relationship. As an intelligent, thinking woman she could do that without courting disaster. All she had to do was keep things in perspective.

As if he sensed her internal decision, Gabriel dragged his mouth off hers. Without a word he pinned her to his side, his arm tightly anchored around her shoulders, and led her back across the sand toward the beachfront home.

He was aware of the trembling in his own hands as he guided her silently through the night. She was going to give him what he needed tonight. A part of him could hardly believe it, and another side of him insisted that there could have been no other outcome. He had to have her.

Deliberately he stopped trying to analyze the conflicting emotions. She was coming home with him. That was all that mattered tonight. With this woman he was learning the real meaning of reckless passion, he tried to tell himself humorously. But it was too close to being reality to elicit even a slight smile. True impulsiveness was something you laughed or cried over after the fact, not during the experience.

Samantha blindly pushed aside her own thoughts. The details could be sorted out in the morning. Right now she only wanted to learn what lay in store for her in an angel's arms. She, too, winced a bit at the faint trembling in her fingertips, and then she forgot about it as Gabriel urged her down the carpeted hall to his bedroom.

He got her through the door and then he folded her into his arms as if he couldn't wait an instant longer. She was fleetingly aware of the uncluttered simplicity of the room, knew that the windows faced the ocean, but all she could concentrate on was the feel of his hands as they went unhesitatingly to the buttons of her black leather jacket.

Holding her mouth damply with his own, Gabriel slipped the leather from her shoulders. A moment later his hands flattened along the slender line of her back and then moved slowly around her waist until they rested just beneath the small weight of her breasts. The thin cotton fabric of her shirt conducted the heat of his palms with startling efficiency. Samantha could feel it burning into her flesh, and she whispered his name helplessly into his throat.

"I want to see you the way I saw you this afternoon," he growled gently, "soft and naked and waiting for me." He buried his lips in her hair, nuzzling the sweet place behind her ear as he worked carefully to undo the tiny buttons of her shirt.

110

He was a precise, step-by-step sort of man, Samantha reminded herself wonderingly as she submitted meekly to the slow, deliberate undressing. Who would have thought that there could be such mounting excitement to be had simply from being undressed so precisely?

He took his time and did it right. Each button down the front of the shirt and then the ones at the cuffs were carefully undone before he eased the material off and set the garment down on top of the leather jacket which had been placed on a nearby chair.

She had worn no bra, and when he turned back to her, Samantha's breasts were bathed in moonlight. "You fit my palm perfectly," he breathed, reaching out to cup the soft weight of one breast in his fingers. "When I first saw you on that massage table, I wanted to pull that towel off of you, turn you over on your back, and just look at you."

Samantha inhaled sharply, her body reacting unbelievably as he lowered his head and curled his tongue lingeringly around each nipple in turn. She felt the round, dark peaks being coaxed forth into an aching tautness that sent echoing ripples of sensation down into her thighs. Slowly Gabriel tasted and cajoled and urged with his tongue and lips until he seemed reluctantly satisfied with the effect he'd had on her body.

"Tell me you want me," he muttered deeply, lifting his head again and taking one of her hands in his. "Tell me that this is a sign of wanting."

Before she quite realized what he intended, Gabriel gently forced her fingertips to her breast, making her fully aware of the ruby-hard evidence of her own desire.

111

Samantha gasped, strangely astounded, even a little alarmed at the incredibly erotic effect the caress had on her. She had thought herself as much in tune with her own body as any other woman, but never before had she been made to touch it under the guidance of a man.

"Gabriel, please," she moaned, putting her face into his solid shoulder to hide the flame in her cheeks. She tried to tug her hand away from his, but he held it to her breast a moment longer.

"Tell me," he urged thickly.

"I want you." The words came in a little relieved rush. It was the truth. There was nothing wrong with wanting a man, she told herself again and again. Nothing at all. But that knowledge didn't cancel the odd fear she experienced when she realized just how much she desired Gabriel Sinclair.

He dropped her hand, and she hastily wound both arms around his neck as he murmured the words of need into her ear. Then she felt the clasp of her jeans being undone, and the denim was peeled away from her hips. A moment later she stood naked in the shadowy room, pressing close as Gabriel slid his large hands hungrily up and down her spine. The rough texture of his sweater teased the already inflamed nipples.

Slowly he rocked her from side to side against his body, brushing her hips with exciting roughness along the outline of the waiting hardness beneath his jeans.

Of their own accord her fingers moved down his shoulders and up under the dark blue sweater to find the bare, warm skin underneath. "You could drive me crazy tonight, do you know that?" he demanded fiercely.

112

"Have you ever been crazy?"

"Not until I met you."

With shaking hands she got his sweater off, dumping it heedlessly to the floor rather than folding it carefully and stacking it on the chair as he had done with her things. "Angel hair," she drawled deliciously, spreading her fingertips through the curling mass on his chest.

"If you like the hair, you'll love the feathers." Gabriel flinched at his own poor joke. He rarely made jokes of any kind, least of all when he was making love to a woman. Carefully he put out a hand and removed her glasses, setting them aside with grave precision.

"Feathers?" Samantha looked up at him through her lashes.

"On my back. Where the wings are, of course."

"I can't wait." With a soft sigh she leaned her cheek against his bare shoulder and trailed her nails down across the flat, masculine nipple. When the caress made him suck in his breath, she continued it boldly, probing at the waistband of his jeans.

"Finish undressing me, Samantha," he rasped, taking hold of both of her palms and fitting them to his waist. He nibbled hungrily at the tip of her ear and along the line of her jaw as she obediently began pushing the rough denim down the flat planes of his hips.

She realized abruptly that just as she hadn't taken the time to pull on underwear before sliding into her jeans earlier, neither had Gabriel bothered with a pair of shorts. With alarming swiftness the full, surging heaviness of his manhood was revealed, his arousal somehow a challenge and a threat.

113

As his jeans fell to the floor at his feet, Samantha stepped back reflexively, but he clamped his fingers into the curve of her buttocks and dragged her close again, eyes gleaming. "I want you, Samantha. So badly I can't even think straight. Touch me, honey. *Touch me!*"

She moaned, fluttering her hands down to rest on the solid, strong line of his thighs. Gabriel shivered in reaction, and his response gave her the courage to continue the bold caress. With tingling lightness she traced the outline of body hair from below his navel to the thrusting shape of his masculinity.

Unsatisfied with the delicate touch, Gabriel pushed himself deeply into her warm palm, urging her to caress him more forcefully. Simultaneously he let his fingers slide tantalizingly into the curve of her buttocks.

"Oh, my God! Gabriel, I . . . I'm going to lose my balance." She panted, releasing him to sink her fingertips helplessly into his shoulders as she sought to steady herself. Her eyes were half-closed and glazed with a passion she didn't fully comprehend.

She felt the throbbing triumph in him as he wordlessly scooped her up into his arms and carried her across to the bed. When she sprawled languidly down on the sheets, he leaned over to cage her possessively between his arms.

"I keep telling myself that we've got the rest of the night," he whispered huskily, "but I don't think I can wait much longer."

"Is that a warning?"

"A statement of fact."

She smiled tremulously up at him with ancient, feminine provocation, holding out her arms. His rocklike weight came down to half-cover her body in a wave of elemental force.

"Oh, Gabriel!" Samantha's eyes squeezed shut against the unexpected rushes of pleasure he began eliciting as his hands wandered over her body, bringing each part of her pulsatingly alive. Her legs shifted on the cool sheets, seeking to entwine him, and the crystalized copper of her nails left tiny marks in his bronzed skin as she began to cling to him more and more demandingly.

"Tell me again how much you want me," he ordered against the soft curve of her breast just before his teeth closed over one rigid nipple. "I need to hear the words."

"I want you, Gabriel. I need you. I have to feel you inside of me." Could he hear the bewilderment she felt beneath her haze of passion? Nothing had prepared her for her response to this man. The pleasure in her body had turned into compulsion. When his heated kisses reached her stomach, she arched her lower body in reaction. "Now, Gabriel, please, now!"

"Not yet, honey. Not yet."

There would be no pushing him, she realized finally. Gabriel Sinclair did everything carefully and thoroughly. When his fingers slid between her thighs, she closed her legs quickly, needing the feel of him there to help ease the growing pressure. Her muscles could not remain locked against the persuasive biting kisses he began to trail through the curling hair which marked the delta of her thighs, however.

"Open yourself for me, witch. Let me know all there is to know about you."

She obeyed, moaning his name again and again as he stroked the petaled, inner reaches of her desire. Her hands locked in his hair, urging him to her, but he held back from the final union.

"Gabriel, please," she whispered impulsively, "I can't bear any more." With all her strength she tugged at the mass of his shoulders, trying to pull him onto and into her body.

Gabriel gloried in the words of her passionate surrender, exploring the dampening heat between her legs with wonder. She wasn't playing any games. There was no artifice in this. Samantha was aching for him, wooing him with the primitive demands of her womanhood. The scent of her body was rich and compelling. He felt at once trapped in her power and magnificently in control of this elusive creature under him.

This woman was his and his alone tonight. The knowledge pounded in his brain and in his loins. He would take her completely, lose himself in her, fill her totally. He felt an irresistible need to imprint himself so thoroughly on her senses that she would never be able to look at another man.

And then he could wait no longer. More roughly than he intended, he pulled her legs apart and lowered himself down onto her until he was poised at the flowering entrance of her body.

"Gabriel!"

He surged fiercely forward, sheathing himself in the thick, tight velvet folds of her. He felt the shock of his entry ripple through her body and heard the soft gasp of startled wonder at the back of her throat.

Gabriel halted at once, his face tight with the conflicting emotions of passion and concern. "Honey, are you all right? Have I hurt you, sweetheart?"

"Hurt me? No," she managed, clutching at his heavy shoulders. "Oh, don't stop, Gabriel, please," she sighed. "Don't stop now."

The concern faded from the tight lines at the corner of his mouth, and he lowered himself heavily to her breast with a muttered groan of desire. Then he was thrusting with a slow, steady rhythm that made Samantha overwhelmingly aware that the solidness of him extended to every part of his body.

The crescendo of his lovemaking mounted, becoming an irresistible spiral of sensation that grabbed at her senses and pulled them headfirst into the final vortex.

Samantha was overwhelmed at the moment her climax took her. Unaware of how deeply her nails raked his back or how tightly her legs wrapped his surging hips, she instinctively sought to bring him into her completely and found herself exploding around him.

Gabriel experienced a purely masculine thrill of satisfaction as he felt the small, internal convulsions shake her. He managed to raise his head so that he could glimpse the sweep of emotion across her face, and then he drank the echo of her cry from her parted lips.

Before he had even swallowed the sound, his own pulsating need erupted. He clenched one hand violently into the flesh of her buttocks, holding her in place while he fed her the full force of his passion.

The tumult seemed endless, and then it began to fade, leaving the pair on the bed in a tangle of perspiration-dampened arms and legs. Languorously Samantha clung to the man who made love like an angel or a devil, she couldn't decide which. She didn't care if the night around them never ended. She wanted to know the pleasant, satisfying heaviness of him spread along her body for as long as possible. The present seemed quite perfect in that moment; the past and future totally forgotten.

When she opened her eyes at last, it was to find Gabriel watching her with an expression of lazy satisfaction that was very male. The look on his face helped bring back reality.

"You seem very pleased with yourself," she murmured, trying to decide exactly how she should be feeling. Stupid? Wanton? Marvelously abandoned? Pleased? What in hell had she done by going to bed with this man? All her sound reasoning dissolved into insignificance as she tried to adjust to the new status of her relationship with Gabriel Sinclair. But her body was too relaxed, her senses too sated to think about it properly just now. She needed a little time.

"I'm only pleased with myself if you are," he told her simply, leaning down to brush her full mouth with his own. "Only if you are."

In spite of herself, Samantha relented, a smile gentling her features. "You must know I am." It was the truth, and there was no reason not to be honest about it. She couldn't be anything less than honest at the moment, anyway. Her natural defenses were down, unable to maintain themselves in the warm aftermath of his lovemaking.

"What are you thinking about?" Gabriel demanded abruptly, twisting his fingers in her hair and holding her head so that she had to face him on the pillow. "And don't tell me it's business!"

"Ah, but it was, in a way," she murmured sleepily.

"S-s-shi—"

"Don't say that!" she protested, hushing his mouth with the tips of her fingers.

"I can't. I never could. Not when I really needed to. When I'm angry or tense enough to make use of it, I'm usually too angry or too tense to get the word out in one piece! What are you laughing at, witch?"

"You, of course. Who else would I be laughing at?"

He let that pass. "Were you really thinking about business?"

She said slowly, "In a way." How could she begin to put her fears and hesitations into words? She didn't have to. Gabriel did it for her.

"You're worrying about having an affair with a man with whom you're trying to do business, aren't you?" he challenged softly. "Afraid that I'll somehow get the idea you're trying to buy my cooperation?"

She felt the heat in her face as he baldly stated the basic problem. "I wouldn't want you to get the wrong idea, Gabriel," she began in a remote little voice.

"Don't worry," he told her roughly, "I won't. I know damn good and well you don't make a habit of doing business like this!"

Her eyes widened slightly at the absolute certainty in his words. "What makes you so sure?" she whispered starkly.

119

His glance traveled from one end of her body to the other, noting each salient feature as if she were a new possession he was intent on enjoying. "I'm not sure I can explain," he admitted. How could he put into words the way he saw her? Too complex, too soft, too intelligent, and just plain too passionate to involve herself in meaningless affairs. "You'd be a different sort of woman if you'd been conducting business that way for the past few years," he said finally. "And then there was the physical part. . . ."

"The physical part!" she exclaimed. "You mean I didn't demonstrate sufficient expertise?" The gold in her tortoiseshell eyes flamed abruptly.

Gabriel answered with a quirking smile, extending his hand so that the pad of his thumb grazed lightly over her nipple. "That's not what I meant at all. It's just that I had the impression it's been a hell of a long time since you've been to bed with a man. You were like a coiled spring, honey. How long has it been, sweetheart?"

"That's not a gentlemanly question, Gabriel!"

"It's been months for me," he said simply, "several."

She flushed, surprised at the confession. It wasn't the kind of thing most men would admit to so readily. It didn't fit with a strong, macho image. "It has?"

"Umm. And what's more, I probably would have plodded along in happy celibacy for quite a while longer if you hadn't appeared on the scene. Samantha, I can't even remember wanting a woman as badly as I wanted you tonight!"

"Oh, Gabriel," she breathed, wondering for the hundredth time why he kept managing to take her off guard.

"You don't have to look so delighted with the news," he chided.

She smiled dreamily. "Well, you're not the only one who's been plodding along in happy celibacy. But for me it's been about three years."

"Three years!" He looked startled.

"I didn't realize what I'd been missing." That much was the truth. "It was never this good before." And that was also the truth. The literal truth. She'd never known anything as all-consuming and as totally satisfying as Gabriel's embrace.

"And was it worth waiting for?" he prodded, watching her expression as if deeply fascinated by it.

"I don't think I ever really knew what true seduction was until tonight," she whispered with a candor that shocked her. "You are a very thorough man, Gabriel Sinclair."

"Only because I wanted you so thoroughly and completely," he growled, his mouth closing over hers in renewing passion.

Samantha had a fleeting recollection of having imagined that Gabriel would make love by the book. But if he did, it was a book he, himself, had written.

CHAPTER FOUR

Samantha awoke to sunlight and a blindingly clear realization of her own stupidity. She sat up in bed, instinctively clutching the sheet, and turned to stare down at the man who slept beside her. Gabriel's dark hair was rakishly tousled, the first time she'd ever seen it anything but neatly combed. The white sheet foamed at his waist as he lay magnificently sprawled like a contented hunting cat on his stomach. Some angel!

What a fool she had been, Samantha told herself in rising self-disgust. What an absolute idiot! What in the world had possessed her? No, scratch that question. It was only too starkly clear in her brain what, or rather who, had possessed her.

Possessed. The word sent her edging hurriedly off the bed, out the door, and down the hallway to the bedroom she should have stayed in last night. Once inside she closed the door, violently aware of her own nakedness, and then gave vent to the anger which was suddenly seething in her. Her closed fist struck the side of her leg in impotent fury.

"Damn! Damn! *Damn!*"

She had traded whatever small edge she'd held for a night of passion.

Now the night was over, and she was left with the intuitive, devastating knowledge that she was no longer in full control of the situation. Months of planning and working and research had hung in the balance, with success depending entirely on how well she handled Gabriel Sinclair. And she'd undoubtedly blown the whole deal within twenty-four hours of coming face to face with the man.

Good God! Was she fated to forever go about making an absolute fool of herself where men were concerned? She could envision Vera Maitland's pitying expression only too well. Thank heaven her mother hadn't known about her plans!

"Samantha Maitland, you are an idiot!" she hissed at herself in the mirror, the gold in her eyes glittering with the force of her feelings.

How could she possibly restore her sense of being the one in charge, the one who was controlling and manipulating the situation after her physical surrender last night?

Surrender.

That was as bad a word as possessed. Both of them were words which had never even had much of a place in her vocabulary until last night. They were words she'd never used to describe the act of going to bed with a man, words her mother would have despised as hangovers from the Dark Ages. Women today didn't surrender to men, not intelligent, independent, thinking women. They might choose to share an evening of mutual pleasure, or they might let themselves relax physically with a man. They might even decide to explore a mutual passion with a man. But they didn't do something archaic and primitive like *surrender* to their partners!

Samantha knew all about sex. She had been taught to view it from a proper perspective long before she'd had any personal interest in the subject. Vera had seen to it that her daughter grew up with a healthy, balanced understanding of the simple biological function. At its best, sex was a mutually agreeable experience to be kept in its proper place. Even during the excitement of the affair with Drew Buchanan, Samantha had never lost her perspective on the subject of sex. It could be boring or fun, exciting or dull, passionate or prosaic.

It was not an act of surrender on the part of the woman.

She turned away from the mirror, too disgusted with her own image to continue berating herself in front of it. How could she possibly put last night into a proper perspective? She hadn't hopped into bed with a man for an evening of fun and games. She hadn't even gone to bed anticipating a night of pleasure to be casually shared with a man who interested her physically.

She had given herself to Gabriel, completely, and if she hadn't known intellectually that it wasn't possible, she would have said irrevocably. Talk about archaic female thought processes!

In the cold light of dawn she could still feel the way her body had been tuned to his. Her muscles even ached a little from the remembered demands of his passionate strength. And to think she had imagined him as an unimaginative lover! He had taken her by storm.

But what really mattered, Samantha told herself grimly as she shoved open the door which led to the bathroom, was that Gabriel had known just how total her surrender had been. Even as she'd fled his bedroom a few minutes ago, she had been aware of the satisfaction and contentment which had etched every line of his relaxed body. And she could still hear the words of claiming and possession he had whispered to her during the night.

"Shit!"

He might not be able to say it, but she certainly could, and the elemental word certainly fit her mood. Samantha slammed into the shower, yanking the tap with such force that the water hit her body like a waterfall.

Talk about giving away the psychological edge! How in hell could she possibly restore the balance of power in the relationship? How could she put matters between herself and Gabriel back on a business footing after last night? He would wake up with the knowledge that he was now completely in control of the situation.

He would tell himself he had only to take her to bed in order to handle her. Samantha groaned at the thought. Gabriel Sinclair was a highly successful businessman. The last thing he would probably be interested in doing was business with a woman who was so obviously at the mercy of her own passions. Men like Sinclair didn't make their mark in the world by involving themselves and their money with women who didn't have as much self-control and hard-edged business sense as themselves. Hadn't he admitted that his relationship with the last woman he'd backed financially had been purely business? Sinclair was the kind of man who would keep the worlds of sex and business clearly separated.

By succumbing so easily to his advances last night, she had proven to him that she wasn't good business partner material. Damn it to hell! Now what was she going to do?

Samantha was aware of a terribly trapped sensation. It was hard to even think clearly. There had to be a way out of the mess she had created. There had to be. Surely all these months of planning weren't going to go down the tubes just because she'd gone crazy last night?

How could she regain Sinclair's respect for her as a potential business partner?

"Samantha?"

She jumped a little at the sound of his voice as he came through the bathroom door. Panic seized her. "I'm taking a shower," she snapped. "I'll be out in a few minutes." Out and running, she added silently.

Was that what she was going to do? Run?

"There's no rush," he drawled softly, pulling aside the shower curtain to gaze at her with remembered satisfaction. "I'll join you." Then he was inside, reaching for her with lazy hunger.

She moved away at once but not before his palm had slid lightly over the dusky rose of one nipple, eliciting a tingling awareness. "I'm through," she announced

126

quickly, trying not to look at the hard planes and angles of his body.

"No, you're not," he countered gently, snagging her wrist. His mouth edged upward at the corners as he regarded his captive with anticipation. "I'm going to scrub your back for you."

"Gabriel, I don't feel like playing any more of your bedroom games," she informed him rashly.

His eyes narrowed. "Games?" he repeated far too softly.

For the life of her she couldn't read his expression. Her chin came up disdainfully as she slipped her wrist free of his grasp and stepped outside the shower. "What do you call little one-night flings?" she asked with a false nonchalance.

He held aside the curtain and eyed her coolly. "You mean little flings like last night?"

The question sounded dangerous to her oversensitive emotions. But she clung to her chosen pose of casual insouciance as if to a lifeline. Wrapping a towel quickly around herself, she started out of the bathroom. "What else?" She shut the door firmly behind her and then raced across the room for her clothes.

A sense of control began to reassert itself as she dressed. The jeans and the rakishly styled white pirate shirt with its drawstring collar and wide-cuffed, full sleeves helped provide a feeling of being more in charge of her chaotic emotions.

Samantha grabbed at the sensation and deliberately began to build on its foundation. Last night had been just a one-night stand. Regrettable, perhaps, from a business point of view, but certainly not a devastating experience. Was there any possibility of convincing Gabriel of that?

One thing was crystal clear. She had to get out of his home today. Staying here would be incredibly stupid. She was packing her suitcase when Gabriel emerged from the bathroom, a towel wrapped negligently around his waist.

"Going somewhere, honey?"

She could hear the steel underlying the question, and it stiffened her resolve. "I have business to attend to, Gabriel, remember?" she forced herself to drawl lightly, stuffing a shirt into the suitcase without bothering to fold it. "I'm going back to Seattle."

He stood filling the bedroom doorway, watching with disapproving eyes as the unfolded shirt was crushed beneath a pair of wadded-up trousers. Samantha could almost feel him itching to take the suitcase out of her hands and repack it properly. Everything would be neatly folded and carefully tucked in, she thought with a fleeting amusement which died quickly.

"Your business was with me," he murmured, following the movements of her sloppy packing as if fascinated.

"It would probably never have been a satisfactory partnership," she informed him gruffly. "You're too neat."

"What the hell's that supposed to mean?"

She'd managed to startle him with that comment, Samantha realized, the knowledge restoring a bit more of her sense of command. If she could put him off-balance even a little bit this morning, there might be a chance of salvaging something from the operation. The first flicker of hope darted through her brain as she turned a brilliant smile on her nemesis.

"It means just exactly what it sounds like. There are two kinds of people in this world, Gabriel. People like me who do things in what seems a slipshod, casual, intuitive manner to your sort. And there are people like you who do everything carefully, neatly, with great attention to detail. Making a partnership work between the two types was probably a hopeless idea from the start."

"Is that so?" he murmured very politely. "Does that mean you've decided to give up your plans for taking on the Buchanan Group? You no longer want my financial backing?"

"You sound pleased by the idea," she challenged.

He watched her for a moment and then shrugged. "I've had my doubts about the project from the start," he admitted.

"I know! You made them abundantly clear." She couldn't quite hide the angry movement of her hands as she crammed the last of her clothing into the suitcase.

"Honey," he began persuasively, "the basic concept of what you want to do isn't bad. It's a little reckless, perhaps, but feasible. It could be done. But it takes a certain kind of person to pull off a stunt like that. Even if I gave you the money, you'd still have to figure out a way to deal with Buchanan if he gets nasty when he finds out who's standing in his way. I don't think you have any idea of the kind of pressure a man like that brings down when he wants."

If Gabriel only knew just how well she understood Drew Buchanan! "You think I'll buckle under pressure? Give in when the threats start?" she demanded.

He frowned. "It's a rough business going up against a corporate s-s-shark like Buchanan."

"I can handle it."

"Honey, you're an information broker, not a power broker! You think you know all about the inside workings of the corporate world because you study them every day in your line of work. But there's a hell of a difference between studying that world from the outside and actually being on the inside. Buchanan is as ruthless as they come. He'll crush you."

"Ah, and then you'd lose all your money, is that it?" she goaded.

"You envisioned me as a silent partner, as I recall," he retorted. "Which means that you'd be the one trying to deal with Buchanan. And from what I know of you, Sam, I'd have to guess that yes, I probably would wind up losing a lot of money."

"I'd pay you off whether or not I make a killing in Phoenix!"

"With what? A lifetime subscription to your computerized business information service?"

"You'd get your money, one way or another, Gabriel," she said stonily and slammed the suitcase shut. The lid didn't close properly because a sock was sticking out on the side. Ignoring it, Samantha forced the latch shut.

"Does it occur to you that I might be concerned with something other than losing my money?" he gritted.

"No," she said savagely, glancing around the room to

see what she'd forgotten. She nearly always forgot something when she packed in a hurry like this.

"How about the fact that I don't particularly relish the idea of seeing Buchanan use you to mop his office floor?"

Her hairbrush. She'd forgotten her hairbrush. It was sitting on the dresser. Samantha started toward it resolutely. "Gabriel, you seem to have gained a somewhat false notion of my personal stamina and fortitude. I can only assume the impression stems from last night. . . ."

His expression eased as she turned to face him, hairbrush in her hand. "Last night I saw the softness in you, sweetheart," he allowed gently. "You're a creature of beauty and energy and incredible passion. You took my breath away when you surrendered in my arms. . . ."

The hairbrush seemed to leave her clenched fist of its own accord, hurtling across the room toward Gabriel's head. He barely ducked in time. It struck the bathroom door behind him and clattered harmlessly to the floor. For an incredulous instant he stared down at it and then lifted unreadable eyes to her face as she glared furiously.

"I did nothing of the kind," she snapped. "I went to bed with you. Women do that sort of thing these days, you know. They go to bed with men when they feel like it. It is a simple case of indulging in a little harmless sex. It's your male ego which chooses to view what happened last night in terms of dominance and submission, surrender and victory. That's not the way it looked from my side at all! Don't you dare try to guess what

131

my behavior outside of bed is like based on my behavior in bed! Is that clear?"

"Am I allowed to make judgments about your behavior outside of bed based on this little scene you're conducting this morning?" he shot back coldly. "Because if I am, I would have to conclude that you are an emotional, unpredictable, excitable female."

Samantha played the only card she had left. Drawing herself up to her full height, she stalked across the room and reached down to grab her suitcase. "I shall have to take care not to give William Oakes the same bad impression, won't I?"

"Samantha!"

She was halfway down the hall and would have been a lot farther but for the heavy suitcase when he caught up with her. Gabriel's hand clamped down on her shoulder, halting her in midstride and spinning her around to face him.

"What the hell is that supposed to mean?" he rasped.

"Guess," she invited succinctly.

"You're going to contact Oakes? Ask him for financial backing?"

"You're very shrewd," she mocked, aware of the rock-heavy weight of his hand on her shoulder but refusing to acknowledge it, "for a businessman."

"I've told you to stay away from him. He'll take everything if the deal goes through, and God help you if he loses money on it!"

"You're starting to sound a little emotional, yourself, Gabriel."

"Damn it, Samantha . . . !"

"Three days, Gabriel. That's how much time you've got. Three days to cut yourself in on my deal or forget about the whole thing. Are you really going to stand by and watch Oakes make all that money with me?" she concluded interestedly. "Because we are going to make a pile, Gabriel. Who knows? Maybe I'll learn a few things from William Oakes in the process. He's good. As successful as you are, according to the computer. But with any luck he'll be more inclined to stick to business instead of giving in to his masculine cravings. I must prefer to do business with men who aren't emotional, unpredictable, and at the mercy of their baser instincts!"

Wrenching herself out from under his hand, she dragged the heavy suitcase down the hall and out onto the front patio.

"Samantha, you're not going to manipulate me, damn you!" Gabriel stalked along behind her, brows set in a rigid line over blazing hazel eyes.

"I wouldn't dream of trying to manipulate you," she scorned, shoving open the wrought iron gate. "I'm just a poor, soft, brainless little female. How could I dream of trying to manipulate a powerful, successful man like yourself?"

"You know damn well you're trying to manipulate me!" he gritted as she opened the car door and slung her suitcase into the backseat. "You're trying to threaten me, trying to force my hand. Samantha, I don't let anyone get away with that."

She slid an icy glance up at his tightly set face as she dropped into the front seat of the car and slammed the key into the ignition. "I believe you," she told him simply.

"Then don't try your luck!"

"Wouldn't dream of it," she drawled, switching on the engine and throwing the little car into gear. "All I'm doing is offering a straightforward business proposition. Three days, Gabriel. That's how long you've got to consider it. After that I'll contact the next name on the list. Oakes. With any luck he doesn't have any weird idiosyncrasies like running around in his front yard wearing nothing but a towel!"

The neatly raked gravel in the drive flew from beneath the sporty car's tires as Samantha sent the vehicle charging back toward the main road. She didn't even glance in the rearview mirror as she departed.

Gabriel stared after her, fighting a silent, savage, internal battle. She was gone. Just like that.

He'd staked a claim on her last night. She couldn't just leave like this! Didn't she realize that? Samantha belonged to him now.

The urge to go after her—and drag her back by her hair if necessary—was astonishing in its strength. It took the full force of his will to bring the seething emotional tide under control. What was the matter with him? He'd never been like this over a woman. Dazedly he stared down at his shaking hands.

Three days.

The little witch would do it, too. She'd go to Oakes with her crazy proposition. And Oakes would find a way of turning the whole thing to his own advantage. He'd use her.

Three days.

How did she dare to lay down an ultimatum like this to him?

"S-s-shi . . . !" Gabriel gave up the attempt and strode back to the house thinking darkly of the buckwheat pancakes and the fresh papaya he had been going to serve Samantha this morning.

She really knew how to screw up a man's plans. Perhaps she was a shrewder businesswoman than he'd thought!

Jeff Ingram paused outside his boss's office and adjusted the subtly striped tie in the mirror wall which lined the deeply carpeted hall of the executive suite. Jeff's personal taste in ties tended toward the more colorful. His taste in suits tended toward styles with a European dash in fabric and shape. But he wore a conservatively cut suit and the quiet tie because that's what Buchanan wore. One of the basic precepts in the corporate world was that a man who wanted to move into the executive suite should dress like the men who already inhabited it.

Jeff Ingram fully intended to wind up with a penthouse office that had a view of the ocean. Just like Buchanan's. He raised his hand and knocked on the heavy wooden door.

After the polite knock he opened the door and walked straight in. His appearance had already been announced by the secretary in the outer office. Buchanan didn't shout permission to enter through his office door.

"I have the update you requested on the Phoenix

project, sir," Jeff began at once as the other man glanced up from a file on his desk. Buchanan did not waste time in office pleasantries, so Jeff always made a practice of coming straight to the point when he made appearances in the head office.

Buchanan was capable of such pleasantries, of course, Jeff reflected wryly as the older man nodded him toward a chair. He'd personally witnessed Buchanan's enormous personal charm on several occasions. It was phony as hell but brilliantly effective. Jeff knew he still had much to learn in that direction. The Buchanan charm was on display at social functions and chamber of commerce meetings. There one saw the gracious, clear-eyed, community-minded Drew Buchanan. Someday that was where and how people would see Jeff Ingram.

Buchanan was nearing forty now, but the thick, tawny hair hadn't thinned, and the flecks of gray at the temples made Jeff envious. That distinguished look worked magic on women. It also served to reassure the men who might otherwise have found Buchanan's open, handsome features a little worrisome. The brilliant "you-can-trust-me" smile also seemed effective with both sexes, young and old. Jeff practiced a similar smile every morning while shaving.

The trick wasn't so much in imitating the smile, Jeff had decided, it was in learning how to make it slice through an opponent like a knife when the occasion demanded. Buchanan was good at it. The man was a bastard and someday, Jeff promised himself, he would be an even more successful bastard than Buchanan.

"Excellent. You're really quite dependable, Jeff." Drew

took the folder from the younger man's hand and flipped it open to the summary page. "You've started closing on our options?"

"This week. We've got the big parcels tied up. Now we go after all the little bits and pieces of Phoenix that we'll need."

Buchanan frowned thoughtfully. "What's left that we haven't covered?"

"An apartment complex and a restaurant along with a couple of small shops. Nothing difficult. I'm not anticipating trouble from any of them, so I left them until the last. The shop owners have already indicated a willingness to relocate, and the restaurant owner is thinking of retiring. We'll have one of our brokers make him an offer soon."

"It's the apartment houses which are always so damn difficult," Drew noted politely, waiting.

"Not in this case, sir." Jeff hid his inner smile of satisfaction. He'd worked hard to anticipate Buchanan on this. "I've done some research on this particular building. The owners are in a bind and more than happy to take a cash offer."

"And the tenants?" Drew questioned softly. "It's not like the old days, Jeff, when one could just go in and evict or quadruple rents and force people out. These days one must keep the corporate image in mind." Buchanan's mouth twisted faintly over that sad fact.

"The place hasn't been renting well for the past two years because the owners couldn't afford to maintain the building properly," Jeff informed him smoothly. "No cash flow and a lot of unhappy tenants. The ones who are left will be more than willing to move into that new complex on the outskirts of Phoenix, especially when we guarantee them three months free rent."

"The Maitland Maneuver?" Buchanan's brow arched with wry interest.

"Yes, sir. It's very effective." Although I'll be damned if I can figure out where you got the name for it, Jeff thought silently.

Drew Buchanan studied his eager, anxious-to-please assistant. He noted the conservative tie and suit. Ingram had his sights set high, and he'd probably make it someday. That was okay by Buchanan. He understood Jeff Ingram, which meant he could trust him. His behavior was predictable. Not like Samantha Maitland, he realized dryly as Jeff's mention of his scheme brought the name to his mind.

"It is effective in situations like this," Drew remarked. "Works almost every time. Did you know that it was invented during the process of obtaining the very chunk of land we're sitting on, Jeff?"

Ingram's eyes narrowed a fraction. He always got uneasy when Buchanan got chatty. True, such times presented some interesting opportunities to pick up a few inside pointers, but Buchanan in a friendly mood was Buchanan at his most dangerous.

"No, sir, I didn't know that," Jeff allowed cautiously.

"The woman who once had your job developed it. I didn't approve of her efforts that first time, but when I realized how much easier and more cost-effective it was to have people leaving willingly, I decided we would make use of the procedure in the future where feasible."

Buchanan saw the wariness in Ingram and smiled inwardly. It never did any harm for people in Jeff's position to know there were others out there who had pleased Drew Buchanan. People like Jeff Ingram should occasionally be reminded that they could be replaced. The idea of a shrewd predecessor having once occupied Jeff's position would give the younger man food for thought. Keep him on his toes. The fact that it had been a woman would probably make the lesson even more salutary. No man liked the idea that he could be replaced by a female or that he had to live up to the performance of a female who had gone before him.

Damned if he was going to dilute the small sting of the lesson by going on to tell Ingram that Samantha had applied her effective techniques out of a bleeding-heart concern for the tenants rather than any realistic business rationale.

The high-rise office tower in Miami which housed the corporate headquarters of the Buchanan Group had a view of the ocean. The former structure on the very expensive plot of ground hadn't been so fortunate. It had been a three-story apartment complex, far too short to afford a view. The inability to see the ocean over the rooftops hadn't bothered the tenants of the building, however. The average age of the residents had been sixty-eight, and they had all been more concerned with their low rents and the tiny gardens allocated to each unit.

But Drew had realized the full potential of the land almost at once. With a little pressure in the right places, he had gotten the zoning laws changed for the neighborhood, and then he had set his intriguing new assistant to work on securing the property.

Samantha. She'd had a real talent for the business world. She'd also been endowed with a rather sweet ass. The combination had been very appealing. When he'd realized who her father was, Drew's interest had sharpened into thoughts of marriage. The prospect of the Thorndyke money was a welcome one at the time. Money had seemed the most important thing in life in those days.

He'd recognized the weaknesses in Samantha right from the start, of course. His ability to zero in on the vulnerable points of others and use them to his own advantage was a skill he almost took for granted now. An instinct.

Samantha's flaws were easily summarized as far as Buchanan was concerned. She had an underlying softness which would no doubt forever blunt the necessary ruthlessness one needed to cultivate for the executive suite. In addition, she had been stricken with a social conscience which was almost amusing at times. That alone would probably have kept her out of the highest reaches of the corporate world. He wondered idly if she'd ever overcome that particular failing. And while her nicely rounded rear had been quite attractive, the tits had always been a little disappointing.

But all of those flaws could have been dealt with, he decided in retrospect. The social conscience could have eventually been quelled. And he could have lived with the less than perfect bustline. After all, there were plenty of women available for the times when he really wanted to indulge his taste in that direction.

Yes, for the sake of the Thorndyke money, Drew could have been reasonably content with Samantha for a wife. But there had been one other nagging flaw in her character which he frankly admitted he'd never been certain he could handle. It was the uneasy feeling that, even though he knew her strengths and weaknesses, he still didn't quite know Samantha Maitland.

You could only really be confident about someone when you knew you had a handle on him or her. When you understood what made that person tick. But Drew knew he'd never had that feeling of absolute certainty about Samantha Maitland. There was a part of her he had never quite pinned down, never quite been able to control. He couldn't even put a name to the unknown factor.

The evidence of the indefinable aspect of her nature was most clearly apparent when she was at work, he decided in retrospect. Give her an assignment and the job always got done. Sometimes brilliantly. But never in a predictable or orthodox fashion. She worked with an intuitive logic that managed to take him by surprise too many times. It was unnerving. Drew wanted skill and creativity in those who worked for him, but he wanted that skill and creativity to be controllable, similar enough to his own way of thinking as to be thoroughly comprehensible. With Samantha it was almost eccentric in nature. And highly unpredictable. Drew did not like unpredictable people around him. He never wanted to be taken by surprise, even when it worked to his own advantage.

And it had worked to his advantage on more than one occasion, he allowed with a wry sense of humor. Take the time he had indulged her and allowed her to go ahead with her bizarre plan for relocating the tenants of that old apartment building which had stood on the site of the Buchanan building. Not only had the scheme saved him a fortune in time and court costs, but the all-out effort to find substitute housing and provide several months of free rent to the dispossessed tenants had made him look very good in the local press.

It was after the business sections of the newspapers heralded his "socially responsible" approach to growth that he'd had the first stirrings of interest in local politics. He owed Samantha for that, Drew decided magnanimously.

She hadn't lasted long enough, however, to learn of his new interest. It had all come to a head the day Thorndyke had marched, unannounced, into his office and told him flatly to forget any notion he had of marrying Samantha. The order had been reinforced by the information that Thorndyke had no intention of leaving anything to his bastard daughter if she married Drew Buchanan.

All points considered, there hadn't seemed much percentage in hanging on to Samantha Maitland. There were other equally capable and far more predictable assistants, and there were other potentially more useful wives.

Jeff Ingram swallowed the subtle warning about being replaced, managing not to grit his teeth too loudly in the process, and leaned forward earnestly to go through the rest of the data in the folder. By the time he had finished, Buchanan seemed quite pleased with progress, and the younger man's enthusiasm was back in full sail.

"I'll get on the last of the details this week. We're buying the larger parcels through the usual dummy corporations," Jeff summarized briskly, "and we'll use a lot of small real estate brokers to pick up the remainder. Didn't want to send out any ripples of warning on this one, so we've been playing it very low key. I see no major problems, sir."

"And the restaurant?"

"The restaurant will be the easiest of all. As I said, rumor has it that the owner wants to sell. We'll make him a generous offer shortly." Jeff allowed himself the smallest of assured smiles. Buchanan didn't like his staff to be overconfident, but he did approve of a certain degree of assured competence. Jeff hoped the smile was right. The son of a bitch could cut you to ribbons for something as small as an overconfident smile. "No problem."

With a nod of dismissal Drew watched Jeff walk out of the office. Then he swiveled the padded leather chair around so that he could contemplate the expensive ocean view. The Phoenix project was on line, which meant he could turn his attention to other matters this afternoon.

Matters such as his date with Carol Galloway that evening. The slow, half smile edged his mouth but never reached the tawny eyes. The smiling eyes were saved for occasions when other people were around. Drew Buchanan had the virtue of utter truthfulness

143

with himself. He was deceptive only with others. It was a crucial factor in his success, and he knew it.

Carol was beautiful. Blond, classical features, good legs, and high, firm breasts. Much better breasts than Samantha had, Drew decided objectively. Samantha had been much too small for his tastes. He really was a tit man at heart.

Carol also knew clothes, and her well-bred grace and social contacts were exactly what was needed in the wife of a man who had discovered during the past three years that he liked mingling with the political elite even more than he liked mingling with the corporate elite. The fact that she was a little cold in bed didn't matter; it was even an asset. He was weary of too much passion in a woman. Passionate women inevitably demanded things like love and passion and fidelity in return. He preferred light, uncumbersome relationships. Another reason why Samantha probably wouldn't have worked out well as a wife, he decided. He'd always had the feeling she wanted too much from him.

But most important of all, with Carol there was never that uneasy feeling of not knowing exactly what she was thinking and what she was likely to do. He and Carol understood each other completely. Each had something the other wanted. It was a well-defined exchange of her family's political connections for his money and clout in the corporate world. A business arrangement, really. He had no fear of being caught off guard in a business arrangement because when it came to business, Drew knew he was damn good. The best. The one in control.

No doubt about it; Carol's dowry was going to be her

well-connected family. She was the daughter of the man who would almost certainly be the next U.S. senator from the state of Florida. Jake Galloway didn't have as much money as Victor Thorndyke had had, but that was no longer important now that Drew had enough of his own.

For Drew Buchanan had learned that there was something even more interesting in life than money. Something called power. Politics was the path which led to real power.

The flight back to Seattle was uneventful, even soothing, Samantha decided. From thirty thousand feet one's problems seemed a little less real, and once back on the ground again there were the welcome distractions of locating her Fiat in the airport parking lot, waiting in line for the ferry which would transport her back to the island she called home, and the rain. It was still raining, just as it had been when she'd left for California.

The weather suited her mood. California had been too damn sunny and cheerful.

The old Victorian house awaited her patiently, but it did not wait alone, Samantha realized as she spotted the black Ferrari in the curving drive. Eric was here. Just what she needed after a long, unsatisfactory business trip. She loved her half brother dearly, but his presence didn't always bode well for her peace of mind. Then again, she could use whatever interruption Eric Thorndyke might be bringing into her life. The alternative was to spend the evening dwelling on the time with Gabriel.

145

She was about as likely to hear from Sinclair in three days as she was to learn how to crochet. The odds were decidedly against either event, she thought morosely as she parked the car.

"Where the hell have you been? I had to pry open a back window yesterday to get into the house. What happened to the key you always leave in the flower box?" Eric met her at the door with a can of beer in one hand and a bag of natural-style potato chips in the other. He was frowning, the Thorndyke blue eyes brooding and impatient. Samantha had inherited Vera's eyes, a fact which had always pleased her mother.

But the son born to Victor Thorndyke and his wife Emily had been a truly legitimate member of the family, unlike his half sister. He had wound up with his father's eyes, near-black hair, and dark good looks. He was one year younger than Samantha and the only member of the Thorndyke clan she could tolerate for more than five minutes.

It was probably the fact that he was so much younger than his older, legitimate brother and sister which had initially accounted for his ready acceptance of Samantha. She had been close to his age, and her natural independence had appealed to the rebel in a young boy struggling for his own identity and style in a domineering family. They had mutually agreed to accept each other from the day they had met when Samantha was sixteen and Eric fifteen.

Samantha had always known her father's name, of course, and clearly understood why her last name wasn't Thorndyke. Vera had made no secret out of it, nor had

146

she seen any reason to pretend for the child's sake that her father had died. Samantha had been forced to learn pride very quickly in the face of the cruel questions of the other children in school. Pride and a fierce defensiveness of her mother. Vera had told her, too, that Victor Thorndyke had another family and Samantha would never be a part of it. Vera explained very carefully that Samantha didn't need her father.

To a large extent, Samantha supposed, that was true. Her mother gave her everything; an excellent education, maternal devotion which, though of a somewhat unconventional nature, was nevertheless quite intense, and the ability to stand on her own two feet. Invaluable gifts for any child.

But even when she had been very young, the curiosity was there, moving about occasionally in the back of Samantha's mind and generating a kind of restlessness. She comprehended the fact that her father didn't even know of her existence, and she understood when her mother explained that a man in Victor Thorndyke's position would not be at all pleased to learn he had an illegitimate daughter after all these years.

Vera even explained that the legitimate members of the Thorndyke family had rights. Samantha was told early on that it wouldn't be very pleasant for Victor's wife and children to have inflicted on them the knowledge of a daughter born to another woman. And it wasn't as if Victor had deliberately gotten Vera pregnant and just abandoned her. It was Vera who had terminated the affair once her goal of conceiving Samantha had been accomplished.

"Didn't you ever think of asking him to divorce his wife and marry you?" Samantha had asked naïvely one day at the age of twelve.

"I had no right to do such a thing!" Vera had retorted at once and had then gone on to deliver an enlightening lesson on the subject of taking responsibility for one's own actions. She had also added a salutary fillip on the topic of the rights of other people such as Emily Thorndyke. "I knew what I was doing when I had the affair with Victor, Samantha. I also knew from the beginning that marriage was not possible. To tell you the truth, I would not have married him, anyway, even if it had been a possibility. Marriage would have stifled me, dear. It would stifle any independent, creative woman. It is an archaic institution which has never benefited women. The only ones who ever got anything useful out of marriage were men. It is basically an economic institution, Samantha, but one which no longer provides even financial security for women. You don't need marriage."

The nagging curiosity about her father had persisted, however, driving her eventually to the public library at the age of sixteen. There, with the help of a reference librarian, she had looked up the Thorndyke name in a huge book which listed all major U.S. companies. There, under the *T*'s was a corporation called Thorndyke Industries. Victor Thorndyke, President.

For several weeks Samantha hugged the newfound information to her, telling herself it was enough and that she could stop there. But all too soon she wanted more. She wanted to meet Victor Thorndyke.

At last, unable to keep her need secret any longer, Samantha had dared broach the issue to her mother. She had started out with a lot of carefully detailed reasons as to why she should be allowed to meet her father and had ended up in tears, begging Vera to make the phone call which would inform Victor he had another daughter. Sensing that if she didn't step in and monitor the situation Samantha would make some wild attempt on her own to achieve the contact with Victor, Vera had reluctantly taken on the task of delicately initiating it.

No one could have foreseen Thorndyke's response, least of all Vera, who had expected to be immediately rebuffed by her ex-lover. Instead he had recovered almost immediately from his astonishment, and then he had demanded to be introduced to his offspring. He never doubted the child was his. He'd known Vera well enough to realize she would never lie about a thing like that. The question in his own mind was how much money she was going to want to keep Samantha's existence a secret. He had taken a plane east, using business as an excuse less than a week after Vera's call.

The eventual meeting had totally unexpected ramifications. Thorndyke had walked into the Maitland home half-expecting to fend off a cheap blackmail attempt and had stayed to be enchanted by his unbearably tense, terribly frightened daughter.

No one could have guessed at the instant rapport which blossomed to life immediately between father and daughter, especially not Vera. Thorndyke had seen at once the resemblance to himself which went far deeper than a superficial molding of features. It was a way of thinking, a way of reasoning, and a natural aptitude for business which made Samantha his true heir in a way duplicated only in his youngest son. He accepted Samantha completely. She was an extension of himself, just as Eric was.

For a time the news of Samantha's existence was kept between the three involved parties. Whenever his business took him east, Thorndyke arranged a visit with his daughter. Samantha had never known for certain whether or not her father and Vera had ever resumed their affair. There was no doubt but that the attraction still flared between the two adults, but they were both far too discreet to involve Samantha in that aspect of their lives.

Then one day Victor had announced his intention of acknowledging Samantha to his California family. Vera had protested angrily, pointing out the trauma it would cause everyone, but Thorndyke had been insistent. In the end, Vera could only demand that Samantha not be forced to face the other Thorndykes in a confrontation scene. Victor had understood and respected that request.

He had flown back to California, and the next time he came east he was accompanied by his youngest son. Fifteen years of age, Eric had been as curious about his new sister as Samantha was about him. They had gotten along from the first.

During the next several years Samantha had had a great deal of contact with her father, although she had never met any other member of his family except Eric. Thorndyke had been the one to guide her when she selected a university which would provide her with a good grounding in business. He had been the one to assist in finding her the first job after graduation.

Vera, to her credit, had learned to accept this new influence in her daughter's life, certain that, having had her to herself for sixteen years, she'd done a solid job of instilling the important tenets Samantha would need to survive as a woman and as a socially conscious member of society. Vera had even been objective enough to realize that Samantha's talents lay in the business world, and she didn't try to force her daughter into the academic environment.

"You can do just as much good on the front lines as you can from the ivory tower, perhaps more," she'd enthused to Samantha. "Capitalism needs to be tempered by a social conscience."

Victor Thorndyke had taken great pleasure in helping plan his daughter's career, especially because he was discovering at the same time that he was going to be denied that pleasure with Eric. Eric was going off on an unexpected tangent, a direction which Victor considered a deplorable waste of talent. Eric had turned into a computer freak.

After helping Samantha choose a school and a first job, Victor had also assisted in the decision to move Samantha on when the position proved limiting.

"Timing is everything in a business career," he'd told her. "Knowing when to move is more important than knowing when to stay."

There was an up-and-coming development firm down in Florida, he told Samantha one afternoon on a periodic trip to the East Coast. Perhaps she should look into it. Working for a dynamic, fast-moving company such as the Buchanan Group provided plenty of opportunity for high-achievers like Samantha. He had not foreseen the possibility of his daughter falling in love with the chief executive officer or that Drew Buchanan would manipulate her as easily as he was manipulating his business ventures.

The eventual meeting with the rest of the Thorndyke clan had occurred two years ago when Samantha had been summoned for the reading of Victor's will. Distraught at the loss of her father, she had been unprepared for the scene in the attorney's office when she came face-to-face with the full weight of her actions that day in the public library when she'd looked up the Thorndyke name.

The resentment and disdain on the part of Victor's widow, Emily, his eldest son, Victor Junior, and his other daughter, Amanda, was a palpable wall against which she had floundered the moment she entered the room.

Samantha had reacted with a savagely cool, defensive arrogance which would have done Vera proud. She'd turned down the money which had been left to her as if it amounted to peanuts instead of a fortune and had walked out of the room without a backward glance.

For some odd reason she knew her refusal to take the inheritance had irritated the Thorndykes as much if not more than the fact that she had been included in the will in the first place. It was as if, by walking away from it, she hadn't proved herself to be the mercenary little bitch they had all been certain she really was. Only Eric had appreciated the gesture. Anything which flew in the face of natural Thorndyke dominance appealed to him. He had envied Samantha's sheer guts in the matter. Looking at him now, Samantha realized she was rather glad to see him again.

"I haven't left the key in the flowerpot since the last time you were here and lectured me about the stupid security habits of the female of the species," Samantha quipped lightly to her half brother as she climbed out of the car and started up the steps with her suitcase. "Do any damage to my window?"

"Nah, it's fine. Your phone's been ringing off the hook." Eric took her bag from her hand as she entered the house. He had a pleasant fire going in the old brick fireplace and a sportscaster's voice boomed from the television set in the corner. The remains of a box of takeout fried chicken littered the coffee table. "Where have you been, Sam?"

"I had business down in California." Automatically she walked over and flipped off the TV. She hated having it on. Someday she would simply toss it into the trash can. To date, however, she hadn't been able to work up the nerve. It seemed wrong, somehow, to cut herself off from any potential source of information when her whole line of work was based on collecting just that. "Did you answer my phone?"

"Nope. I knew who was calling. I listened in while your recording machine took messages."

"You computer freaks are born snoops, aren't you?"

she grumbled, slipping off the black leather jacket. "Have you left anything for dinner?"

"Sure. I went shopping. What were you doing down in California?" He traipsed after her as she made her way into the kitchen and watched hopefully as she surveyed the shambles he had made of the room. Samantha knew she wasn't a model of neatness, but Eric could not give her pointers.

Eric could afford the best, as was evidenced by his beloved Ferrari, but he had his image as a maverick computer wizard to maintain. The jeans he wore were old and faded, the gaudy leather belt scarred and worn. He steadfastly refused to wear a suit to work, maintaining that genuine computer wizards simply didn't do that sort of thing unless they happened to work for IBM.

"I wanted to discuss business with a . . . a client who lives down there." Samantha opened the refrigerator door, forbearing to comment on the chaos in the kitchen. She found herself wondering what Gabriel would say if he saw the place. He'd probably go into shock.

"There's a pizza in the freezer. I picked it up yesterday. Why don't we have that?" Eric offered helpfully as he watched her standing morosely in front of the denuded refrigerator.

"I guess it's either that or we go out to dinner, and I don't feel like doing that," Samantha muttered. "I expect you to replenish my larder before you leave this time, Eric. After your last visit I had to restock completely, and it cost a small fortune!"

"I needed a lot of energy while I was playing with

154

that sort program on your computer. I don't see any bugs crawling in the program. Had any trouble with it?"

"No." Samantha smiled for the first time as she slid the frozen pizza out of its box. "I've been able to do a lot with it. Very flexible."

"Good." Eric looked briefly pleased because he had, after all, designed the program for Samantha. Then the brooding look descended once again. "Want a beer?"

"Have I still got some wine left?" she inquired blandly, turning on the oven.

"Of course. You know I prefer beer. I'll open a bottle of that zinfandel I saw down in your cellar."

"That will be fine." What would Gabriel say if he saw this pizza? she wondered, wrinkling her nose at the array of frozen cheese and tomato sauce. He would probably have chucked it out the window and made his own from scratch.

"How's your mom?" Eric demanded politely, returning with the bottle of California zinfandel. He had no trouble opening the wine. Eric had had the benefits of an excellent education, even though he flaunted them occasionally.

"Last I heard she's enjoying herself working up a battle plan to stall the licensing of a new nuclear plant that's supposed to be coming on line next June in the Midwest somewhere. I haven't talked to her for a while." Like over a month. The closer the plans for cornering Drew Buchanan approached completion, the less Samantha wanted to talk of her mother. Vera knew nothing of the project. Samantha wanted the whole matter to be a fait accompli which she could casually lay at her mother's feet.

"What about your family?" Samantha remembered to ask politely, although they both knew she couldn't have cared less about general Thorndyke welfare. At least Samantha liked to think she couldn't have cared less.

"You'll find out for yourself when you turn on the telephone recorder and listen to the playback," Eric told her wryly.

Samantha sent him a sharp glance as he handed her a glass of the dark red zinfandel. "That's why my phone's been ringing? And why you haven't bothered to answer? Your family is trying to get in touch with me?" Just what she needed.

"Afraid so." Eric threw himself down into a white, ladder-back kitchen chair and gulped from his can of beer. He looked disgusted and dejected, and Samantha knew her first twinge of genuine concern. Eric had sometimes elected to use her residence as a place to hide from his family in the past, and it always meant trouble for Samantha because the Thorndykes had learned where to come looking.

Without another word Samantha walked over to where the recording machine sat on the end of the pleasantly cracked tile counter and flipped the device to rewind. Then she sat down in the chair facing her half brother and sipped the wine while they both listened in silence to the string of increasingly annoyed Thorndyke voices on the tape.

"Samantha? This is Emily Thorndyke. Is Eric with you? Please have him call home as soon as possible."

"Samantha, this is Mrs. Thorndyke again. We want to reach Eric, and we know he's probably staying with you. This is *family* business and has nothing to do with you. Please do not get involved!"

"Samantha? Mrs. Thorndyke. I insist you have Eric get in touch at once. If you don't, I'll have to ask Victor Junior to take a hand in this."

It was the ultimate threat. Samantha was only mildly amused that Eric's mother still called her eldest son "Junior" even though his father had been dead for two years. The woman was a creature of habit.

Emily's voice came on the tape three more times before she made good on her threat and had her son make the call. Victor Thorndyke Junior's deep tones held all the dynamic disdain his position as president of Thorndyke Industries had given him. He was thirty-eight years old, and he didn't care very much for Samantha. But, then, none of the Thorndykes did, except for Eric. Samantha didn't blame them. Every time they came into contact she managed to annoy them.

They'd liked her even less after she'd accidentally gotten wind of the take-over attempt planned by a Thorndyke rival shortly after Victor Thorndyke had died. For no good reason that Samantha could think of, she kept Thorndyke Industries on her list of continually monitored companies, and when the hints of take-over activity had filtered through her rapidly expanding information network, she'd passed the word even though the firm was not a subscribing client.

Actually, Samantha reflected, it was facetious of her to say she didn't know why she monitored Thorndyke

Industries now that her father was dead. She did it precisely because the company was her father's legacy. It had been his creation, a businessman's work of art which he had left behind as a testimony to his genius. Samantha felt an odd loyalty to the firm even though she had never been actively involved in it. When she had provided the take-over warning, Victor Junior had successfully used the extra time she had bought him to counter the attack. There had been no thank-you note from the Thorndykes, Samantha recalled dryly. None was expected.

"Samantha," Victor Junior's voice declared with all the firmness he normally applied to incompetent staff members, "I must insist you stop playing games. This is business. Have Eric call me at once."

There were no more calls on the tape. Samantha rose and shut off the machine with a long-suffering sigh. "Well, Eric, what are you up to this time?"

He stared at her for a long moment as if trying to line up the right words. Then he said slowly, "I'm leaving the firm, Sam."

She arched an interested eyebrow, unsurprised. She only wondered what had taken Eric so long to make the decision. "Going to become the first Thorndyke on welfare?"

"Sam, this isn't funny! The only way to make it on your own terms in this world is to make it on your own terms! The way you and Dad did."

"You've been studying elementary philosophy? That was a very profound statement." She chuckled.

"Don't laugh at me, Sam."

158

"You know I always laugh at Thorndykes. It's good for the digestion."

He ignored that, watching her with a grim set to his mouth. There was a hardness in his eyes that Samantha had never seen there before, and she wondered at it. "I had my way out all planned, Sam. I've been working on it for months. I had developed a product to market, and I was going to set myself up in business somewhere here in the Northwest." His hand closed into a taut fist on the table.

"Had?" Samantha questioned very gently. "Past tense?"

"Vic stole it."

"He *what*?"

"He stole it!" Eric repeated in a tight voice. "He took the software packages I'd been working on and patented them in the name of Thorndyke Industries."

"Eric, what are you talking about? What software packages?"

"They're called 'application generators,' Sam. A new idea in the computer world, and they'll make millions for the people who develop and market them. I've been working on mine for ages, and they were absolutely brilliant! Beautifully simple. Most of the bugs worked out. Incredibly adaptable. . . ."

"Okay, okay, I'll buy all the glowing adjectives. Tell me what they *do*."

"Application generators are little modules of preprogrammed software which you can plug into any new program that's being developed. Saves countless hours of routine programming."

"But every program is unique. Made to do a special

159

job like crank out payroll checks or produce an inventory list. How could you preprogram sections of them?"

"Because even though every company wants its computer programming to do jobs which are unique to that company, there really are a lot of similarities in the tasks involved," Eric told her impatiently. "All payroll-writing programs have certain things in common, no matter which firm they're designed for. They all have to figure deductions, vacation pay, stuff like that. I'm designing little modules which a programmer can simply plug in whenever he gets to the routine part of his program. Instead of having to write out all the lines of code it takes to tell a computer to deduct social security taxes, he simply inserts the lines of code I've already written."

"Can that be done? Can programs be written that are interchangeable for different computers?" she asked.

"That's the magic part. Making them adaptable to a variety of computers," Eric told her with great satisfaction. "I can do it."

"Sounds good, Eric," she said slowly.

"It *sounded* good," he corrected heavily. "It sounded like my ticket out of Thorndyke Industries. It sounded like the perfect way to start in business for myself."

"So what went wrong?" she asked gently.

"What went wrong is that, thanks to another guy in the computer department at Thorndyke, Vic found out just how valuable those program modules of mine might be."

"He hadn't known you were working on them?" Samantha frowned.

"Oh, he knew, he just didn't pay much attention to what I was doing. He agreed to let me play with the computer on my own time, and he agreed that anything I developed during that time would be mine. He didn't seem to care what I did as long as I handled Thorndyke business during regular working hours on the computer."

Samantha waited, knowing from what Eric had said in the past that Victor Junior had probably brushed off his brother's computer talents, considering them rather clerical in nature. The family had more than once tried to pry Eric out of the computer room and into the front office as a vice-president, deeming that role more in keeping with the status of a Thorndyke. But Eric hadn't budged, and his desire to stick with computers had been grudgingly tolerated.

"Go on," she finally prompted.

"Well, Vic found out from this other guy about the potential value of what I was doing, and the first thing I know he hauls out an old, standard form everyone, including me, signs when they go to work for Thorndyke."

Samantha winced. "The kind of form which clearly states that anything developed by an employee during his tenure with the company belongs to the company?" It was a fairly standard contract in most technologically oriented businesses.

"Yeah." Eric stared grimly at the counter across from him. "Everything happened very quickly after that. Vic can move fast when he wants to. With the help of my so-called friend in the department, tapes were made of my little programs, patent applications were filed, and

161

Vic graciously offered me the great honor of being promoted to vice-president of Research and Marketing for the new Thorndyke Industries product."

"Oh, Eric." Samantha sighed sympathetically.

"He *knew* I wanted out of the firm, and he guessed I was going to use my inventions as a way to start over on my own. But he never said a word until I had everything done and ready to go!" Eric slapped the table in fury and frustration. "But I'm not going to let him trap me this way, Sam!"

The buzzer on the stove sounded, indicating the pizza was ready, and Samantha got to her feet to check on it. Eric's eyes followed her across the room. "What are you thinking of doing, Eric?" she finally asked quietly.

"I handed in my formal resignation before I left to come up here," he began steadily.

Samantha nodded as she gingerly plucked the tray of bubbling pizza from the oven. "So you quit? Hence all those calls on my answering machine?"

"Yeah, but Vic and Mom and Amanda don't know the half of it yet."

"I'm listening," Samantha said in resignation.

Eric drew a long breath. "I decided that, since Thorndyke Industries deprived me of my ticket out, it was only fair that it finance my new start in some other way."

Samantha finished slicing the pizza with one of her very dull knives and picked up the pan with pot holders, starting back toward the table with her burden. "How?"

"How much, Sam, do you think West-Land Equipment would pay for a spread-sheet showing the wholesale costs of all the parts and materials Thorndyke buys to build its new submersible pumps?"

"Eric! My God! What have you done?" Samantha was shaken. The pizza slithered precariously on the tray as she came to an abrupt halt halfway to the table and stared at him. "You're talking about industrial espionage!"

"I've got that financial information, Sam. I went into the Thorndyke computer and pulled it out before I left Los Angeles two days ago. I made a printout of it, and I can sell it to West-Land for enough to set myself up in business as a computer consultant anywhere in the country! Don't you see the beauty of it? Thorndyke's going to wind up financing my career, all right, and on my terms!"

Samantha read the agony of suspense in her relative's taut features, knew instinctively that he was somehow seeking her approval and support for what he had done. But before she could think of anything to say, the pizza gave up its attempt to cling to the tray and slid off onto the brown-and-white-checkered floor, landing in a squishy splash of cheese and tomato sauce.

Wordlessly Samantha glanced down at the mess at her feet. It crossed her mind that this sort of thing would probably never have been allowed to happen in Gabriel's kitchen.

Then she raised her eyes again to meet the urgent blue gaze of the young man who had just announced his intention of selling the family secrets.

"How do you know West-Land will pay so much for what you took from the Thorndyke computer?" she whispered.

"Because the deal's already been made, Sam," he explained in a stark-sounding voice that told her just how uneasy he was over what he had done. There was a tense pause, and then Eric ground out savagely, "Don't look at me like that! I couldn't call if off now, even if I wanted to!"

"Why not!" she demanded.

Eric's mouth twisted. "Because the whole arrangement was made through a . . . a kind of broker. A man who does this sort of thing for a living. He found the buyer when I contacted him and told him what I had. He takes a cut."

"And if you were to change your mind?" she pressed anxiously.

"Sam, I can't change my mind! This broker isn't exactly a pillar of the business community! Don't you see? He's like a loan shark or something. If I don't deliver the goods on time, I've had it. He will send someone to come and collect what I promised to provide. Forcibly!"

"Oh, my God, Eric. *What have you done?*"

"I'm trapped, Sam. I can't change my mind now. I have to go through with the deal."

"Eric, you can't!"

He stared at her for a long, anguished moment, and then he closed his eyes. "I know. I've known since yesterday. A man doesn't betray his own family, no matter what they've done to him. Christ, Sam. What am I going to do?"

CHAPTER FIVE

The really annoying thing about this, Gabriel decided laconically, was the thought of Samantha's expression when she opened the door to find him standing humbly on her doorstep, checkbook in hand.

He hooked one foot over the bottom deck rail and leaned his elbows on the top one. Far below, the white wake foamed around the hull as the Washington State ferry slid placidly through the cold gray waters of Elliot Bay. Behind him the Seattle waterfront receded slowly, the aggressive new skyline half-hidden in the mist.

Jesus! It was cold! How the hell did Samantha survive this chilled, damp weather? Gabriel huddled deeper into the lightweight windbreaker and thought briefly of the sunshine and warmth he had left behind in California. Down there the Pacific was an inviting blue. Here it was steel-gray.

She lived on an island. Figured. Count on Samantha not to live like a normal city person in a high-rise apartment building in downtown Seattle. Judging by the number of cars parked belowdecks, a lot of people around here lived on islands. There were literally hundreds of chunks of land scattered throughout the waters of Puget Sound. It had taken a while to find the right ferry for the island on which Samantha lived.

Gabriel considered again the reception he was likely to receive when Samantha opened the door to him. This was the third day, the last day she had allowed in her ultimatum. Had she been getting anxious? Or had she simply been making plans to contact Oakes?

Whatever her present state of mind, Gabriel knew exactly what would go through her quicksilver brain the moment she opened her door to him.

"Little witch," he muttered, lifting the Styrofoam cup of hot coffee to his mouth. "You're going to think you've won, aren't you? You'll probably be impossible to live with until we get a few things straightened out between us."

He could read the delighted arrogance and feminine satisfaction in those gold-flecked tortoiseshell eyes already. His mouth kicked upward in a wry grimace. It was going to take some work to convince her that just because he had arrived, money in hand, she wasn't one hundred percent in the driver's seat.

And it was going to be a little hard to explain to her exactly why he had succumbed to the pressure of her feisty ultimatum. Not that he didn't comprehend his own motives quite thoroughly, Gabriel thought grimly. He'd realized almost as soon as she'd left his house that morning that he'd go through hell to keep her from getting tangled up with William Oakes. Good God!

166

Together Oakes and Buchanan would have screwed her to the wall! The woman didn't have the foggiest notion of what she was getting into when she talked of forming an alliance with Bill Oakes. She probably didn't have a very realistic idea of what it took to go up against a man like Buchanan, either. A lamb among wolves.

But a very arrogant little lamb who wouldn't have sense enough to run when the wolves started closing in on her. Gabriel's eyes narrowed as he studied a mist-shrouded island slipping past on the starboard side of the ferry. No, Samantha wouldn't run. She didn't lack courage.

He sighed and downed the last of the coffee. So here he was, the angel Gabriel to the rescue. Except that he didn't feel particularly angelic about the whole thing. What he really felt was a distinct hardening of his body below the belt when he thought about having Samantha within reach again.

Some angel.

And Samantha definitely wasn't going to look upon this as a rescue operation. She was going to take one look at him and think he had come all the way to Seattle for the sake of the deal she had offered. She was going to assume that her threat had worked.

Which left him with the task of making her understand that just because he was prepared to back her financially, he was not prepared to be a silent partner. Gabriel intended to have a very vocal say in the plans she was formulating. Damned if she was going to assume she was the one in command.

But it was going to take some doing to teach her

otherwise, he reflected, turning away from the rail to head back to the glass-walled cabin in the ferry. He figured his best chance of regaining the upper hand would be to put Samantha flat on her back in bed. The empty Styrofoam cup crumpled with a soft crunch as his left hand tightened reflexively.

It wasn't easy finding the house along the narrow, winding road which circled the island. It was almost hidden among the heavy growth of pine and fir, but when it came into view, Gabriel decided the old Victorian monstrosity suited Samantha perfectly. Eccentric, fiercely independent, and even arrogant, but like its owner, offering a promise of cozy warmth inside.

There were two cars in the drive. Gabriel frowned as he parked his rented Buick. The Fiat had to be Samantha's but the black Ferrari looked like a man's car. He knew it in his bones. Oakes? Would she have contacted him already? Damn it to hell, she was the one who had said three days. She could damn well honor her own time limit.

He slammed the door of the innocuous Buick, shoved his chilled hands into the pockets of the windbreaker, and headed toward the porch steps. Was he going to have to kick Oakes out on his ass? Or did the Ferrari belong to some other man, a lover, perhaps?

No. Not a lover. The only lover in Samantha's life right now was himself, whether she realized it or not. But if there was a man hanging around who had opinions to the contrary, Gabriel decided he'd have to set the record straight immediately.

"Now who's sounding arrogant?" he chided himself

half under his breath as he raised his hand to clash the huge brass eagle which appeared to serve as a door knocker. He was rather appalled at the grim resolution he was feeling. Possessive jealousy wasn't at all characteristic of him. But, then, neither was this business of chasing after a woman and begging her to take his money!

Samantha glanced up from the computer printout she was studying, a wave of trepidation assailing her as the eagle on her door clanged demandingly. For an instant she stared into her brother's tense eyes as Eric, too, lifted his head. He turned away from the computer screen where he'd been furiously working on a financial spread-sheet program.

"It's probably just some friend of yours, Sam. They can't know where I am. Not this soon!"

"Your family knows where you are," she reminded him tightly, her heart pounding as she considered just who might be standing on the other side of her door. She didn't fear the possibility of finding another Thorndyke out there. Thorndykes were irritating but manageable. She feared another sort of visitor entirely.

The deadline Eric's industrial espionage broker had given her brother had slipped by last night. Eric hadn't delivered the promised financial information.

"My family knows, but the people I'm dealing with wouldn't contact them to find out where I am," Eric hissed. "And no one else knows where I am!"

"Okay, okay. I'll see who it is." Samantha got to her feet, feeling a little shaky as she faced the prospect of answering her door. "Eric, we've got to call the police.

I can't live like this, worrying every time someone knocks on my door!"

"You think the police can handle this crowd?" he scoffed unhappily.

"Well, what are we going to do? If you really think they'll be after you . . ."

"I'm working on it, Sam. Don't worry. By tomorrow I'll have this doctored spread-sheet ready. West-Land won't be able to tell it isn't the original version! I'll turn it over and we'll be out of this mess."

The idea had come to Eric and Samantha yesterday as the deadline for delivery drew near. Samantha had known from the first that her brother wouldn't be able to follow through on his act of corporate espionage. Rage and a driving sense of injustice had pushed him into rashly making the deal, but the ties of family loyalty and his own personal decency had reasserted themselves. He was not Victor Thorndyke's son for nothing.

But the plan for extricating him from the web he had woven was taking time to prepare. The substitute data sheets with the phony financial information had to look good if they were to fool both Eric's shadowy contact and West-Land. He had been up most of the night restructuring the original spread-sheet. Samantha had spent the night beside him, doing what she could to help. The thought of time having run out on them was terrifying.

The clash of the eagle came again, and Samantha drew in her breath. The door had to be answered.

"Sam," Eric called after her urgently.

"Yes?" She paused in the doorway and glanced back at her brother's disturbed expression. He was scared, too, she realized.

"Sam, if you don't recognize whoever's out there, don't open the door," he ordered starkly.

"Believe me, I won't!"

"I wish you'd gotten a dog, a big one, like I told you to a few months ago," Eric muttered, sliding out of his chair and moving forward to follow her into the living room.

"Oh, shut up and stay out of sight," she gritted irritably. "It's probably only your brother or one of his minions come to take you home."

"A large dog wouldn't be a bad idea in that case, either."

Samantha padded across the floor in her fluffy house slippers. She was wearing a pair of faded jeans which fit like a glove and a loose, plaid flannel shirt. Her hair was knotted carelessly on top of her head, slightly askew. The long, hard night showed in the drawn look of her features and in the unnatural brightness of the brown and gold eyes.

Restlessly she prodded her glasses higher on her nose and peered through the tiny peephole built into the old wooden door.

"Gabriel!" The name was a soft, startled exclamation. She blinked rapidly, stepping back from the door. "It's Gabriel Sinclair!"

"Who the hell's that?" Eric frowned from across the room, watching the shocked expression on his half sister's face. "You know him?"

171

"You could say that. Good grief! I never thought . . . I mean, the most I expected was a phone call. I didn't dream he'd turn up on my front porch!"

"Who *is* he?"

"A . . . a business acquaintance," Samantha began awkwardly as the eagle clashed once again.

"Well, for God's sake let him in," Eric grunted in relief. "I'm going back to work." He swung around the corner, heading back down the hall to the parlor where the computer equipment was housed.

Samantha reached for the doorknob with trembling fingers. Gabriel had come. In her heart of hearts she hadn't really expected him to show up. Not like this. Wordlessly she flung open the door and stood staring up at the man in front of her.

Gabriel's gaze ran assessingly over her drawn, too-tense features and came to rest on the widened tortoise-shell eyes. "Mind if I come in?" he finally drawled when she just stood there, saying nothing. "It's damn cold out here."

"What are you doing here?" she whispered hoarsely.

"What do you think I'm doing here? You could have used a few more days at the spa, Samantha. You look like hell. Or do you owe this delightfully haggard appearance to the man who drives that Ferrari parked outside?"

"Actually," she managed flippantly, recovering from her initial shock, "that's not far off the mark. Come in, Gabriel. Somehow I wasn't expecting to see you."

He moved through the doorway, the dense, restrained power of him intimidating her senses as she tried to

172

readjust to his unexpected presence. Her plans for Drew Buchanan had taken a temporary back burner as the crisis involving her brother had materialized. And she had flung the ultimatum at Gabriel more out of self-defense than any real expectation that it would work.

It had worked!

The full meaning of that began to dawn on her as she watched him shrug out of his jacket. His eyes moved almost aggressively around the pleasantly cluttered room. She found herself remembering the pristine neatness of his own home.

"Don't worry, no rats or cockroaches, Gabriel. A little cozy sloppiness never hurt anyone!" She took his lightweight jacket and hung it in the hall closet, aware that he was watching her now with an intensity that was unnerving. "Can I get you a cup of coffee?" she demanded brightly, turning to confront him.

"Who is he?"

"Who?" She honestly didn't know who he was talking about. Her head was filling up too fast with all the possibilities of Gabriel's presence. He had come to seal their partnership. She could hardly believe it.

"The man who drives that Ferrari parked outside," Gabriel explained with a patience which sounded as if he was willing to stand there in her hall until doomsday waiting for the answer.

"Oh, him!" Was Gabriel a little jealous? Good Lord, how much power did she really have? "That's Eric. Come along, Gabriel, and I'll make the coffee."

Before Gabriel could answer, Eric's voice came loudly

173

from the back parlor. "Make some for me, too, Sam. I need another cup!"

Gabriel eyed Samantha for a second and then swung around on his heel and headed down the hall, following the sound of Eric's voice.

"Gabriel, wait!" Samantha yelped anxiously, realizing the unstoppable force she had unleashed. "Eric is my . . ."

The words died on her lips as his broad back disappeared. Samantha glared at the empty hall. "Well, hell! Who's in charge around here, anyway?" The sight of Gabriel on her doorstep had caused her to believe she might be once again in command. Obviously it was going to take some effort to stay in that position. She stomped down the hall toward the back parlor, rounding the corner just in time to see Gabriel come face-to-face with a mildly surprised Eric.

"If you're not the computer repair man, we might have a problem," Gabriel said evenly.

Eric arched one black brow, his fingers drumming gently on the computer console in front of him. "Then it's lucky I am the computer repair man, isn't it?"

"Gabriel, stop it!" Samantha hurried up behind the two men, not caring for the cool way they were assessing each other. "This is Eric Thorndyke, my half brother. Eric, this is Gabriel Sinclair, a . . . a business acquaintance."

"No kidding," Eric murmured, blue eyes gleaming in spite of the exhaustion in them. "Since when did you go for the heavy-handed macho type, Sam?"

"Business makes strange bedfellows," Gabriel said calmly.

"Gabriel!" Samantha's dismayed exclamation made Eric's brow rise another half inch.

"So he's that type of business acquaintance, hmm?"

"Cut it out! Both of you! Damn it, Gabriel is here on business. Aren't you, Gabriel?" she challenged, whirling to confront him.

He stared at her, drinking in the sight of her furiously flushed face and disheveled clothing. "You could say that."

"I am saying it. Now do you want some coffee or don't you?" she snapped.

"I do, even if he doesn't," Eric volunteered, staring moodily at his terminal screen. "I think I've got another long night ahead."

Samantha shook her head urgently, anxiety flaring in her gaze as she was recalled to her brother's far more critical problem. "Eric, I think you should get some sleep. You can't work efficiently when you're this tired."

"Believe me, Sam, I wouldn't sleep a wink," he retorted dryly, punching a button on the machine. "Go get your 'business acquaintance' some coffee. Sounds like the two of you have a few things to talk about in private."

"For a computer type, your brother displays an amazing amount of people sense," Gabriel declared firmly, taking hold of Samantha's arm and guiding her forcefully out of the parlor. "And I could use a shot of brandy with that coffee if you've got it. I'm chilled to the bone. It's going to take me hours to warm up!"

175

"Gabriel, you can't simply come charging in here and acting as if you have a right to give orders like this!" Samantha's protests were somewhat diluted by the fact that she was being hustled down the hall. "If you're here to do business . . ."

"Oh, I am, I am."

"Then you can damn well act a little more business-like!"

"You never told me there was a third party involved in your little scheme, Samantha. Where do you keep the pot?" He released her as they walked into the kitchen.

"What third party? Just sit down, will you? You're making me nervous, the way you're charging around here like a bull in a china shop!"

"I'm making *you* nervous! That's a switch." But he sat, lowering himself into one of the ladder-back chairs at the kitchen table. He watched Samantha as she began shoveling coffee in large quantities into the automatic drip machine. "Tell me about Eric."

"What's to tell?" she grumbled, measuring water in a rather rough fashion. "He's my half brother. He's staying here for a while," she added with sudden firmness. If Gabriel thought there was going to be another person in the house tonight, he might not press to stay here himself. The last thing she needed on top of everything else was to be confronted by the possibility of another night in bed with Gabriel Sinclair. She was damn well going to keep whatever edge her ultimatum had given her!

"He's helping you with your big plans for taking on

176

Buchanan? Samantha, that's going to be lousy coffee." He got to his feet. "Here, let me do it."

She let herself be gently shouldered aside, too tired physically to fight him. "Eric isn't helping me with the Buchanan deal. Is that what you meant by having a third party involved?"

Gabriel nodded, pouring the coffee back out of the machine and remeasuring it carefully. "If he's not part of your scheme, then what in hell have the two of you been doing all night on that computer? You both look exhausted."

Samantha moved uneasily, taking the chair he had just vacated. "Eric is working on an important program that he wants to finish and take back with him to Los Angeles." Poor, but she really couldn't think very straight at the moment. The long hours of the night and the morning were beginning to tell. She wondered how much longer Eric would be able to go on without sleep. He had been laboring twice as hard as she had.

"Must be one hell of a program to keep you both up all night! Come on, Samantha, what's going on? I get the feeling that whatever you and your brother are working on, it's important to you, as important even as our deal."

"Eric's project just happens to have a deadline on it, that's all. My deal will wait a couple of days," she mumbled. Then she brightened a bit. "Gabriel, have you really decided to back me after all?"

He finished pouring carefully measured water into the machine and turned on the switch before answering. She studied his back, aware of the solid breadth of his shoulders. Disturbing memories of how those hard, smoothly muscled shoulders had blocked out the moonlight as Gabriel had lowered himself into her body that night in California jangled alive in her mind. Ruthlessly she squashed the images. This was business.

"If you're still determined to try your hand at outwitting Buchanan, I'll back you financially," Gabriel said very seriously. He turned away from the coffee machine, leaning back against the counter and folding his arms across his broad chest. He looked, Samantha thought, awfully implacable for a man who had just surrendered to an ultimatum. She eyed him from beneath lowered lashes. "There are, however," he continued, "a few conditions."

"The hell there are," she sighed wearily, closing her eyes completely and leaning back in the uncomfortable chair. Her jean-clad legs stretched out in front of her. "Tell me about the conditions, Gabriel." Samantha groaned.

He hesitated. "Somehow you just don't look like you're up to doing business," he observed mildly. "Do you always exhaust yourself like this when you're working on a crash project?"

Her eyes flickered open and she regarded him balefully. "Tell me about the conditions, Gabriel."

The brackets at the edge of his mouth tightened ominously. It occurred to Samantha that this man had a little practicing to do in his role of supplicant. She had to keep reminding herself that he had come running after her, asking for a partnership.

"Condition number one," Gabriel growled, "is that I

am not going to be a totally silent partner. I'm not going to simply turn the money over to you, Samantha, and let you handle everything. I'll want a full voice in every decision that needs making."

Her eyes narrowed. "You think I'll louse it all up and you'll wind up with half interest in a restaurant instead of several hundred thousand dollars in interest on your money?"

"I try to limit the risks," he drawled.

"Working with me is a risk?"

"I couldn't have put it better myself."

"But you're willing to take the risk of financing me because you can't bear to turn your back on all that nice, easy money and the chance of getting even with Buchanan, right?" she concluded in satisfaction.

He pulled himself away from the counter and reached for a couple of coffee cups as the machine finished its task. "Samantha, honey, I know you think you're in the driver's seat at the moment, but don't go getting too uppity on me, okay? I haven't written out the check yet."

She didn't care for the slow, even way he said that. "Here, give me one of those cups," she murmured gruffly. "I'll take it in to Eric."

He filled the cup and handed it to her silently. Samantha grabbed it and hurried out of the kitchen, grateful for the excuse to get away from him for a moment. The way he seemed to fill her kitchen made her feel strangely restless and a little jittery. Or perhaps the jitters were just a result of all the coffee she had drank today, she decided reassuringly.

"Here you go, Eric. But I really think that you should quit. Have a bite to eat and get some sleep. Surely that horrible man will give you a day or two of grace! He doesn't even know where you are, for heaven's sake!"

"Who knows what he'll do?" Eric reached for the coffee cup with gratitude. "I've never dealt with this crowd before. But believe me, I get the feeling they don't extend a lot of grace periods!"

"How on earth did you ever find such a person in the first place? Where does one go looking for a broker in industrial espionage?" Samantha demanded unhappily.

"I don't know where most people go looking," Eric told her wryly, "but I went looking in a computer. I tapped into some of those information sources you use like the newspaper indexes and a few sources you *don't* use."

"You tapped into . . . But, Eric, you were using the Thorndyke computer, and I know Thorndyke doesn't have a subscription to any of those information sources. Victor was too cheap to buy the services."

Eric regarded her pityingly. "Sam, for someone like me, a paid subscription isn't really necessary. I just used a telephone link to connect with the particular computer I wanted to search and then I went in and took what I wanted."

Samantha stared at her half brother in awe. "You just casually invaded a bunch of computer memory banks? Long distance? My God, Eric, you must be a genius. A real genius! I've heard of people who know how to get into other people's computers, but I've never actually met one! And to think my own brother can do it!"

180

Eric shrugged, taking his talent for granted. "Look where it got me. In trouble with a man who probably moonlights for the Mafia! Jesus! How could I have been so stupid?"

"You found this . . . this person in one of the computers you searched?"

"I found some cases of industrial espionage which had been kept on file in the computers of a couple of private firms who had, uh, used this guy's services. Once his name cropped up, I knew who to contact. For all the good it did me." Eric gulped coffee. "I'm glad your friend Sinclair will be staying the night."

Samantha shook her head in automatic reaction. "Who said he was staying the night? Eric, I keep telling you, he's a business acquaintance, nothing more!"

"Sure." But his blue eyes smiled with weary perception.

"Eric, I'm warning you, don't turn into a pesky younger brother at this stage in the game!"

He sobered. "I mean it, Sam. I'm glad he's here. I'll feel better about staying another night now that there's another man in the house. I was thinking about moving out to a motel."

"What on earth for?"

"So that you won't be involved if the wrong people come looking for me!" he snapped abruptly, setting down the coffee cup and going back to work on the computer. "But Sinclair looks as if he could handle trouble if it walked in the front door."

Samantha's mouth fell open as she stared at her half brother. "Gabriel Sinclair is not staying the night!"

"Yes he is," Gabriel said, coming through the door behind her. "That's condition number two, Samantha."

She whirled around. How much had he heard? Only her last sentence, apparently, because he wasn't demanding explanations of Eric's cryptic words. Aware of a trapped sensation, Samantha tried desperately to regain control over a situation that seemed to be rapidly slipping out of hand. And to think that for a moment or two when she'd seen him standing on her front porch she'd gained the impression she was in command again! Men! It was a constant battle to keep them from walking all over you. Vera was right. The male of the species had his uses, but a woman had to struggle constantly to keep him in his place.

"Gabriel, I would like to remind you that you are the one who wishes to do business with me. Don't forget that I still have other alternatives." She ignored his arcing brows as she reminded him of William Oakes. "If you start putting too many unbusinesslike conditions on our arrangement, you can damn well forget the whole thing!"

"Don't pay any attention to her, Gabe," Eric remarked, not glancing up from the computer screen. "She's just a little tired. She gets grouchy when she's tired."

"From what I've seen of the contents of her refrigerator, I get the feeling s-s-she hasn't been eating well, either. Come on, Samantha. Let's go into town and get some decent groceries for dinner. You and Eric both look as if you need a good meal."

The familiar stutter over the 'sh' sound disarmed Samantha for a crucial instant. Why on earth should she be vulnerable to the small imperfection in his speech? Because it gave her the comforting illusion that he had weaknesses?

"I have plenty of good meals stashed in the freezer," she informed him in a voice so cold it might have been stored there itself. "Frozen turkey pot pies, frozen TV dinners, and frozen pizza. I stocked up yesterday!"

"I said you need a decent meal, not a frozen pizza." He put out a hand and snagged her wrist. "Let's go."

He moved with placid, unalterable intent, dragging her out of the parlor and down the hall to the living room where he patiently located his windbreaker and her black leather jacket in a closet.

Samantha made one more halfhearted attempt to protest his high-handedness, but somehow she was simply too exhausted to fight him over such a small thing as what to have for dinner. In spite of herself she remembered the fabulous meal he had prepared for her that night in California.

"We can go shopping if you insist, Gabriel, but you might as well know that I can't cook nearly as well as you do! Believe me, you're better off eating a frozen pizza when you eat in my house." As soon as the words were out of her mouth, she realized just how much ground she had lost. If she let him stay for dinner, she was going to wind up letting him stay the night.

"I'll be safe enough if I do the cooking."

An hour and a half later the rich fragrance of a lamb stew began to waft through the kitchen. Samantha sat, feet propped on a chair, sherry in her hand, and watched sleepily as Gabriel added cream and eggs to the scone mixture he was preparing. It was an oddly pleasant sight. A comforting one. Perhaps Eric was right. It might be nice to have Gabriel in the house tonight. At least they'd eat well!

"I hope," she mumbled as she sipped at her sherry, "that you don't have any misconceptions about where you're sleeping tonight, Gabriel."

"I'm staying here." He kneaded the scone dough for a few seconds, his touch light. He didn't look up. It was easy to ruin scone dough with too much kneading. One had to pay attention.

Samantha realized she was taking second place to the scones and sighed inwardly. "I have an extra bedroom. I suppose you can use that."

"Your graciousness overwhelms me."

"You're a little overwhelming yourself. What made you change your mind and come to Seattle, Gabriel? Did you really start worrying about losing out on a good deal? Which was more important? The money you stand to make or getting even with Buchanan?" She didn't know why she was pressing for the answer. Perhaps for future reference. You never knew when you might be able to use this sort of information. Any clue into Gabriel Sinclair's motivations was potentially useful. It was plain she was going to need all the weapons she could get in the ongoing struggle to maintain the balance of power between them.

"What if my reasons are even simpler and more straightforward than that, Samantha?" he asked quietly as he shaped the individual scones and placed them on the baking tray. "What if I said I decided to come all this way and lay all this money on the line for the sake of another chance at getting you into bed?"

She chilled. "I wouldn't believe you. Men like you don't get where they are by doing dumb things like that."

"Don't they?" he asked vaguely.

"Gabriel, stop teasing me! I'm exhausted and I'm not in the mood for your sexual innuendoes. If you actually came all this way thinking I'd go to bed with you in exchange for your money, you can turn right around and head back to California. And you damn well know it!"

His mouth crooked upward in self-mockery. "Let's just say I've decided to go along with you and leave it at that for the time being, s-s-shall we?" He put the tray of scones in the oven and then picked up his own glass of sherry. As he sat down across from her, she saw the cool, speculative expression in his eyes. "I know what you're after, witch. You want to know exactly what makes me tick so that you can control me. But I'm not going to give you any help in that direction. It would be like putting a sword in your hand."

"If you think I'm such a vicious person, why are you even willing to do business with me?" she grated, stung by the accusation of manipulation. It was true enough, she supposed, but she was only trying to manipulate him out of self-defense. For he was surely trying to do the same to her. Had *already* done it on one unforgettable occasion! The memory of her night spent in his arms still burned in her head. Talk about being manipulated!

185

"I don't think you're a vicious person at all," he mocked gently. "I think you're bright, daring, and resourceful. You'll use whatever you think you can get away with using to keep me where you want me."

"And where's that?" she challenged, wondering absently if the sherry was going to her head on an empty stomach. Damn it, she had to find out exactly what was motivating him. There was a nagging suspicion that she didn't fully understand all the factors involved here.

"You want me under control." Gabriel lifted one shoulder in polite acceptance of that simple fact and swallowed another sip of sherry. "I don't blame you."

Suddenly Samantha's sense of honor bounded to the surface through the waves of exhaustion. "Very magnanimous of you. You don't blame me because you're trying to do the same thing in reverse. You're trying to control me."

"S-s-should make for an interesting partnership, don't you think?" Gabriel lifted his sherry glass in salute, and out of sheer bravado Samantha did the same. The crystal rims chimed as they came into contact, but it was difficult to hear the soft tinkling sound because at that moment a dazed, red-eyed Eric came trooping around the corner and into the kitchen.

"Something sure smells good in here. Dinner ready?"

Gabriel looked at him critically. "Just about. Sit down here with your sister and I'll serve. The two of you are a real pair, you know that? You look as if you've been partying for a week."

"I wish!" Eric muttered, stumbling into his seat and rubbing his eyes.

Samantha got to her feet to help set the table even though Gabriel tried to wave her back down into the chair.

"What have you two been working on in there?" Gabriel dished out the fragrant lamb stew and carried the plates to the table.

Samantha thought she would faint from the sheer bliss of the aroma of the stew as it was carried past her nose.

"Just something I've got to have done as soon as possible," Eric said offhandedly as he dug into the meal. "Scones! Geez. I haven't had scones in ages. You know, it would be great if you could teach Sam how to cook. Her mother didn't think it was a good idea for girls to learn."

Gabriel grinned, and Samantha realized how much she had missed that rare smile. "Why not?"

"She doesn't have anything against good cooking, mind you," Samantha hastened to assure him. "It's just that she was afraid a woman who learned too many traditional homemaking skills might find herself trapped in a traditional female role."

"So what else can't you do?" Gabriel inquired interestedly.

Samantha thought about it, remembering the unconventional days of her childhood. "Well, I can't knit or crochet or sew. I never learned to make my own Christmas decorations. And I'm a lousy housekeeper," she finished on a note of defensive triumph.

"She's also bossy as hell at times," Eric confided.

Gabriel glanced sideways at Eric. "What *can* she do?"

To Samantha's astonishment her half brother took the question seriously. "She's got nerve. And guts. The kind of guts it takes to face down the entire Thorndyke family. She considers the rest of us a nasty, condescending bunch. Which Thorndykes, by and large, are. Let's see, what else? She's got some weird ideas about loyalty."

"Weird?" Gabriel questioned, his eyes on Samantha, who was concentrating heavily on her stew.

"Yeah, she's even loyal to Thorndykes although now that Dad's gone she has no reason to be. Saved Vic's ass a year ago. Vic's my older brother. He's president of the family firm now. There was a threatened buy-out, and Samantha got wind of it through her computers. She warned Vic in time for him to salvage Thorndyke Industries. If I'd been her, I would have let it go under. Vic didn't even bother to thank her."

"Eric, that's enough," Samantha interrupted briskly. "Your family doesn't owe me a thing. I'm an embarrassment to them, and it's better for all concerned if I stay out of their way."

"She's also damn independent," Eric went on musingly. "Let's see. Oh, yes. I'd trust her with my life. That's about it. Other than that she's a real washout as a female. But I expect the right man could make something of her," he concluded optimistically.

"I'll keep that in mind," Gabriel murmured very politely.

"If the two of you have finished assassinating my character, would you mind passing me the butter and honey for the scones?" Samantha fixed them both with a cold eye and then went back to her meal. "If there's one thing I can't abide, it's men who gossip!"

Gabriel's delicious feast disappeared rapidly. The man could cook, Samantha allowed privately as she polished off the last tender chunk of lamb. God, she was sleepy. So much had happened in the past few days. How did Eric keep going? From the looks of him, he wouldn't. Not for much longer. Her brother was running on the ragged edge.

"I think you should at least take a nap for a few hours," she said quietly as she helped Gabriel clear the table. "I'm beat and you've been working twice as hard as I have."

"I can't stop, Sam. There's no time left." He got up from the table. "You go ahead and get some rest."

"You're both dead on your feet," Gabriel announced coolly, coming up behind Samantha. "S-s-surely whatever it is you're working on will keep until tomorrow morning?"

"I don't know if it will or not," Eric returned wearily.

"You're not going to be able to accomplish much in your present condition," Gabriel pointed out. "Get a few hours of sleep, Eric."

Samantha looked anxiously at her brother. "He's right, Eric. What's the point of working when you're this far gone? It's liable to come out all gibberish."

"Maybe you're right." Eric faced both of them, strain and tension and outright exhaustion plain in his face. "Maybe a couple of hours of rest would help. I'll use the couch in the computer room. Thanks for the meal, Gabe. It was terrific."

"You're welcome," Gabriel said softly, watching the younger man leave the room. He turned to Samantha. "For the last time, Samantha, are you going to tell me what the hell's going on here?"

"It doesn't concern you or our deal," she replied stubbornly. "Don't worry about it. I think I'll take your advice and go to bed. Come with me and I'll show you a room you can use." Without waiting for his consent, she led the way out of the kitchen and up the stairs to the bedrooms.

Gabriel followed obediently, not protesting when she showed him a room that was several doors down the hall from her own. "It's a little early for me yet," he said calmly as he saw her back to the door of her own bedroom. "I think I'll read for a while downstairs."

Samantha nodded. "Suit yourself. In the morning we can talk. Good night, Gabriel. Thanks for dinner." Very firmly but very gently she shut the door in his face.

Gabriel stood quietly on the other side, staring unseeingly at the antique woodwork as he pondered the situation, and then he went slowly back down the stairs and into the computer room. Eric was already sound asleep on the old Victorian fainting couch in the corner. He'd dimmed the lights before collapsing.

Thoughtfully Gabriel walked over to the desk on which the computer terminal sat and began shuffling idly through the piles of printouts lying near the printer. What had he stumbled into? What the devil was Samantha involved in now? He picked up a large stack of the most recent printouts, the ones Eric had been making just before dinner, and carried them out into the living room.

Sitting in front of a dying fire, a glass of Samantha's excellent brandy near at hand, Gabriel settled into a huge, old, overstuffed chair and began taking a serious look at what he had found.

Samantha Maitland was one surprise after another.

CHAPTER SIX

Loyalty. Nerve. "I'd trust her with my life," Eric had concluded, outlining his sister's redeeming characteristics.

He'd forgotten to mention one other aspect of Samantha's personality, Gabriel decided an hour and a half later as he tossed aside the last of the printouts in disgust. She was definitely a little soft in the brain.

Because unless he was totally misreading the situation, it looked very much as if Eric was engaged in faking a whole set of Thorndyke Industries financial data. And he'd called on Samantha to help him.

Gabriel gazed deeply into the embers of the fire, his mind pulling together all the facts and figures he'd just been through. What was Eric up to? Sabotaging the family firm? Stealing from it? Doctoring its computer files of financial data? Or was he preparing to steal from another firm's computer files?

What the hell was going on?

But that question, he freely admitted, didn't bother him nearly as much as the fact that Eric had involved

Samantha. He'd come scurrying up here to Seattle to drag Samantha into whatever scam he had going.

And because somewhere along the line in her crazy family history Samantha had decided she owed her half brother her loyalty, she had let herself get mixed up in God knew what for his sake.

Gabriel thought about that kind of loyalty. Eric had claimed he'd trust his sister with his life. The embers glowed on the hearth for a few more minutes as Gabriel followed the path of his own logic to its ultimate conclusion.

He wanted that kind of loyalty for himself.

With an unfathomable hunger, Gabriel realized abruptly that he longed to possess Samantha's loyalty. He wanted to be able to say he could trust her with his life, his fortune, his honor.

His large, competent hand curled into a fist as it rested on the tattered arm of the chair. In return for those invaluable gifts he was prepared to protect her. He would keep her safely out of the clutches of men like William Oakes or Eric Thorndyke. Her first loyalty would lie with Gabriel Sinclair. After that fact was established in her head, she would no longer be vulnerable to others.

The wave of possessiveness and masculine hunger rolled over him in a pounding fury, leaving behind a cold determination that was shocking in its intensity. He had known he wanted Samantha, had realized he wanted to guard her from the dangers her own impulsive nature would lead her into, but he hadn't admitted until now just how completely he wanted to claim her.

He wanted to be able to sit at the dinner table and casually announce with absolute conviction that Samantha owed her loyalty first and foremost to him, Gabriel Sinclair. Then he would tell mooching half brothers like Eric Thorndyke to get lost. Samantha was no longer vulnerable to men who would take advantage of her.

Loyalty. Nerve. Trust. He'd married once without taking any of those qualities into consideration. He'd married for other kinds of reasons entirely. Thoughts of Glenna stirred up a few ashes in his mind now, but no glowing embers. It was difficult to feel any warmth for a woman who'd demonstrated no bonds of courage or trust.

What Glenna had going for her had seemed enough at the time. She was a beauty. Gabriel remembered the sight of her undressing for bed, her long black hair falling down the length of her slender back as she brushed it in front of the mirror. Green eyes that reminded him of a cat had watched him in the mirror, reflecting Glenna's knowledge of what her naked image did to him.

Yes, they reflected her awareness of her own sensual beauty, but those eyes had never mirrored a passion of her own, merely a pleased satisfaction at the knowledge of her power. Gabriel allowed himself to luxuriate in the memory of the undisguised desire and need which had blazed in Samantha's eyes that night in California. His body grew warm just at the thought.

Glenna's charms were only skin deep. Gabriel had soon grown frustrated and then bored with the games she played in bed. After a while her beauty had no longer commanded his body's reaction. By the time the political and social disaster had engulfed his father, there had been little left of the marriage to Glenna. She had taken quick action to avoid being caught up in the widening ripples of the Sinclair family financial calamity and ensuing social humiliation. Weston Sinclair's political career had been destroyed. Glenna had felt no loyalty toward Gabriel who, by the mere fact that he was Weston Sinclair's son, had been involved in his father's scandal. She had left town the day the first headlines had hit the newspapers and had filed for divorce from the sanctuary of her parents' Boston home. Gabriel had been too busy trying to deal with disaster to bother fighting for a woman who owed her loyalty to no one but herself.

The factor which had always been missing in his relationships with women, he realized, was commitment. He supposed he couldn't really blame a woman for not wanting to commit herself completely to a man, especially a man such as himself. His mouth tightened. But that didn't lessen the fact that he wanted that kind of commitment from Samantha. He was proud enough, egotistical enough, uncompromising enough, to go after it.

She had only whetted his appetite with their night of lovemaking. Now he ached for a far more thorough commitment. He wanted her to give herself completely, no strings attached.

Which, when you thought about it, was one hell of an unlikely possibility, given the fact that Samantha Maitland had been raised to be an independent woman who didn't need a man. How was he supposed to go about asking this creature of nerve and dash and energy to yield herself to a man who offered a plodding sort of protection in return?

He got the distinct impression that Samantha wasn't even interested in being protected. She was far too accustomed to standing on her own two feet. She'd fight any man who tried to tell her she needed him.

With a decisive surge of resolute energy, Gabriel thrust aside the printouts and got to his feet. Out of habitual caution he checked the screen on the fireplace, closing it properly, and then he walked through the living room, turning out lights in order.

When he reached the staircase, he started up the steps with a firm, steady pace that reflected his own inner decision. He knew he had a battle on his hands taming Samantha on an intellectual level, but his body remembered all too well that he had already gained her physical surrender. He could at least give himself the satisfaction of having that much again. His pulse began to pound heavily as he contemplated Samantha's room at the top of the stairs.

In the darkness Samantha lay very still, listening to the sound of Gabriel's footsteps on the staircase. For an hour and a half now she had been shifting restlessly in bed, her tension too great to allow for sleep. She should have been exhausted after being up most of the previous night. She *was* exhausted.

But the thought of Gabriel Sinclair's presence in her home was more than enough to keep her awake. He wanted her. She had seen it in his eyes the moment she had opened the door, had felt her own reaction to the desire in him.

It was crazy, idiotic, to lie here wondering if he would try her door or go on down the hall to his own room. What was the matter with her? She had barely regained some small edge of control in their precariously balanced relationship. How incredibly foolish it was to even think about succumbing once again to the undeniable attraction which had flared between them.

Damn it, she thought, sitting up to pound the pillow into a more comfortable shape; everything was getting so complicated. What would Vera say if she saw the emotional chaos her daughter was in because of a man?

That thought hardened Samantha's resolve. She was a fully adult woman, in charge of her life and of her revenge. Furthermore, she had her hands full at the moment helping Eric out of his mess. She had no business lying anxiously awake like some primitive woman in a cave awaiting the arrival of the male animal who owned her.

That image was ludicrous enough and sufficiently mortifying to restore her tension-distorted perspective. Cave woman, indeed! Samantha smiled grimly to herself and flopped back down on the abused pillow.

At precisely that instant Gabriel's steady footsteps in the hall came to a halt, and Samantha's door opened.

Samantha lay blinking in the shaft of light which angled across her bed and silently cursed old houses with bedroom doors which no longer locked because the keys had been lost. She didn't dare move. The atavistic reaction which causes a hunted creature to freeze at the approach of the predator seemed to have a hold on her muscles.

Gabriel stood filling the doorway, his face in impenetrable shadow. His solid physical presence overwhelmed her senses, and Samantha remembered the way she had once let herself cling to him.

"Gabriel?" she finally managed faintly, gathering the courage to try and break the ancient spell with a prosaic question. "What do you want?"

He moved into the room and shut the door behind him, leaving them both in deep shadow. "Some answers," he replied, coming slowly, inevitably toward the bed. "But most of the questions can wait until morning."

She looked up at him, trying to see his expression. He was a dark angel standing there beside her bed, half threat, half promise. "If the questions can wait," she dared softly, her blood racing in her veins, "then why are you here now?"

"The questions can wait, but I can't," he said simply. Then he calmly sat down on the edge of the bed and began taking off his immaculately polished shoes.

The very mundane, very routine action finally jarred Samantha out of her near-trance. "Gabriel!" she hissed, levering herself up on one elbow and clutching the sheet to her throat.

"I told you. I can't wait." He tugged off one shoe and began unlacing the other.

"Damn it!" she snapped. "You can't just walk into my bedroom and start undressing as if we've been married forty years. I'll yell for Eric if you don't behave yourself. We're business partners, Gabriel Sinclair. Not lovers!"

"We were lovers before we finalized the business side of this arrangement," he drawled gently, setting the shoes very neatly to one side. He began unbuttoning his shirt. "As far as I'm concerned, nothing has changed with the first part of that arrangement." He hung the shirt carefully on the bedpost of the old four-poster bed, standing up to take off his slacks. "I want you, Samantha. And I've been remembering the way you wanted me. I can't get the thought of it out of my head."

"Gabriel, I mean it. I'll call Eric."

"You don't need Eric to protect you anymore, honey. You've got me. I'll take care of you." He stepped out of the slacks and folded them precisely across a nearby chair. "I know you don't think you need me as anything except a silent partner, but I can make your body need me." With one lean fingertip he flipped a tendril of hair from her shoulder. "I'm a patient man. I can wait for all of it."

Samantha's eyes widened as he stood before her, unselfconscious, magnificently naked. Why did it have to be this man? After three years of wary aloofness toward all males, why did all her defenses collapse at his feet? She *did* feel like the primordial cave woman of her imagination. She had to break the hold he had on her senses before it was too late.

"No, Gabriel, I won't let you do this to me!" She flung the sheet aside, scrambling toward the far edge of the bed in a flurry of tangled nightgown and disarrayed hair. She wasn't fleeing from a pleasant physical attraction. She was running from the chaotic depths of a passion which mystified her. Better to stay clear of it rather than risk being engulfed again as she had been that first time.

The bed behind her gave beneath Gabriel's weight. Just as she reached the unpromising safety of the opposite edge, his hand closed in a huge, gentle manacle around her wrist.

Again, as she had that night on the beach, Samantha had the impression she had been chained to granite. A sense of inevitability overloaded her normal thought channels, blocking out coherent protest or angry diatribe.

"Samantha, I need you. I'm going to make love to you tonight because on this level, at least, you belong to me. Don't fight me, honey. Please don't fight me!"

He yanked her quite gently down onto her back. She sprawled on the sheet beneath him, violently aware of the extent of his arousal. He was a man of such powerful, uncompromising passion, she thought dazedly. And he had the power to tap an answering level of passion in her. Samantha stopped struggling, not only because it was useless against his rocklike strength but because she had known tonight was going to be like this the moment she had opened the door to him this afternoon.

Carefully he pinned her wrists on either side of her head, lowering himself across her body until his chest crushed her small, soft breasts. She saw the dark glitter of intent in his eyes, and then his mouth was on hers. The groan of aroused hunger which emanated from deep in his throat caught at her senses.

The musk of his body filled her senses as Samantha surrendered her lips. It was a heady, tantalizing scent, every bit as primitive as the sexual need in him. Against her thigh she could feel the unyielding pressure of his hardening body. His tongue thrust forcefully into her mouth, establishing a rhythm that presaged the cadence of another kind of penetration.

"Oh, Gabriel, *Gabriel*!"

"Did you really think I'd go quietly to my own room tonight, witch?" he growled, trapping her writhing legs with his heavy thigh. He nibbled hungrily along the line of her throat, one hand moving down her body to the point where her hiked-up nightgown revealed the curve of her hip. His incredibly sensitive hand clenched into her flesh and then moved aggressively to the shadowy tangle of hair between her legs. "My God, woman! How can you pretend not to want me when you're already warm and wet and waiting?"

Samantha shivered uncontrollably as he stroked his fingers into her heat. She was burning for him. How could she deny it? Convulsively she used her free hands to clutch at the hard, bronzed shoulders above her, and her lower body arched against his hand.

As soon as he felt her response, he withdrew his probing fingers, leaving the damp, satin flower between her legs unsatisfied and aching with desire. She moaned and sank her teeth lightly into his shoulder. "Touch me again, Gabriel. Please touch me like that again."

"How do you want me to touch you, sweetheart?" he taunted coaxingly as he removed the tousled nightgown. He bent to catch hold of one budding nipple with his mouth, circling the dark aureole with the tip of his tongue. Samantha felt the fire flaring in the pit of her

201

stomach and gasped aloud. "Take my hand and show me how you want me to touch you," he repeated more urgently.

"Gabriel!" His name was a small cry of protest against the boldness he asked of her and a plea for him to end the torment.

"Show me," he invited once more, his voice as heavy with passion as the rest of him. He spread his hand across her stomach as his tongue continued to tantalize her nipples. "I only want to please you, sweetheart."

"You only want to *tease* me," she corrected a little savagely. "Gabriel, finish what you started. I ache so . . . !"

"I always finish what I start." He let the ball of his thumb travel through the tangled thatch of hair until it hovered just above the throbbing point of her desire. "Just show me what you want."

Samantha thought she would go crazy with wanting. Desperately she arched her hips again, exultant when the action briefly brought his thumb to exactly the right place. "Oh, yes, *yes!*"

But he withdrew his hand almost at once, seeming to take a blatant satisfaction in her pleading need. Through the haze of her mounting desire it dawned on Samantha exactly what was happening. Gabriel Sinclair was prepared to go on teasing her all night. He was going to make her pay for the attempt to deny her own attraction to him.

"You're punishing me!" she accused, wrapping her arms tightly around his neck and drawing his head close so that she could nip somewhat viciously at his ear. "You're not a very kind man."

He groaned as she savaged his ear, a husky sound thick with masculine arousal. When her nails raked his back, he sucked in his breath, lifting his head just far enough so that she could see the warning glitter in his heavy-lidded eyes. "Being kind wouldn't do me much good around you, witch. But then, kindness is not what I need from you either."

"What?" she hissed, her body's reactions slipping out of her control as she responded to the dark intent in his eyes.

"I need to hear you beg me to take you. I need to have you take my hand and guide it exactly where you want to be touched. I need to know that you know how badly you want me!" He punctuated each command with a light, stinging kiss on the soft undercurve of her breasts.

And he wants to know I won't be able to deny him again the way I tried to do this afternoon, Samantha thought wildly. But she was beyond worrying about the balance of power in this dangerous relationship. The future was the last thing she could think of now. There was only this burning need, this craving for the fulfillment he offered.

"Damn you, Gabriel. Someday I'm going to—"

"But not tonight," he told her evenly.

"No, not tonight. . . . Touch me, angel. Here and *here!*" She felt the heat in her face as she grabbed his hand with an awkward desperation and led him to where she needed the feel of him. In the process she was made forcibly aware of the damp, flowing warmth between her legs, and the flush in her face grew hotter. He had a way of forcing her to acknowledge her own earthy sexuality. It was both exciting and shocking. It was also a new experience. Her sensual encounters three years ago had all been conducted on a more sophisticated, more deliberately romantic plane. Drew Buchanan, bastard that he was, also made it a point to play the charming gentleman in bed. Samantha had never realized just how elemental the act of sex could be.

Now the knowledge consumed her, stripping away any pretense or hope she might have had for keeping the encounter with Gabriel Sinclair on a light, not-to-be-taken-too-seriously basis. She gave herself to him once again in an act that she knew later would have to be labeled as surrender. At the moment it simply didn't matter. The driving urge to satisfy and be satisfied overrode all caution. And there was no hope of disguising that urge.

"Ah, Samantha," Gabriel rasped against her flesh as he stroked and tantalized the softness of her. "I think I would kill to keep you in my arms like this!"

She heard the incredulity in his words and realized vaguely that he was as stunned by the level of their mutual passion as she was. Then she could think no more. He was sliding down her body, his warm tongue searching out the places his fingers had been thrilling.

"Oh! Oh, my God, *Gabriel!*"

Her thighs parted wantonly for him as he pushed them farther apart with his large hands. For excruciatingly exciting moments he drove her again and again to the brink of satisfaction, only to cease the delicious torment at the last possible instant.

At last when she thought she could bear no more, he came to her, his heavy weight gliding up along her body like an irresistible ocean wave. His manhood forged a path through the petals of her flowering softness, and the answering cry in Samantha's throat was silenced as Gabriel drank the sound of it from her lips.

She was already so close to the edge that the slow, driving rhythm Gabriel established sent Samantha over almost immediately. She arched almost violently in his arms, felt the sting of his nails on her buttocks, and then gave herself up completely to the mindless climax of passion.

Somewhere above her she heard her name muttered in a thick, rasping voice. Heard, too, the dark, exciting words of urgent desire, and then Gabriel was following her into the temporary, velvet oblivion. His release was total and physically overwhelming. Samantha felt crushed into the bedclothes as he collapsed completely along the length of her.

It was a long while before Gabriel's heavy weight was shifted. Even as he rolled onto his side, he kept his hold on Samantha, his hand resting with warm possession on her breast. When she opened her lashes slowly to meet his eyes, she found him watching her. There was an instant of stark silence, and then Samantha tried desperately to rally the scattered forces of self-defense. If he gloated, even for a moment, she would strangle him.

"Don't look at me like that," he begged, amusement lighting his eyes along with pervasive, leonine satisfaction.

"Like what?"

"As if you're trying to decide whether or not to go for my throat." He reached out to draw a lazy finger across the base of her own throat.

"You're very perceptive," she dared.

"Do you really want to tear me apart because of what just happened?" he challenged whimsically.

"Not because of what happened but because of what I expect you'll read into the whole thing!" she retorted, goaded. He knew, she thought anxiously. He knew and understood completely the extent of his power over her. So dangerous.

"Don't be afraid of me, Samantha." The amusement faded from his eyes as he smoothed back a tendril of her hair. "I'm on your side, remember? We're partners."

"Uh huh. Just don't get the idea that you're the senior partner merely because of . . . of . . ." She broke off, unwilling to put her own surrender into words.

"Because I've been on top when we make love?" he drawled, taking great pleasure in being able to meet her anger with a humorous sally. "You can get on top next time—I think I'd rather like that."

"Damn it, that's not what I meant and you know it!"

"Honey, any relationship between us had to include more than just the business angle. If you're honest with yourself, you'll admit that much. I wanted you from the start. And once I found out you felt the same about me, I could no more have ignored the information than fly."

"You're supposed to be good at flying, remember? All angels fly," she grumbled.

He grinned, and there in the depths of her huge four-poster bed the expression was unbelievably endearing and dangerous. "Then let me put it this way: I don't intend to ignore the information. Even if I could."

"You think you can use it, don't you? To control me."

"A good businessman uses whatever it takes to keep a handle on a volatile deal. You're one very volatile woman, Samantha Maitland."

Suddenly a thread of hope wove itself into her head. Her golden brown eyes slitted consideringly. "Are you afraid of me, Gabriel Sinclair? Is that why you're so anxious to prove your dominance in bed?"

"Did I prove it?" he retorted interestedly.

"Go to hell," she muttered.

"I can't. Not hell." He settled onto his back, drawing her close to the perspiration-damp length of his hard body.

"I seem to recall one angel who got kicked out of heaven," she mused sleepily. Lord, she was exhausted. Too tired to go on fighting Gabriel. She'd settle this with him in the morning, she promised herself. In the morning.

No, in the morning she had to help Eric. Poor Eric. Had he awakened yet and gone back to work at the computer? She really should go downstairs and give him a hand. But she was so sleepy. . . .

"Gabriel?"

"Mmmmm?" He sounded just as sleepy. Satiated and content.

"You said you had questions?"

"I said they could wait. Go to sleep, honey. We'll sort it all out tomorrow."

"I'm not going to answer any questions that don't relate to the Buchanan deal," she vowed softly. She knew instinctively he wanted to know about Eric's situation and what was going on downstairs in the back parlor. But her loyalty in this instance was clear-cut. Eric had it all. He was her half brother.

"You'll answer them," Gabriel told her very gently. "And then I'll get you out of whatever idiotic scheme Eric's dragged you into."

"You don't understand!"

"I understand more than you think. Go to sleep, Samantha." He cradled her closer so that her face was pressed against his chest, effectively silencing her.

Samantha gave up the small battle and succumbed to sleep.

Gabriel dozed for a time, his body relaxing completely in the aftermath of passion, but as the immediate physical lethargy faded, it was not replaced by sleep. Instead, forty minutes after Samantha had fallen asleep beside him, he found himself still awake. How much control did he have over the woman who lay curled in his arms? How much control did any man have over a woman? Would he really have enough to keep Samantha from being used by Eric? Or enough to stay in charge of the scheme she had developed for dealing with Buchanan?

She was so damn independent. So determined to follow her wild and reckless plans wherever they might lead. And she had no patience with the steady, cautious, rather dull way he went about things.

But she responded to him in bed. In bed she was his. Totally.

Clinging to that small reassurance, Gabriel allowed his mind to drift, seeking the solace of sleep. He would be busy enough in the morning when he took on brother and sister.

The splintering, thudding crash downstairs half an hour later brought Samantha bolt upright in bed, her heart pounding, her body shivering with instinctive, startled fear. Blindly she put out her hand, seeking the comfort of Gabriel's solid strength even as she tried to orient herself in the darkness.

"Gabriel! What on earth . . . ?"

But he was already sliding out of bed, heading for the door. "Stay where you are!" he ordered, his voice a bare whisper as he cracked the door an inch.

Eric's startled shout echoed up the staircase just as Gabriel got the door open. There was another sickening thud and then the sound of savage male voices.

"You're late, punk. Real late. You think Mr. Kirby plays games with suckers like you?"

Another crashing blow, and this time Samantha had pulled herself together enough to realize in horror what was going on.

"Eric!" She gasped, leaping from the bed and running naked to the door even as Gabriel shut it firmly and swung around to catch her. "Let me go! They're after Eric!"

"S-s-shut-up!" Gabriel snarled, clamping his hand

across her open mouth. He held her in a grip of iron as she struggled desperately to free herself. She had to get to Eric. But fighting Gabriel's implacable grip was fruitless, and when she realized he wasn't about to free her, she collapsed limply against him. Almost at once the palm across her mouth was lifted. His eyes blazed down at her, narrowed and infinitely dangerous.

"Who's down there? Who's after Eric?"

"I can't explain it all now! Take my word for it, they're going to hurt him. We've got to help him!"

Even as her eyes pleaded with him for understanding and aid for her brother, one of the invader's voices sounded from the living room. "I'll get the woman. Don't want her doing anything dumb like calling the cops." The next instant heavy, pounding footsteps sounded on the stairs.

Gabriel didn't hesitate. "Come on." He dragged Samantha toward the window, scooping up her nightgown and his neatly folded slacks as he went by the chair. Samantha had the impression that if the clothing hadn't been convenient, he wouldn't even have bothered to stop for a second and find some. As it was, she found herself being hauled, still naked, out onto the balcony, which stretched the full length of the house. All of the bedrooms opened onto it.

"It's freezing!" she gasped, stunned by the impact of the windblown rain as Gabriel shut the window behind them.

"I've been saying that since I got here," he gritted. "This way."

It was ludicrous, Samantha thought hysterically, running naked along a balcony at one o'clock in the morning in the driving rain of a winter night. Gabriel's hand was clamped around her wrist, however, and the sight of his rain-slick nakedness wasn't ludicrous at all. He looked like some savagely male animal intent on getting his woman to safety.

But it wasn't her safety she was concerned about. "Gabriel, wait! We've got to help Eric."

"Quiet, Samantha. Do as you're told. The way I see it, this whole mess is your fault, anyway."

"My fault!"

He came to a jarring halt then in front of the last window on the balcony. He shoved at the stubborn frame of the old glass, applying a steady, irresistible force that quickly broke the old lock inside.

Samantha stared in amazement. "You're awfully strong," she whispered.

"You've got awfully weak locks. Now get inside." He pushed her through the window, not coming in behind her.

"Gabriel, what are you going to do?" A new fear assailed her as she realized he was staying out on the balcony. "That man will realize I'm not in the bedroom. In a few seconds he'll be out there on that balcony looking for us!"

He saw the panic in her eyes and heard the frightened lilt to her voice and reacted. Very carefully he reached through the window and gave her a violent shake, his fingertips biting into her shoulders.

"Stay in this room until I come to get you. Don't make a sound. Not a damn sound, do you hear me?

And if you ever think of leaving the room to go help Eric, I will beat the living daylights out of you when this is all over!" Samantha nodded, momentarily speechless as he shoved her nightgown at her along with his slacks.

Then he grabbed for his pants again as a thought occurred to him. Quickly he yanked the belt free of its loops. Without pausing to give Samantha a chance to recover from the blunt, brutal command in his voice, Gabriel whirled and started back along the balcony, belt in hand. The slacks stayed with Samantha.

"S-s-shi . . ." He gave up and gritted "Damn it to hell" from between clenched teeth as he realized what that look in Samantha's eyes had contained when he'd turned from her. It had been outright fear he'd seen for a few seconds in those huge tortoiseshell eyes. Fear for him? he wondered.

There was no time to contemplate that question. The man on the staircase would be reaching the top of the stairs now, trying the first closed door. He'd push it open and discover the empty, rumpled bed. It wouldn't take any genius to figure out that the only route out of the bedroom was the window.

"Jesus! Talk about freezing your ass off!" Gabriel grunted pithily to himself as the chilling rain whipped his bare body. Thoughts of sunny California flashed through his brain even as he slammed to a silent stop beside the window of Samantha's bedroom and plastered himself flat against the wall of the house.

What the hell was he doing here turning his ass into a popsicle in the middle of the night because of some crazy woman and her screwy half brother? He was a businessman, for God's sake! Not Nick Carter or James Bond.

He pulled the end of the belt through the buckle, creating a large loop of leather. Crazy broad. When this was all over, he was really going to lay down the law. He was willing to tolerate a few surprises out of her, but this was carrying things to extremes.

The window of Samantha's bedroom crashed open and the nose of an automatic pushed through. Well, hell, Gabriel thought fleetingly. It was now or never. He whipped the loop of his belt around the blue-black steel shaft of the gun and yanked for all he was worth.

Gabriel was astonished at how easily the gunman seemed to follow his weapon through the window under the fierce pull of the leather cinch. The turkey didn't even have enough sense to drop the automatic until it was too late. The weapon went flying as Gabriel dropped the belt and grabbed for the other man's arm.

With both hands clamped around the attacker's forearm, Gabriel hauled him through the window and out onto the balcony. The man opened his mouth to yell, but it was too late. Gabriel already had a fist descending toward the assailant's jaw. He held back nothing, wanting only to silence the guy and keep him silent. With his full strength behind the blow and goaded by the realization of just how much danger Samantha was in, Gabriel's fist lashed out at the target.

The gunman crumpled to the balcony, unconscious.

For an instant Gabriel simply stood staring down at his victim. He'd never hit a man before.

Just one surprise after another, he thought savagely as he turned on his heel and raced back along the balcony to the room where he had left Samantha.

His feeling of savagery increased as he spotted Samantha leaning out of the window, anxiously watching him return. "I told you to stay inside!" He leaped over the sill, pushing her back in ahead of him.

Samantha, who had just learned the meaning of having one's heart in one's throat, threw herself into his arms. The nightgown she was now wearing swirled around her ankles and tangled with his hair-roughened legs. "Gabriel! Are you all right? My God, you scared me half to death!"

He stared at her for a split second and then quickly put her from him and reached for his slacks. "Other than the fact that I'm going to have frostbite in a few very inconvenient places, I'm fine. Damn it, Samantha, you've really gone too far this time, do you know that?" He closed the fastening of the slacks.

She assayed a shaky smile. "I'll help you warm up the frostbitten parts," she volunteered, realizing that this was a side of her angel she hadn't seen before. It fit with the rest of him. Implacable, stubborn when crossed, reassuringly strong. She'd seen the way he'd dropped the gunman with a single blow. And the catch on the window hadn't been all that weak, either. Solid, strong, dependable. Her angel Gabriel. Tonight he was the answer to a prayer.

"Turning on the cute, sexy act isn't going to save

your ass, lady. When this is all over I'm going to—" He broke off abruptly, his head coming up with a snap as the second man's voice howled up the staircase.

"Come on, Tony. We haven't got time for fun and games. You can screw the broad later. Get her down here!"

Samantha shivered in sudden horror at her intended fate. "What are they going to do to Eric?" she breathed.

"I have a feeling you're in a better position to answer that question than I am. Come on, we haven't got much time. That other joker is going to come looking for his friend. I don't suppose you have a gun around the house?"

"Of course not!"

"Too bad," he sighed morosely. "I lost my chance at that other guy's gun when it went flying off the balcony. Something tells me I won't get away with that balcony scene twice."

"Where are we going?" Samantha whispered anxiously as he clamped a hand around her wrist once more.

"The kitchen."

"The kitchen!"

"Kitchens are loaded with useful things," he growled. "The trick is getting down there without being seen."

Samantha hesitated, not knowing why the goal was the kitchen but willing to trust him now. "These old Victorian homes have all sorts of interconnecting rooms. This room connects with what used to be the nursery, and from there we can get to the old sewing room. There's a set of stairs from there down to the back porch."

"And that opens off the kitchen," he concluded with a short, frowning nod. "Okay, let's get going."

"There's something else which might be useful on the back porch," Samantha whispered, thinking. "The fuse box."

"Be careful, Samantha, you're starting to s-s-show evidence of a small bit of brain. Fuse box, hmmm?"

"There's no need to be insulting! I've tolerated quite a lot from you already this evening." Her fingers went to the still-stinging side of her cheek in annoyed memory. "Do you always go around battering your business partners?"

"No. I made an exception in your case because you need a little business sense knocked into you. Now s-s-shut up and try not to make a sound."

He led her through the nursery and into the old sewing room which Samantha had converted to a plant-filled atrium. Her mother never had thought sewing a good hobby for a modern woman, but she'd had no objection to gardening. Samantha had inherited Vera's green thumb.

The back stairs creaked, Samantha remembered at the last minute and put out a hand to halt Gabriel. "They squeak," she mouthed in the shadowy light.

He nodded and started down them very carefully. She followed just as cautiously, marveling at how such a solidly built man could move so well. She wasn't going to get an apology for that shaking, she realized. It had really been a very controlled blow, not one delivered out of rage, although he had been angry at the time. She hadn't had a chance to explain that she wasn't going to succumb to hysteria. Samantha supposed he'd had a right to assume the worst. When this was all over, she'd explain to him very carefully that Vera Maitland hadn't raised a daughter prone to hysteria.

The blow Gabriel had delivered to the intruder was an altogether different story. Samantha chewed her lip, reflecting on the unrestrained force which had gone into it. Did Gabriel even realize his own strength? He was not the sort of man who'd gone around testing it or himself in a physical sense. She doubted that he'd ever been active in sports or that he took much interest in spas and gyms. But as that venerable torturer Miss Carson had noted. Gabriel didn't look like he needed any spa treatments.

Perhaps he swam a lot in the ocean in front of his home?

Good Lord! Where was her mind wandering to? Eric was in terrible danger, and she and Gabriel were hardly in the clear.

"Goddamn it! Tony! Get her down here. We ain't got all night!" The other intruder's voice called harshly, an edge on it that made Samantha realize the man was beginning to recognize that something was wrong. Then there was sudden, absolute silence. What had they done to Eric to keep him so quiet during all this?

On the dark enclosed back porch Samantha fumbled momentarily and then indicated the fuse box. Unhesitatingly Gabriel went to work on it, slamming the master switch. An instant later the entire house was plunged into darkness.

"Tony! What the hell—?" Almost immediately the

intruder realized the stupidity of giving away his position in the dark by yelling for his hapless companion. Once more, silence descended.

"Now for the kitchen," Gabriel muttered half under his breath. He dragged Samantha, who by now could barely feel her numbed feet, into the warmth of the shadowy kitchen. Her eyes were adjusted enough to the darkness to make it possible to discern familiar shapes.

In fact, she could just barely make out Gabriel's arm reaching for the heavy old cast-iron frying pan which hung on the wall. Her eyes widened, but she resisted the urge to demand an explanation. Then he gripped her arm, giving her a slight, urgent shake, and brought his face very close to hers.

"Stay here." The words were not quite a sound, but she understood.

Samantha nodded mutely. She damn well wasn't going to stay behind in the kitchen while Gabriel and Eric were in such danger. But there was no point alarming Gabriel further with that news. He clearly had enough on his mind at the moment.

Then he was gone, his dense, dark form gliding down the hall on incredibly quiet bare feet. The silence in the house was eerie, almost unnatural. Even the small noises of the night outside seemed to have ceased. At least, thought Samantha, Gabriel had the advantage of knowing the layout of the downstairs portion of the house a great deal more intimately than the other man did.

Where was the other? Had he followed his friend Tony upstairs? Another dismaying thought flitted through

Samantha's mind. She and Gabriel had only heard two different voices, but what if there was a third stranger in the house? Still no sound from Eric. What on earth was Gabriel going to do with that skillet?

As stealthily as possible, Samantha pulled open the cutlery drawer and removed a small paring knife. She had no real idea of what she could accomplish with it, but there was some reassurance in having it in her hand. Then, hardly daring to breathe, she padded silently down the hall in Gabriel's wake.

She hadn't gone far before she realized that she had no notion of where the others were. The intruder might be hiding behind the closet door ahead. Or he might have dropped in back of the old couch in the living room, waiting for some shape to materialize out of the darkness. Where was Gabriel?

On instinct Samantha paused in the hallway, violently aware of the adrenaline pounding through her. The primitive fight-or-flight reaction of the human being under stress, she consoled herself. It wasn't true that anyone else could actually hear her heart beating or be aware of the fine trembling in her hands.

She peered into the living room. In the deep shadows she could make out the familiar bulk of the couch, the overstuffed chair by the hearth, and even the leering shape of the tall palm near the window. There were no human shapes. Samantha stayed where she was, sunk in the shadows of the hall.

The back parlor which housed the computers was down the hall which branched off to the right. Was Eric still there? Tied up, perhaps, or unconscious? Maybe she should make a dash for the parlor. It was the one room in the house which still had a locking door.

Even as the thought occurred to her, Samantha realized the impossibility of carrying through with the idea. It would leave Gabriel alone out here in the darkness to face the intruder. There was no question of abandoning him, regardless of whatever condition Eric was in at the moment.

There was a click and then a horrendous roar as a gunshot shattered the stillness. Samantha started, the fear-induced adrenaline pumping more madly than ever. Then she froze. The shot had come from the top of the stairs. She had seen the brief flash out of the corner of her eye.

"Don't move!" the intruder shouted, more than an edge in his voice now. The man was coming unglued, Samantha decided. Perhaps that would work to their advantage. "Don't anybody move or I'll kill you!"

When he got no reply, he waited a few more heart-stopping seconds. Was he trying to decide whether or not he had an audience? Perhaps he was convincing himself that whoever had decked good old Tony had now fled?

Then he started down the stairs. Samantha couldn't yet see him, but she heard the familiar creak in the third step from the top. Where was Gabriel hiding? My God, the man was already halfway down the stairs. What was she going to do when he made it to the bottom?

The assailant seemed to regain his confidence with every step. Or perhaps he had simply succumbed to

the urge to get out of what had become a highly
untenable situation for him. Whatever the reason, he
was moving very quickly by the time he reached the
last step.

So quickly that he didn't even notice the broad, male
shape which surged out of the pit of darkness beneath
the staircase.

Frozen in the hall, Samantha saw what happened
next as a rapid play of dark forms against an even darker
background. Gabriel hurled the heavy iron pan at the
man on the stairs, who screamed in panic and pain as
the skillet struck him.

Then Gabriel was lunging toward his staggering victim,
who had dropped the gun under the impact of the
frying pan. A split second later both men crashed to the
floor at the foot of the stairs in a writhing, savage tangle
of flailing arms and legs. The tinkle of breaking glass
told Samantha that the small vase on a nearby end table
hadn't survived the jarring thud of the men as they hit
the floor.

She watched in horror as the two rolled over and
over across the old, worn Oriental carpet, each struggling for dominance. Gabriel was recognizable in the
darkness only because of the lighter shade of his bare
upper torso. The contours of his broad shoulders materialized on top as he momentarily gained the advantage.
Then, with a vicious grunt of pain and rage, the other
man managed to reverse the position.

Another vase was sent hurtling to the floor along with
a dainty tri-legged table and a stack of books which had
been resting on it. Samantha felt the violence in the air

as if it had a life of its own. It was a palpable aura surrounding the two battling men. Savage, primitive, and overlayed with a life-or-death desperation.

The ferocity of the battle struck deeply into Samantha's awareness. She had never seen men literally at each other's throats. At that moment it was difficult to remember that the civilized world existed, the primitive instincts were so very close to the surface.

Suddenly, above the grim sounds of the battle on the floor, another, much fainter noise pulled at Samantha's attention. The third step from the top had creaked again.

Helplessly Samantha stayed in the shadows as the other gunman began to groggily descend the staircase. He had apparently recovered somewhat from the blow Gabriel had dealt him earlier.

"If you think," Samantha muttered to herself, "that I'm going to let this fight become two against one, you're out of your head!" Her fingers tightened on the small paring knife. Damned if she would let the other man go to his friend's aid.

The man called Tony reached the last step, one hand on his jaw as he squinted into the darkness, trying to determine exactly what was happening. At that moment Gabriel's bare back became visible as he heaved himself once more on top of his opponent. Apparently Tony, too, realized how to tell one fighter from the other in the darkness, because he started forward at once.

Samantha waited no longer. Without giving herself a chance to think, she leaped out of the hall and onto

Tony's back, clinging there like a limpet as she brought the paring knife down against his shoulder.

The small blade just managed to penetrate the jacket and shirt Tony was wearing. Less than an inch of steel actually made it into the shoulder muscle, but the surprise assault from the rear, together with the unexpected, stabbing pain, produced a roar of anger and panic from Samantha's victim.

He swung around, dislodging her so that she dropped to her feet. Tony's momentum carried his hand through a violent arc which brought his fist crashing against the side of Samantha's face, the same cheek Gabriel had slapped earlier. The wild blow brought a cry from Samantha as she staggered backward under the impact.

"Samantha!"

As if her shout had given him the impetus he needed to end the battle on the floor, Gabriel freed one fist and brought it awkwardly but with tremendous power against his opponent's head. As the man went limp beneath him, he leaped to his feet, charging blindly toward the man who was attacking Samantha.

But Tony had had enough. He backed away toward the open front door, dancing quickly away from Gabriel.

"Tony, wait! Help me, you bastard!" The man on the floor struggled to his knees and then shakily to his feet. "How many of them are there?"

"I don't know!" Tony had already reached the door. It was obvious he was of two minds about assisting his partner, but when the other man lurched toward him, he grabbed his arm and yanked him out the door.

Gabriel stood groggily, gasping for breath and feeling

pain seeping through every pore. He reached for Samantha, trying to see her face in the darkness.

"Are you all right? Samantha! Are you okay?"

"Yes! Yes, Gabriel, I'm fine. Oh, my God, what about you? That man was hurting you so!"

He stared down at her as her palms came up to cup his ravaged face. Even in the shadowy light he could see the terrified concern in her widened eyes. Her hands felt marvelously light and gentle on him, and for a long, bewildering moment he wanted only to stand there and let her go on touching him like this.

"Eric." He got the name of her brother out huskily. How could she have forgotten Eric? How could she be standing here trying to soothe him when her precious half brother was in God-knew-what condition in the back parlor?

"Yes, yes, I'll get to him. But what about you, Gabriel? Are you all right? You should lie down. There's the possibility of shock, isn't there? Are you bleeding? Oh, damn! I can't see a thing!" she wailed helplessly.

He caught her hands in his own and gently tugged them away from his face. "I'm okay, honey. Go see about Eric. I'll get the lights."

She hesitated a moment longer, and then she whirled, heading down the hall toward the back parlor.

Gabriel stood for a second watching her flying night-gown trail out behind her like a gossamer ghost, and then he pulled himself together and started toward the porch.

Even as he relocated the fuse box and got the lights

functioning again, he was still telling himself not to read too much into Samantha's actions.

Still, anyway you sliced it, the facts came out the same. In the crunch, with both her brother and himself needing her attention, Samantha's first concern had been for him, Gabriel reflected. She had stayed to deal with his hurts first before racing off to check on Eric.

The cut on his lip grew even more painful as Gabriel found himself smiling with savage satisfaction.

CHAPTER SEVEN

The reason for Eric's silence throughout the siege became evident as soon as Samantha raced into the parlor. He lay bound and gagged on the floor, his alarmed eyes asking frantic questions as she knelt by his side and began untying him. The lights came back on just as she got the gag off.

"Christ, Sam! Are you all right? What happened out there? I've been lying in here feeling like a stupid, helpless fool for getting you into all this! Where's Gabe?"

"Right here." Gabriel's laconic answer brought Samantha's head around sharply. He was leaning against the doorjamb, massaging the bruised and battered side of his face. "And I couldn't agree with you more, Thorndyke. You are a stupid fool for getting yourself and Samantha into this mess."

"It's not his fault!" Samantha protested automatically, undoing the last of Eric's bonds. Instantly she regretted the defensive words. Gabriel's hazel gaze swung to her, pinning her coldly.

"If by that you mean not all of this is his fault, that you're as much to blame as your brother, I might be inclined to agree with you."

"Gabriel, you don't understand!" she cried, getting to her feet as Eric shakily stood up beside her.

"I understand enough to know that both of you are playing out of your league." His eyes ran down the length of her body. "Go put some clothes on, woman. I don't feel like hashing this out while you're running around half-naked! Come on, Eric. I think we both need a shot of some of Samantha's brandy. I could probably use the rest of the bottle, now that I think of it."

"Gabriel, let me help you clean up first," Samantha said quickly, her heart wrenching at the sight of the blood on his mouth and the swollen redness under his eye.

"I said go get dressed!" he barked.

Her eyes narrowed as she realized just how thin his temper was at this point. But she prudently said nothing, moving to slip past him and head for the stairs.

"What the hell . . . ?" He grabbed her arm as she moved past, yanking her to a quick, urgent halt. "Your cheek!"

Her hand came up to her abused face as she remembered Tony's blow, and her first impulse was to answer Gabriel with some snide remark. A fitting reply for his foul temper.

But he looked so incredibly stricken as his eyes moved over her swollen cheek she relented, tortoiseshell eyes softening. "Don't be silly, Gabriel. It probably looks a lot worse than it feels. That second man, the one you decked on the balcony, hit me.

"Besides." Samantha lifted her chin with a trace of arrogance as she faced her now-frowning angel. "Weren't you threatening to damage another portion of my anatomy earlier, Gabriel?" she managed lightly. The relief which crossed his face was mixed with a decided degree of sardonic warning.

But all he said was, "Go get dressed, Samantha. The three of us have a lot to talk about." She was halfway down the hall when he called out softly behind her. "You're right. I remember the conversation now. But if and when I take to beating you, I won't make a habit of giving you black eyes. Just a black and blue ass."

Samantha didn't glance back over her shoulder, but as she went around the corner she deliberately added an extra flounce to her stride, aware that Gabriel's gaze was focused on her retreating derriere. The nightgown didn't provide much concealment.

As soon as she was safely in her room at the top of the stairs, she regretted the sassiness. This was hardly the occasion for it. Her bruised face hurt, Gabriel looked in much worse shape, and Eric was already feeling horribly guilty for the disaster he had brought down upon her house. Gabriel, she suspected, was going to go out of his way to make Eric feel even worse.

And the basic problem remained. True, thanks to Gabriel, the two toughs had been sent packing into the night, but what was to prevent their return? Eric had to get that phony financial data finished and turned in to the mysterious contact the intruder had called Kirby. It was their only hope.

But first came the explanations to Gabriel. There was, Samantha realized grimly, no way around them now. She'd seen the implacable intent in him when he'd told her the three of them were going to have a talk. Ah, well. In a way it was going to be something of a relief to talk to him about the whole mess.

Fifteen minutes later, bundled in her very untantalizing yellow terry cloth bathrobe and seated beside Eric on the overstuffed couch, Samantha changed her mind. It was not going to be a relief at all to talk to Gabriel Sinclair about the problem. It was very unpleasant, indeed.

"You're a pair of fools." Gabriel sat across from them on the old chair near the hearth. The pile of computer printouts which represented much of Eric's work was stacked beside him on the table. Gabriel took another sip of his brandy and leaned his head back against the cushion, lashes lowering briefly over weary eyes. "A pair of fools."

In spite of her own immediate reaction to being labeled a fool, Samantha's heart turned over at the sight of his battered face. Gabriel had taken a lot of punishment. No man had ever come close to doing half as much on her behalf before.

"Gabe, you don't know the whole story," Eric said dully. He, too, was taking large swallows of brandy and looked more exhausted than ever.

Without opening his eyes, Gabriel replied, "I can see from these printouts that you're up to something with a

229

lot of cost data that applies to Thorndyke-type equipment. You're faking up an entire spread-sheet."

Eric hesitated and then asked bluntly, "How can you tell it's faked?"

There was silence, and then Gabriel opened his eyes and stared at the younger man. "The same way Kirby will be able to tell. The numbers are too far off to be anywhere near plausible."

Eric grimaced. "Oh."

Gabriel's glance swung to Samantha. She shrugged. "I don't know plausible-sounding figures for pumps. That's not my field of expertise."

"If you're going to get into industrial espionage in a big way, you'd better be a bit more thorough in your research, don't you think?" Gabriel asked with a savage cool that unnerved her. "Your casual, offhand ways aren't going to assure you a very lucrative career in that field, honey. People like Jackson Kirby play for keeps. And they tend to put a premium on accuracy."

Samantha chewed anxiously on her lower lip, aware of just how angry Gabriel really was.

"Don't take it out on Sam," Eric urged bleakly. "She's not involved in this. If you knew her at all, you'd know this mess is hardly her style."

"I know her well enough to know that, while s-she might not have gotten into something like this on her own, s-she s-s-sure as hell could be hauled into it by a conniving half brother who convinced her s-she had to do it for his sake!"

The heavy stammer was ample evidence of his rising temper, Samantha thought, but that didn't keep her from taking fierce exception to the implication that she was easily manipulated. "For heaven's sake, I can think for myself! I was trying to help Eric get out of a mess, not into a career in industrial espionage! If you want to hear the whole story, why don't you stop telling us how dumb we are and let us tell you what really happened!"

"Excellent idea. Talk. Eric first."

Under that penetrating gaze Eric sighed and began his story from the beginning. Samantha felt a wave of sympathy for her brother as he bluntly told Gabriel the entire truth. Eric was humiliated and chagrined, and Gabriel didn't make it any easier for him. But to give her half brother credit, he didn't try to gloss over any of the facts. He told the tale in a straightforward manner, and when he had finished, Gabriel's first question astounded Samantha.

"Why did you change your mind?"

"About selling Thorndyke secrets?" Eric shrugged. "Ask Samantha. She understands."

When Gabriel's probing eyes moved to her tense, still face, Samantha, too, lifted a shoulder in a resigned shrug. "It would have been like betraying Dad. As soon as Eric realized that, he couldn't go through with it. No matter how nasty Vic Junior was to him."

"Dad built that company from scratch," Eric explained softly. "I'm his son. As soon as I'd gotten over my rage at Vic's high-handed treatment, I realized I couldn't go through with the deal with Kirby."

"But by then it was too late," Gabriel concluded flatly.

Samantha and Eric sat silent. The reality of that

231

statement was eloquent enough. But Gabriel's next words brought Samantha's head up in shock.

"They'll be back, you know," he said almost conversationally. But the hard, unrelenting lines of his face were not casual at all.

"Those two bastards who broke in here tonight?" Eric clarified uneasily. "But if I can give Kirby something that looks like what he wants . . ."

Gabriel shook his head wearily. "You can't give him something 'close' to what he wants. It's got to be the real thing. Buying and selling this stuff is how he makes his living. If he starts selling unreliable information, he'll be out of business just as fast as Samantha would if she started giving her clients false data."

Samantha winced. "I hadn't realized how similar my profession was to Mr. Kirby's!"

Gabriel took another sip of the brandy. "Information, legal or illegal, is the name of the business game. It's why even little one-man business operations are buying computers. It's why conglomerates employ armies of people who do nothing but correlate financial and statistical data. Based on information of one kind or another, people like Drew Buchanan gamble millions of dollars in development projects. And it's because of certain information you acquired that you're going to try and take advantage of his move."

Samantha frowned, shifting uneasily under Eric's questioning look. "It's business, Eric. I'll explain later. I told you Gabriel and I were business associates, remember?"

Eric arched one brow. "Given the fact that he just

saved both of us from God knows what at the hands of Tony and friend, I'd say he's something more than a business associate."

Before Samantha could reply to the obvious, Gabriel was interrupting coolly. "We got lucky tonight. I trust both of you realize that? We're not likely to get that lucky again. Kirby's people only expected to find you and Samantha here this evening. Next time they'll be prepared."

"I wish you'd stop talking about a next time!" Samantha stirred restlessly, aware of a gathering sensation of helplessness.

Gabriel's temper snapped unexpectedly. "You think you can make 'next time' go away by pretending it won't happen? Hasn't it sunk in yet that Jackson Kirby plays hardball? He'll make an example out of Eric if your brother doesn't produce what he promised to produce! God knows what he'll do to you just because you happen to be in the vicinity!"

"How do you know so much about Jackson Kirby?" she flung back, frightened.

"Word of his sort gets around. You don't think Eric conjured him up out of thin air, do you? There are enough rumors and gossip about the man to lead people in your brother's situation to him."

"Well, what are we supposed to do now? Let Eric sell out? Is that the only way to call Kirby off?" she snapped furiously. Desperation was fueling her temper. My God, she thought. What if Gabriel hadn't been here tonight? What will happen the next time?

"That's one way," Gabriel agreed evenly.

Eric looked stricken. "I can't!"

"You should have thought of that before you contacted him!"

Samantha jumped in quickly. "What do you mean that's 'one' way? Is there another? Can we buy him off?"

Gabriel's mouth crooked briefly in acknowledgment of the idea. "That's not a bad thought, really. Unfortunately, I don't think it would work in this case. He knows he's got Eric under his thumb now. Even if you bought Kirby off this time, he's the kind who might very well decide to look Eric up again in the future. And next time he'd have a little blackmail to use against him in order to gain his cooperation. He would have proof, you see, that Eric had paid him off the first time."

Samantha stared at him, her mouth going dry. "You seem to have a fairly good idea of how people like Kirby work."

He met her eyes, the hazel gaze cold and unreflective. "I do."

She sat very still, clutching the lapels of her yellow robe, and knew she wasn't going to ask just how Gabriel came to know so much about Jackson Kirby and his ilk. There were times, Samantha thought in a flash of realization, when Gabriel Sinclair could be a little frightening. Every time she thought she had this man under control and well in hand, he did something disturbing and unsettling.

A week ago she would have said that Gabriel Sinclair was the last man on earth capable of truly surprising her. How was it possible that such a predictable, organized, methodical person as Gabriel kept taking her unawares?

"All right, Gabe," Eric interposed softly. "It's obvious you've got some idea of how to handle this mess. What do you suggest we do?"

"I can think of only one practical, foolproof approach," Gabriel told him slowly, as if the idea in his head was not a pleasant one, even if it was workable. "I don't have the power to call Jackson Kirby off. But I know someone who does."

Samantha's eyes went very wide. With sudden intuition she knew exactly who he meant. "Emil Fortune?" she breathed.

"Who's Fortune?" Eric demanded.

The other two ignored him. Gabriel made a small, flat gesture with his left hand, leaning his head back again on the cushion as he stared thoughtfully at the ceiling. Samantha wished violently that she could read his mind. What was he thinking? Was he afraid of Fortune? Or afraid the friendship between them wasn't strong enough to ask this kind of favor? What was wrong? She knew an impulse to comfort Gabriel and didn't have the vaguest notion why she should feel that way. What was wrong in Gabriel's mind about enlisting his friend's assistance? It seemed like an eminently reasonable idea to her.

"Damn it, who's Fortune?" Eric asked again.

"Someone who will know how to get Kirby off your back. He's a friend of mine," Gabriel concluded quietly.

"No kidding!" Eric looked intrigued. "You must know some interesting people!"

"A man doesn't always have a choice in his friendships." Gabriel set down the empty brandy glass and looked at Samantha. "Why don't the two of you go back to bed?"

It wasn't a suggestion; it was an order, and Samantha's instinct was to protest it. "Gabriel, I'm not a child to be sent to my room while the grown-ups conduct business. You're going to call Fortune tonight, aren't you?"

"Go to bed, Samantha," he repeated softly.

"Come on, Sam. I'm zonked and you must be, too." Eric took charge, getting to his feet and reaching down to prod his sister to hers. "Let's do as the man says, okay? He's got a right to give a few orders after what he went through for us tonight."

Samantha started to dig in her heels, but something about the unyielding expression in Gabriel's eyes convinced her to allow Eric to lead her toward the staircase. But she knew in her bones she shouldn't be leaving her dark angel alone like this. She should be staying down here while he made the phone call. Samantha wasn't certain why she should feel that way, but she did. And there was another aspect to the situation. Damned if she would let Gabriel relegate her to the role of useless female. He needed her, whether he was willing to admit it or not.

Beside her Eric suddenly stumbled over a small object on the carpet. "What the hell . . . ?" He bent down and scooped up the tiny paring knife. "It's got blood on it! Where did this come from?"

"From the same place that frying pan came from," Samantha muttered, indicating the cast-iron skillet which lay on the floor beside the stairs. "The kitchen. You'd be astonished, Eric, at how many useful things there are in a plain old kitchen!"

Behind her Gabriel growled, "You used that little knife on that man? Good God, woman! What did you think you were doing?" She heard the sharp disapproval in his words and tossed a deliberately goading glance back over her shoulder.

"Actually, I don't think I did too badly for someone who's not very good in the kitchen!"

Gabriel felt the unwilling gleam of amusement and admiration which threatened momentarily to light his eyes. "Samantha, honey, you may have more domestic talents than people give you credit for!" he drawled.

He watched her ascend the stairs, noting the proud tilt of her tousled head and the way the old bathrobe pulled pleasantly taut around her well-shaped rear. Part amazon, part businesswoman, part soft, clinging female. He realized he was beginning to feel precariously in possession of the soft female because of her response to him in bed. He also felt tentatively in control of the businesswoman because of the financial arrangement between them. But what chance did he have of controlling the amazon? That fierce loyalty and feminine strength which was so much a part of her was not going to be a simple matter to claim. He consoled himself once more with the memory of how she had run to him first instead of her brother after the battle that evening.

Then, with a sigh, he reached into the back pocket of his slacks and removed the wallet which had somehow stayed in place during the excitement. Somewhere, buried behind his credit cards was a little slip of paper with Emil Fortune's phone number on it. It wasn't a number he had called frequently enough to have memorized.

And he'd never called it with the intention of asking the man on the other end to repay a favor. Was this how his father had gotten in so deep? Was this how it all started? Friendships which led to favors which led to disaster?

Even as he dialed, Gabriel acknowledged the simple truth. Only for Samantha would he do this. The woman was well and truly in his blood now. Which left wide open the question of who was really controlling whom, he thought grimly.

There was silence from the top of the stairs as the phone started to ring on the other end of the line. Gabriel leaned back in the oversized chair, his legs stretched out in front of him, and tried to think how he would handle the coming conversation. Somehow, all he could really think about was his father. . . .

It was a while before Emil Fortune came on the line. Patiently Gabriel explained to the sleepy voice which originally answered that it was important Emil be told who was calling. After several minutes of resistance, it must have become apparent to the other person that Gabriel was not going to give up and that the cool, polite request to speak to Emil Fortune would be repeated endlessly until it was satisfied.

"Gabe, my friend. What's wrong?" Fortune's soft query was straight to the point.

"I need a favor, Emil. A big one," Gabriel said with a calm that surprised him.

There was a pause on the other end. And then, "You mean you need a favor repaid, Gabe. I am the one who owes you, remember? You have only to ask. Even if I did not feel in your debt, you are my friend, and the same condition would apply. You have only to ask."

Gabriel massaged the bridge of his nose in a slow, tired gesture. "Emil, this is rather complicated."

'I had the feeling it might be or there would be no need to call at this hour of the night, would there?" Emil Fortune said gently.

Gabriel drew a long breath. "There is a man. Jackson Kirby. Have you heard of him?"

"No, but don't let that stop you. I can find out whatever I need to know about him within the hour."

"Your sources are pretty good, aren't they?" Gabriel realized he was shaking his head in silent, wry admiration. What had he been saying earlier about the importance of information to just about everyone in business? Any kind of business?

"They have to be good or I would not be as rich as I am, would I, Gabe?"

"Good point. Okay." Gabriel sighed. "Here it is in a nutshell. Kirby is a broker of sorts. Deals in industrial espionage. Buying and selling. He's very big but keeps a very low profile. He's also very powerful. Sometimes resorts to rather crude business methods."

"How crude?"

"Crude enough to send armed gunmen into a private home in the middle of the night and threaten a young man who was foolish enough to think he could deal with Kirby."

"Ah. A young man. A friend of yours?"

"He's Samantha Maitland's half brother," Gabriel admitted stonily. There was no way to avoid bringing her name into this. "You met her on one occasion, I believe."

"At my sister's spa. She was having a small problem checking out, as I recall." There was a trace of humor in Emil's voice as he recalled the incident. "I liked her, Gabe. So she did, indeed, manage to shake you out of your rut, hmm?"

"She's a bundle of surprises," Gabriel grated feelingly.

"Some pleasant, I trust."

"The mess involving her brother is not one of the pleasant ones. He got furious with his older brother who runs the family firm and decided to sell a rather crucial spread-sheet to a competitor. Got cold feet within days after he realized exactly what he was doing. But by then Kirby had been contacted."

"Ah, the reckless, hot-blooded ways of youth." Emil sounded suspiciously reminiscent. "Young men are so volatile, aren't they?"

"I wouldn't know. I seemed to have missed that stage in my development," Gabriel rapped.

"Don't worry. It sounds as if you are getting another crack at it. Due to the charming Samantha."

"Emil . . ."

"Please, Gabe. There is absolutely nothing to be concerned about. This Mr. Jackson Kirby will not be bothering your friends again. Believe me."

"No further questions?" Gabriel's knuckles whitened around the phone.

"You want him called off, correct? I will see to it that he gets the message."

"Emil. Listen to me," Gabriel said very carefully. "I don't want anyone to suddenly turn up missing. Do you understand?"

"Relax, Gabe. Your Mr. Kirby strikes me as a businessman. As such he will, I am sure, prove eminently reasonable. There will be no embarrassing disappearances. Things are not done that way in the international community of financiers."

"Uh huh. What about the international community of the Fortune family?" Gabriel retorted.

"Gabe, you must not form too harsh an opinion of my family simply because there are a few skeletons in the closet. All families have their black sheep, do they not?"

"Some families," Gabriel noted dryly, "are made up almost exclusively of black sheep and skeletons."

Emil must have detected the grim humor in the words because he laughed deeply on the other end of the line. "It makes for interesting reunions. Enough of that. Tell me. What happened when Mr. Kirby's small army invaded Samantha's home? That's where you're calling from now, isn't it?"

"Yes." Gabriel didn't bother to ask his friend how he had arrived at that conclusion. Emil Fortune was a highly logical man. "I got a little cut up. Samantha is going to have a black eye in the morning, and her brother is all right."

"But you are all right?" There was a new, no-nonsense thread of steel overlying the soft, gentle voice now.

"Yeah. Between us, Samantha and I managed to send them packing. The little witch used a paring knife on one," he added, sardonically aware of the pride in his own voice. "She scares the hell out of me sometimes, Emil."

"I told you she was good for you," Emil responded in tones of great satisfaction. "And you? What was your approach to the subject of violence?"

"You know me. I'm good in the kitchen," Gabriel grumbled. "I used a frying pan. The dashing man of action!"

"I would like to have been there." Emil chuckled.

"You have a morbid sense of humor."

"All international financiers have a morbid sense of humor. Goes with the territory. Good night, Gabe. Go and have Samantha bathe your manly wounds and tell her not to worry about Jackson Kirby. Neither she nor her brother will hear any more of him."

"Emil," Gabriel began urgently and then ran out of words. "Thanks." It sounded lame.

"Why must I keep reminding you that I'm not doing you any favors? Only repaying one. Good night, friend." Emil Fortune hung up the phone with a gentle, final-sounding click.

For a long moment Gabriel sat with the dead receiver in his hand, thinking once again of his father. Then he slowly replaced the instrument.

He saw the bit of yellow bathrobe out of the corner of his eye and turned his head completely to find Samantha standing at the foot of the stairs, her hand resting tensely on the banister. She was watching him with deep intensity, her eyes soft and luminous behind the lenses of her glasses. How long had she been standing there?

In that moment there was no trace of the amazon or the businesswoman or the soft, hot, clinging female he had held in his arms a few hours ago. This was the woman who had cradled his bruised and battered face between tender hands after the battle with the gunmen. Another side of Samantha, Gabriel thought in fleeting wonder. And one he wanted to have come forward and gather him close. He needed her.

His body still ached from the beating it had taken, and his mind was unsettled from the business he had just conducted with Emil Fortune. This wide-eyed, intensely feminine creature swathed in an old bathrobe was the cause of all his aberrant behavior. Did she realize that? Did she know just how much he wanted to be cradled and soothed and fussed over? Did she have any idea of how badly a man needed a woman's comfort after the ravages of violence? Didn't she see that he had a right to her comfort?

Comfort and cradling and soothing solace were among the few things that couldn't be taken from a woman by force. They had to be freely given. But damn, how he needed her now.

Samantha loosened her grip on the banister and started across the room in response to the silent hunger she read in Gabriel's eyes. It was not a conscious decision to go to him. It was not a decision at all. She went forward because there was no alternative.

"My poor battered Gabriel," she whispered, touching the side of his face with delicate fingers. "What have you done? I knew I should never have left you alone to make that call." She sank to the carpet beside the overstuffed chair, kneeling so that she could continue to stroke the line of his cheek. The brooding masculine eyes never left her face. He didn't move as she reached out to touch him, but Samantha had the deeply intuitive feeling that it was because he was holding himself in some sort of rigid grip.

Every instinct in her warned that Gabriel was suffering, and not just from the physical beating he had taken earlier. In that moment Samantha wanted only to comfort and cherish. "Gabriel, why was that call so hard for you? What have you done by calling in Emil Fortune? Have you compromised yourself now in some way?" she asked in sudden anguish as that possibility dawned on her.

He reached up and caught one of her hands roughly in his, squeezing it tightly. "No. Emil is, in his own way, a man of honor. *And he is my friend.*"

She looked up at him, bewildered. "Then why are you so upset?"

"Am I?"

"Gabriel, please don't play games with me. Tell me what's wrong!" she pleaded.

He shut his eyes briefly, and when the mahogany lashes flickered open, she still could not read the expression there. "Nothing's wrong. Emil says to tell you there is nothing to worry about. Kirby won't bother Eric again."

"But will Emil bother you?"

His mouth kicked upward for a few seconds. "He isn't a Godfather type, honey. Not in the sense you mean. In any event he owed me a favor. As far as he's concerned, he's merely repaying a debt, not putting me in debt."

"What could he possibly owe you? Oh!" She fit the evidence together quickly, bypassing a few logical routes in order to come up with the perceptive answer to her own question. "His sister's spa? He's grateful to you for helping her?"

"Something like that. Emil is closer to his sister than he is to anyone else in the world. When she determined to set herself up in business without any aid from the Fortune family, he was very upset. But Donna wanted a clean start with no strings attached which might embarrass her later. She came to me with a strictly legitimate proposition. I had no idea of who she was or how she was connected. I loaned her the money and the expertise she needed to get started. When Emil found out what I had done and that I hadn't taken advantage of Donna somehow in the process, he decided I was a man he could trust." Gabriel shrugged. "Emil doesn't have many friends he can trust. During the past couple of years he has come to value our acquaintance."

"And the favor he feels he owes you? That's based on his gratitude for your having helped his sister?"

"I know it's not strictly logical. My deal with Donna

was merely another business proposition to me at the time. But Emil felt he owed me something for taking care of his sister during a time when she wouldn't accept any help from the Fortunes. And he likes me. I like him. We're friends. I don't know how else to explain it."

"Then if you're not alarmed at having asked Emil for this favor for Eric . . ."

"For you," he ground out with sudden fierceness. "I'm doing this for you, Samantha. Not Eric."

She swallowed. "I understand. You make a very useful partner," she tried to say lightly. "I have this sinking feeling that any of the other financial backers on my list would have abandoned me as soon as those two jokers walked in the door tonight!"

"But none of those other potential backers would have found himself in your bed when the incident occurred, would he?" Gabriel shot back with calculated certainty. His eyes glittered for a moment with possessiveness and a definite warning.

Samantha found herself swallowing again, and this time her mouth felt very dry. Damn it to hell! The man risks his neck for me, and now he figures he has a right to turn possessive. More than possessive. He's looking at me as if he thinks he owns me. "You sound very sure of that."

"Are you telling me I s-shouldn't be so s-s-sure of it?"

He was so tense, she realized. The stammer was harsher than usual. He looked weary and in pain, and yet Gabriel looked as if he was prepared to fight this particular battle all night if need be. Samantha knew she couldn't bring herself to lecture him on rights and equality and the fact that their relationship outside of business was supposed to have nothing to do with their partnership. Not tonight. Tonight her instincts urged he to offer comfort, not a Vera-Maitland-style lecture.

Besides, Samantha acknowledged wryly. When all was said and done, she owed this man one hell of a lot. How had a relationship which started out as a simple business partnership gotten so damnably complicated?

"Samantha?"

He wanted some recognition of the claim he obviously felt he had on her. It was, Samantha told herself, a small thing to give him tonight after all he had done. "You know very well there wouldn't have been any other professional venture capitalists in my bed tonight," she said with a lightness she was far from feeling. "Most venture capitalists aren't nearly as venturesome as you are!"

"And you don't make a habit of combining business and the bedroom," he finished for her. "I'm the exception." He stroked the sensitive inside of her wrist with the ball of his thumb in an absent, sensuous gesture. "So why was it so difficult to call Emil Fortune?"

"Persistent little thing, aren't you?" He groaned, resting his head against the wing of the chair and continuing to massage her wrist. "The truth is, I kept thinking of my father. This is how it must have been for him. I never really understood, Samantha. I did my duty. I stood by him. But I never really understood."

"Understood what, Gabriel?" Samantha ached for him, responding now to the pain in his voice.

247

Gabriel took a long breath. "My father is Weston Sinclair. Does that ring a bell?"

She frowned, trying to think. "Should it?" But something nibbled at her memory.

"Only if you're a devotee of old political scandals. Dad was a congressman on his way to being a senator. Everything fell apart for him about ten years ago."

"Wait a second. I seem to recall my mother discussing a scandal about a congressman who got himself involved with . . . with, oh, Gabriel." She groaned, remembering. "With the mob?" You couldn't grow up with Vera Maitland and not have a high degree of political awareness drummed into you. Samantha no longer followed the political scene with Vera's avid fervor, but in those days she had still been spending a lot of time in her mother's home, and there such discussions were as routine as the morning milk delivery.

"Dad had some very dangerous friendships," Gabriel said simply. "They eventually ruined his political career. The resulting scandal hit everything he had built, including his business. I was working for him at the time. I saw the whole house of cards collapse. Creditors were so thick on the ground you couldn't move without running into one. Dad had been ignoring the business in favor of running his political career, and financially things were pretty weak. All of a sudden, when the scandal erupted, he found himself facing bankruptcy. Every warning I had given him about the business became a dire reality. It all caved in on him. On top of that, all his so-called friends, the social circle that politicians always move in, disappeared. It nearly sent my mother into a nervous breakdown."

"And you?" she whispered.

"My wife left me because she couldn't bear to be associated with the Sinclair family," Gabriel told her dryly. "She came from good Boston stock. From people who didn't get involved with underworld figures."

"But it wasn't you who was involved, was it? It was your father? Why did she leave you?"

"Samantha, marriages involve whole families, not just the individuals. Especially marriages which are made for social or political reasons. There was no way she could remain with me and stay unmarked by what was happening to my family."

"If she'd loved you she would have stayed!" Samantha muttered rather violently.

He looked at her. "I guess she didn't really love me, hmmm? Oh, Samantha, you're not that naïve. Mushy, nebulous concepts like romantic love don't hold people together during times of real stress."

She stared at him. "Then what does hold them together?"

"Hard-edged ideas like loyalty," he said evenly. "Loyalty, honor, commitment."

"Those ideas only have strength if the one promising them can be completely trusted," Samantha said slowly.

He stared at her with a flat, uncompromising stare. Samantha felt herself tremble slightly under the impact of that look. "Wise witch," Gabriel murmured softly. "You're absolutely right."

"Did you . . . did you trust your ex-wife? Could you

have asked those things of her?" Why was she asking him such incredibly personal questions? But Samantha felt a driving need to know the answers.

"Glenna could not have given me the kind of commitment it would have taken to keep our marriage intact. I knew, once I'd had a chance to really think about it, that I couldn't have asked those things of her. It wasn't in her to give them."

He was still pinning her with that glittering, hawklike stare. It was almost unnatural in its intensity, a little feverish. "Gabriel," she got out huskily. "Are you feeling all right?"

"I'm not in shock, if that's what you mean."

"But you hurt, don't you?" Feeling very womanly, almost maternal, Samantha touched his bruised face.

"I hurt."

"And it's all because of me." She shook her head, overwhelmed with a feeling of guilt. "If it hadn't been for me, you would never have had to go through what you did tonight. You'd be safe and sound in your immaculate house by the sea. Oh, Gabriel, I'm so very sorry!"

"Don't expect me to play the gentleman and tell you it's nothing. I ache too much to say it was nothing," he rasped softly.

"And phoning Emil brought back too many painful memories of your father for you to be able to say it's nothing," she added sadly.

"Yes."

He made no attempt to mitigate her guilt. Now that Eric was safe, all she could think about was how unfair it was to have involved Gabriel in the mess. But God!

What would she have done without him? She owed him. There was no way around that knowledge. The debt was mammoth in size, and she knew by the way he watched her that he wanted to be repaid.

"Gabriel, how can I repay you for what you did tonight?" The question was a tremulous whisper of sound in the quiet room.

His fist tangled abruptly in the seal-brown length of her hair, holding her head so that she could not look away from him even if she tried. Samantha felt the atmosphere charged with the same primitive, barbaric element she experienced when Gabriel made love to her, and she knew a frisson of fear. He was going to bind her to him further, somehow. She didn't know how or why, but she sensed the inevitable outcome even before he spoke.

"Your brother says he can trust you," Gabriel observed in an astonishingly neutral tone. "With his life."

Helplessly she lifted one shoulder. "He's my brother."

"I'm not your brother."

"Hardly," she managed huskily.

"I want to be able to trust you, too." His grip on her hair tightened as he searched her taut face. "With my life. With everything. I want to know you'll be completely loyal to me, Samantha Maitland."

She stared at him uncomprehendingly.

"You asked how I wanted to be repaid," he gritted, the neutral tone vanishing. "This is what I want. Tell me that from this night forward I can trust you. Tell me that you owe as much loyalty to me as you do to that damn fool brother of yours!"

The breath was tight in her chest. "Would you believe me if I promised those things?"

"I'd believe you. You're dangerous in some ways, reckless, a little foolish at times, but I think that if you promise me loyalty, you'll give it."

Her bewilderment grew. Was Gabriel afraid she'd sleep with someone else while he was her lover? Was he afraid she would try to cheat him on the Buchanan deal? Was he nervous of the possibility that he might lose control of her during the term of the partnership and that she would do something stupid and ruin everything? What was he after?

It didn't much matter what he was after, Samantha thought as the silence stretched out between them. She owed him, and he had told her how he wanted to be repaid. She really had no choice. "Gabriel," she said gently, "you can trust me. I won't cheat you."

"Either in bed or in business," he clarified grimly.

"No." She felt the grip in her hair relax, realized some of the tension was seeping out of him. "You're hurt, Gabriel. Come upstairs and let me take care of you. You need to be in bed, and I have some ointment I can put on those cuts and bruises."

Resolutely she got to her feet and reached down to tug at his arm. For a second he seemed disinclined to move, and she realized she would never get him out of the chair unless he cooperated. The man weighed a ton!

"Are you going to fuss over me?" he asked whimsically. "Cosset me and salve my manly wounds?"

"I think you may have taken one too many blows to the head," she retorted dryly. "I'm not the domestic type, remember? Come on, Gabriel. Upstairs." She heaved again, and this time he came up out of the chair with a groan.

"Jesus, honey, I'm not used to this sort of thing!" He gingerly touched his bruised side. "I hope you don't expect me to just be the muscle part of this partnership."

"Why not? You concentrate on that, and I'll be the brains of the outfit."

"We're lost before we even begin," he complained, leaning heavily on her as she slipped an arm around his waist and started him up the stairs.

"Have a little faith, Gabriel. Angels are supposed to be blessed with lots of faith. Live up to your namesake!" She staggered a bit under the weight of his arm across her shoulders.

"Believe me, honey, I'm operating on pure faith already." The words were heartfelt. "It's s-s-surely not common sense that's gotten me into this situation."

"Are you going to spend the entire duration of our partnership making snide remarks?" She edged him through the door of her room and watched in sympathy as he sprawled gratefully on the tousled bed.

"They are not snide remarks." His eyes closed as he laid his head carefully on the pillow. "They are pithy little commentaries on the vagaries of the human condition. Especially my condition. Come and soothe my fevered brow, Samantha. I hurt."

Samantha hurried to the bathroom to collect what little she had in the way of first aid remedies.

*　　*　　*

The next morning Samantha was up long before either Gabriel or Eric stirred. Dressed in a pair of narrow wool slacks and a hugely overscaled dolman-sleeved shirt done in red velour, she went downstairs to investigate the damage which had been done to her front door. Behind her she left Gabriel sleeping soundly, a condition he had fallen into rather quickly under her first aid ministrations.

There had certainly been no further sexual demands from her battered angel, she thought in affectionate amusement as she studied the broken, splintered lock on the front door. Gabriel had wanted and needed more practical help last night after the fight. He had fallen asleep while she was still applying ointment to the bruise on his ribs. He was going to be black and blue in a few places this morning.

But nothing, she decided grimly, would match the shiner under her right eye. She grimaced at herself in the hall mirror and then straightened her facial expression at once when it proved painful. Her only consolation was that she had dealt out as good as she had got.

Eric was the first downstairs, sniffing hungrily as he strode into the kitchen. "Bacon and eggs. Smells great. Who says you can't cook?"

"You said it, for one." She prodded the yellow mass in the pan on the stove. Scrambled eggs were tricky, she had learned. They tended to be either too slimy or too hard. Still, they were simpler than poached or fried eggs, and over the years she had gotten fairly good at catching them before they went from just right to rubbery.

"Geez, you're sure a sight." Eric studied her right cheek with a critical eye. "It looked bruised last night, but it looks a lot worse this morning!"

"Bruises always look worse a day or two later. How do you want your eggs? Hard or sort of hard?"

"Sort of hard." He sat down at the kitchen table and poured himself coffee. "You and Gabe made some team last night."

"Some team. If it had been up to Gabriel, I would have stayed locked up in the guest room. He thought I was going to go hysterical on him. How many strips of bacon do you want?"

"Three. You're not the hysterical type."

"I know that and you know that, but I guess Gabriel didn't. He was under a little pressure at the time."

"I'll bet. He saved both our asses last night, Sam. We owe him a lot." Eric sipped his coffee reflectively.

"I've already started making payments on the debt," Samantha said half under her breath. Loyalty. Trust. What else would Gabriel ask of her?

"What?"

"Never mind. Have some more bacon. It's going to burn."

"Are you really doing business with the man?" Eric asked conversationally, digging into his sort-of-hard eggs. He paused after the first bite to go to the refrigerator and get a bottle of catsup, which he poured liberally over his plate.

"Yes. He's backing me financially in a deal I have going in Phoenix."

"Sam, why did he happen to bring up Buchanan's

name last night? And don't tell me it was sheer coincidence. Does your business deal with Gabe have something to do with Buchanan?"

"In a way," she responded shortly, not wanting to discuss it. Eric knew of her short-lived engagement to Drew Buchanan, but he didn't know of the taste for revenge she had been nurturing for three years. No one did.

"Does Gabe know about you and Buchanan?"

"No. And I'd appreciate it if you would kindly keep your mouth shut about it!"

"Why?"

"Because I don't want him thinking there's anything personal in this deal. He might decide not to back me if he thought that I had some personal reason for tackling Buchanan!" she said in exasperation. "I mean it, Eric. I don't want you dragging that three-year-old mess into the conversation. Understand?"

"I understand." He looked up at her. "Is there?"

"Is there what?"

"Anything personal in this deal you're setting up?"

"No! Damn it, it's strictly business. I worked for Buchanan, remember? I know how he thinks and how he operates. I have a plan that will enable me to take advantage of a certain situation in which he's involved. That's all. Furthermore, if anyone's got anything personal at stake in going up against Buchanan, it's Gabriel. Drew's company aced him out of a major deal a few years ago. Gabriel's quite happy to have a little business revenge."

"You know what I think, Sam?"

"I'm sure you're going to tell me."

"I think you're playing with fire. Better be nice to Gabriel. He's the only one I know who might be able to keep you from getting burned. Any more of those sort-of-hard eggs?"

"They have all gone quite hard," she retorted nastily.

It was Gabriel's voice which came next. "Sounds like s-s-she's in a great mood this morning," he remarked calmly as he walked into the kitchen.

Samantha looked up in consternation, but a quick glance at his face assured her he had overheard nothing about Buchanan. She relaxed at once. "Good morning, Gabriel. Want some scrambled eggs?"

"Why not? Since I've met you, I've started living dangerously. Dish 'em up." He sat down across from Eric and looked prepared for the worst.

"Start with the coffee," Eric advised. "It helps pave the way."

"Thank you for the advice. Samantha, your face looks like hell."

"You and Eric both have such a way with words at this hour of the morning," she muttered. "You don't look so terrific yourself."

"I'm the one who came out of this with the fewest bruises," Eric said very seriously. "I owe you, Gabe."

"Your sister's already agreed to pay the tab," Gabriel told him laconically.

Neither he nor Samantha was prepared for the angry flush which welled up in Eric's face. "You mean by sleeping with you?" he asked harshly.

Samantha nearly choked on the bite of bacon she had been chewing. "Eric!"

"No," Gabriel told the younger man very softly. "S-she was already sleeping with me before last night's little punch-up, remember?"

"Gabriel! Eric! Stop it right this minute! I will not have my private life discussed over the breakfast table like this!" Samantha stood angrily on the other side of the kitchen, her hands on her hips, her cheeks burning.

The men ignored her, watching each other like circling wolves. Samantha vaguely understood that something was being settled this morning between the two of them. Something which would determine how Gabriel and Eric dealt with each other in the future.

She recognized Eric's instinctive rejection of the idea that his sister might be sleeping with Gabriel in order to pay off some sort of debt. She also saw Gabriel's implacable decision to have his relationship with Samantha be fully accepted for what it was. He was claiming a lover's rights and making his position clear to the one member of Samantha's family who might feel an obligation to protect her.

"What you and Samantha have between you," Eric began slowly, "is your business as long as you're not planning on forcing her to sleep with you because of what you did for me."

"Samantha and I are quite capable of working out our own relationship. You're not involved, Eric. What I did last night was for her."

"You don't give an inch, do you?" Eric said almost

admiringly. "It's take me as I am or get the hell out of Dodge, right?"

"Right."

Eric let out his breath on a long sigh. Then he smiled crookedly. "I don't know why I got worried there for a minute. You made it pretty clear last night that you'll take care of her. Just chalk it up to a brother's natural protective instincts."

Gabriel nodded once, shortly. "All right. I'll accept that."

"I guess," Eric mused consideringly, "that lovers tend to be a little protective in their own right. Which is probably why you aren't sure you like me. You blame me for the mess Sam got into last night."

"I'll admit that was my initial reaction," Gabriel allowed sardonically.

"Well, I can't say I blame you," Eric grunted. "It was my fault."

Gabriel relented. "I have it on the best authority that young men tend to be a little wild at times and land themselves in trouble."

Eric grinned as the tension between the two men broke. "Don't you remember what you were like ten years ago, Gabe?"

"I seem to have been somewhat retarded in my development. I'm making up now for lost time." Gabriel sighed. He glanced across the room at a stony-faced Samantha. "Are my scrambled eggs hard enough, honey?"

"Like rocks!" she hissed.

"I can't wait."

CHAPTER EIGHT

"What the hell do you mean, the restaurant's been sold? You told me everything was under control, Ingram. I'm not paying you for screw-ups like this! If we've got trouble on this Phoenix deal because you didn't keep on top of the situation, your ass is going to be on the firing line."

The thing about Drew Buchanan, Jeff Ingram decided with a strange sense of detached admiration, was that he could make chopped liver out of you without ever raising his voice. Ingram drew a long, steadying breath. He had been dreading this scene since early this morning when the agent in Phoenix had relayed the news that the parcel of land with the restaurant on it had suddenly gone off the market. It had been sold, and no one yet knew who the new buyer was. Ingram had been so sure that the restaurant wasn't going to be a problem. So sure that the old man who owned it wanted to sell and would do so at a more than reasonable price when the Buchanan Group made its offer through its agents.

But Jeff Ingram hadn't made the offer in time. Someone else had scooped the old, dilapidated Mexican restaurant and along with it a chunk of land that was crucial to the group's forthcoming development project.

So here he was getting the full Buchanan coal-raking treatment. And the bastard never even raised his voice. Every word had been delivered in a cold, emotionless tone that conveyed the man's displeasure far more effectively than any amount of chest beating and yelling would have done. Ingram had no doubt at all that his job was on the line because of that goddamned restaurant.

"It's probably just a coincidence, sir," he tried carefully.

Buchanan arched one brow. "Coincidence, Ingram? There are no coincidences when you're talking seventy-million-dollar deals."

Ingram tried again, striving to keep his own voice as cool and logical as Buchanan's, just as if the thought of losing a forty-thousand-dollar-a-year job didn't bother him in the least. "Sir, the owner of that restaurant has been wanting to sell for some time. We figured there was no rush to make him an offer because there isn't much of a market for run-down taco stands in Phoenix at the moment. We didn't think anyone else would be interested, and if we'd rushed in too enthusiastically with an offer, people would have gotten suspicious."

"So you let the least attractive properties wait until last."

"Of course. Otherwise too many questions would have been raised about why unattractive parcels in downtown Phoenix were suddenly going like hotcakes."

"You should have taken an option on that restaurant,

261

Jeff," Buchanan remarked, swiveling his chair around so that he could view the ocean.

"Taking an option would have had the same effect, sir. It might have alerted someone. We already had so many options going . . ."

"Do you know who bought the restaurant?"

Ingram ground his teeth in silent frustration and then said softly, "Not yet. We're working on it. Should have the information by noon."

"Jeff, when people are on the verge of lousing up seventy-million-dollar deals, I do not like to hear them using the word 'we.'"

Ingram clenched his fist and then consciously un-clenched it. "*I'll* have the information by noon."

"A little sooner, perhaps, Jeff?"

"I'll do my best, sir."

"Your best has been sadly lacking lately, hasn't it?" Buchanan swung the chair back around, his eyes clear ice. Ingram wondered fleetingly if the man ever got excited or showed any real passion of any kind. He probably faked something up for that chesty Galloway woman when they were in bed together, but Ingram was willing to bet that it was pure theatrics—the right words, the right sounds, but, above all, controlled. Of course, Carol Galloway didn't exactly come across as the wanton, melt-in-your-arms type, either. Jeff had seen her a couple of times on Buchanan's arm, and while he had to admit there was a lot to be said for a nice pair of breasts, he, personally, liked a little warmth in a woman's eyes to go along with them.

Perhaps he'd outgrow that idiosyncrasy when he got

to Buchanan's level, he decided sardonically. Then again, if he didn't salvage that damned restaurant deal, his trip to the executive suite was going to be badly sidetracked.

"Sir, I regret this foul-up with the restaurant. But I still think it's probably just an unfortunate coincidence. The old man found someone who would take the place off his hands, and he sold out. We'll get it back."

"I know we'll get it back, Jeff," Buchanan said silkily. "The question is how much will I have to pay to get it back. If whoever bought that restaurant knows the true value of the land to me, it's going to cost. We're in too deep to back out of the project, and if the son of a bitch knows what's going on, he'll know that, too. That restaurant should have cost no more than thirty or forty grand. If the new owner knows the real value, they could hold out for half a million or more. I don't like being made a fool of, Ingram. I don't like having some joker think he can take me to the cleaners."

"I understand, sir."

"Find out who bought that goddamn taco stand." Buchanan dismissed his assistant with a disdainful nod. "I want to know by eleven o'clock this morning."

"Yes, sir."

Jeff Ingram walked out of Buchanan's office with his usual brisk, efficient-looking stride, but inside he knew he was already running. He had to get that information, and he had to get it fast. And then he had to pray to whatever gods watched out for up-and-coming-fast-track executives that whoever had chosen to go into the taco business in Phoenix didn't know what a gold mine he was sitting on. Shit. He doubted he'd ever eat a taco again.

*   *   *

The information was relayed from Phoenix by a phone call from one of the real estate agents the Buchanan Group had been using. It came in at ten forty-five, just as Ingram found himself understanding why so many of his colleagues had prescriptions for Valium. Fifteen minutes before the deadline. Talk about taking things down to the wire.

But the name he jotted down on his notepad wasn't reassuringly anonymous. Maitland. Where the hell had he heard that name? Surely not the same Maitland who'd once had his job? Christ! Wasn't anything going to go right today?

With deep foreboding Ingram made his way back up to Buchanan's office. There, feeling as if he might very well be signing his own death warrant, he handed the piece of paper with the scribbled name on it to his boss.

And for the first time since he had met Drew Buchanan, Jeff had the satisfaction of seeing the man's unwavering control momentarily shattered.

"The bitch!" Buchanan ground out as he read the name. "That damned bitch. What the hell does she think she's playing at?"

Ingram waited, uncertain how to deal with the unexpected flash of frustrated rage. It was so unlike Buchanan. When Buchanan simply continued to sit there, staring at the name on the paper, Jeff finally decided to say something. "Shall I check into the matter further? Want me to locate her?"

Slowly, suppressing his fury with a supreme effort of will, Buchanan lifted his head. "Of course I want you to locate her. Don't worry, it won't be hard. She wants to be found now."

Ingram swallowed, hiding the nervous reaction manfully. "You think this is all deliberate, sir?"

"Oh, yes," Buchanan said very evenly, totally back under control. "It's quite deliberate. I taught Samantha Maitland everything she knows about business, *real* business. And now she has the gall to think she can use it against me."

"Sir, I don't understand. Why would she want to tackle the Buchanan Group? How could she have known about the Phoenix deal?"

"The woman had her weak points, but lack of intelligence wasn't one of them," Buchanan grated. "Get out of here, Jeff. I want to know where she's staying, what she's doing for a living these days, who she's sleeping with, and what kind of car she's driving. I want to know everything you can find out by five thirty this afternoon."

He swung the swivel chair back around to face the window, listening as Ingram quietly left the room. Then he looked down again at the piece of paper in his hand.

Samantha Maitland, you little conniving bitch. I always knew you'd throw me a curve someday. But I've been playing hardball a lot longer than you have, lady. You don't lack nerve and you don't lack brains but I know your weaknesses. I'll find the right one to use to crush you.

He crumpled the paper in his palm and slammed it into the garbage can. Who the hell did she think she was to pull this kind of play on him? There was only one reason for it, of course. She wanted revenge.

Revenge. He repeated the word in his head. A woman who wanted revenge must still be carrying a torch. Samantha was a woman scorned, and that meant she was at the mercy of her own emotions. She wouldn't be thinking with total clarity. Not that he'd ever really been able to comprehend exactly how she *did* think, he reminded himself grimly.

But a woman's desire for revenge on a man should be a fairly simple, clear-cut situation. She must still want him on some level, or she wouldn't be investing the emotional energy it took to get even.

Whatever her feelings toward him, they had to be strong. Good God! She must have been watching his movements for the past three years! To have gotten a handle on the Phoenix deal so early, she must have been lying in wait for him. He'd been stalked all this time and hadn't even been aware of it.

The knowledge wasn't pleasant. Drew Buchanan liked to be totally in charge of every aspect of his life. How had the bitch snuck up on him like this?

Was he prepared to watch a multimillion-dollar deal become completely snafued because of Samantha Maitland? At the very least she would hold him up for a fortune. At the worst she might simply refuse to sell at all.

Either way his ego and his bankbook were going to take one hell of a beating. He had to break her and do it quickly before she had a chance to become too high on her own power.

The way to break a woman was through her emotions. He'd held her in the palm of his hand once; he could do it again.

And if seducing her didn't work, he'd find the weapon which would. Samantha had her vulnerable points. Everyone did. He'd find the soft spots and use them against her.

At five thirty Jeff Ingram's report was almost complete.

"Here's her Seattle address, sir. Some island in the sound. She's got a going little concern peddling business news and information to a bunch of client firms who pay her well for the research she provides. The car's a Fiat. There's just one thing I couldn't pin down," he concluded hesitantly.

"What's that?" Buchanan pulled the report toward him and scanned it rapidly.

"Well," Jeff cleared his throat. "There doesn't seem to be any indication of a particular man in her life. She dates but . . ."

"But she's not sleeping with someone on a regular basis? Good. That should make things easier," Buchanan growled, turning over the second page of the short report.

"Easier, sir?"

"Never mind. Have my secretary book me on a flight to Seattle tomorrow."

"Yes, sir. Uh, do you want anything else this evening?"

"Get lost, Ingram. You've done enough damage for one day."

Gabriel would be arriving the day after tomorrow.

Samantha pressed the button which turned off the printer and collected the neatly piled stack of reports she had just generated from the computer. This week

267

most of her clients were going to be pleased. The indications were that the big grain deal with the U.S.S.R. was going to go through, the stock market had settled down to a more normal pace, and the heavy storms in the Midwest were finally abating. Beneath all those unrelated facts lay a wealth of financial news. The business world was hungry for information. It needed it to survive in a way that no other field of endeavor did.

Almost everything and anything was of interest to someone, somewhere in business. Fundamental medical research news was of prime interest to drug companies. Information on weather patterns led huge agribusiness firms to make crucial crop decisions. Political situations in the Middle East determined the price of American oil. The death of a world leader could totally disrupt the stock market. It was all incredibly interrelated, impossibly complex, and wonderfully stimulating intellectually for Samantha on most days.

But today she wasn't concentrating with her usual precision. Gabriel had phoned last night and said he would be in Seattle the day after tomorrow. Samantha recognized the curl of intense anticipation in the pit of her stomach and wondered at it.

How had such a man managed to invade every area of her life so thoroughly? Stupid question. Gabriel Sinclair was a very thorough sort of man. She shook her head bemusedly as she prepared the individualized research reports for mailing.

She should be thinking of the next stage in her plans for revenge. By now Buchanan must know who had swiped the restaurant out from under his nose. If he didn't find out this week, she would be astounded. She'd worked long enough in his offices to know just how good his own sources of information were.

Gabriel had left the day after the confrontation with Kirby's men. He'd gone back to California to set the wheels in motion which would provide the cash needed to buy the restaurant in Phoenix. To be on the safe side, he'd told Samantha he would have the actual purchase concluded by a lawyer he knew in Phoenix. Samantha's name was the one listed as purchaser. Gabriel preferred to continue his habitual practice of maintaining a low profile in such arrangements.

"Which does not mean I consider myself a silent partner," he'd warned her once again as he'd prepared to take his leave a week ago.

"No." She half-smiled as she stood beside the Buick and watched him feed the key into the ignition. "You've been anything but silent during this whole process."

"Self-defense," he explained succinctly. "I feel like I have to stay one step ahead of you for both our sakes!"

"Do I really scare you, Gabriel?" she murmured wistfully.

He hesitated instead of switching on the ignition. Then he reached out a massive hand and dragged her head down to his level. Leaning through the window he kissed her soundly. "You terrify me, witch. I feel like I'm riding a tiger. I don't dare get off, and I'm not at all sure what my fate will be if I stay on! But at least I know now that I can trust the beast." And then he grinned his rare, shark's grin. "Besides which, there are times when the ride is very pleasant, indeed. Good-bye, Samantha. I'll call you tonight."

He'd called her every night since he'd left. Samantha had come to look forward to the phone calls with the greatest anticipation. It was true that Gabriel almost always discussed business, telling her the state of the Phoenix situation and related details. But before the conversation ended, he always managed to remind her of the claim he had staked on her body. No matter how subtle the remarks Samantha always hung up the phone with vivid memories in her head of how it had been to lie in his arms.

The day after Gabriel had left, Eric had decided to go back to California long enough to make peace with his family.

"They've stopped calling every day," Samantha pointed out when he told her of his decision. "And at least you managed to keep Vic from sending a private detective to my door."

"Only by telling him I'd be back by the end of the week." Eric grunted. "God, if he only knew what I almost did!"

"He doesn't ever have to know," Samantha told her brother stoutly. "No one ever has to know. Some things are better kept to oneself."

"I've hardly kept it to myself! I managed to involve you and Gabriel and somebody named Emil Fortune whom I have the distinct impression I'd rather not meet face-to-face!"

"Actually, he's rather nice face-to-face." Samantha

chuckled. "A sweet little man who looks like he wouldn't hurt a fly. Very gallant, too."

"International arbitrage, hmmm?"

"That's what Gabriel says."

"Well, I for one am not going to ask how some international financier knows who to call to get a character like Jackson Kirby off my back! I'm just going to be grateful from a distance. Sam, what did Gabe mean the other morning when he said you'd agreed to pay my tab?"

"He was just being deliberately cryptic," Samantha assured him, clearing the table of the remains of the hamburgers she and Eric had been eating. How could she explain that pact she had made with Gabriel Sinclair? She wasn't even certain herself exactly what he had been asking of her.

He had wanted to know she wouldn't cheat him in bed or in business, but she had the feeling it was more far-ranging than that. But until she knew herself what the contract meant, she certainly wasn't going to try to explain it to Eric.

She only hoped she hadn't bound herself in a way which would someday come to haunt her in a way she couldn't yet foresee. Gabriel had been so intense that night. And she, caught up in the emotional turmoil of gratitude, passion, and sympathy, probably would have promised him anything he asked at that point.

It occurred to Samantha as she generated address labels from the computer that Gabriel was astute enough to recognize just how vulnerable she had been that night. Gabriel Sinclair was not a stupid man. He simply insisted on moving at his own pace and doing things in his own thorough way. He was, in fact, quite brilliant. And, too, there must be a streak of ruthlessness in him somewhere or how else could he have gotten as far as he had?

Angels were not always easy to understand. They were proving to be full of surprises and perhaps even dangerous.

Samantha chewed on that thought for the remainder of the afternoon.

It was as she crawled alone into her bed that night that Samantha realized she had spent a great deal more time lately thinking about her relationship with Gabriel Sinclair than she had about her plans for the Buchanan Group. The knowledge was astonishing. How had Gabriel managed to overwhelm so many aspects of her life so suddenly?

The next morning, however, when she opened the door to find Drew Buchanan on her front porch, everything fell rapidly back into perspective. Reality came thundering in on her.

It was raining, as usual, when the old brass eagle on her door sounded commandingly throughout the house. Samantha, sitting at her terminal, started a little. She had been concentrating intently on the Soviet grain harvest reports outlined on the screen, and the sound of the old eagle jerked her almost violently out of her study.

Gabriel was not due for another day. Eric, as far as she knew, was still placating the other Thorndykes. A neighbor?

Even as she walked down the hall to open the door, Samantha's intuition went into high gear. By the time she unlocked the door, she was already half-prepared for who she would find on her doorstep.

"Well, Sam, you finally managed to do it, didn't you? You took me by surprise."

She looked up at him, and a hundred memories together with the tangled emotions surrounding them crashed through her head. He was as handsome as ever, the pleasant, terribly deceptive all-American look enhanced now with a touch more of the distinguished gray at the temples. For her the charm had been turned on, she saw at once, the easy, laconic smile in place, rueful amusement in his eyes. The elegantly tailored suit he was wearing emphasized his height and the leanness of his body. She guessed he still worked out religiously at a health club, as he had when she last knew him.

As she stood there taking in the sight of him, letting herself taste the first hard, bright morsels of victory, a part of Samantha insisted on noting the physical difference between Drew Buchanan and Gabriel Sinclair. It was an easy difference to summarize. Drew was lean, dynamic, polished, and sophisticated.

Gabriel was . . . Gabriel. Solid, hard, dependable. He was just *there*, taking up more than his share of space and quietly forcing the world around him to accommodate itself to him wherever he happened to be.

"Hello, Drew," she drawled with exquisite politeness. "How nice to see you again. Here on business?"

"Ah, Sam." He sighed wryly. "I can see you're deter-

273

mined to get your pound of flesh out of all this, aren't you?"

"Actually, I was thinking more in terms of seven hundred and fifty thousand. Money is so much more useful than flesh."

"Seven hundred and fifty!" For just an instant the indulgent amusement faded a bit in those charming eyes. For a fraction of a second, Samantha saw the cold, emotionless man behind the facade, and she shivered a little at the enormity of what she had undertaken. Gabriel had been right when he'd accused her of playing out of her league. But when the stakes were high enough, a woman played the game that had to be played.

"Seven hundred and fifty," Drew repeated, this time on a dry whistle of admiration. "You're really going for the top, aren't you? I was thinking more in the neighborhood of three hundred and fifty thousand. Half a million, max."

"What's another few hundred grand when you're already into a project for seventy million?" She smiled brilliantly.

He shook his head in seemingly rueful amazement. "You always were pretty good at research. Where'd you get that figure, Sam?"

"Oh, it took some calculation. I had to add up a lot of little figures to get it. Close?"

"Seventy million for the Phoenix job? Oh, yes. Quite close. Are you going to keep me waiting out here in the rain, Sam, while you negotiate?" He gave her that wonderfully endearing smile that was supposed to make a woman see the little boy beneath the surface. It made her realize that Gabriel's rare shark's grin was a lot more honest.

"Come in, Drew. I wouldn't want you to get those lovely shoes wet." Italian leather, probably a few hundred dollars for the pair. No, he hadn't changed at all.

He stepped through the door as she moved aside, and his eyes slid lingeringly the length of her body. She was clad in jeans and a western-style white shirt, the rolled up sleeves and open collar giving her a rakish air. The brown mass of her hair was held back behind her ears with two red clips.

"Interesting, but not quite the way I remember you."

She tilted her head slightly as she led him into the living room and waved him to a chair. "How do you remember me, Drew?" The question was as cool as she could have wished, as if she didn't give a damn about the answer.

Which was, Samantha realized on a strange tide of relief, very close to the truth. It was only then as she sank into the overstuffed chair across from him, her legs casually outstretched and crossed at the ankles, that Samantha acknowledged to herself she'd been hiding a sense of unease about this confrontation. She hadn't wanted to admit consciously that when she finally came face-to-face with Drew Buchanan again she might still find herself attracted to him.

Now the moment had arrived, and she was discovering that her most secret fear had no real existence. How much of her freedom from that danger was because of Gabriel? When a woman had lain in an angel's arms, the devil was no longer much of a temptation, she thought whimsically. She owed Gabriel more than his share of the profit on this deal. She owed him something for having made sure in his own, overwhelming manner that when the final confrontation came she would have no lingering attraction for Buchanan to weaken her resolve.

All at once Samantha felt marvelously in control; an avenging huntress or an ice-cold, righteous goddess. She was going to restore the pride that had been in tatters around her three years ago. Something of her unalterable intent must have shown in her eyes or in the set of her chin, even, perhaps in the flickering smile which edged her mouth because Drew Buchanan was studying her rather intently before responding to her question.

"I remember you in neat little suits and leather pumps. You used to wear your hair in a no-nonsense little coil at the nape of your neck, as I recall." His eyes gleamed with deliberately seductive reminiscence. "And I also recall how pleasant it was to remove the pins."

"That was the interesting thing about our relationship, wasn't it, Drew? It never got beyond the pleasant stage for you. You save your passions for more important things, like business, don't you?"

"I don't remember you complaining about my passions three years ago," he murmured, his eyes narrowing faintly.

Samantha could feel his assessing gaze as if it were a physical probe. He was sizing her up after three years, looking for the weak spots, seeking out the old ones and trying to reactivate them. Why hadn't she been able to see this man so clearly three years ago?

"Three years ago I was less perceptive about some things," she remarked dryly, answering his comment and her own question at the same time.

He hesitated and then said calmly, "Did Thorndyke ever tell you what happened that day in my office when he played out the outraged father scene?"

"Oh, yes. He told me that he'd warned you I wouldn't receive a dime if I married you. That was all it took, apparently, to convince you that I wasn't the bargain you had first thought." The words came easily, considering they formed part of the motivation for a passion as strong as revenge. Why was it that today she could sit here and admit to both of them that she had simply been younger and dumber three years ago?

"By not marrying you, I helped make sure you got your inheritance, Sam. Doesn't that count for anything? Isn't it conceivable that I may not have wanted to deprive you of what was rightfully yours?"

She grinned suddenly. "I never did get the money, you know."

He looked momentarily startled. "You didn't? Thorndyke really did decide to leave his sweet bastard daughter out of his will? I'm surprised. What did you do? Turn around and run off with some other unacceptable suitor?"

"I turned the money down. There was a lot of it, too. But it was worth it . . . though I certainly don't expect you to understand." Did that condescending little laugh really come from her?

He shook his head in mock dismay. "Still the same impetuous, go-to-the-wall-over-a-principle Samantha. What an idiot you are," he added in amusement. "How have you managed to survive in the real world for the past three years?"

Her mouth kicked upward again at the corners. "Well, lately I've had a guardian angel. Very useful."

He frowned, sensing that something besides flippancy lay behind the remark. "An angel?"

"Umm. Never mind about that, however. Tell me how you plan to talk me out of fleecing you over that restaurant," she invited complacently. "I can't wait to hear your strategy."

"You're so sure I have one?"

"You wouldn't be here otherwise. You really could afford to simply pay up and chalk it off to experience, you know. But instead I find you standing on my doorstep within days of learning who now owns a certain taco stand in Phoenix. You must have some plans."

"You seem equally sure they won't work."

"They won't." She shrugged.

"I'm not going to simply shell out that kind of money to you, Sam," he told her gently. "And not because I can't afford it."

"But because it would gall you unbearably to succumb to what is essentially blackmail. Blackmail from someone you once thought you could control completely. I understand perfectly, Drew. Quite perfectly."

"You're awfully sure of yourself. It must have taken you months of planning to pull off this coup. Were you that badly hurt three years ago?" He leaned back in his chair, watching her face intently.

"Oh, the pangs of unrequited love died quite quickly, as a matter of fact," she told him musingly, thinking about it.

"But the feeling that I'd made a fool out of you didn't die so quickly?"

"You always were very perceptive about other people, Drew. It's one of the reasons you're so successful. You know how to strike just the right notes from them. But you play them for your own pleasure and advantage. You're not a very nice man, Drew Buchanan."

"And you're hoping that you're going to teach me a lesson? Show me the errors of my ways?" he drawled.

"I don't delude myself that what I'm doing will cause you to change your ways. I just want you to know that you can't trample over everyone and get off scot-free every time. Some of us will fight back, Drew."

"Because of your pride." He nodded.

"Something like that. It would be difficult to explain to you."

He moved his head in a negative gesture. "No, it's not. Don't you think I understand pride?"

"A man's pride, perhaps. Not a woman's," she told him simply.

"Is it so very different?"

"It takes a slightly different form in every woman. And it's a more flexible thing, I believe." She smiled. "Some women will banish it completely for a man, for example."

"But not you?"

"No, not me." When you had a woman like Vera Maitland for a mother, you couldn't banish pride. Especially not for a man.

"So I'm going to have to pay through the nose to soothe your ravaged pride," he concluded with a nod that was entirely too understanding.

"I'm going to make sure you remember the occasion," she agreed dryly.

"Where did you get the cash, Sam?" he asked abruptly.

"The cash?"

"That restaurant was purchased for cash. I'm just curious about where you got that much of it. I understand the asking price was fifty thousand dollars. If you turned down your father's money a couple of years ago and spent the time since you left the Buchanan Group building up a business from scratch . . ."

"Your sources are very good."

"You should know. You used to work for me. You used them, yourself, quite frequently, as I recall."

"One of the many things I learned from you," she agreed pleasantly, "was how to build an information network. I took that basis of information and expanded it considerably with a computer. Now I am in the information business."

"Yes, I know," he said, the faintest edge of impatience to his voice. He'd realized, apparently, that she'd just sidestepped the question. "As I said, I'm told you've been building up your little business, and I realize what it takes to keep even the smallest of businesses going through the first two years."

"Nice to know you still appreciate what the little guy

has to go through struggling to survive these days," she said conversationally.

"Oh, I do, Sam. I do. Which brings us back to the basic question. Where did you get the spare cash to buy a fifty-thousand-dollar restaurant in Phoenix?"

"You don't really believe I'm going to tell you any more than I have to in order to complete the deal, do you, Drew?" she demanded sweetly. "That was another thing I learned from you. Never provide unnecessary information to the opposition."

"Are you afraid the information in this case might be used against you?" he countered swiftly.

"Not at all. I'm just following your own general policy of not going out of my way to hand out details." Which was the truth. Gabriel preferred to keep a low profile simply because that was the way he operated. He didn't invite attention. But there really wouldn't be anything Drew Buchanan could do even if he did discover that Gabriel Sinclair was her financial backer. Gabriel was simply involved in a business deal. There was nothing which could be used against him.

Drew sighed, his eyes momentarily hooded and gleaming with a malevolent intent he couldn't quite hide. "It would appear I'm at your mercy." He didn't sound as if he believed it, however, and Samantha took warning.

"So it would appear. Care to write out the check right now?"

"Ah, Sam. You always were impetuous. One doesn't conduct deals of this magnitude quite so hastily."

"Unseemly?" she hazarded brightly.

"Very."

"How does one conduct them?"

"Over dinner. Will you have dinner with me tonight? For old times' sake?"

"I love that charmingly wistful note in your voice. Just the right touch. God, you are really an incredibly good actor, Drew. Perhaps you missed your calling after all. Then again, I suppose you find the skill very useful, don't you? You'll find it even more useful as you move into your new career of politics."

For the first time she managed to catch him slightly off guard. He recovered almost instantly. "You really have been paying attention to my comings and goings during the past few years, haven't you?"

She shrugged, saying nothing. His association with a politician named Galloway hadn't been hard to turn up. The fact that Galloway had a tremendously effective political machine which he had inherited from his father had also soon come to light. Buchanan, if he could insinuate himself into that machine, could probably easily take control of it. After that there would be little to stop him. It didn't surprise her that Drew had developed a taste for power on a large scale. It was bound to come with success. Wasn't she herself rather enjoying the feeling of power she had today? Perhaps the stuff was addictive!

"Dinner, Sam?" he prompted very softly, a husky, deeply masculine note in his voice.

She had known this was coming, of course. It was obvious that one of Buchanan's approaches would be to try a little seduction. After all, he had been so eminently successful at it three years ago. Men like Drew who had no reason to question their technique with women tended to mobilize that sort of approach first. It was the easiest as far as they were concerned.

And she had fully intended to let him try it just for the satisfaction of stringing him along a little further. Yes, it would be wonderfully satisfying to laugh at him as he practiced his sophisticated, superficial sensuality.

So why was she hesitating over the dinner invitation?

Because, she realized with a new, very distant sense of dismay, thoughts of Gabriel were starting to infiltrate her thinking. Thoughts of Gabriel and the strange promise he had bound her with were pouring out of nowhere into her mind. Ridiculous! She wasn't about to cheat him either out of his half of the deal or by going to bed with Drew Buchanan. In fact, the last thought was decidedly unpalatable, almost more so than cheating Gabriel out of his share of the money would have been! Good God! How far gone was she in her relationship with Gabriel Sinclair that the notion of sleeping with another man was deeply abhorrent?

A sense of rising unease stirred in the pit of her stomach. For the first time since Drew had walked in the door, Samantha began to lose her sense of being totally in command of herself and the situation.

But she *was* in charge of both, she reminded herself fiercely. And she was in no danger of breaking her promise to Gabriel even if she chose to linger over her victory by having dinner with Buchanan.

She swallowed, unwillingly aware now that what was really starting to bother her was a distinct feeling that somehow she would be violating the pledge she had made to Gabriel, that she had already violated it.

Damn it! What was the matter with her? She had done nothing which required either an explanation or an apology or a sense of guilt. Still, the first nibbling of panic could be felt at the edge of her mind. What would Gabriel say if he knew she had dinner with Drew Buchanan tonight? What could he say? What right would he have to say anything at all? She certainly wasn't contemplating actually going to bed with their opponent!

Suddenly Samantha found herself wishing she'd explained her own, personal motivation in this deal to Gabriel. Things would be so much simpler now if he knew the full story.

Only he probably would never have agreed to get involved with her financially if he had known the full story. Catch twenty-two.

Well, shit. It was too complicated to sort out while she sat here staring at Drew Buchanan's wryly amused face. She needed to think, and she couldn't do that with her enemy here in the house.

"I'm afraid dinner isn't possible," she murmured politely. "Even for old times' sake. I have other plans." Like getting out a frozen pizza!

"Plans that are more important than discussing a great sum of money?" he mocked, and she could have kicked herself. He was choosing to interpret her refusal to dine with him as cowardice. The dismaying thing was that he might be right in a way!

She smiled, the expression every bit as false as his own. "Dear Drew, we both know you have no intention of discussing terms this evening. You only want to see if you can get me into bed. Frankly, I've got more interesting ways of spending the evening. Why don't you run along now and let me know for certain when you've decided to make out a check?" She got to her feet as a means of encouraging him to leave and also because she was beginning to feel uncomfortably restless. She wanted him out of the house.

But her unexpectedly hasty dismissal must not have fit in with his plans at all. Another chunk of the facade slipped as he stood up quickly and reached for her.

"I wonder why I never realized until this week what a little bitch you are," he said coldly. His hands bit into her shoulders.

Samantha lifted her head, unflinchingly meeting his icy expression. "But, Drew, you're the one who taught me everything I know."

"And I always knew you didn't have enough of that ruthlessness to make it to the top, love." The polished seducer was back in charge as he lowered his mouth to take her lips. "You're soft, Samantha. Baby soft. Don't you remember?"

She stood still for a moment beneath the touch of his mouth, curious to see how different his kiss would be for her now than it had been three years ago. There was nothing. It was all too contrived, too jadedly sensuous, too deliberately provocative. There was none of the elemental power that captured her so easily when Gabriel took her in his arms. And there wasn't any indication that Drew was more than superficially involved in the caress. With Gabriel there was never any doubt but that he was succumbing to the passion of the moment just as he forced her to surrender to it.

Gabriel. What the hell was she doing standing here in Drew Buchanan's arms? Even if the embrace meant nothing, she had no business letting this man touch her.

A strange kind of panic seized her. The overwhelming need to free herself of the spurious caress drove her into sudden, wild protest. She threw up her hands, pressing furiously against Drew's chest, and at the same time snapped her head away from his.

"Get out of here, Drew. Don't bother contacting me again until you're ready to sign a check! Get the hell out of my house!"

He had the nerve to smile. It was a slow, cool, satisfied smile, which told exactly how he was viewing her actions.

"Don't you trust yourself to even kiss me, baby?" he murmured smoothly, stroking his fingers along the line of her shoulder. "Are you so afraid of finding out that the old magic still exists?"

God! He thought she was fighting him because she was terrified of losing her control. The monumental ego of the man. But none of that mattered as much as getting him out of her home. She should never have let him in the front door. It was all wrong. She had violated the spirit if not the letter of her midnight pact with Gabriel, and the feeling of revulsion was almost sickening.

"Get out, Drew." She kept her voice utterly calm, stepping away from him and striding toward the front door. "Don't come back. Why don't you have one of your assistants contact me for the final details? That way you won't have to disturb your busy schedule any further."

His smile became even more satisfied. "You're running scared, baby, and I know you. You're the one who just told me how perceptive I am, remember? I'll keep pushing buttons until I find the one that works." He moved slowly toward the door. "And I will find it. You know I will. I always do. You haven't got a chance of standing up to me, Sam. You of all people should know that."

"Get *out*!"

"I'm going. But I'll be back. Believe it. I'll see you tomorrow."

He strode outside to where his car was parked as if he hadn't a concern in the world. As if he had Samantha in the palm of his hand.

Samantha watched him leave, beginning to breathe normally now that he was off the premises. Running scared, was she? He didn't even have an inkling of how unsettled, how nervous, how *scared* she really was! But even if he had deduced the truth, he was going to tell himself that it was because she was terrified of her own reaction to him.

The only terrifying thought was how she was going to explain all this to Gabriel Sinclair when he arrived in the morning.

CHAPTER NINE

"It's about time you got here!"

Samantha came down the front porch steps with quick, restless steps as Gabriel's rented car pulled into the drive. The explanations were clearly outlined in her head and had been ready for hours. After a night spent tossing and turning as she tried first to talk herself out of the strange guilt and then, when that effort failed, tried to figure out how to convince Gabriel she wasn't really guilty of anything, Samantha was not in a good mood.

Gabriel perused her slowly as he climbed out of the sedate car. Samantha could literally feel him taking in every aspect of her from the overbright sheen of her eyes glittering at him from behind the lenses of her glasses to the tension in her figure and the hectic flush on her cheeks. The bad night's sleep showed, she thought disgustedly. Then, after absorbing the evidence of her obvious agitation, Gabriel's eyes moved deliberately to the rounded curve of her hips tightly sheathed in jeans.

288

"Nothing like a warm welcome from his woman to make a man forget this damn rain," he drawled as he paced through the mist toward where Samantha had come to a stop on the bottom porch step.

She stared at him, astounded that he could tease her even a little when he must realize something awful had happened. Her mouth tightened at the sardonic expression in his eyes when she made no move to kiss him hello.

"Oh, Gabriel, I'm sorry!" Samantha groaned.

"About what? The rain or the unencouraging greeting I'm getting?" He reached her side and leaned down to take her mouth in a brief, hard kiss.

"I have to talk to you." She stepped back nervously, leading the way into the old house.

"About what?" he asked again, sounding more patient than ever. He set down his leather travel bag and followed her toward the warmth of the kitchen.

His very calmness fed her anxiety, Samantha thought irritably. It was annoying to be so keyed up, so tense, and have the object of all that tension acting as if he were some kind of salesman home after a week on the road.

"It's very complicated, Gabriel." She sighed. "Sit down. I'll get you some coffee."

"Tea sounds more soothing. You sit down, Samantha. I'll make it." His large hands descended on her shoulders, and she was pushed gently but firmly onto one of the kitchen chairs.

She watched morosely as he set about collecting all the things he needed for tea and then began making it in his careful, precise way. God, she couldn't even make tea the way he liked it, let alone cook or keep house or conduct business in a fashion of which he approved. Self-pity hovered in a dark cloud over her head.

"You should have picked another woman, Gabriel."

He didn't pause as he methodically warmed the china pot with hot water, but Samantha thought the broad shoulders tensed a little beneath the conservatively cut pinstriped shirt he wore.

It was funny, she thought vaguely, both Drew and Gabriel wore conservatively tailored clothes but for entirely different reasons. Buchanan chose the look because it fit the image he strove to maintain of respectable corporate power. Gabriel chose it simply because it suited his personality. Samantha couldn't imagine him dressed any other way.

"One who can cook?" he jibed in response to her mumbled comment.

"This isn't a joke, Gabriel. Buchanan's here. He arrived yesterday," she snapped back baldly. "And he's coming back here today."

Gabriel's hand stilled for a moment before he went through with the action of putting the kettle on the burner and switching on the heat. It was typical of the man, Samantha realized. He never let anything put him off course. She felt a sense of wistful admiration for his deliberate, unhurried ways. He always finished what he started, even something as small and insignificant as putting the kettle on the stove. Despite the shock of her announcement, nothing impeded the flow of the tea-making ceremony.

There was something wonderfully reassuring about Gabriel Sinclair. Why the hell had she tried to finesse the business arrangement between them? This wasn't the kind of man a woman wanted to manipulate or finesse. This was the kind who should be treated as an equal and dealt with openly and honestly.

"Oh, Gabriel," she whispered raggedly, "I'm sorry."

He turned slowly to face her, leaning back against the counter and folding his arms across his chest. His face was an unreadable but infinitely calm mask. Too calm. It wasn't human to be that calm. It wasn't even particularly angelic. Samantha's nervousness increased considerably.

"Okay, Samantha. Tell me about Buchanan."

"It's so damn complicated!"

"Probably not as complicated as it seems to you at the moment," he retorted dryly.

"You're right," she admitted quietly, bringing herself back under control. "It isn't really complicated, it's just rather messy. Gabriel, there's something I haven't explained to you about this business deal of ours. Something I didn't think really mattered because it didn't have anything to do with the financial arrangements between you and me. It *still* doesn't," she added insistently.

"Who are you trying to convince, honey? Me or yourself?"

"Myself. Gabriel, three years ago I was engaged to marry Drew Buchanan." She lifted her eyes defiantly as she waited for the angry explosion. Gabriel just looked at her, his gaze pensive.

"I see."

She took a breath. "Do you? What I'm trying to explain is that I had other motives for concocting this deal than the ones I explained to you. I'm not just out to make a quick financial kill."

"You're out for revenge."

"That's the part that gets complicated." She groaned. "I am out for revenge but not the sort Drew thinks."

"And what, exactly, does Buchanan think you want?"

He sounded so unmoved and so unalarmed she thought wonderingly. Didn't he see how she had misled him? Wasn't he furious that an emotional motive like feminine revenge was at the heart of her whole plot? He had to be annoyed, to say the least, to find out that he hadn't been given the whole picture right from the start.

"He thinks I must still be carrying a torch for him. He sees me playing out the role of a woman scorned."

"And you're not?"

Her eyes hardened. "Of course not. He's not worth three years of plotting and planning and research!"

"Who is?"

"My mother."

"I think," Gabriel noted calmly as he turned to the stove in response to the teakettle's whistle, "that I'm beginning to see a light at the end of this crazy tunnel. Keep talking, Samantha."

Her shoulders moved in an uneasy shrug. "There's not much else to explain. I'm in this because I'm trying to show Vera Maitland that she didn't raise a failure and a fool of a daughter."

"Are you sure that's how she thinks of you?" He poured the hot water into the warmed pot.

"I saw the look in her eyes after my fiasco of an engagement was broken up by my father," Samantha said bitterly. "It was as if I had betrayed every tenet she had taught me by making a fool of myself over Buchanan. It's been three years, Gabriel, and I can still see that expression in her eyes. I didn't turn out strong and independent and brave like my mother. I turned out to be a weak little idiot who managed to let herself be blinded by a slick, sophisticated playboy who uses everyone, including women, for his own ends. When I saw him yesterday," she went on in a lower tone, "I couldn't believe I'd been so stupid three years ago. My mother was right to be appalled at what happened."

"So this whole elaborate maneuver down in Phoenix is solely designed to prove to your mother that you, too, can be as hard as nails?"

Samantha's eyes narrowed at the cool mockery in his words. "I think I'm trying to prove it to myself, too. I want Vera to know I can take care of myself, and I want to know I can do it. I won't be stomped on."

"Tell me about that engagement, Samantha," Gabriel ordered quietly as he carried the tea things over to the table and set them down. He sank heavily into the chair across from her and began to pour, his eyes on the pot.

He had a right to know, she decided grimly. So she told him as concisely and as honestly as possible. She even told him exactly how it had ended. "Vera called in my father, who did his duty and bailed out his daughter before she actually found herself married to Drew Buchanan. He did it in a typically Victor Thorndyke fashion, naturally. No holds barred. Walked into Drew's office and told him I wouldn't inherit a dime if he married me. Drew was no fool."

"He called off the engagement?"

"With his usual finesse and style. I hardly knew what was happening, only that things were changing between us. Very quickly it was all over, and I was forced to accept the fact that I'd made a fool of myself."

"And the worst aspect of the whole situation was that you hadn't lived up to Vera's image of a daughter?" Gabriel sipped his tea, seemingly only casually interested in the answer.

"Or my own image of Vera Maitland's daughter! My mother has never made a fool of herself in her life. And certainly not over a man," Samantha noted proudly.

"Sounds like an amazon."

"She is." Samantha smiled obliquely. "I was raised on tales of amazons."

"And you're out to prove you've inherited the mantle." There was a long silence while Gabriel sipped tea before he finally spoke again. "Well, that does fill in the missing piece of the puzzle," he murmured.

Samantha eyed him cautiously. "What puzzle?"

"I never could quite figure out what was going on behind the scenes in this little deal of ours. There was always a piece missing."

She frowned. "You knew I was holding something back?"

"Let's just say I knew I didn't have all the pertinent facts. I'm coming to accept that as normal with you, honey," he told her coolly. "You're just full of little surprises."

The tip of Samantha's tongue moved briefly across dry lips as she continued to watch his unreadable face. The man could certainly play poker if he ever wanted to and play it well. She couldn't even begin to tell what he was thinking.

"You don't seem overly concerned about that fact," she finally ventured, genuinely puzzled now. "I mean, I rather thought this little confession scene today was going to have a slightly different effect on you."

"Really? What sort of effect did you expect it to have?" She didn't like the placid way he asked the question.

"It did occur to me," she retorted, "that you might be a bit upset about the whole thing. Angry, perhaps. Absolutely infuriated, in fact!"

"Why should I be infuriated?" he asked, raising one eyebrow.

"Because you're not the sort of man who likes little surprises! For God's sake, Gabriel, why are you taking this so calmly?" Her hand clenched into a small, frustrated fist. This wasn't going the way she had imagined it would at all. But, then, things rarely did around Gabriel. When was she going to realize that?

"Well, I can't say I truly enjoy having a lot of little rabbits pulled out of hats when I've invested a reasonable sum of money in the lady magician," he said wryly, "but I covered the situation by taking out insurance."

"Insurance!" She stared at him uncomprehendingly.

"Gives a man a lot of peace of mind," he explained equably. "More tea?"

"Gabriel, what the devil are you talking about? What insurance?" She ignored the offer of tea.

He sighed at her slowness, helping himself to another cup of tea. "Samantha, what made you decide to tell me all this today? Why do I arrive in the rain after a boring flight to find my business associate greeting me with the mea culpa routine?"

"I told you! Buchanan came to see me yesterday!" Why was he being so dense?

"And?"

"And I realized I hadn't been completely straightforward with you," she mumbled, subsiding back against her chair. "There were reasons, you know," she went on defensively.

He nodded, as if understanding perfectly. "You were afraid I wouldn't go through with the deal if I knew there were emotional rather than purely business motives involved."

"Well? Would you have gone through with it?" she challenged.

"Once I realized you were going to go through with it with or without me, yes. I wasn't operating with a purely business attitude either, I'm afraid. Or hadn't you noticed?"

She slanted him an assessing glance through her lashes trying to figure out his meaning. "If you're talking about the fact that we've slept together," she said stiffly, "then that doesn't make any sense. You and I both agreed that the physical side of this relationship was totally unconnected with the business side."

"I lied."

Samantha blinked in astonishment and then in gathering anger. "You said you weren't backing me just for the dubious benefit of sleeping with me!"

"I'm not. But that doesn't mean I can divorce the business side of this from the bedroom. Can you?"

"Of course I can!"

"Then why are you going through this grand confession scene?" he asked again, endlessly patient.

"Gabriel, you are deliberately confusing me," she shot back accusingly. "I've told you that Buchanan came to see me yesterday!"

"And that event made you decide to confide all your motives to your business partner?"

"Well, yes, in a way. . . ."

"In what way?" he persisted.

Samantha was almost out of patience. "Because I realized when Drew tried to seduce me that I was in a somewhat untenable position!" she gritted.

Something very unangelic moved in Gabriel's eyes at the word "seduce," but he simply concluded the confession for her. "You realized that you were suddenly very close to violating the promise you made to me last week."

She stared at him. "How did you know?"

"That promise of loyalty I got out of you that night was my insurance, Samantha."

"Your insurance!"

"I knew that the one way to be sure I didn't find

myself facing one surprise too many was to shackle you with your own sense of integrity. You live by your own rules, apparently, but you do stay within them. I had been through a lot that night, I'm afraid, and I decided I'd better make sure things weren't going to get worse. I needed the reassurance." He half-smiled in grim memory.

"You put a hell of a lot of faith in that oath you forced on me!" she crisped, feeling abused and outmaneuvered.

"The only thing I want to know, Samantha," Gabriel went on with a dangerous softness in his voice, "is which line you were suddenly afraid of crossing. Tell me about the seduction."

"You want to know which it was in, business or bed, that I found myself on the verge of betraying you, don't you?" she muttered resentfully.

"Just tell me what happened. Buchanan figured he could play on your old attraction? Thought he could handle you by seducing you all over again?"

"You don't have to sound so matter-of-fact about it!"

Gabriel lifted one broad shoulder. "It sounds like a logical approach for him to try under the circumstances. Was it in danger of working? Is that why I'm getting this little scene today?"

"How can you be so damn cool about all this?" she stormed, incensed.

"Sorry. I thought you realized I tend to be rather unexpressive in my reactions. Am I making this all too dull for you? Would you rather I beat my chest and then beat you? Shall I do a bit more kicking and screaming?"

Quite abruptly Samantha found herself stifling a small surge of sardonic humor. "You don't have to liven things up for me, Gabriel," she muttered dryly. "I'm quite aware of the fact that I should be grateful you're taking all this so calmly. It was the business end of things I started to get nervous about yesterday."

"Not the bedroom end?" He was still watching her with that imperturbable, assessing gaze.

"Definitely not!" She smiled very coldly. "But I had planned to let Drew try his little games. I wanted to string him along a bit; let him think I was still attracted. Ah, Gabriel, I had such plans for that confrontation with Drew Buchanan. After three years of working toward it, I had intended to wring the most out of it. Instead, when he asked me out to dinner, I suddenly realized I was beginning to panic. All I could think about was that I hadn't been completely honest with you. That I had used you, I guess. I couldn't get him out of the house fast enough. So much for three years of scheming!"

"What about the business end? Did you give him your price for the restaurant?" For the first time she thought she detected satisfaction in his voice.

"I, uh, upped it a bit from the one you and I had discussed." She eyed him warily, remembering the plan to set a five-hundred-thousand-dollar tag on the land.

He closed his eyes, clearly begging a higher authority for patience. "How much?"

"Seven hundred and fifty thousand dollars."

That brought his eyes open in a hurry. "Seven hundred and fifty!"

"That's what Drew said," she drawled. "And in exactly that tone."

"I'll bet. You're probably lucky he didn't do something more drastic than try to seduce you! Three quarters of a million. You've got nerve, honey, I'll give you that. Jesus! One more s-s-shock like that and I'll probably collapse!"

"I guess I got carried away." But that was the one aspect of the situation for which she didn't intend to apologize. Damn it, she had a right to salvage something from the grand scheme which had gone grandly haywire.

Gabriel saw the glint of defiance in her eyes and decided not to push the matter. The damage had already been done. He would just have to keep an especially close eye on Samantha now because Drew Buchanan wasn't going to take kindly to the notion of being truly fleeced. He might have accepted something around the three-hundred-fifty-thousand to half-a-million figure with a certain fatalistic business equanimity. He'd have made a few attempts at applying some pressure, but in the end he would have decided it wasn't worth fighting. Not when he realized Samantha wasn't involved in this alone. But the outrageousness of asking for a lot more was going to make the man furious. People got unpredictable when they got emotionally involved to that extent, he reminded himself laconically.

Just look at his own behavior!

"Gabriel," Samantha said hesitantly, interrupting his thoughts.

"Hmmm?"

"You don't seem especially upset, and while I'm grateful for small favors, I find myself asking why I'm getting off so lightly."

His mouth lifted reluctantly upward at the corner. "Like I said. Nothing like a little insurance to give a man peace of mind. I'm sitting here thanking my lucky stars that we had that midnight chat last week."

"The only difference it made was that I decided against having dinner with Buchanan!" she pointed out in annoyance.

"I happen to consider that a major difference."

Her eyes narrowed, and Gabriel could have kicked himself. He had been handling her all right up until now. Now things were threatening to get sticky. She was like a stick of dynamite this morning, he decided uneasily, trouble looking for an excuse to explode.

"I can see that you do consider it important. Which brings up something I'm beginning to think we need to discuss, Gabriel."

Hell. He'd let her off the hook, and now she was going to push her luck. He could see it coming. With an inner groan of dismay, Gabriel poured himself another cup of tea and waited patiently for disaster. "You got a good scare last night, didn't you?"

"Drew didn't scare me! He left when I told him to."

"I don't mean Buchanan scared you. He's got more sense than to rough you up. That's not his style, from what I know of the man." Gabriel pushed that notion aside. "What scared you was how you found yourself reacting." He tried to think of a way to defuse her uncertain temper. "That's what you want to discuss,

301

isn't it? The way you found yourself feeling bound to me? So much so that you were unable to deal with Buchanan the way you had planned to deal with him?"

"It was a very awkward sensation, Gabriel," she told him flatly. "I think we need to define our relationship a little more closely. I should have felt free to deal with Buchanan anyway I wished last night, and instead I lost control of the situation because I started worrying about what you would think! I shouldn't have had that feeling, Gabriel."

He looked down at the cup of tea cradled in his hands, searching for a diplomatic way of saying what had to be said. Diplomacy, unfortunately, was not one of his strong points. He didn't take well to tiptoeing around an issue. "It's too late, Samantha" was all he could think of to say. He said it as gently as possible, but it was like lighting the fuse of the dynamite.

"It is *not* too late!" she exploded, leaning forward intently. "Gabriel, we are going to set some reasonable and highly explicit ground rules for this relationship of ours, or else we are going to call the relationship off! Do you know what I felt last night? I felt as if you had claimed some sort of territorial rights over me! As if I shouldn't be making a move, without consulting you! I felt as if I were your possession or something! Believe me, that's not the sort of relationship I want with a man; any man. And it all happened because of that vague promise you had me make. I want that promise clarified, Gabriel. I want both of us to know exactly where we stand and what we can expect from each other. I don't want this nebulous, all-encompassing feeling that I somehow belong to you!"

He shook his head, knowing nothing he was going to say would pacify her. She had indeed had a scare last night. She had come face-to-face with the conflict between her passion for revenge and her passion for him. "What do you want me to say, honey?" he asked softly. "That we can conduct our affair as if it were a business contract? Do you want me to say that yes, there are loopholes and you're free to take advantage of them? I'm not going to say that, Samantha. I'm not leaving you any loopholes. I'm not going to release you from the promise you made me the other night."

"Damn you, Gabriel, you're deliberately taking advantage of a promise I made at a time when I was very emotionally involved!"

"Honey, that's the only way you ever are in a situation. Very passionately involved. You're passionate in your revenge, in your business dealings, in your feelings of loyalty, in your sense of honor. You're also very, very passionate in bed. Do you really expect me to give up all that now that I've got it?"

For a moment she simply sat, stunned by his bold claim. Gabriel could feel the simmering fury in her and thought about pointing out another of her passionate traits. Then he decided it was not the best time to discuss her far from placid temperament.

"Of all the outrageous, chauvinistic, pigheaded, *masculine* things to say!" she finally managed, jumping to her feet. "You don't own me, Gabriel Sinclair! Do you hear me? If you want a relationship with me, an *affair* with me, then it's going to be on my terms! I won't be caught again in the situation I was in last night!"

He looked up at her incensed expression "You mean you don't want to find yourself having to put our relationship ahead of your thirst for revenge?" he asked calmly. "I can't help you there, Samantha. The relationship comes first. Ahead of everything else. I want you and I have you. I won't release you."

The teacup left her hand and went sailing past his head, landing with a shattering crash against the kitchen wall. She hadn't really been aiming at him, Gabriel realized, or else she would have hit him. He was sitting too close for her to miss. The action was a grand gesture of frustration and fury at the trap in which she found herself.

"The hell you *have* me!" she hissed, her hands on her hips.

Gabriel wasn't sure what he would have said next, probably nothing especially helpful. But the words died on his lips as the old brass eagle sounded on Samantha's front door. He watched the impotent look of outrage cross her face as she realized the grand scene toward which she had been building was going to be delayed. If he hadn't had a fairly sure idea of who was probably at her door, Gabriel would have felt vastly relieved by the reprieve. As it was, he had to act quickly to get control of the situation.

"Samantha, listen to me. That's probably going to be Buchanan," he snapped, leaning forward to plant his hands flat on the table between them. "He'll have some new tactic in mind, and this time he'll find out he's dealing with me as well as you. Leave it to me, do you understand? I'll handle him."

"I set this whole thing up! I'm the one who's going to handle him!" she got out tersely, turning on her heel to stride for the door.

He caught her just as she reached the hall, clamping a sure hand around her arm and pulling her to a halt. "Samantha, you and I can have our battle in private later. Right now we have to stand together, no matter how annoyed you happen to be. Is that clear? Everything's going to ride on convincing Buchanan that he hasn't got a chance in hell of pressuring us."

"And you think you can do a better job of convincing him than I can?" she mocked savagely.

"Frankly, yes."

She struggled for a moment longer, and then he saw the recognition of the reality of the situation hit her. "Later, Gabriel," she warned him stoutly as she shook herself free of his grip.

He didn't pretend to misunderstand. "Later," he agreed with a sigh. But nothing was going to be different later, didn't she realize that? He had a claim on her, and he wasn't relinquishing it regardless of what happened between them later.

Now there was Buchanan to deal with. Buchanan, who thought he was about to be held up to the tune of seven hundred and fifty thousand dollars. Buchanan whom Samantha had once loved. Christ! What a morning.

Gabriel stood behind Samantha as she opened the door, just out of the line of sight the visitor would have as he stood on the threshold. A few seconds of time in which to observe the other before making his own presence known was all he was going to get. But it should be enough to tell him what he was dealing with, Gabriel thought.

"Good morning, Drew," Samantha said with a chilling politeness Gabriel had never heard from her. The amazon in action.

He took an instant to reassure himself with the knowledge that even when she was thoroughly annoyed with him she had never turned that feminine ice on him. Then he focused all his attention on the tall, lean man filling the doorway.

Drew Buchanan was, Gabriel saw at once, the kind of man women would always be pursuing. That lazy smile, the open, handsome features, and all that corporate power were bound to be one hell of a lure. Something about Buchanan promised moonlight and roses, dinners at the most elegant restaurants, and a sophisticated sensuality. And something about Buchanan was as phony as a three-dollar bill. Samantha professed a total lack of interest in the man himself, claiming she only wanted her revenge in order to prove something to herself and her mother. But was she really free of the man's charm?

Gabriel watched Samantha's intended victim through narrowed, assessing eyes and realized belatedly that he had formed a fist with his hand. Deliberately he unfolded his fingers. Small, highly significant gestures such as that would not go unnoticed by Buchanan. Furthermore, Gabriel thought grimly, he'd never been prone to such blatant, outward displays of his own emotional state. Then again, he rarely experienced highly emotional states. Only Samantha had the power to elicit such drastic responses, he realized with an inner sigh. And watching her confront her ex-fiancé was not going to be easy on his nerves. The worst part, though, was that he had the distinct feeling she didn't know quite what she had unleashed here this morning. She was probably going to be in for a shock.

"Good morning, Sam," Buchanan said with lethal charm. Gabriel found himself hating the familiar way the other man shortened her name. "I've been doing a little thinking, and I have an idea or two you might want to consider. May I come in?"

"Of course." She stepped aside with ready grace. "There's someone here I want you to meet, anyway."

Gabriel heard the barely concealed note of expectancy in her voice and almost winced. Samantha was about to pull another rabbit out of the hat, and this time he, himself, was going to be the grand surprise. He had time to wonder sardonically just how terrifically surprised Buchanan was going to be, and then Samantha was turning to make the introductions. Gabriel felt a pang of helpless protectiveness as he saw the fiercely satisfied expression lighting her eyes. Helpless because he couldn't protect and defend her in a way she would approve. He could only do it his way, and given the fact that he was dealing with Buchanan, she was going to feel a little battered by the time it was all over.

"Drew, this is Gabriel Sinclair. I knew you'd be interested in meeting him." Gabriel felt his arm taken in an unexpectedly possessive grasp. "Gabriel is the venture capitalist who is my partner in the restaurant deal."

Buchanan's gaze flickered rapidly over Gabriel, assessing and summarizing his opponent just as Gabriel had done earlier. Now they were even. Neither man offered a hand in greeting. Instead they both inclined their heads in polite acknowledgment of the open warfare which existed between them.

"I did wonder how Samantha scraped together enough cash to pick up on that option," Buchanan drawled rather idly.

"She's sharp," Gabriel murmured noncommittally.

"Thank you," Buchanan said, smiling broadly as he prepared to take the first lunge with the verbal sword. "I taught her everything she knows . . . and not just about business."

Gabriel sensed rather than heard Samantha's small, angry gasp, but he didn't divert his attention from the other man for a second. He did experience a mild surge of irritation, though. What did she think this kind of confrontation was going to be like? A polite exchange of masculine pleasantries over a glass of sherry? He had news for her: It was going to get a lot nastier.

"I understand," Gabriel said with an air of complacency as he led the way into the living room. "That explains a few of the gaps in her education. Naturally, I'm doing my best to eradicate some of the unfortunate misconceptions she arrived with when she came to my bed."

"Gabriel!" His name emerged as a mixture of fury

and dismay from her lips. He didn't look at her, having his hands full with Buchanan.

"I wasn't aware I had left her with any misconceptions," Drew said with a clinical glance at Samantha's whitening face. She was standing frozen in the doorway as the two men sank down across from each other in the overstuffed chairs.

"A few major ones, I'm afraid," Gabriel drawled, leaning forward to lace his fingers between his knees while he studied the other man intently. "Such as the notion that it's never quite as good for the woman as it is for the man. I think that I've managed to persuade Sam otherwise. Samantha," he applauded softly, "is a very fast learner."

Out of the corner of his eye Gabriel saw Samantha absorb the shock of the tactics he had applied to Buchanan. He knew she was finding herself speechlessly enraged in the face of such crude male savagery, but he also knew there was no choice. Buchanan had chosen the weapons, starting off by declaring a contest over which of them could claim Samantha. That Samantha herself undoubtedly did not wish to be claimed by either man was beside the point. God knew he was going to pay dearly later for putting her through the ordeal.

Buchanan's eyes were blank and cold as he made no effort at all to translate his smile to them. "Perhaps one of these days I'll get around to finding out just how much you've actually taught her."

"Ah, well, I'm afraid that won't be possible." Gabriel sighed with mock regret, glancing down at his loosely locked hands. "Samantha, it turns out, is a one-man woman. After s-s-she finds the right man, naturally." Damn it to hell! Why hadn't he planned that sentence ahead in his mind!

"And you think she's found the right man now?" Drew murmured. Gabriel knew from the gleam in his eyes that the other man had found the slight stammer very interesting. The last thing he wanted to do was betray any sort of weakness, and Buchanan was certainly the type to interpret such a shortcoming.

Time to draw this unpleasant scene to a conclusion. Gabriel nodded at the still-silent Samantha. "Ask her."

But the simple, challenging words proved to be the catalyst Samantha needed to unstick herself from the doorway. Gabriel saw the angry fire in her eyes as she came toward him, but it was the only indication of her emotional state. The rest of her was under complete control, right down to the cool little smile she gave him and the small intimate gesture of resting her fingertips on his shoulder as she came to a halt beside the chair. She looked at Buchanan.

"There's no need to ask, Drew. Gabriel is a little heavy-handed about such things at times, but he's quite right, you know. Our, uh, partnership is a complex one, to put it mildly. You really don't have a snowball's chance in Hades of seducing me."

"Your tastes have changed, love," Drew said far too casually.

"They've become more discriminating," she agreed easily.

Gabriel saw the flash of quickly controlled fury in

310

Buchanan's eyes and knew there was still a long way to swim to shore if Samantha was to be protected from this particular baracuda, but she, herself, had taken a major step toward constructing her own defense by picking up on his cues.

And for that he could only be grateful because in her current mood one took a risk by expecting her to be thinking rationally. Still, she seemed to have recognized how crucial it was to show no chips in the mortar of their combined front. Gabriel's fingers tightened momentarily as he thought again of the scene which would take place when Buchanan finally left. Samantha was going to tear very wide strips off him, he knew, and he wondered fleetingly whatever had happened to his status as an angel. It had been rather short-lived. Pity. He had been coming to enjoy it.

"Now that the fundamentals have been dealt with," Gabriel announced smoothly, "perhaps we can get down to business. You need that land on which our restaurant is sitting, Buchanan. The only question left is how badly do you want it."

"I'm sure you know the answer to that," Buchanan said softly, "or you would never have agreed to back Sam in this little revenge plot."

Gabriel felt Samantha's fingertips tremble slightly where they rested on his shoulder. "Your understanding of Samantha's little scheme is as off base as your understanding of other aspects of her character, but we'll let that pass. The problem at hand is money."

"Seven hundred and fifty thousand in ransom, I believe," the other man growled.

"Not a bad price, actually, considering what potential that chunk of real estate has for your development project." Damn Samantha and her decision to up the ante. It was going to be tricky negotiating back down to a more reasonable figure without making himself look weak and thereby jeopardizing the deal altogether. Perhaps he'd tear a few stripes off her sweet hide during the coming battle. Why should she have all the satisfaction? "Samantha and I are reasonable people, however. . . ."

"Meaning that's an asking price? Not a firm one?"

Again Gabriel felt Samantha's hand tremble on his shoulder, and he knew it was from frustrated anger not nervousness or fear. She didn't want to negotiate. She wanted to take Buchanan to the cleaners. But at least she had the sense to keep her mouth shut.

"We would, of course, be quite interested in hearing any offers." Gabriel watched the other man's eyes for any kind of information he could get.

"Try a hundred K. Double what you paid for the taco stand." Buchanan sat back and waited.

It was Samantha who spoke before Gabriel could reply. "Come now, Drew. You know very well you're not the only potential buyer out there."

"Who else is going to give you a hundred thousand dollars for that old restaurant?" he challenged.

"Someone else who knows you're eventually going to need that land and is willing to buy it off of us and turn around and sell it to you. Perhaps for *more* than seven hundred and fifty thousand."

"You'd sacrifice it at a hundred grand rather than negotiate with me for a higher figure?"

Gabriel took a hand. "Samantha is overstating the case a bit. We're willing to talk, Buchanan. But we're not going to let you have any bargains."

Buchanan studied the pair of them, the quiet, reserved man in the chair and the willful, temperamental woman who stood beside him. The unknown factor in this new equation was Gabriel Sinclair. Buchanan was too much a businessman to make a move before checking out all the unknowns. He got to his feet in an impatient movement.

"I'll let you know my best offer in a few days." He gave Samantha a level stare. "You're not going to have this all your own way, baby. And you should know me well enough to realize that." He flicked Gabriel a disdainful glance. "You're welcome to her, you know. Frankly, when her father said she'd lose her inheritance if she married me, she managed to lose her main appeal. Or perhaps you enjoy following a woman around like a tame lapdog as she hatches one crazy scheme after another?"

"Why, you bastard!" Samantha's tone was low and threatening.

Gabriel grabbed for her wrist as she started toward Buchanan. "Stop it, Samantha!" he grated, jerking her to a halt. But not before he'd spotted the curiously satisfied look which flared in Buchanan's eyes as the other man turned his back on both of them and strode out the front door.

"He called you a tame lapdog!" Samantha whirled to

face Gabriel as he held her wrist tethered between his fingers.

Gabriel arched one brow quizzically, examining the outrage in her eyes. "Is that why you went for him? Because he called me a lapdog? I thought it was because he deliberately insulted you."

"Well, he did! But he also managed to insult you, in case you didn't notice!"

"I've been called worse." He shrugged philosophically. So she'd taken offense on his behalf. That was a rather pleasant thought, especially considering that he wasn't exactly in her good graces at the moment. Then he wryly mocked himself for the thought. When a man found himself wanting a woman as badly as he wanted Samantha, he tended to seize at the smallest bits of comfort. Maybe he was becoming something of a lapdog!

"What are you smiling at?" Samantha freed her wrist, absently rubbing it as she stalked stiffly across the room.

"The possibility that Buchanan may be right. I do seem to find myself trailing around after you, trying to pretend I'm in charge of this nutty scheme and only succeeding in getting myself more mired down in the process."

"Are you going to stand there and insult me, too? On top of that horribly macho scene you just put me through?" She lifted her head, fixing him with an infuriated glare. "I will never forgive you for that, Gabriel. I would never have expected such locker room behavior from you!"

"Buchanan started it." He didn't really expect the

protest to make much headway, and he wasn't disappointed.

"We were supposed to be conducting high-level financial business with him! And you sit there and brag about your performance in bed!"

"Was I bragging?" he heard himself ask wistfully.

Samantha nearly choked on her own words as her outrage threatened to overwhelm her. "Don't you dare look at me like that!" she ordered fiercely.

"Like what?"

"Like some damn tame lapdog!"

"Which approach do you prefer?" he asked conversationally, starting toward her. "The lapdog or the locker room machismo?" He started toward her, knowing now exactly what he was going to do. Why should he stand here letting her rant and rave when he was the innocent party in all this?

She must have seen the intent in his eyes because she blinked quickly a couple of times in angry confusion, and then she took an instinctive step backward. "Gabriel?"

"Do you know what I'm going to do?" He paced closer, his resolve permeating every step. "I'm going to put a halt, even if it's only temporary, to all the temperament and outrage I've had to witness today. I'm going to buy myself a little peace and quiet. I deserve it, you know. I've got it coming, and you're going to give it to me. I am not an adaptable, easygoing sort of man, Samantha," he went on half-apologetically as he closed the distance between them. "I find that constant upsets in my life tend to make me long for moments of quiet and relaxation. I find I want to reestablish, if only for a short time, some illusion of being in control."

"Gabriel, I'm warning you, don't you dare touch me!" She backed another step, sliding toward the hall entrance.

Gabriel read and understood the confusion, astonishment, and anger in her expression. She was spoiling for a fight, and he was going to give her something else entirely. "Do you know the easiest way for a man to regain a feeling of being in control of a woman, Samantha?"

"Don't you threaten me with those caveman tactics!" she slung back defiantly, edging one step closer to the door.

"I'm not going to call it that. You, naturally, are free to call it anything you choose. One way or another, though, I'm going to restore a little of the natural order around here."

"We're supposed to be partners, for God's sake!"

There was something enormously satisfying about that look in her eyes, Gabriel decided as he slowly closed the distance between them. The wide tortoiseshell gaze reflected the beginnings of feminine wariness, perhaps even genuine fear, and he knew damn well it wasn't because she was actually afraid of him. That anxious expression reflected another kind of wariness, the kind that told him that what she really feared was her own response when he took her in his arms.

Very satisfying, Gabriel told himself again. He'd never had a woman watch him in quite that way. It fed the primitive side of his nature as nothing else could have done.

Only Samantha had the power to make him forget anyone could ever call him methodical and uninspired. When she looked at him as if she knew damn well she would find herself melting in his arms in a few more minutes, he felt as if he could handle anything, including her.

"Partners, Samantha? Your idea of a partnership is a bit vague, I'm afraid. Partners don't keep important information from each other. Partners don't start delicate negotiations on their own, tossing out an entirely different price tag than the one on which said partners had already agreed. Partners don't try playing dangerous little games of revenge without warning each other."

"I've explained all that! Gabriel, listen to me. I haven't tried to cheat you in any way."

"I know that. But you also haven't tried to be a real partner in this little endeavor, either, and you know it. You had all your private schemes going on the side, and I was just supposed to quietly finance the whole production without asking too many questions. That's not a partnership, Samantha. That's you trying to use me."

Guilt flashed into her eyes, and she bit down hard on her lower lip. "Oh, Gabriel, I'm sorry. I've already told you I'm sorry. But, damn it, we've been through all of this before. Be honest—if I had laid it all straight out in the open from the start, wouldn't you have backed away from the deal entirely? I even had to threaten to go to William Oakes. That's what it took to make you decide to back me. You couldn't bear the thought of losing out to Oakes!"

He reached her then, closing his hands around her shoulders just as she made one last futile dive for the doorway. Gabriel held her still, staring intently down into her anxious, upturned face.

"You little idiot," he rasped, his body already reacting strongly to the feel of her as she stood captive, "do you really believe I'm going through all this just to keep from losing a deal to Oakes? You must be crazier than I thought if you think that's why I've let myself get taken through the mill on this wild scheme of yours."

She stood rigidly beneath his hands, her head tilted with pride and defiance. "You've already said that sleeping with a woman isn't reason enough to do business with her either! So why are you here, Gabriel?"

"Beats the hell out of me. Charity work, I guess. For some asinine reason, the logic of which escapes me at the moment, I had this crazy notion that you needed a little protection from people like Oakes and Buchanan.".

"Protection!" The word seemed to inflame her. "I don't need any man's protection! I can damn well take care of myself. Do you think I could have built up this business of mine so fast and so successfully if I was incapable of taking care of myself? Do you think I could devise a plan like that Phoenix deal if I was incompetent? Do you think I could have lured you into backing me if I was really unable to handle my own business affairs? *Protection!*"

He saw the slap coming but stoically stood his ground, not making any attempt to block the short, hard blow.

As his face reddened beneath the imprint of her fingers, he tightened his hands on her shoulders. "Is it really such an insult to say I felt protective toward you?" he whispered harshly.

Already the remorse was filling her eyes. He saw her lips tremble slightly as she lifted her hand again to his face, this time to soothe the place she had struck. "Oh, Gabriel, damn it, I'm sorry. I always seem to be saying that to you, don't I? But it is an insult, you know!" she went on more firmly.

"Samantha . . . can't you admit that you need me in some way?"

Her face stilled, only the wide, searching gaze showing any sign of expression. And Gabriel couldn't read the one he did see there. A sense of rising frustration made him dig his fingers roughly into her shoulders.

"I would," Samantha said very carefully and with absolute precision as if she was just in the process of formulating the realization, "admit I needed a man *in some way* if he could admit he needed me . . ." She let the sentence trail off into nothingness as they continued to face each other.

She meant, Gabriel knew, that she would admit to her sexual need of him if he pushed her and if he was willing to give her the same assurance. It should have been enough. But it wasn't. He already knew he could make her want him with a passion that reached out to inflame them both. *But it wasn't enough!*

"You're so damn cautious, aren't you? For a woman who thinks nothing of jumping headlong into every-

319

thing else, you're one hell of a coward about taking a risk on me," he said bitterly.

Before the words were completely out of his mouth, she was impulsively crowding close, her hands sliding up his chest and around his neck. He felt the urgent, warm pliancy in her body and saw the sudden tenderness invade her eyes.

"You're the idiot in this partnership if that's what you believe," she murmured. "I've been taking risks on you since the day your name came up in my computer! It was a risk choosing you over William Oakes in the first place. With all the information about Oakes available, he was a much safer bet as a business partner than an unknown man in California who seemed to have become quite successful without making any of the usual waves!"

"Samantha," he began huskily, only to be silenced once more.

"And I took one hell of a chance letting you seduce me that first night. I know men don't see it that way, but I certainly do! Most women do. Furthermore, there was that ultimatum the following morning. You could so easily have ignored it, and I knew that. Then there was the risk of continuing to have an affair with the man who's supposed to be only my financial partner. A man who makes a very tricky partner in the first place because he keeps trying to be the one in charge. He does crazy things like saving my brother's neck, and then he demands vague midnight promises which aren't very clear in meaning until the chips are down and it's too late to back out of them. Oh, Gabriel, talk about putting everything on the line for a person!"

He drew a long, uneven breath, his hands sliding up to curve around her throat. She could probably feel the way his fingers were shaking, he thought fleetingly. "I seem to have gotten a rather one-sided view of this whole thing," he admitted throatily. "I hadn't looked at it from your viewpoint, honey. I guess we've both been taking some risks lately." It was a novel idea, he realized, this notion that Samantha had taken a chance on him. Women didn't behave that way about Gabriel Sinclair. There was nothing particularly risky about him. But Samantha didn't seem to know that.

That thought was almost as satisfying as the realization that she knew she would surrender in his arms. Gabriel groaned, shaping her face with his hard hands and crushing her mouth beneath his.

"Damn it to hell, sweetheart, the only time I feel as if I'm in control is when I have you lying underneath me and your legs are wrapped around mine!"

"That's a very chauvinistic attitude," she chided gently, but her fingers were gliding through his hair, and her mouth was soft and parted and only half an inch from his.

"I'm only a man." He was compelled to confide that as an excuse for the elemental way he felt about her. Carefully he reached up and removed her glasses, leaving her eyes wide and strangely vulnerable.

"Your halo does tend to slip now and then," she whispered as he nuzzled the soft skin behind her ear.

"Lord knows you provide enough provocation to keep

it permanently out of alignment!" He began a pattern of increasingly warm kisses down the length of her throat. It wasn't hard to sense that Samantha wanted to resist further, perhaps talk out some of the tensions which still hung between them. He felt her try to stiffen and pull herself back. But that was the last thing he could tolerate. Not now. Not when his body was already heavy with arousal and the desire was beginning to run like fire in his veins.

"Gabriel? Gabriel, we should talk a little more. What happened this morning was very serious."

"Yes." He didn't try to deny it, but he didn't cease his assault either. Let her talk. It would keep her busy while he was going about more important things such as undressing her. His hands found the buttons of the jonquil-yellow shirt she was wearing, and he began undoing them with great care.

"I . . . I don't want you to get the idea that all of our problems can be solved in bed," Samantha was saying urgently as he finished the last button and pushed it off her shoulders.

"No," he agreed absently. Hell, she wasn't wearing a bra. And she'd known he would be here this morning. She almost always wore a bra. A slow smile of raw pleasure touched his eyes. He flattened his palms above her small breasts and slowly moved them downward until the budding nipples were pressing into the centers of his hands.

"Gabriel, are you listening to me?" Her voice had a breathless quality to it, and he sensed she was having a hard time focusing on what she wanted to say. A shiver coursed through her as he slowly rotated his palms across the hardening berries which tipped her softness.

"I'm listening, sweetheart." And he was, to the sound of her quickening breath, to the edge of desire underlining her words, and to his own instincts which told him that in a few minutes she would be moaning her need of him.

"It's important that we understand each other. We've both made some serious mistakes in this partnership of ours."

"Yes." She sounded so intense, so anxious to get her point across. He slid his hands down the warm side of her ribs and then around to find the fastening of her jeans. Her fingertips fell to his shoulders, and she let them sink into the fabric of his shirt. It was an unconscious, kneading gesture which reminded him of a cat, and it fueled the growing heat in him.

"Gabriel," she whispered huskily, her lashes lowering as her passion mounted, "about what you said to Drew . . ."

"Ummm?" He had the jeans unzipped now and was pushing them slowly down her hips, loving the shape of her buttocks beneath his hands. As the denims fell to the floor at her feet, he followed, kneeling in front of her to taste the warm silk of her stomach. The rising scent of her desire told him all he needed to know. Deliberately he pushed his hand against the dampening heat between her legs. Above him she sucked in her breath, and suddenly she was bracing herself with her hands on his shoulders as her thighs trembled.

"You shouldn't have made it sound the way you did," she tried to say. He could hear her struggling to get the words out properly. "You shouldn't have . . . Oh, Gabriel!"

His name was a sigh as she tumbled to her knees in front of him, unable to stay on her feet any longer. He groaned as he caught her mouth with his own and pulled her naked form close to his own, opening his thighs to drag her between them.

"Don't you understand, Samantha?" he grated fiercely, cupping her buttocks and straining her into the aching hardness of him. "You belong to me now."

She didn't argue. She was beyond arguing, and he took advantage of the fact to push her gently down on the frayed Oriental carpet. With one hand he traced rough patterns on her breasts and stomach while he freed himself from his clothing. She writhed beneath his touch, reaching upward to pull him to her as soon as his slacks were off.

Still wearing his shirt, which he'd only managed to get unbuttoned, Gabriel came down on top of her. He knew a savage pleasure in the way she parted her legs for him, and then he felt the touch of her fingers on his manhood as she guided him to the heart of her desire.

His last coherent thought before the waves of sensual need engulfed them both was to wonder who was surrendering to whom.

Drew Buchanan gave the assignment to Jeff Ingram as soon as he walked in the door of the Buchanan building.

"I want to know everything you can find out on Gabriel Sinclair. Venture capitalist working on the West Coast. And I need it yesterday."

But the information he needed didn't come from Ingram; it came from Carol Galloway that night as she and Buchanan faced each other across a snowy tablecloth in an elegant, intimate restaurant that overlooked the harbor. Drew had only mentioned the name in passing as he gave her a brief, severely edited version of his trip to Seattle.

She sipped her Chardonnay thoughtfully as he talked, sensing the anger which lay beneath the polite facade. Whatever had occurred in Seattle had not been fully satisfactory. In a few minutes she learned why.

"Sinclair." She took another sip of wine and frowned beautifully. "Gabriel Sinclair. You say he's working on the West Coast? A venture capitalist?"

Buchanan watched her closely. "That's right."

"Not by any chance related to the Weston Sinclairs, is he? They had a son who, I believe, had a talent for money. The last I heard he'd left the family business and headed for California. That was a few years ago."

Buchanan couldn't believe his luck. "You know him?"

"I'm not sure. Dark, red-brown hair, a rather solid sort of build? Certainly lacking in the social graces, considering his background."

"And with a stammer?" Buchanan realized he was holding his breath.

Carol nodded slowly. "Now that you mention it, I believe there was some speech problem."

325

"What do you know about him?" Drew demanded quickly.

"Not much, really. His parents and mine were friends for a time. Weston Sinclair was in politics. We met them on the Washington party circuit. His son didn't really fit in. But he was married to a woman who dearly loved the Washington scene, and occasionally she dragged him along to some of the cocktail parties and such. Poor dear."

"Sinclair?" Buchanan frowned.

"No." Carol chuckled. "His wife. She longed so to take her place in society, and all her husband wanted to do was stay at home and manage the family business. I know she was bored to tears with him. Left him, as I recall, when everything fell apart for the Sinclairs. We never saw any of the family socially after that, of course, but I do recall hearing that after he'd salvaged what was left of the Sinclairs' business for his father, Gabriel had headed for the West Coast."

Buchanan only had one question. "What do you mean, after things fell apart?"

Carol arched an eyebrow in surprise. "Don't you remember all that hubbub about Weston Sinclair's connection to underworld heavies? Ruined his political career when they came to light. One has to be so careful these days," she added almost regretfully. "The public demands such a ridiculously high standard from its elected representatives. Once the media gets hold of some juicy tidbit, it's very difficult for a politician to recover."

"Tell me," Buchanan said slowly, "about the Weston

Sinclair scandal. I didn't follow the Washington scene that closely in those days."

"Well, I did." Carol smiled. "Can't help but do it when you're raised in a political household! Let me see, what do I remember? The facts, of course, would have been in the papers at the time."

"I'll have my assistant start digging through the library in the morning."

Carol nodded absently. "Now what else can I tell you?" she mused. "It's a little difficult to remember Gabriel Sinclair. My chief recollection, I'm afraid, was that he was quite dull."

"I assure you, at the moment, he is making my life anything but dull!" Buchanan reached for his wine and listened attentively to everything Carol Galloway could recall. Christ, he was lucky to have found her! The perfect politician's wife.

And Carol, who had been raised from infancy to be precisely that, spilled out everything she could remember about Weston Sinclair and his family. If there was one thing a survivor on the Washington social circuit learned in a hurry, it was to have a retentive ear for gossip. Careers were made or broken on gossip in that world. She had been only twenty at the time, but her parents had trained her well.

The man sitting across from her was going to provide her with her proper place, the position she'd been groomed for since infancy. She would no longer be the daughter but would be the wife of a prominent politician. A much more powerful position.

And Daddy would see that Drew became prominent.

Daddy liked Drew. Carol was astute enough to know that it was probably because the two men were so much alike.

Across from her, Drew contemplated how he would stop Samantha in her tracks, and then his imagination went farther. The little fool needed to be taught a lesson. When this was all over, he'd make sure she got it. No one, least of all an emotional little piece like her, was going to get away with trying to score off him. He'd give it a few months before he went after her. Give the relationship with Gabriel Sinclair a chance to cool off so that Sinclair wouldn't feel obliged to come to her rescue. And that relationship was bound to cool eventually. Carol said the man was as dull as dishwater, and Samantha was anything but. She'd grow tired of him. Or else, Drew told himself with savage humor, Sinclair would grow tired of her antics.

One way or another, Samantha would probably be on her own in a few months time, and then she would be vulnerable.

Destroying her would be a pleasure. Buchanan smiled to himself. An interesting exercise in power.

CHAPTER TEN

"The important thing, Gabriel," Samantha announced two mornings later as he prepared to leave for California, "is that you don't get the idea you can control me with sex."

"No," he agreed in a rather vague tone as he packed his shaving kit with immaculate precision.

Samantha watched the careful process of packing as Gabriel practiced it and hid an indulgent smile. "I mean, I wouldn't want you getting the notion that anytime we disagree you can simply march in here and . . . and . . ."

"And lay you down on your Oriental rug and make love to you until you stop arguing?" He straightened abruptly, zipped the shaving kit shut, and turned to face her. His eyes were gleaming with suppressed laughter, a laughter that was entirely too wicked for Samantha's peace of mind. "I wouldn't think of it!"

"Darn you." She sighed, throwing herself into his arms and blissfully letting his strength absorb the impact.

"You're impossible. And I wish you didn't have to go back to California today."

He cradled her head with his hand, holding her close. "I wish I didn't have to go back, either. But I've got a couple of things which have to be watched down there. Interesting as this deal of ours has proven to be, it is not my only ongoing project."

"Do any of your other ongoing projects involve women?" she mumbled into his shirt. She inhaled the scent of him, storing up the intimate taste of it in her mind.

"Would you be jealous if they did?" he said.

She could sense the expectant waiting in him. "Yes!"

He seemed inordinately pleased by the confession. She felt the chuckle deep in his chest. It was good to feel the laughter in him. When she'd first met him, Gabriel hadn't been the type to laugh very often. Samantha experienced a pleasant satisfaction at being able to bring out that particular emotion.

"Samantha," he whispered, holding her so that he could look down into her face. "There's no one else. You know that, don't you?"

She nodded mutely. The thing about Gabriel Sinclair was that you could trust him implicitly.

"And there's no one else for you, either," he concluded evenly.

She shook her head, again without saying a word.

"When I come back from California the day after tomorrow, we'll have to talk about that," he stated.

"Talk about what?" she demanded softly.

"Honey, I can't keep running up and down the coast

every week," he affirmed dryly. "We need to discuss a more convenient arrangement."

"Gabriel . . . ?"

"I've got to go, honey, or I'll miss the ferry. If I miss the ferry, I'll miss my plane." He pulled her close and kissed her hard on the mouth. "And if I miss my plane, I'll be in trouble down in California. Things are at the critical stage down there with a new computer design firm I'm backing. I'll be back the day after tomorrow. Then we'll sit and wait to hear from Buchanan. He should be making up his mind to play the game our way by then."

"You don't think he'll call sooner than that?"

"I doubt it. He'll want us to sweat a bit. It's the only weapon he's got left. If I'm wrong, though, and he does call, just find out what he's offering and tell him you'll consult with me. Then hang up and call me, understand? I don't want you bargaining with him on your own!"

"I don't want you giving away that restaurant, either," she retorted. "We can get the seven hundred and fifty thousand out of him if we just hold our breath longer than he can."

"Honey, in a situation like this things go much more smoothly if we give a bit. Believe me, I know what I'm doing."

"If you say so," she agreed dubiously.

"I say so." He kissed her again, this time on the forehead, and reluctantly put her aside to pick up his overnight bag. "I'd better be going," he said, groaning.

She walked him out to the car, watching morosely as he climbed inside and started the engine. "Good-bye,

Gabriel," she murmured wistfully, realizing just how reluctant she was to see him go. "Hurry back."

"I'll do that." He smiled. "And this time I hope there won't be any major surprises waiting. I'm not sure I could take it."

"Nonsense," she assured him cheerfully. "You can handle anything, Gabriel."

He grinned, that fleeting, wolfish grin, and then he put the car in gear and drove sedately toward the main road. Samantha watched him until he was out of sight and then turned and slowly walked back into the house.

A more convenient arrangement. What was he going to suggest? That she move down to California, or that he move up here? Samantha mulled the idea over and knew it made her uneasy. The affair with Gabriel Sinclair was the most exciting thing that had ever happened to her. He aroused passions she wouldn't have dreamed existed and he elicited softer emotions in her as well.

But did she really want to live with him? It sounded very much like marriage, and marriage was a state she had been so determined to avoid since the disaster with Buchanan. Her mother was right. A woman could only be really free as long as she didn't commit herself to marriage.

The relationship with Gabriel was too new, too fragile, to warrant such a serious step as moving in with him. Or was it simply that, deep down, she feared that step because of what it would cost her?

Gabriel would be as possessive as any husband. He would insist on getting involved in her business. She was sure of that. He felt she needed a little polish and professional guidance. Scratch that "little." He felt she needed a hell of a lot, and knowing him, he'd see to it that she got it even if he had to force it on her.

No, if she moved in with Gabriel, nothing would remain the same. He would invade every aspect of her life. And she would insist on fighting him every step of the way, especially when it came to running her own business.

Wouldn't it be a hundred times smarter and safer to keep the affair long distance? At least for the foreseeable future? They needed time to work out some of the bugs in their relationship.

That's what she would tell him, Samantha decided as she closed the door behind her and started down the hall to the back parlor. She would tell him they needed a little more time.

The unexpected call from Drew Buchanan, the one Gabriel had assured her wouldn't come so soon, came the next morning.

It changed Samantha's whole life.

Buchanan didn't even give her a chance to adjust to the situation. He had seen the look in Samantha's eyes when she had stood beside Sinclair that morning in her living room. He'd seen the way she'd leaped to the other man's defense when he'd called Sinclair a lapdog. And he knew which buttons to push when it came to dealing with Samantha Maitland, and he pushed them without any compunction.

"Call it off, Sam. Take the hundred grand I'm willing

to give you and call it even. There aren't going to be any negotiations."

She heard the chill certainty in his voice, and something inside her panicked.

"What are you talking about?" she managed coolly. But she knew disaster had struck. Drew wouldn't be sounding this positive if he hadn't found another weapon. Oh, God, what had he come up with now, and would she and Gabriel be able to find a way to deal with it? Of course they would, she told herself in the next breath. Her fingers tightened on the receiver.

"I'm talking about Gabriel Sinclair being Weston Sinclair's son. His only son. I'm talking about a scandal which erupted a few years ago when it came to light that Weston Sinclair was hanging out with mobsters. I'm talking about a political career in ruins and how that scandal could very easily be resurrected if you and your lapdog go through with trying to take me for seven hundred and fifty thousand dollars. And if you don't think it will be easy to make it sound as though the son has followed in the footsteps of the father, you're naïve, Sam. Even more naïve than I thought."

"You're lying!"

"You want the facts and figures? I've got them all right here in front of me. Sure you want to hear them? They're pretty brutal, Sam. Your partner's father really made a mess of things. Should have covered his tracks a lot more carefully. Consorting with known underworld figures, questionable business contracts, hints of payoffs, you name it."

"You're slipping." She forced a lightness into her

voice she did not feel. "You can't possibly hurt Gabriel with that kind of old news."

"Want to bet?" Buchanan was smiling on the other end of the line. Samantha could almost see that cold, hard smile. "Not only can I resurrect all the mud surrounding his father, which certainly wouldn't do Weston Sinclair any good now that he's finally back on his feet, but it would be damn easy to give the Arizona papers the impression that the old "family friends" are still helping out the Sinclairs' son and heir. Call it off, Sam, or I'll smear your backer's name all over Phoenix. It sure as hell won't do his career any good, will it?"

Samantha thought with horror about Gabriel's friend Emil Fortune. At this point even Drew Buchanan probably didn't realize how lethal a weapon he held. If he did reopen the old scandal and imply that Gabriel was involved with his father's questionable friends, how long would it be before his relationship with Emil Fortune came to light? Even if Gabriel could escape the mud which had once been slung at his father, how could he ever explain away his relationship to Fortune?

Furthermore, by involving Gabriel in Eric's mess, Samantha had unwittingly caused Gabriel's association with Fortune to become even more awkward.

Shit!

"You really are one hell of a bastard, aren't you, Drew?"

He laughed on the other end of the line. "And you're a soft-headed little fool who won't have the heart to let her lover take the flak off this scandal. I'll crucify him, Sam. I'll nail him to the wall, and it will ruin him. No one will do business with him again. No reputable concern will want to borrow money from a possible mob associate. No one except the type who normally deal with that kind of lowlife anyway. He won't be a venture capitalist any longer, Sam. He'll be a frigging loan shark. Quite a comedown, hmmm?"

Samantha slammed down the phone, shaking from head to foot. As quickly as she did it, it wasn't quick enough to prevent her from hearing Drew's satisfied laughter on the other end of the line.

She paced the house for the next hour, frantically searching for a way out. But there was not a way out. Buchanan had neatly closed the trap, and the only way she could free herself was to sacrifice Gabriel.

Sacrificing Gabriel was unthinkable.

Samantha came to a halt beside the potted palm in the living room, staring blindly out into the Seattle mist. Unthinkable.

She couldn't hurl Gabriel Sinclair to the wolf because she loved Gabriel. Loved him far more than she loved the idea of proving herself in the eyes of her mother. Loved him far more than proving to Buchanan that he couldn't treat her the way he had three years ago and get away with it.

Her taste for revenge was as nothing next to her commitment to Gabriel. She had more or less coerced him into her life, and once there he had proceeded to dominate it. Compared to her feelings for him, revenge played a pretty poor second. Samantha closed her eyes on that thought and then opened them again, suddenly able to see everything very clearly. The only really crucial factor in this whole mess now was saving Gabriel. The decision was made with an abrupt and absolute conviction, the kind of intuitive certainty which left no room for doubt. She would protect Gabriel whatever the cost.

Only yesterday she had been planning ways of talking her angel into giving the relationship more time. With all the time in the world ahead of them, it had been easy to be hesitant, to want to be sure. Samantha shook her head wryly.

Buchanan had just taught her that there was no question of her feelings for Gabriel Sinclair. None at all.

With grim resolution she picked up the phone and asked for the number of the Buchanan Group's headquarters in Miami. When Drew eventually came on the line, she didn't give him a chance to speak.

"You can have the restaurant for a hundred thousand," she told him dully.

"I thought you'd see reason. I'll have my lawyers draw up the purchase agreement this afternoon. Look at it this way, Sam. I could have made you hand it over for virtually nothing. I'm being generous under the circumstances. For old times' sake."

"You're going to rot in hell Drew." She put the phone gently down in its cradle, and then she lifted the receiver again and dialed her travel agent.

"No, I'm not going back into that damn spa! Just get me on a plane to Santa Barbara. I'll arrange my own accommodations for the night."

News like this had to be explained in person. She wasn't going to tell Gabriel over the phone what she had just done. It was far too complicated. And she couldn't stand to wait until the next day, when he would be returning to Seattle. She would go crazy overnight.

The travel agent phoned back a few minutes later to tell her she was booked on an early afternoon flight to California.

The house on the coast was just as she remembered it. Secluded, sheltered by its heavy landscaping, open only to the sea, it provided Gabriel with the peace and the solitude he craved.

She had brought him very little of either, Samantha thought sadly as she parked the car in the drive and sat staring at the iron gates for a moment. He'd been awfully patient with her, considering how little he cared for upsetting factors and surprises. She'd blown his placid routine to smithereens, and she had almost shattered his hard-won privacy for good. If Buchanan had gone through with his threats, Gabriel would have gone through hell watching his parents' life vandalized again by the press and he, himself, would have lost the low profile he had worked so hard at maintaining. He would suddenly have a reputation hanging over his head, one that would undoubtedly have crippled his career.

And it would have been all her fault.

Samantha shivered at the thought and climbed out of the car. She was almost at the gate, preparing to ring the bell, when he opened the front door and stared at her in astonishment.

"Samantha! What in the world . . . ?"

He started toward her, and Samantha took in the sight of him, loving every solid, conservative, stubborn inch. Tears pricked at her eyes, and her lips quivered as she clung to the iron gate with both hands.

"Oh, Gabriel, I'm so sorry. . . ."

"Oh, s-s-shi . . . shi . . . Damn it to hell! Samantha, I warned you. I can't take much more of this. What the hell is going on this time?" He flung open the gate, and Samantha almost went with it, remembering at the last minute to release her grasp on the curving bars.

And then she was in his arms, holding him fiercely, whispering his name over and over again as she buried her face against the solid reassuring warmth of his chest. His wonderful, huge hands soothed her with infinite care, threading through her hair and massaging her tense shoulders.

His words, however, were anything but soothing. "Jesus, woman! Let me have it quickly. The waiting is killing me!"

"I sold the restaurant to Buchanan for a hundred thousand."

There was a suspended moment of total shock from the man holding her, and then his voice came in a low snarl unlike anything she had ever heard from him in the past. *"You did what?"*

She was seized by the arms and held far enough away from him so that his gaze could burn into her. Samantha swallowed rapidly, knowing the moments of comfort had evaporated.

"I had no choice, Gabriel. Buchanan pulled the one trick he knew would work on me." She attempted a small, shaky smile, pleading for understanding with her eyes.

But there was no understanding in Gabriel's expression, only cold, implacable anger. "What trick?"

"You."

"*Me!*" He looked thunderstruck. "Samantha, what the devil are you talking about?"

"He knows, Gabriel," she whispered. "Somehow he found out about your father and the scandal a few years ago. He knew everything, and he was going to resurrect the whole mess and give it to the Arizona papers."

"Oh, my God!" He shook his head dazedly, and then he shook her. "Samantha, you folded because of that threat?"

"What else could I do?" she asked simply. "He knew so much that could hurt you and your family. What if he'd dug farther and found out about your friendship with Emil Fortune? Don't you see? We're lucky to be out of it with the hundred K."

"You spent three years plotting this deal!"

"I wasted a lot of time, didn't I?" She half-smiled. "No, I take that back. If I hadn't gone after it at all, I would never have found you."

"Was finding me so important?" he asked unsteadily.

"Finding you is the most important thing that's happened to me out of this whole mess, Gabriel," she told him gently. "I love you. I realized that this morning when Drew called. I suddenly knew what was really important in this whole mess."

He uttered an inarticulate sound and hauled her back against him, wrapping her so tight and close she knew

she would feel the ache in her muscles when he re
leased her.

"Samantha!" He buried his face in her hair, and she
felt the tremor that went through him. "Samantha. Oh,
my God, lady, you are the only person on earth with
the power to completely traumatize me. Life was so
peaceful before you came along."

"I know. I know, Gabriel. I'm sorry."

"Samantha, if you apologize one more time I s-s-shall
probably beat you. Just s-s-shut up, will you?"

"Our partnership would never have worked anyway.
You're always giving me orders. It's just as well the
business arrangement between us is over. Sooner or
later I would have gotten tired of taking orders."

"You never did take them very well. Samantha, are
you aware of what you have done?"

"Yes."

"Did you take into consideration the thought that you
might have called me for a consultation before agreeing
to Buchanan's price?"

"No."

"Did it occur to you that Buchanan made the threat
to you instead of me because he knew I might not go
along with it?" Gabriel grated.

"Yes. Drew is very adept at reading people. He knew
you would have stuck by me to the end, regardless of
the threat."

"But you, on the other hand, caved in at once. Because you love me." He sounded as if he were trying to
get all the facts straight, to put all the pieces of the
puzzle together before dealing with the issue at hand.

ypical Gabriel Sinclair approach to a problem. Methodcal.

"Yes."

"Samantha, was I really more important to you than having your revenge on Drew Buchanan? More important than proving yourself your mother's daughter?"

"Yes."

"I can't take it in. That you gave up everything you've worked for during the past three years for the sake of what you feel for me." He hesitated, as if mulling it all over in his head. "Oh, hell, it was that damn promise I made you swear that night, wasn't it? Oh, Samantha, I'm the one who's sorry. How could you think I ever meant that oath to force you to give up everything you've been working for?"

"I didn't even think about the promise. I just knew I couldn't do anything to hurt you." She lifted her hands to cradle his face. "Stop worrying about it, Gabriel. I'm not going to regret this. Some things I'm absolutely sure of. And I'm sure that I'll never regret falling in love with you. Although," she added as a whimsical afterthought, "you may very well regret it. Darling Gabriel, I'm not exactly right for you, am I?"

"You're absolutely perfect for me." He breathed heavily. "And you must know by now that I love you." He wrapped her closer, molding her to him as if afraid that she might somehow evaporate.

"Do you, Gabriel?" Samantha surrendered to the enveloping embrace. "Do you really love me?"

"Come inside and I'll show you."

She laughed up at him, happier than she had ever

been in her life. "Are you going to make mad, passio
ate love to me on the floor in the living room?"

"No, I'm going to make you the best pasta primavera
you've ever tasted in your life!" he vowed, pulling her
against his side and starting toward the door.

"And then?" she prompted happily.

"And then I will make love to you. But not on the
floor in the living room. This time I think we'll use the
bed."

The thing about Gabriel Sinclair, Samantha reminded
herself for the hundredth time, was that you could trust
him completely. And he'd said he'd loved her.

A long time later, after the incomparable pasta and
the even more incomparable lovemaking, Gabriel lay
with Samantha cradled in his arms and gazed thoughtfully up at the ceiling of his bedroom. Tucked in his
arms, she slept peacefully, her leg entwined with his
and the tip of one breast pressing lightly against his
chest.

She loved him.

He still couldn't quite believe his luck. He realized
vaguely that he must have fallen in love with her almost
from the beginning. What else could account for his
crazy actions? Where was the line between desire and
love? Not that it mattered. He'd crossed it long ago
with Samantha.

She'd walked away from three years of stalking and
planning just because of that bastard Buchanan's threats
to the man she loved.

Sweet idiot.

o, that wasn't fair, he told himself indulgently. There s nothing lacking with her brainpower. She simply ad a set of principles that sometimes got in her way and a sense of loyalty which did the same. He'd seen what she would do out of loyalty. Her determination to help Eric was evidence and so was her confession the other morning about the real reason behind her plot against Buchanan.

He knew he could trust her. But he hadn't dared to dream that the mutual trust they shared would grow into love. He'd had no right to expect so much.

He shifted slightly, rolling over onto his side. Samantha mumbled a sleepy protest and snuggled more closely against him. For a long moment he studied her as she lay beside him tangled in shadows and sheets. She was a woman he would be able to trust for the rest of his life.

He knew in that moment that he would do anything for her. She was truly his, and he would take care of her, even when she didn't particularly want to be taken care of. A smile edged the line of his mouth as he considered what living with Samantha was going to be like.

But there were other matters to be cleared up first before he informed Samantha that she was moving in with him.

"Samantha," he whispered huskily.

She didn't stir.

"Samantha," he tried again, putting a hand on her hip.

"Mmmmmf."

"Honey, wake up. We have to talk." He lightly patted the intriguing curve of her rear.

She ignored him. Very carefully Gabriel changed the light pat into a small slap.

"Must you always resort to Neanderthal tactics?" she grumbled, flopping over on her back and opening her eyes.

"It does have the merit of getting your attention."

"Well, you've got it." She yawned, one hand straying into the tangle of hair on his chest, giving it a playful tug.

"Ouch! Now what was so important that you had to wake me up in the middle of the night?"

The smile faded from his mouth to be replaced by a more serious expression. "Samantha, we're going to have to clean up a few loose ends before we can forget Buchanan."

"What loose ends? I sign the papers, and he hands over a check for a hundred thousand dollars. That's it." She wrinkled her nose at his sober look. "I know you're not going to make much money on this deal, Gabriel, but at least you'll recover your investment, and if we split the other fifty thousand, we'll still make twenty-five apiece. I think I'll use part of my half to repaint the front porch," she added thoughtfully.

"Which front porch? Yours or mine?" he asked cautiously.

"Mine, naturally. Yours doesn't need it. Besides, you don't actually have a front porch. You have a deck."

"Samantha," he said, sighing, "are you planning on staying on that island of yours?"

He felt her sudden stillness. "Were you going to suggest a different arrangement?" she finally asked with seeming carelessness.

"You know damn well I'm going to ask you to move in with me. No"—he moved his head once in a short negative—"not *ask, tell* you to move in with me. I'm not going to commute to Seattle every couple of days from here. Don't look so damn stricken, Samantha."

"I don't know, Gabriel. Maybe it would be better if we did commute, at least for a while. We're so different in so many ways. I'm liable to drive you crazy with the way I do things."

"Don't worry, I'll take care of the cooking." He chuckled.

"It's not just that. I have a business to run, and I want to run it in my own way. Can you honestly see yourself keeping your hands off it? Or are you going to want to 'guide' me?"

His stomach tightened as he realized she was seriously concerned. "For Christ's sake, honey, what are you afraid of? That I'll take over completely?"

She hesitated and then said wryly, "The thought did cross my mind. For my own good, of course."

He stared at her. "I can't believe this! You're actually afraid I'll try to run your business for you?"

"Well, you've made it clear that you don't think too much of my business ability," she muttered.

"I think you were in over your head taking on Buchanan, yes! Most people would be! That doesn't mean I don't have a lot of respect for your ability to run your information service and run it well. Samantha, I never quarrel with success, and anyone who can get a business on its feet and running at a profit in only a couple of years with very little capital investment has my complete admiration. Don't you think I, of all people, know what the odds are against the beginning entrepreneur? I've made it my life's work to finance people like that, remember? I know competency when I see it."

She looked at him in confusion. "But you didn't want to finance me on the Buchanan deal."

"That's different. As you've just discovered," he added deliberately. "People like Buchanan play rough, and you do have your soft points, sweetheart."

"Soft *point*." She sighed. "You."

"Apparently." He grinned lovingly. "Not that I'm complaining. Which does bring us to the reason I woke you."

"Ummm?" It was obvious she was still mulling over what he had said about her business ability.

Gabriel gave her an impatient shake, trying to get her full attention. "Honey, I made a bad error in judgment that morning when I made it clear to Buchanan that you belonged to me."

"It was rather disgustingly possessive!"

"It also happens to be true!" he retorted. "Unfortunately the tactic backfired on me. I had meant to give Buchanan the idea that you had protection, namely me. But he immediately discovered that I wasn't your shield, I was your weak point. You have to hand it to the bastard; he's as sharp as they come."

"Well, it doesn't matter now as long as we hand over

the restaurant. Don't worry, Gabriel, you and your family are safe," she assured him quickly.

He studied her, feeling a rush of affection and desire and indulgent impatience. "What would you say," he asked carefully, "if I were to tell you that Buchanan can't hurt me?"

She gave him a startled glance. "But he could if he started spreading rumors and if he were to find out about Emil Fortune. . . ."

Gabriel shook his head. "Samantha, there's no way he could smear me in the Arizona papers without smearing himself as well. Don't you see? If he implies I'm involved with organized crime, then he also implies he's dealing with organized crime. Didn't you get suspicious when he volunteered to give you twice what you paid for that damn restaurant? If he'd really been sure of himself, he would have made you hand it over at a loss! He just wanted out and figured the fastest way to do that was threaten me and then follow it up with enough money to partially placate you."

Her eyes widened. "Oh, my God, Gabriel, I never thought of it that way. You're right. If he starts spreading rumors in the Arizona papers about you, then people are bound to start wondering why he was dealing with you in the first place. Very bad for the image, and heaven knows Buchanan has to watch out for his image!"

That caught his attention. "Really? Any particular reason other than keeping the corporation name clear?"

"He's got his eye on a political career," she told him absently, still thinking over what he had just said. "Hell, Gabriel, I really let myself get hustled by that con man, didn't I? Again." She bit her lip. "But what about the threats against your family, though? You wouldn't want to see their names dragged through the mud again."

"Honey, there's nothing older than ten-year-old scandals. Buchanan would never be able to find a newspaper interested enough to reprint the story. Not unless there was some tie-in to a current scandal, and that would mean the Arizona deal. And once he involves the Arizona deal . . ."

"He involves himself," she concluded in dismay, rolling off him to throw herself back against the pillows in disgust. She stared morosely at the ceiling. "What a fool I was. What a complete idiot!" Her hand clenched at her side. "And if you say 'I told you so,' I swear, I'll . . ."

He stopped the words with a gentle hand across her mouth. "Samantha, how can I call you an idiot or a fool when this whole mess wrung a confession of love out of you? You could have gone on in this relationship for months before committing yourself that far, couldn't you? You're so damned cautious about relationships! And thanks to your mother, I'll probably have a hell of a job talking you into marriage!"

"Marriage!" she mumbled from under his palm. The tortoiseshell eyes filled with astonishment as she pushed his hand away. "*Marriage!* Gabriel, how can you talk about marriage? We've only known each other a couple of weeks, and I'm not really the marrying sort, anyway. I've explained that—"

"You've explained that you don't consider marriage

one of life's necessities," he agreed dryly. "And neither do I. Except in certain circumstances."

"Such as?" she demanded forebodingly.

"Such as when I'm taking on the task of trying to handle a woman who's part amazon, part businessperson, and part soft, sexy female. I think marriage is the third link in the chain I need to hold you."

"And what, may I ask, are the other two?" she hissed.

"I figure I can hold the soft, sensuous female with sex. She seems totally unable to resist me after I get her flat on her back," he drawled outrageously.

"Such arrogance!" Samantha breathed.

"Ummm. And I think I've got the businesswoman under control with that midnight promise of loyalty I had her agree to honor."

"You don't think a businesswoman might conveniently forget an oath like that on occasion?" she dared.

"Not one descended from Victor Thorndyke or Vera Maitland."

"You've never met either of them!" she protested.

"I've met their daughter. I know all I need to know about both of them from watching her in action."

"I see," Samantha said far too pleasantly. "And the amazon? How are you going to hold her?"

"That's where marriage comes in," he explained equably. "Nothing like marriage to tie down an amazon."

"I've got news for you. Amazons don't get married," Samantha informed him with relish. "They kidnap men and use them for certain limited purposes."

"But in this case, I've reversed that process, haven't I? And this kidnapped amazon is going to stay kidnapped.

She can, of course, use me for certain limited purposes. I'm a generous man."

"Gabriel, you're finally beginning to make some sense in this conversation," Samantha whispered admiringly as she put her arms around his neck and drew him down to her. "Come here and let me use you for certain limited purposes."

She felt his body begin to awaken once more, pushing against her with familiar demand. Under his hand her nipple stirred eagerly in its burrow. There was something else she wanted to talk about, Samantha realized, something which had begun teasing her thoughts earlier when they had discussed Buchanan's own vulnerability. Ah, well, it could be handled just as easily in the morning. Right now there were more important things in life.

But long after Gabriel had drifted off to sleep beside her, Samantha lay awake, turning the new idea over and over in her mind, trying to examine it for obvious flaws. It wasn't until she decided there weren't any that she finally snuggled into Gabriel and went to sleep.

The next morning as she let him serve her buckwheat cakes and fruit topped with an incredible honey-yogurt mixture, Samantha carefully explained what she intended to do. Gabriel turned from the stove to stare at her in astonishment.

"You're serious, aren't you?" he finally growled, half in admiration, half in dismay. He brought the plate of buckwheat cakes to the table.

"I'm not going to let him get away with it, Gabriel.

He's threatened both of us. The man needs a lesson, and I've finally found a way to see he gets it."

"You're talking about revenge, not business."

"I'm big on revenge, remember? And I have a growing impression that you're not always so angel-pure in your motives, either."

He shot her a thoughtful, hooded glance, and it occurred to Samantha that the rosy-cheeked modern version of angels, the kind one saw on Christmas cards, really bore very little resemblance to the original model. The originals tended to carry flaming swords and wielded catastrophic power. They were quite capable of avenging wrongs and generally did so with devastating impact.

"Why are you smiling at me like that?" Gabriel demanded abruptly.

"I was thinking about avenging angels. You're furious with Buchanan for the way he used you to get to me, aren't you?"

"Let's just say I don't approve of the way the man does business."

"Interested in my plan?" she taunted gently.

"I hate to admit it, because it's as good as admitting that you've managed to corrupt my normal approach to business, but, yes, I am. Frankly, it might also be a way to take out a little insurance," Gabriel said slowly.

"Insurance!"

"You remember how fond I am of insurance?" He smiled at her crookedly.

"Why do you need insurance against Buchanan?"

"Because he's quite capable of casually crushing your

new business in a year or so as a way of teaching you a lesson."

"Destroy Business Intelligence? But how? Why?"

"The how is easy enough, and even I probably wouldn't be able to protect you. If he starts a campaign to ruin your reputation for reliability and analysis, he might very well succeed. A few words in the ears of the honchos of some of your most important clients. A few comments to the business press. Rumors. Innuendoes about possible conflict of interest situations in which you sell information gained on one company or another. Hell, I don't know what he'd do, but I do know he's capable of it, and I think your nasty little scheme has a good chance of tying his hands." Gabriel nodded to himself as he forked up a large bite of buckwheat cake. "A very good chance. Okay, honey, let's spread it all out on the table and take a good look."

"We're talking about very hardball, here, Gabriel," she felt obliged to warn. But the excitement was bubbling in her, and she thought she sensed it behind the deceptive placidity of his gaze. They looked at each other for a long moment.

"How do you know," Gabriel said gently, "that I don't normally play the game this way?"

"Because you're not the type!" she exclaimed in surprise.

"Maybe I've learned a few things hanging out with you?" He grinned.

"I'm not sure I understand you this morning, Gabriel. I thought I'd have a heck of a job talking you into this. I've never seen you quite this way before."

"You've never seen me in a lot of ways, Samantha," he told her gently. "Including at work. I think, because you handled me so easily when you tried to induce me to finance you, that you somehow got an erroneous impression of the way I normally do business. Normally," he emphasized sardonically, "I don't let myself get pressured with such tactics as blackmail."

Samantha sucked in her breath, still startled by the unexpected edge of steel she had uncovered. "You let me get away it," she finally pointed out cautiously.

He grinned again, this time showing lots of teeth. "I have been well compensated."

"Gabriel, I think your flaming sword is showing," Samantha told him very seriously, aware that she did not know all there was to know about him and even more aware that she would have her hands full holding her own in the future. "Under certain circumstances you could make me very nervous."

"We're even, honey. Sometimes you scare the daylights out of me, too." He went to work on the last of the buckwheat cakes. "So what's our first step in your little plan?"

"Get a little professional expertise. I'm going to call in that wild-eyed computer maniac of a half brother of mine. He can tell us whether or not we can get the information we need, I think."

"He can use your computer to do the job," Gabriel said thoughtfully. "Why don't you phone him after breakfast and have him meet us at your place in Seattle?"

"You really think my idea has possibilities?" she queried with just a trace of hesitancy. In a partnership, one liked to have the enthusiastic support of the other partner, Samantha realized.

"Believe me, Samantha, if there's one thing I learned from my father, it's how vulnerable a politician can be, especially one with Buchanan's instincts and temperament. There's no way he could have stayed clean for the past few years. I think you're right. All we need to do is find the dirt."

Samantha shivered, staring at Gabriel as if he'd made the transition from angel to devil in one easy step. "I don't think I would like to have you for an enemy, Gabriel Sinclair."

"You don't," he retorted. "You have me as a friend. And as a lover."

"And as a business partner." She chuckled.

"One of life's more stable relationships."

Avenging angels, Samantha decided, were far more interesting and a great deal more dangerous than one would have supposed.

Two days later at one A.M. in the morning, Samantha carried coffee into the back parlor of her old house. The room was lit by the eerie glow of the computer console screen, and illuminated in the soft glare were the two men who had sent her in search of coffee.

Her brother sat hunched before the keyboard, entering commands with the intuition and skill of a born genius. He was so deeply involved in what he was producing on the screen that he didn't even bother to glance up when Samantha entered.

Gabriel, who was stretched out in the chair beside

ric, his feet propped carelessly on the desk and his
shirt opened at the throat, did look up, and he also
smiled fleetingly.

"Did you make it exactly the way I told you?" He
took a mug from her hand and sipped experimentally.

"After all the junk food you two have eaten this
evening, you're not likely to notice the bouquet!" she
retorted. "I would never have believed I'd see the day
when you'd stoop to eating frozen pizza, Gabriel. And
look at you, you're positively disarrayed!" she added,
eyes gleaming as she took in his wrinkled shirt, tousled
hair, and casual sprawl.

"The things a man will do for a woman," Gabriel
murmured comfortably.

"Getting closer, Eric?" Samantha asked.

"I've found the file on the zoning stuff," Eric mumbled absently, his attention so glued to the screen that
he didn't notice the coffee Samantha set down beside
him.

"We don't want the main file, we want some other,
buried file on the same subject," Gabriel said quietly.

"Are you actually inside the Buchanan computers?"
Samantha asked in awe as she sat down next to Gabriel
and stared at her brother's hunched form.

"That part was easy. I simply dialed up the Buchanan computers on your telephone. You're gong to
have one hell of a phone bill, though." Eric chuckled,
never taking his eyes off the screen. "I've been in
contact for over three hours."

"This is so illegal," Samantha breathed shakily.

"It's a blast," Eric corrected her, entering anoth command which brought up more files of information.

"The fact that other people's computers can be searched long-distance by folks like Eric, here, is definitely a security flaw," Gabriel observed calmly, sipping at his coffee. "But useful."

"Aren't there any safeguards?" Samantha asked uneasily.

"Sure," Eric responded. "Lots of them. All kinds of electronic safeguards. That's what makes it interesting. It's a real challenge to get beyond them."

"Uh huh. Let's hope the challenge doesn't land you in jail someday, Eric Thorndyke!"

"Buchanan's people will never know they've been invaded," Eric assured her. "I'm not leaving any tracks behind. I'm not trying to play with the records they've got filed in the computer, I'm only searching them."

"Don't worry about Eric," Gabriel advised. "Besides, he owes you this."

"He doesn't owe me!" Samantha protested angrily. "You're the one who got Kirby off his back."

"He's right, Sam." Eric took a second to gulp down his coffee. "I owe you this. Not just for helping me out when I came here to hide from Kirby but for a lot of other help you've given me down through the years. You're my sister. My *real* sister," he concluded simply.

Gabriel leaned forward to examine something on the screen. "And besides, he loves his work, don't you, Eric?" he drawled wryly.

"Yup."

I think," Gabriel said absently as he peered more
⸰sely at the line of computer print, "that when this is
1 over we'll have to talk about setting you up in the
⸰omputer security advising business. Something tells
me that if we don't channel this flair of yours for computers into a legitimate area, you're going to come to a
bad end sooner or later."

That brought Eric's head up from the screen, and he
stared at Gabriel in astonishment. "What? You're going
to help finance me? Help get me started in a business
of my own?"

"That's how I make my living, remember?" Gabriel
said calmly. "For a percentage of the profit, of course."

Eric's face reflected his astounded enthusiasm and
pleasure. "Christ, Gabe, that's fantastic. You really mean
it?"

"I mean it." Gabriel was still staring at something on
the screen, frowning intently. "As I told your sister, I
recognize competency when I see it. Of course you'll
have to be willing to take a little advice along the way
as far as the management end of things goes."

"You bet! Don't worry about me listening to your
advice!"

"Good." Gabriel nodded once. "Knowing your sister
that point does concern me a little because I was a bit
worried that her bullheaded tendencies might run in
the family."

"You know the two of you are thrilled to pieces
tonight because I've given you an excuse to do something so illegal it's disgraceful. If I were an upright
businesswoman, you wouldn't have had the chance to

play computer detectives." She peered over her l
shoulder. "Hey, wait a second, Eric. . . ."

Gabriel leaned forward, his eyes on the same
ment record. "Eric, I think we're on to something l
Back it up and let's see that record on the zon
commission meeting just before this one."

Samantha and the two men traipsed back and fort
through the files of the Buchanan Group. It was
incredible, she reflected, the huge quantity of information it took to run a large business these days. She had
had many occasions to use the Buchanan computers
when she was working for Drew, and it hadn't been
hard to point Eric in the right direction for the sort of
information needed. But she no longer had the codes
and passwords for getting into the regular files, much
less these very-private-looking files.

Eric had found his way past all the barriers, however,
with an ease that both delighted and shocked her.

"Here?" Eric asked.

Gabriel nodded. "Isn't it amazing how often during
the past several years various members of various zoning commissions across the country have changed their
minds about Buchanan properties? How many times
tonight do you think we've seen commission members
change 'no' votes to 'yes' votes in favor of the Buchanan
Group? A few too many."

"Drew always was very good at making his case for
development projects to zoning commissions and other
people in city governments," Samantha observed dryly.

"A little too good. Buchanan, I think, has discovered
an easier route than convincing people with environ-

359

...pact statements and economic arguments. Your
... has been making payoffs for years, Samantha.
...een buying the votes he needed when he couldn't
...em any other way; I'll stake my food processor on

...Then I was right. The question now is whether or
...t he was dumb enough to leave some records of those
...ayoffs, hmmm?"

"People like Drew Buchanan keep records on every-thing," Eric volunteered confidently. "You should know that."

"Even information that could hurt the firm?" Samantha shook her head.

"That kind of information is kept in great detail," Gabriel said dryly. "But not usually together with the legitimate stuff."

They found what they were looking for at three forty-five in the morning. As soon as Eric retrieved it, the phone connection linking the two computers across several thousand miles was cut off by the simple process of unhooking the phone from the computer modem and restoring the receiver to its cradle.

"Just like that," Samantha said wonderingly. "Just like my brother can gain access to any major computer in the nation."

"Well, it does take a bit of talent and intuition," Eric pointed out with grave modesty. He looked as exhausted as he had the night he tried to fake up the Thorndyke spread-sheet. They were all exhausted.

"It takes," Gabriel said, rising stiffly from his chair and stretching broadly, "sheer genius. You, Eric Thorndyke, can go far if you find a legitimate outlet for your talents and if you'll listen to my advice."

Eric summoned up a tired grin. "Don't worry. I'll listen. I can't wait to tell my brother Vic that I'm starting my own business. He still thinks computer experts are only glorified electronic clerks."

Samantha staggered a bit as Gabriel dropped his arm heavily around her shoulders and pulled her toward the door. "Bed, everyone. This kind of business takes a lot out of you. Christ, I'm tired."

"So am I." Samantha yawned.

"You s-should be." Gabriel laughed. "This was all your idea, remember? In your own way, you're as much of a genius as your brother is."

Samantha smiled smugly, inordinately pleased with the compliment. Coming from Gabriel, it meant something.

They made their way upstairs, undressed, and climbed into bed. Samantha curled into Gabriel's hard, reassuring strength with sleepy pleasure. She was almost asleep when Gabriel murmured in her ear.

"When this is all over . . ."

"Ummm?"

"I think it's time I met your mother. See if s-s-she's interested in meeting her future son-in-law."

"Mom's not real big on son-in-laws," Samantha warned, too tired to argue.

"S-she's going to love me. Didn't you tell me yourself the first day we met when I poured tea for you?"

Samantha could feel him smiling complacently, his

in resting on the top of her head. She had just tacitly agreed to marry him, and they both knew it.

"I'll phone her this week."

Because she was going to marry Gabriel Sinclair. Samantha made the decision with her usual sudden conviction, and then she went to sleep.

CHAPTER ELEVEN

"I'll make my reservations for Miami after breakfast."
Gabriel calmly helped himself to another of his perfectly cooked poached eggs while Samantha dropped
her fork with a small crash.

"*Your* reservation? What about mine?" Her eyes
turned suddenly fierce.

"I think it would be best if I handled this last face-to-
face meeting alone, Samantha. It isn't going to be
pleasant," Gabriel declared very seriously. He didn't
appear too fazed by the simmering warning in Samantha's
gaze.

"I'll be damned if you're going to handle the grand
finale without me! This was my scheme, remember?
You are not getting on that plane to Miami alone.
We're partners!"

Frowning, Gabriel appealed to Eric, who was happily
wolfing down poached eggs on toast. "For Christ's sake,
Eric, talk to her. Tell her s-s-she's being an idiot."

"You've been doing a pretty good job of it yourself,

and it never seems to have much impact," Eric observed. "I don't know what you expect me to do. Besides, I can't use logic on her because she's got a perfectly logical reason for going."

"What logical reason?" Gabriel gritted.

"She's going to protect you." Eric shrugged.

"I don't need protection!"

"Tell her that."

"Cut it out, both of you," Samantha ordered briskly, polishing off the last of her toast and egg. "I'm going with Gabriel because this was my idea originally and because Gabriel and I are business partners. That's all there is to it. Now, if you will excuse me, I'm going to get dressed."

Gabriel watched broodingly as she strode regally toward the door of the kitchen. Just before she reached it, he growled, "You didn't particularly enjoy it the last time Buchanan and I met," he reminded her flatly.

She smiled unconcernedly at him over her shoulder. "I shall trust you to find some way to keep the mentality out of the locker room this time." Her yellow terry robe whipped about her ankles as she made her exit.

Eric followed Gabriel's narrowed stare toward the empty doorway. "Sorry, Gabe, but when she's made up her mind like that, there's not much that can stop her."

"Damned amazon." Gabriel sighed, folding his napkin very precisely and putting it back on the table. "You can do the dishes, Eric. I've got to get ready."

"Hey, Gabe. . . ."

"Yes?"

"Don't worry about it," Eric said very seriously. "She's

a good one to have in your corner sometimes. I know she's kind of small and she's a female and all, but she'll go to the wall for you now, believe me."

Gabriel groaned. "I do not particularly want her up against the wall! I'm trying to make s-s-sure s-she's going to be safe in the future, not out in the line of fire, goddam it!"

"She's just as anxious to protect you," Eric explained, trying to pacify the older man.

"We shall probably strangle each other in the process!" Gabriel exploded and stalked out of the kitchen. But he knew he wasn't going to keep Samantha off that plane to Miami, and other than the fact that the scene with Buchanan was liable to be vicious, there was no real reason to forcibly prevent her from being present, and he knew it. She was his business partner, as she had been reminding him all morning, and she had a right to be in at the kill.

He just hoped she wouldn't faint at the sight of blood, he told himself furiously. Then he remembered how she'd sunk that little paring knife into Tony's arm that night Kirby's men had intruded. No, she wasn't likely to faint at the sight of blood. Damned amazon.

Samantha had almost forgotten the bright glare and the pervasive warmth of Miami. It inundated her as soon as she and Gabriel got off the plane and it followed them into the cab. The cab's air conditioner was not sufficient to deal with the humidity, and by the time the Buchanan building came in sight on a palm-lined street, Samantha's turquoise blouse was starting to stick to her body. She didn't think it was noticeable beneath ne summer white suit she was wearing. It had been a long time since she'd dressed like this, she reflected as Gabriel escorted her into the lobby of the building. Her hair was pinned neatly at the nape of her neck, her suit was elegantly tailored, and her expensive leather pumps added an extra two inches to her height. Even Gabriel had felt obliged to comment on the outfit.

"Hell, lady, you're rather formidable in your battle dress, aren't you?" he'd growled as he'd driven to the airport in Seattle. "I hadn't realized how very *professional* you could look."

"This is the way I had planned to look for our first meeting at the spa," she retorted. "It's not my fault that the first time you saw me I was only wearing a towel!"

That drew a reluctant smile from him. The first smile he'd managed all morning. "Personally, I s-s-shall always have some fond memories of that first meeting."

"I'll bet if I'd been wearing this suit instead of that massage table, you'd have had a much better impression of my business ability!"

"Maybe. But I'm pretty s-s-sure that I'd still have noticed that cute little ass, suit and all."

"Gabriel!"

The chiding humor which had sprung up briefly between them on the drive to the airport, however, had vanished completely en route to Miami. Gabriel was solid business by the time they reached the Buchanan building.

In spite of herself, Samantha found she was looking around the steel and glass high-rise with a certain professional interest.

"Is this where you used to work?" Gabriel asked evenly, seeing her attention to the building.

"No, it wasn't completed by the time I left Miami. I was the one in charge of getting the land, though. Used to be an old three-story apartment building on this spot. A lot of the tenants didn't want to move," she murmured, remembering. A lot of memories were crowding back, and she didn't particularly care for any of them.

"You had to kick the tenants out?" Gabriel asked perceptively.

"I managed to relocate each of them. It wasn't easy." She sighed.

"I'm surprised Buchanan cared enough to worry about relocating people."

"Somehow I managed to prove it was a cost-effective procedure," Samantha explained dryly.

"Was it?"

"No. I scrambled the facts and figures a bit before I handed in my final report. Lied through my teeth, to tell you the truth," she admitted ruefully. "But the papers got hold of the story, and they loved it. Buchanan came out looking like a real corporate hero. Since then, as tenants have become more informed about their rights, the procedure has become genuinely cost-effective in many cases. Cheaper than going to court with each and every tenant you want to remove."

The elevator they were riding purred to a stop at the top floor and opened with a hushed whisper. Across an expanse of plush silver carpet a poised receptionist glanced up in polite inquiry.

"Miss Maitland and Gabriel Sinclair to see Mr. Buchanan," Gabriel murmured politely.

"Is he expecting you?"

"No, but I think he'll see us."

"If you'll have a seat, I'll check," the woman began austerely, only to be interrupted as a rather harried-looking young man emerged from the inner office.

"Alice, can you get me Daniels down in Accounting? We've got a problem with the paperwork on that damned restaurant in Phoenix," he began intently and then halted as Gabriel said evenly, "No rush, Alice. There are one or two more problems which are going to crop up on that damned restaurant."

"Who the hell are you?" Jeff Ingram demanded, frowning.

"Buchanan's problems." Gabriel smiled.

Ingram glanced from his face to Samantha's. "Don't tell me," he muttered. "I'll bet you're Samantha Maitland. And this is Sinclair, right?"

"How did you guess?" she said brightly.

Ingram closed his eyes in despair. "Never mind. Alice, call me when these two have gone, will you? That is, if I've still got a job left." He left without a backward glance.

"Poor man," Samantha said sympathetically. "How well I know that look."

Alice was already using the intercom to contact her boss. She had been a secretary long enough to know when to delay and when not to delay. Whoever these two were, they weren't salespeople.

A moment later Samantha and Gabriel were ushered

into Drew Buchanan's panoramic office. He looked up with mocking resignation as Samantha dropped lightly into the seat across from him.

"Jesus, Sam. Aren't I ever going to be rid of you?"

"You'll be rid of me just as soon as we conclude negotiations on the restaurant," she informed him with a bland smile as Gabriel took the chair beside her. "But there seems to be some question about the price. We thought we'd come to Miami and clear it up in person."

"You and I have already agreed on a price." Buchanan leaned back in his chair, eyes watchful.

"Unfortunately she neglected to consult me before agreeing on that price," Gabriel broke in placidly. "And since the two of us are partners, it's necessary that we both agree before signing any papers."

"We've discussed the matter and decided that, under the circumstances, we're willing to be reasonable," Samantha announced easily. "Four hundred thousand is our final figure."

"Like hell."

"Take it or leave it, Buchanan." Gabriel drawled.

Buchanan studied the other man's quiet, unyielding features for a moment and then switched his gaze to the one he perceived as the weaker member of the "partnership." "Sam," he said very softly. "You know I'll go through with it, don't you? You worked for me long enough to know I don't bluff."

"Which was probably why I caved in so easily the other morning when you called," she responded smoothly. "I have since learned, however, that you *do* bluff on occasion."

"You think I won't ruin him? And you, too, while I'm at it?" Buchanan smiled with indulgent amusement.

"You can't touch me without involving yourself," Gabriel told him. "That was something Samantha didn't realize immediately. I will admit, however, that you do have some potential for hurting her business at some point in the future."

"I'm glad you see that," Drew responded coolly. "I was counting on you figuring that out if she did go to you and tell you about my little bluff. You're absolutely right, Sinclair. I can crush her fledgling little business with no more effort than it takes to swat a fly. Get in my way one more time and I'll do it. You know goddamn well I'll do it!"

"Which brings us to the reason Gabriel and I are here in person, Drew," Samantha interrupted calmly. "As he has pointed out, you are an armed and dangerous man. We're here to disarm you so that we can all continue to do business together with a certain amount of integrity."

"Should I laugh now or later?"

"Save it for later," Gabriel suggested. "Let us explain to you exactly why Samantha and I now expect you to do business in good faith. I think you'll be interested."

"You call holding me up for several hundred grand dealing in good faith?"

"Come on, Buchanan, s-she outmaneuvered you. But s-she did it by the book. There was no intimidation, no questionable business methods on her part, no illegal moves. Samantha used good research and sound business sense to corner you on that restaurant deal. Admit

it. S-she's good." Gabriel didn't regret the stammer th[...]
time. Let Buchanan interpret it as weakness. It would
set him up for the fall.

"So tell me why I'm not going to be in a position to
crush her when this is all over," Buchanan invited, his
eyes on Samantha's composed face. Hell, both of them
looked so damned sure of themselves this time, he
thought uneasily. What were they up to now?

"Because," warned Samantha conversationally, "make
one move toward either of us, and we'll make sure you
never leave Miami for Washington, D.C. It's that
simple."

Buchanan froze, but the cool smile on his lips stayed
firmly in place. "And just how would you go about
stopping me?"

"With this." Gabriel reached into the small case he
had brought with him and handed a set of papers across
the desk. "Look familiar?"

Buchanan glanced down at the records of payoffs
which went back five years, and a cold sensation settled
into the bottom of his stomach. Who the hell had
talked? Who knew all of these facts and figures? He had
been so careful. Only he knew where that information
was stashed away in the computer. Damn it, there was
no one who could have talked! Not to this extent. No
one else knew this much. Only the computer. . . . Jesus
Christ. If this stuff got into the papers, Galloway would
desert him with no questions asked. It wasn't that
Galloway's methods had been any cleaner down through
the years, but he'd done a pretty fair job of hiding the

ɔdies. He would expect any man he sponsored to be
qually good at hiding the remains.

Samantha read the still, shuttered expression on her
ex-boss's face with the unerring accuracy of someone
who had once worked for the man. The accuracy of a
woman who had once believed herself in love with him.
Drew knew he was beaten.

"It goes into a safety-deposit box, Drew," she said
quietly.

He looked up, eyes savage and frustrated. "You really think you'd have the guts to use this stuff? Come
on, Sam. I know you too well."

She smiled at him, and Gabriel, who was intently
watching her face, saw the amazon make her appearance.
He had been about to interrupt, but the sight of that
smile made him close his teeth around the words. There
were times when his woman could definitely take care
of herself.

"A man like you has a tendency to mistake principles
in an opponent for weakness," Samantha commented
musingly. "A mistake that can be quite costly at times."
She paused. "Quite frankly, smearing your name across
the Miami papers wouldn't faze me in the least."

Buchanan stared at her, frustrated fury beginning to
fray the edges of his outward calm. Who the hell did
these two think they were to get in the way of Drew
Buchanan. "I've worked long and hard to get where I'm
going, Sam," he hissed. "Do you think I'll let you stop
me?"

"I'm not trying to stop you," she said with a little
laugh. "Just trim your sails a bit. Free-ranging capital-

ists sometimes need a few controls placed on them, just like my mother once said."

Buchanan shot to his feet, eyes blazing. "Six months from now you won't have Sinclair to protect you, Sam!"

"Gabriel will be around six months from now," Samantha announced calmly, aware of Gabriel's small, certain smile. "The partnership will exist six years from now. It will exist indefinitely. It's for life."

"And what if something happens to your precious partner, Sam? What if something very unpleasant happens to him? I've got friends, bitch. Friends who will handle little matters like getting rid of people who are in the way!"

Samantha blinked, appalled in spite of herself. Murder? Was Drew Buchanan actually talking about murder? He was enraged, she realized. More frustrated and enraged than she had ever seen him. A small chill went down her spine, and then Gabriel was calmly interrupting.

"Now, now, Buchanan. First of all, if you haven't learned by now, the lady can take care of herself. However, just in case your temper has gotten the better of you, it might be a good idea to consider that a couple of other people will know the location of the safety-deposit box which will contain copies of the information we have on you."

After a moment of deafening silence Samantha said, "I think we've cleared up all the loose ends." She rose to her feet, preparing to leave, as Gabriel quietly rose to stand beside her. "Try to block us again, Drew, and I'll use that information to destroy you without a second thought. Shall we go, Gabriel?"

White-faced with impotent rage, Buchanan stared at his uninvited visitors. "You bastards."

Gabriel sighed. "And here Samantha made me promise I'd try to keep the language above the level of the locker room. Sorry, darling."

"Have the papers sent to Samantha's home, Buchanan," Gabriel added easily, taking Samantha's arm. "And remember, the final price is five hundred thousand." Suddenly he grinned his deep-sea smile. "You ought to be grateful to me, you know. If I'd let Samantha have her way, you'd be s-s-shelling out seven hundred and fifty thousand instead of only five hundred. You got a deal."

"Get the fuck out of my office!" Buchanan roared.

One week later Samantha opened the door of her home to Vera Maitland.

"Run this one off, Mom, and I'll never forgive you," she told the handsome older woman who stood on the doorstep as she hugged her.

"If I can run him off, he's not worth having, is he?" Vera Maitland retorted practically.

"I never run when I can walk," Gabriel murmured from the hallway behind Samantha. "How do you do, Ms. Maitland? I'm Gabriel Sinclair."

He stood patiently beneath the assessing gaze from the eyes that were so like Samantha's, and then he smiled. "Why don't you come on in to the kitchen? I was just making tea."

Vera glanced at her daughter as Gabriel turned and

walked away from them. "There's something rather ma‑
sive about him, isn't there?"

"My first thought exactly. Strange, isn't it? I mean,
he's not that tall and there's no fat on him. He's just
sort of *there*. Very reassuring at times."

Maternal anxiety flickered briefly in Vera's eyes. "Sam,
honey, are you sure you know what you're doing this
time?"

"Wait until you taste his cooking." Samantha grinned,
guiding her mother into the kitchen.

The shortbread was still warm from the oven, and
Gabriel was carefully pouring tea when Vera and
Samantha walked into the inviting room. He glanced up
and smiled complacently. "Lemon or sugar, Ms. Mait‑
land?"

"Lemon," Vera told him, watching closely. "And call
me Vera, Gabriel."

He nodded, concentrating on the task at hand as
Vera and Samantha took their chairs. When the tea was
properly poured and the pot set precisely on its trivet,
he sat down and picked up the plate of shortbread. He
extended it politely to Vera, who hesitated and then
helped herself to a thick wedge.

"You made this?" she inquired cautiously, sampling
the warm, crumbly cookie.

"The man cooks divinely," Samantha assured her.

Gabriel smiled benignly. "Fortunately. Otherwise this
marriage might be in bad shape. Samantha's culinary
abilities seem to be limited to frozen pizza, Vera. You
did a lousy job on certain aspects of her education."

Vera gave him a level glance. "I taught her the important things."

Gabriel nodded. "I won't argue there. Some of those things you taught her are a few of the reasons I'm marrying her."

"Why *are* you marrying her, Gabriel?" Vera demanded coolly.

Samantha winced. Her mother in this quizzing, aggressive mood could be quite formidable. Gabriel didn't even falter, however, under that aggression.

"I'm marrying her because, even though the woman can't cook, she has a few other attributes I happen to value."

"Such as?"

"I can trust her implicitly. She's utterly loyal, and she's one hell of a business partner when the chips are down. I suppose I have you to thank for teaching her those things." Gabriel glanced with a sidelong glance at Samantha, who was munching on her shortbread with delicate greed. "Some of the other reasons I love her aren't exactly things you taught her. She was born with them."

"Don't be crude in front of my mother, Gabriel." Samantha reached for her tea.

"And some of the things I love about her didn't come from you or from genetics. Some talents she just appears to have developed on her own, like her remarkable ability to fill my life with various and assorted s-shocks and surprises. It's been a struggle trying to cope at times, but I realize now that it does add another dimension to my rather humdrum little world."

"Don't let the man fool you," Samantha advised her mother. "His world hardly qualifies as humdrum. He's managed to take me by surprise on more than one occasion. And I used to think he was such an angel," she added with mocking wistfulness. Across the table her eyes met Gabriel's, and a message of loving amusement flashed between them.

Vera Maitland didn't miss the exchange. "I am pleased," she began thoughtfully, "that you recognize some of the qualities I tried to instill in Samantha. I wanted her to grow up with a sense of pride and integrity. I wanted her to know the meaning of honor and loyalty. . . ." Her voice trailed off as she glanced at her daughter. "But. . . ."

"But you didn't expect her to throw all that away on a man, did you, Vera?" Gabriel asked softly. "You hoped s-she'd apply them to the worthy causes of this world. But Samantha is not another you, Vera. Not completely. You commit yourself to great battles; she makes her commitment to people."

Vera stared at him, her teacup halfway to her mouth. For a long moment she studied the man her daughter would soon be marrying. "Do you know, Gabriel Sinclair, you may be right," she said at last. "You may very well be right. I never thought of it that way."

"Of course, I'm right." He handed her the plate of shortbread. "It's much riskier, you know."

"What is?" Vera asked sharply.

"Committing yourself to people instead of causes. You can always walk away without too much regret when a cause turns sour. You can't walk away from

people so easily. Much more of an emotional investment involved."

"For a businessman," Vera observed as she helped
herself to another piece of shortbread, "you have a
surprisingly interesting grasp of the fundamentals of
human dynamics. If you are right, then I can only be
grateful my daughter has found a man who appreciates
what he's getting."

"S-she has," he assured her equably. "And may I say
that for a lifelong radical you have a surprising amount
of sensitivity to people."

"If I could interrupt for a moment," Samantha broke
in with mock politeness, "perhaps I could have another
cup of tea?"

Vera smiled. A wide, brilliant smile that Gabriel had
seen on her daughter on occasion. "I wouldn't mind
another cup myself, Gabriel. And don't worry dear,"
she directed toward her daughter. "I'm going to accept
the marriage. I get the feeling I couldn't run Gabriel off
if I tried."

"As I said, Vera," he murmured, "I rarely run. The
only excess energy I have expended lately has been in
pursuit of Samantha. The effort has quite exhausted
me. I won't be doing any unnecessary exercise for quite
a while."

The move to Gabriel's house was decided with a toss
of a coin. Gabriel groaned when Samantha suggested
that simple technique of deciding which of them was to
move where. When his beachfront home won the toss,

he worried about whether Samantha really would be happy in California.

"I can't wait to get into that lovely, neat house of yours and muss it up a little," she assured him zestfully.

Gabriel groaned again, but there was a gleam of amusement in his eyes this time. It was going to be interesting to see what Samantha would do. Maybe, just like his life, his house could use a few surprises.

The keys of the old Victorian were handed over to its new resident, Eric Thorndyke, and Samantha and Gabriel set off on the drive to California one cold, rainy morning.

The move had gone with remarkable smoothness as far as Samantha was concerned, but that was undoubtedly because Gabriel had organized it. It was true the packing had taken much longer under his supervision, and the various arrangements necessary for setting up her corporation in California seemed to take forever, but both were done with a thoroughness which assured they had been done right.

One hour into the drive south Gabriel asked the question he had been mulling over in his mind since Vera Maitland had left a few weeks earlier. "Why didn't you tell your mother about the coup you pulled on Buchanan?"

A tiny smile edged Samantha's mouth. "Somehow it just didn't seem all that important. I stopped needing the revenge somewhere along the way. We didn't wind up going after Buchanan for revenge, anyway. We went after him to protect our partnership."

"To protect each other," he agreed calmly. "I love you, Samantha."

"I love you, Gabriel." Proving herself her mother's daughter simply didn't matter anymore, Samantha thought. She was quite content to be herself.

Which was, of course, the most important lesson her mother had tried to teach her. Samantha had learned it on her own.

On their first night back in the seaside home, Samantha suggested a walk on the beach after dinner. The meal had been superb, as usual, and she was feeling pleasantly stuffed on trout with caviar cream sauce, a watercress and cucumber salad, and a luscious lemon meringue pie which Gabriel had insisted on making in honor of the first meal he had served her.

With her arm wrapped around his waist and Gabriel cradling her close to his side, Samantha walked in silence for a time, drinking in the fresh salt air and the moonlit darkness. Underneath her feet the sand was firm and resilient.

Gabriel's hand tightened around her, and she was pulled a little closer to the hard line of his thigh. It occurred to Samantha that in a few more minutes she wasn't going to be in a mood to talk. Once Gabriel started to make love to her, she was really quite helpless to resist, she thought in satisfaction. Therefore what she had to say had best be said quickly.

"I've been meaning to talk to you about something," she said quietly.

"Ummm?" Gabriel's voice was a rumbling purr of masculine content.

"A business matter."

Some of the contentment went out of Gabriel's tone. "Go on."

"Well, I've been thinking about the old man down in Phoenix. The one we bought the restaurant from."

"And?" She could hear him waiting for the punch line and smiled to herself. Poor Gabriel. He was already preparing himself for another bombshell.

"I think we ought to split the five hundred thousand with him, Gabriel. After all, if it hadn't been for him, we'd never have made that deal work."

"Split it with him!" He swung to a halt and turned to eye her closely in the darkness. "Split it with the taco stand owner? But, Samantha, we gave him fifty grand for that place, and it wasn't worth more than thirty at the most! He was delighted with the deal!"

"He didn't know what we knew, though. He didn't realize how much the place was worth," she pointed out. "We sort of took advantage of him, Gabriel."

He gave her a very stern look. "Samantha, I think I'd better explain a few business facts of life to you, honey. When you've pulled off a coup like the one we did down in Phoenix, and when all the moves have been legal and aboveboard, there's really no need to go around distributing a percentage of the take to every passerby!"

She twined her arms around his neck and smiled dreamily up at him. "We can talk about it in the morning if you'd rather."

"Samantha . . . !"

"But we are going to split with him. Don't worry,

381

Gabriel, I won't make a practice of giving away the profits. It's just that in this case I think it's only right to share with that old man."

"How much," he asked forbiddingly, "were you thinking of giving the former owner?"

"Oh, say a hundred thousand. We split the rest between us."

"You still owe me my fifty thousand investment," he reminded her on a growl.

"Gabriel, we're *partners*. You're supposed to think of that fifty thousand as a mutual investment made by both of us."

"Strange, mine was the only name on the check."

"Details," she scoffed lightly.

"Samantha," he warned, his large hands slipping around her waist, "if you're going to start giving away my portion of our investments, then you're going to have to make it worth my while." His fingers tightened meaningfully.

She frowned. "Gabriel, I'm not ready yet. I'm still talking business."

"In a partnership," he breathed, his mouth hovering an inch above hers, "you can't always have everything your own way."

"Gabriel, wait, I wanted to . . ."

But the words were sealed in her throat as his mouth took possession of hers. Samantha gave up the effort to discuss business and surrendered to the inviting warmth of him.

Gabriel felt the way her body softened against his hardness and sighed his satisfaction into the honeyed cavern of her mouth. Time enough in the morning to explain a few basic principles of venture capitalism. Right now the only thing which was really clear in his head was the need to take his woman to bed.

He found the fastenings of her leather jacket and undid them slowly, thrusting his hands inside to find the curves of her unconfined breasts. He heard her small, kitten-soft moan, and the desire surged through him. She was his. She would always be his. All he had to do was put his hand on her at any hour of the day or night and she would smile and come to him. He'd never had such power or known such extraordinary comfort.

But, then, neither had he ever been held in such thrall before, either. Because the other side of the coin showed him as deeply in this woman's power as she was in his.

"Samantha," he muttered huskily against her ear, "from the very beginning I wanted to lay you down and make you mine. Then I realized I wanted to protect you from your own recklessness and from people like Buchanan. But I never thought to ask who was going to protect me from you."

"Do you want protection?" she murmured, smiling up at him with love.

"No. I prefer to operate under the ridiculous illusion that I can handle you." He chuckled softly. He dropped his hands from the warmth of her breasts and refastened her jacket. Then he caught her wrist and started back toward the house. "Come home with me, sweetheart. I want to go over some of the details of this contract we have between us."

"You're so good at details."

"You must let me know if I'm in any danger of boring you," he drawled, "with my habitual thoroughness."

"Avenging angels are never dull," she told him on a note of laughter. "They always seem to unsheath their flaming swords whenever things need livening up!"

"Veiled sexual innuendoes yet!" he complained as they reached the door of the beachfront home. "As a business associate you lack a certain sober, responsible, conservative attitude, you know that, don't you?"

She went into his arms as they stepped through the sliding glass door, her eyes very brilliant in the moonlight. "And as your woman?"

"As my woman," he rasped heavily, his mouth coming down on hers with familiar, rough passion, "you're quite perfect. The partnership, Samantha Maitland Sinclair, is for life, you know that, don't you?"

"Oh, yes. You're a very thorough man, remember? I expect nothing less than the most binding of contracts."